# Jessamine
## A Novel

*by*

Marion Harland

Double 9
BOOKS

# Jessamine
## A Novel
## by Marion Harland

ISBN: 978-93-62205-30-8

**Published by**

# DOUBLE 9 BOOKS

2/13-B, Ansari Road
Daryaganj, New Delhi – 110002
info@double9books.com
www.double9books.com
Tel. 011-40042856

# ABOUT THE AUTHOR

Marion Harland, also known by her pen name, was an American novelist who was prolific and bestselling in both fiction and nonfiction. Born in Amelia County, Virginia, she began writing essays at the age of 14 under numerous pen names until 1853, when she settled on Marion Harland. Her debut novel, Alone, was published in 1854 and became a "emphatic success" with a second printing the following year. She was a prolific writer of bestselling women's novels, known as "plantation fiction" at the time, as well as countless serial works, short stories, and magazine essays for fifteen years. Terhune married Presbyterian preacher Edward Payson Terhune in 1856, and they moved to Newark, New Jersey, where she spent the rest of her adult life. They had six children together; three of them died as babies. In the 1870s, shortly after the birth of her last son, Albert Payson, she released Common Sense in the Household: A Manual of Practical Housewifery, a cookbook and household guide for housewives that became a tremendous bestseller, selling more than one million copies over multiple editions.

# CONTENTS

# CHAPTER I

A young girl lay upon a lounge in the recess of an oriel-window. If disease held her there, it had not altered the contour of the smooth cheek, or made shallow the dimples in wrist and elbow of the arm supporting her head; had not unbent the spirited bow of the mouth, or dimmed the glad light of the gray eyes. Most people called these black, deceived by the shadow of the jetty lashes. They were wide open, now, and the light of a sunny mid-day streamed in upon her face through the window, yet the upper part of the irid was darkened by the heavy fringe that matched in line the well-defined brows. Her hair, also black, with purple reflections glancing from every coil and fold, was braided into a coronal, and about the heavy plait knotted at the back of the head was twisted a half-wreath of yellow jessamine. Her skin was dark and clear, but she had usually little color; her forehead was not remarkable for breadth or height; the nose was a nondescript, and the mouth rather piquant than pretty, with suggestions of wilfulness in the full, lower lip, and the slight, downward lines at the corners. Her dress was white muslin, with no ornament beyond the gold clasp of her girdle, and a spray of jessamine at her throat.

The casement was canopied with the vine from which this last had been plucked. Hundreds of bright bells were swinging lazily in the warm breeze, and were tossed into livelier motion and perfume by the kisses of brown-coated bees and vivid humming-birds. Heightening the glow of the tropical creeper, while they relieved the eye of the spectator, drooped still, lilac clusters of wisteria, and these the girl put aside with impatient fingers when she raised herself upon her elbow to obtain a better view of the outer scene. A flower-garden, lively with Spring blossoms, opened through a wicket in the white fence into a church-yard—green and level on the roadside—green likewise, but swelling into long ranks of unequal and motionless billows behind the building. This was an ancient structure, as was shown by the latticed windows with rounded tops, and the quaint base of the steeple that yet tapered gracefully into a shimmering point against the pale noon of the sky. But loving eyes had watched it, and reverent hands guarded it against decay. The brick walls were sound, the masonry of gray stone about windows and doors smooth and solid with cement made hard as the stone by years and weather. The sward was shaven evenly, and the two great elms at the entrance to the rural sanctuary were the pride of the region. A double row of these trees bordered the road for a hundred yards in either direction, and now offered shade and coolness to an orderly herd of horses tethered beneath them. A few handsome equipages were there, two or three stately family carriages and several jaunty buggies, but most of the vehicles which the animals were attached, bore the stamp of rusticity, hard usage, and infrequent ablutions, while the preponderance of roadsters and ponderous draught-horses over blooded stock, betokened that in this, as in other agricultural districts, the beautiful was held in subordination to the useful. The little church, thanks to the taste of the present pastor and the economical proclivities of past generations, had escaped the vulgarizing influence of "a good coat of paint." Slow circles of lichens, hoary and russet, had toned down the original ruddiness of the bricks, and green mosses dotted the slated roof. It stood on the edge of a cup-like valley, surrounded by mountains. So near was the lofty chain on the north-east, that the rising sun sent the shadow of the Anak of the range—"Old Windbeam," across the graveyard to the foot of the sacred walls; so remote on the west that the Day-god looked his last upon the fertile pastures, winding streams, and peaceful homesteads, over hills round and blue with distance.

The watcher in the oriel-window saw neither flowers nor elms; noticed the throng of patient dumb horses and motley collection of carriages as little as she did the mountains, near and far. Every feature was stirred with exultant wistfulness, and her eyes never moved from a certain window of the church from which the inner shutters had been folded back. The house was densely packed with living beings—she could see through this—galleries and aisles, as well as pews, and dimly, in the dusky interior, she discerned an upright and animated figure—the orator of the occasion. Into the heat and hush of high noon—heat fragrant with waves of odor from resinous woods, and clover-fields, and garden-borders—a hush to which the tinkling bells of browsing kine in the meadows, and the hum of bird and bee close by, brought a deeper lull instead of interruption—flowed a voice sonorous and sweet; now calm in argument or narrative—now, breaking into short, abrupt bursts of impassioned declamation; anon, rising with earnest, majestic measures, most musical of all, that brought words with the varied inflections, to the rapt listener. Smiles and tears came to her with the hearing; light that was glory to the eyes; softness that was tenderness, not sorrow, to the sensitive mouth.

When the speaker's tones were drowned by the storm of applause that shook the church, and the mass of human heads swayed to and fro as did the cedars in Old Windbeam's crown on gusty Winter nights, the girl fell back upon her cushions and fairly sobbed with excitement.

"My hero! my king!"

A slight bustle in the hall distracted her attention, and warned her of the necessity of self-control. A man's voice questioned, and a woman's — provincial and drawling — replied, and steps approached the parlor.

"Here's a gentleman wants Mr. Fordham, Miss Jessie," said an ungainly country girl, opening the door.

A tall figure bowed upon the threshold.

"I am an intruder, I fear," he said, taking in at once the facts of the young lady's inability to rise from her sofa, and the confusion that burned in her dark cheek at the unexpected apparition. "But they told me at the hotel below that I should find Mr. Fordham here. He is my cousin."

The glow remained in all its brightness, but it was painful no longer, as she held out her hand.

"Then you are Mr. Wyllys?" smiling cordially. "You are very welcome."

She waved him to a chair near her lounge with an air of proud, but unconscious, grace, that did not escape the visitor.

"I am sorry you did not arrive in season to participate in the celebration of our Centennial. You know, I suppose, that Mr. Fordham is the orator of the day?"

Warily observant, with eyes that habitually looked careless, and were never off guard, Mr. Wyllys remarked the smile and glance through the window at the church, which accompanied this bit of information, but his reply evinced no knowledge of aught beyond what was conveyed by her words.

"I should be ashamed to confess it, but I was not aware until this moment that any public celebration was going on, unless it were a religious service in the church — a saint's day or other solemn festival. Is this, then, the Anniversary of a notable event in the history of your lovely valley?"

There was a tincture of commiseration for his ignorance mingled with her surprise at the question that must have diverted the stranger if his sense of humor was keen. Her answer was grave as befitted the importance of the subject.

"The founder of this colony among the hills was a direct descendant of the Scotch Covenanters — one David Dundee, from whom the settlement took its name. He emigrated with a large family of sturdy boys and girls, and his report of the rich lands and genial climate of his new home drew after him many others — all from his native land — most of them his former friends and neighbors. They cleared away forests, built houses, dug, and ploughed, and reaped, and worshipped God after the fashion of their fathers, having, within fifteen years after David Dundee's establishment of himself and household here, erected the substantial church you see over there. At the time of the breaking out of the French and Indian war, there was not a more prosperous and happy community in the State. In response to the call to arms, the bravest and best of the young and middle-aged men formed themselves into a company and marched away to fight as zealously and conscientiously as they had felled the woods and tilled the ground. A mere handful—and most of these infirm from age and disease—remained with the women and children, upon whom devolved much and heavy labor if they would retain plenty and comfort in their homes. They were literally hewers of wood and drawers of water; they sowed the fields and gardens, and gathered in the crops with their own hands—these heroic great-grandmothers of ours!—herded their cattle and repaired their houses, besides performing the ordinary tasks of housewives. And—one and all—they learned and practised the use of fire-arms, kept muskets beside cradles and kneading-troughs, and when they met for worship on Sabbath, mothers carried their babies on the left arm, a gun upon the right. One day, late in April—perhaps as fair and sweet a day as this—news came to this secluded hamlet that a large body of of 'the enemy'—chiefly Indians and half-breeds—was approaching. Providentially, old David Dundee was at home on a furlough of three days—he asked no more—that he might rally somewhat after the amputation of his left arm in hospital. He had the church bell rung (it was a present from a Scottish lord, and it hangs still in the steeple), and after a brief consultation upon the green in front of the 'kirk,' with the wisest of his neighbors—a council of war from which women were not excluded—he collected the entire population into the church, first allowing them one hour in which to bury or otherwise secrete their valuables. The feebler women and the children were sent, for safety, into the cellar, which extends under the whole building; the lower parts of the windows were barricaded with feather-beds and mattresses, with loop-holes through which guns could be thrust, and these stout-hearted matrons and young girls volunteered to defend. The men were mustered in the galleries. A sentinel from the bell-tower soon gave warning that the foe was in sight. From their loop-holes the colonists saw their houses and barns fired, their horses and other stock maimed and butchered, gardens, fields, and orchards wantonly laid waste; but not a woman wept or a man swore or groaned in the crowded church. On they came, flushed with success, ravening for human blood. David Dundee spoke twice before the uproar without made hearing, even of his stentorian voice, impossible. 'Haud your fire 'till ye hear me gie the word!' he said, when his small army looked to

him for orders, as savages and half-breeds rushed forward to surround the building. A minute later—'The Lord have maircy upon their souls, for we'll hae nane upon their bodies! *Fire!*'

"The fight was a fierce one, and lasted until nightfall."

"'Then,' says the chronicler of the story—'seeing that the enemy had withdrawn a little space, we thanked the God of battles, and took some refreshment; then set about caring for our wounded and preparing for the renewed attack we believed the savages were about to make. Finding the hurt of our leader, David Dundee, to be mortal, and that our ammunition was well-nigh exhausted, and being, in consequence, sore distraught in spirit, we gave ourselves anew to prayer—*then, stood to our arms!*'

"Wasn't that grand!" the girl interrupted herself to say—her wide eyes all alight with fire and dew.

"Glorious! One likes to remember that upon such a foundation as your Dundee and his followers our Republic was built," assented the listener. "And, then?"

"And, then,"—taking up the words with singleness of interpretation and a grave simplicity that nearly provoked the auditor to a smile—"the darkness closed down and hid the foe from their sight. With the dawn came a glad surprise. The invaders had retreated, bearing their dead and wounded with them. The garrison had lost but twenty in all—five of them being women. They were buried in the graveyard over there—with the exception of the rugged old chieftain, who was interred directly under the pulpit. All this happened a hundred years ago. When Mr. Fordham was here, last summer, the committee having the centennial anniversary in charge, requested him to deliver the oration."

"I am somewhat surprised that he has never mentioned this new distinction to me, although I knew his modesty to be equal to his ability," said the visitor.

The black brows were knit and the lip curled.

"It is 'no distinction' to him to deliver an historical address to a crowd of yeomen, you may think—and rightly! His consent to do this is a proof of his kindness of heart and willingness to oblige his friends. I understand as well as you do, that our pride in the one event that has made our valley memorable in the history of our country, may seem overstrained to absurdity in the eyes of others. But there are some in Mr. Fordham's audience who appreciate his talents, and all admire. Listen!" her forehead smoothing as the applause broke forth again.

Mr. Wyllys was too well-bred to recall to her mind what she should have learned from his frank avowal of ignorance of her cherished tradition,— namely—that the "one event" had been, in that hurrying modern age, forgotten by the world outside the noble amphitheatre of hills. The country girl had told the story well; her face had been an engaging study while she talked, and there was novel refreshment in her naïve belief that the tale must interest him as much as it did herself. Otherwise, he might have found the recital a bore.

"You misunderstood me if you imagined that I intended to sneer—did me an injustice you will not repeat when you are better acquainted with me. The highest honor that can be awarded the American citizen is the opportunity to serve the people. And my cousin—any man—might well be proud of the compliment conveyed in the invitation to be speaker on an occasion like this. The theme should be, of itself, inspiration. I am disposed to quarrel with him for excluding me from the number of his hearers. His reserve on the subject of the appreciation that meets his worth and talents everywhere is sometimes trying to the temper of those who know how to value these, and the reputation they have won for him."

"He is singularly modest. But that is a characteristic of true merit," said the young lady, laconically. "You came down from Hamilton to-day?"

"I did!" with a slight shrug of the shoulder and a comic lifting of the eyebrows. "Actually arising at four o'clock to take the train. I saw the sun rise, for the first time in twenty years. Your home is very beautiful, Miss Kirke."

"We think so. I ought to, for I was born here and have known no other. But I am not Miss Kirke—only Miss Jessie. My elder sister is in the church. When she comes home, she will play the hostess better than I do."

"Excuse me for saying that you are scarcely a competent judge on that point."

She met the gallantry with the half-petulant expression and gesture that had answered his allusion to his cousin's "new distinction."

"I did not say that to provoke flattery. Apart from the truth that my sister is my superior in nearly everything that goes to make up the dignified lady, she is, just now, in better physical trim than I can boast. I sprained my foot a week ago," smiling, and blushing so brightly as to arouse the spectator's curiosity—"and I am forbidden to use it, as yet."

She turned her face to the window as the crash of a brass band proclaimed that the oration was at an end. While she beat time on the sill to the patriotic strains the visitor inspected the room and its appointments.

It was a square parlor, low-browed and spacious, and wainscoated with oak. Venerable portraits adorned the walls, and the furniture belonged to the era when mahogany was plentiful and upholstery expensive, if one might judge from the disproportion in the quantity of polished wood and that of cushions. A modern piano was there, however, and the carpet was new and handsome. The lounge on which Jessie lay was evidently the workmanship of a neighborhood carpenter, but was far more comfortable than the stately sofas at opposite ends of the apartment, being broad and deeply cushioned, and covered with a pretty chintz pattern. An old china bowl, full of pond-lilies, was upon the centre-table; tall vases of the same material and antique style stood on the mantel, and a precious cabinet of carved wood—Mr. Wyllys wondered if the owners knew how precious— was in a far corner. The most conspicuous ornament of the room was a large picture that hung over the mantel. It was a portrait of the second daughter of the house, taken several years before, for it represented a girl of sixteen, kneeling beside a forest spring. She had just filled a leaf-cup with water, and, in the act of raising it to her lips, glanced at the spectator with a smile of saucy triumph,—a face so radiant with roguish glee as to win the gravest to an answering gleam. The likeness was striking still, and the painting excellent. The figure was spirited, the attitude one of negligent grace, and the accessories to the principal object were well brought in. A vista in the woods revealed the craggy front of Windbeam, and about the old beech, shading the spring, clung a jessamine in full flower.

Mr. Wyllys got up to take a nearer view of the picture, and Jessie looked around.

"That is one of my father's treasures," she said, without a tinge of embarrassment or affectation at seeing him intent upon the scrutiny of her portrait. "It was painted by H——" pronouncing a celebrated name. "He spent a summer in this neighborhood, four years since. He was with us on a picnic to the wishing-well—every county has a wishing-well, hasn't it?— and there made the first sketch of that picture."

"A neat way of informing me that he was struck with her attitude and face, and asked the favor of reproducing them upon canvas!" reflected the guest.

"It is a masterpiece!" he said aloud.

He marvelled, inwardly, at the paternal devotion or extravagance that had tempted the master of the unpretending manse to make himself the owner of what he knew must be a costly work of art.

Jessie answered as if he had spoken.

"Mr. H— — gave it to my father, who had been attentive to him during a severe illness."

She scanned the new-comer narrowly while his regards were engaged by the painting, never dreaming that he was quite conscious of the scrutiny, and prolonged his examination purposely that she might have time and opportunity for hers. He stood fire bravely, for his mien of easy composure did not vary by so much as the nervous twitch of a muscle; his attitude was one of serious attention; his eyes did not leave the picture.

A tall, lithe figure, with a willowy bend of the shoulders, slight, but perceptible, especially when he spoke, or listened to her; fair, almost sandy hair; blue eyes; a pale, and by no means handsome face, inasmuch as the forehead was narrow, the cheeks thin, the mouth large, and the luxuriant beard had a reddish tendency in the mustache, and where it neared the under lip,—each of these particulars and the *tout ensemble* awoke in Jessie's mind disappointment, which found vent in a little sigh and a droop of the corners of the mouth as she withdrew her eyes.

Then, silence abode between them for awhile. The music of the band had ceased, and whatever were the concluding exercises of the celebration in the church, they were inaudible in the great parlor, where cool shadows slept in the corners, and the scent of pond-lilies and jessamine steeped the air into languorous stillness. It would have seemed like a dream to a romantic or imaginative man, and the glory of the place and hour been the figure among the pillows on the couch, her dark cheeks stained red as with rich wine; the sultry yellow of the blossoms in her hair and upon her bosom making more black her wealth of hair, more clear her olive skin, the while, forgetful that she was not alone, she watched with parted lips and eager, love-full eyes, for the coming of her lord.

We shall have abundant proof, hereafter, that Mr. Wyllys was the reverse of romantic, and that his imagination never misled his judgment, but esthetic's was a favorite study with him, and his taste being good, he decided within his calm and patronizing self that the hour spent in the "best room" of the Dundee parsonage was not utterly wasted.

He had had a study in color—and of more kinds than that which met the eye—if nothing else.

# CHAPTER II

"Here they are!"

The low exclamation, fraught with delight and ill-suppressed impatience—genuine and artless as a child's—drew Mr. Wyllys to join Jessie's lookout at the window.

The road and church-yard were full of the retiring crowd, and a group of three persons was at the wicket-gate. A white-haired man, of dignified and benign presence, bowed somewhat under the weight of his threescore years and ten, walked with his arm about the shoulders of one youthful and erect, who retarded his gait to suit the measured tread of his companion.

"Stand back! don't let him see you until he comes in!" ordered Jessie; and Mr. Wyllys retreated without having made other observation of the lady at Mr. Kirke's side, save that she was of medium height and neatly dressed.

Mr. Fordham's face brightened with pleasure and amazement at sight of the figure standing at the head of Jessie's sofa.

"Orrin! you here?"

"In body and in spirit, Roy!"

Jessie's eyes were busy, as their hands lingered in the hearty clasp of greeting.

"What a contrast!" she thought, 'twixt pity for the one and exultation in the other.

The epithet most aptly descriptive of Roy Fordham's features and bearing was "manly." The broad brow; the hazel eyes, rather deeply set, that looked straight into those of the person with whom he talked; the resolute mouth and square chin; his upright carriage, stalwart frame, and firm step—all deserved it. His height did not equal that of his cousin, but he seemed taller until they stood side by side. Without relinquishing the visitor's hand, he turned, with serious courtesy that became him well, to the lady who had entered with him.

"Miss Kirke, allow me to present my friend and relative, Mr. Wyllys!"

It was a formally worded introduction, for Miss Kirke was punctilious in these matters. She bent her head graciously, but with no effusive cordiality such as had gushed forth in her sister's welcome to one with whose name she was pleasantly familiar.

"We are happy to see any friend of Mr. Fordham in our home," she said in a clear monotone that accorded perfectly with her calm face and reposeful demeanor. "My father, Mr. Wyllys!"

The back of the latter was to the lounge when Miss Kirke had committed him to the host's care, and betaken herself to some other part of the house; but he knew that Roy was bending over his betrothed, smiling tender reproach into eyes that filled with happy, foolish tears at his query—"Have you been very lonely?"

"Not at all! I have enjoyed the morning intensely. I could see into the church very plainly, and hear much that was said. It was almost as good as going myself."

"I told you you would be reconciled to the disappointment by noon."

"But not in the way you meant!"

The wilful ring was in the voice, loving as it was.

Mr. Wyllys' visage was a model of bland deference, and his answers to Mr. Kirke's remarks pertinent, the while he was reflecting,—"You are likely to have lively work on your hands, my good cousin, with your Kate. I should hardly have cast the part of Petruchio for you, either."

"I think I will have mine brought to me here, to-day!" he heard Jessie say, softly, when dinner was announced.

Roy's reply was to lift her in his arms and carry her across the hall to the dining-room, where one side of the table was taken up by a settee heaped with cushions. She pouted and laughed as he laid her down among these.

"I believe you imagine that I am losing moral volition as well as bodily strength! I have taken my meals in this *à la* fairy princess style for seven days," she added, to Mr. Wyllys, when they were all seated—"have personated Cleopatra and Mrs. Skewton to my own content and my friends' amusement. I find it so comfortable that I shall regret the recovery which will doom me to straight-backed chairs, drawn up in line of battle against the table. If you want to know the fulness and delight of the term, *dolce far niente*, practise clumsy climbing among our steep hills, and the fates may send you a sprained ankle—a not intolerable prelude to a month of such luxurious indolence and infinitude of spoiling as I am now enjoying."

"The indolence and the petting, might be less to his taste than they are to yours," replied her father, indulgently.

"Don't you believe it!" said Jessie, with a saucy flash of her great eyes across the table at the guest. "I have a notion that both would be altogether to his liking. Unless I am mistaken, he has had Benjamin's share of these luxuries already."

"You have been telling tales out of school, Roy!" said his cousin, threateningly, as Mr. Fordham laughed.

Jessie anticipated the reply.

"You are wrong—and the accusation is unflattering to my perceptive powers. You betray your ease-loving propensities in every motion and accent. Don't frown at me, Euna! I am complimenting him, although he may not suspect it. Indolence—not laziness, mind! but the graceful *laisser-faire* which sometimes approximates the sublime—is the least appreciated of the social arts." Mr. Wyllys answered by a quotation:

"'Surely, surely, slumber is more sweet than toil—the shore
Than labor in the deep mid-ocean.'"

"The gospel of ease, of which Tennyson is the apostle!" said Roy. "Sleep is never sweeter than when it comes to the laboring man, nor is the shore so welcome to him who never leaves it, as it is to the mariner who has gained it by toiling through the deep mid-ocean."

Jessie made a dissenting gesture.

"*Le jeu—vaut-il la chandelle?*"

"Yes—if rest and ease be the chief goods of life," was the rejoinder.

It was made gently and affectionately, but Jessie appealed to Mr. Wyllys, in whimsical vexation.

"Wouldn't anybody know that he is a college professor? He is a merciless logician, and logic was always a bore to me. I don't know the difference between a syllogism and a sequence. Poor Euna! what a fearful trial she had in her pupil!"

"You use the past tense, I observe!" Mr. Wyllys remarked, demurely.

Everybody was tempted to badinage in talking with her.

"Because my days of nominal pupilage are over. The trial remains in full force."

"*You* may say that, my dear." Mr. Kirke laid a caressing hand upon her head. "Your sister and I would hear the slander from no one else."

Miss Kirke said nothing,—only smiled in a slow, bright way, peculiarly her own. While Jessie could not speak without action, the blood leaping

to cheek and lip as did the fire to her eye and ready retort to her tongue, her sister sat, serene and fair, observant of every want of those about her, graceful in hospitality, hurried in nothing, careful in all she said and did. She must have been twenty-five years old, Wyllys decided, but she would look as young at forty, after the manner of these calm-pulsed blondes. The soft brown hair was put plainly back from her temples; her features were like her father's, Greek in outline, but more delicately chiselled; her eyes were placid mirrors—not changeful depths. Her dress was a dun tissue that yet looked cooler than Jessie's muslin, and her lace collar was underlaid and tied in front with blue ribbon. Mr. Wyllys had an eye—and a critically correct one—for feminine attire, down to the minutest details, and he approved of hers as befitting her age, position, and style.

He noted, moreover, with surprise and approval, that there was not a touch of rusticity in the appointments of the table and the bill of fare. Old-fashioned silver, massive and shining; china that nearly equalled it in value, and cut-glass of the same date, were set out with tasteful propriety upon a damask cloth, thick, snowy, and glossy, and ironed in an arabesque pattern. From the clear soup, to the ice-cream, syllabubs, and frosted cake which were the dessert, each dish bespoke intelligent and elegant housewifery. Yet the only servant he saw was the lumpish girl who had admitted him. She removed and set on dishes without a blunder, decent and prim in a white cape-apron, directed, Mr. Wyllys was sure, in every movement, by the mistress' eyes, unperturbed as these seemed.

Crude brilliancy—mature repose—thus he described the general characteristics of the sisters' behavior, by the time the meal was over. Both were strong, both women of intellect and culture. One was as self-contained as the other was impulsive. He had never before—and his acquaintance with the various phases of American society was extensive—met the peer of either in farm-house or country parsonage.

"I should as soon have looked for rare orchids in a daisy-field," was his figure.

The cousins went out for a walk in the afternoon, a ramble that led them by a zig-zag path, to the summit of Old Windbeam. They had climbed the hugest boulder of his knobby forehead, and sat upon it in the shadow of a low-spreading cedar, smoking the cigar of contentment, and surveying at their leisure the magnificent panorama unrolled beneath them, when Orrin laid his hand upon his friend's knee, with a half laugh that had in it a quiver of wounded affection.

"Why have you left me to find all this out for myself, old fellow? Did you doubt my sympathy, or my discretion?"

Roy did not turn his head, but his fingers closed strongly and lingeringly upon his cousin's.

"I doubted neither. There was nothing I could tell you until very lately. I came to Dundee, last September, to pass my vacation at the hotel in the village below. There were excellent hunting and fishing hereabouts, I had been told, and I brought letters of introduction to Mr. Kirke from Dr. Meriden and Professor Blythe, who were his college friends. Before my return to Hamilton, I asked and obtained his permission to correspond with his younger daughter, confiding to him my ulterior motive for the request. He consented and kept my secret. Our letters were such as friends might exchange, and mine were usually read aloud to her father and sister. When I reappeared here at the beginning of our intermediate vacation ten days ago, she received me without suspicion or embarrassment. She never knew what my real feelings toward her were until last week—the day of the accident. We were walking together when she slipped and fell. In the alarm of the moment, for she nearly fainted with the pain, and I thought the hurt far more serious than it afterward proved to be, I spoke words that could not be misunderstood nor recalled. Not that I would recall them! They secured for me the great blessing of my life."

His voice changed here. Up to this sentence the story was a quiet recitative he might have learned by rote, and uttered at the bidding of one he felt had a right to hear it. The lack of spontaneity did not offend the auditor. He appreciated his cousin's richer and fuller nature sufficiently to understand that the most abundant springs of affection and passion lay too far below the surface to be easily forced into view. He saw, too, that the confession of his wooing and winning was made with pain; that the spirit to whose exceeding delicacy of texture and sentiment few did justice, shrank from the revelation, even to his nearest of kin. He doubted not that when the "alarm" of which Roy had spoken, cleft the sealed stone, the hidden waters leaped to the light with power that swept reserve, humility and expediency before them; that Jessie had listened to pleadings more fervent, to vows more solemn than are poured into the ear of one in ten thousand of her sex.

"Does she recognize this truth?" he speculated within himself. "Or does she—the petted darling of an old man and an only sister—receive all this as the tribute due her charms? account her flippant talk, flashing eyes, and schoolgirlish arts an equitable exchange for this man's whole being and life?"

His tact was marvellous to womanliness. His tone took its key from that which last met his ear;—was slightly tremulous—purposely subdued.

"Thank you for allowing me to share in your new happiness! I need not tell you how heartily I congratulate you—how fervent is my wish that your wedded life may be all sunshine. I believe the lady of your choice to be worthy of your regard. I am sure she will have the best husband in the land."

Roy gripped his hand hard.

"You are kind to say it. It is a step I might well tremble to take—this asking a young girl who has lived in an atmosphere of love and indulgence, and known care only by hearsay, to share my toils, to divide with me the burden of whatever sorrow Providence may send me in discipline or judgment; to endure my caprices, be patient with my faults—be loving through and above all."

Orrin held down his head to hide a smile.

"I am continually reminded when the theme of our discourse is 'dear, delightful woman,' of what Willis says of his chum in his 'Slingsby Papers': 'It is seldom one meets with a spark of genuine chivalric fire nowadays. Job lit his daily pipe with it.' If another lover were to talk to me as you do, I should accuse him of rank affectation. I believe you feel all you say. Miss Kirke should be a proud and happy woman."

"She cannot abide that title," said Roy, smiling. "And, indeed, it suits her as ill as it sits well upon Eunice."

"Is that the elder sister? I thought she was 'Una.' *That* would be a fitting name for the chaste beauty. I glanced down, involuntarily, for the tamed lion couchant beneath her chair, when Miss Jessie spoke it."

"She is 'Eunice' to everybody else. They had not the same mother, and there is a difference of ten years in their ages. The first Mrs. Kirke was, I judge, a sedate pastoress who looked well after her household and her husband's flock. Her praise is still in the churches of this region. She died when the little Eunice was at the age of five. Four years afterward, Mr. Kirke brought to the manse a beautiful woman—city born and bred, refined, accomplished, and delicate. She fell into ill-health very soon. Bland as this climate seems to us who live so much further North, it was harsh to her. She was a South Carolinian, and her fondness for her old home grew into longing during her residence among these mountains. Her invalidism became confirmed after the birth of her babe. In memory of the sunny bowers in which her girlhood had been passed, she gave it the fanciful—you may think fantastic—name of Jessamine."

"It is odd, but pretty, and it suits her."

"Her fondness for the vine and fashion of wearing the flower may appear to you and to others a girlish whim. In reality, they are the motherless child's tribute to the memory of the parent whom she recollects with fondest devotion, although she was but five years old at her death."

"She told me she had known no home but this valley. The sisters were not educated in the country, I take it?"

"The elder graduated with distinction at Bethlehem. It was her mother's dying request that she should, at a suitable age, be sent to the Moravian Seminary at that place. She was thorough and conscientious in her studies, as in everything else, cultivating her talents for music and modern languages with especial diligence that, as she has told me, 'it might not be necessary to send little Jessie from home to school.' The younger sister has had no teachers except Eunice and their father, who is a fine classical scholar."

"And a man of far more than ordinary ability, I should suppose. Why has he buried himself alive in this out-of-the-world region?"

"Because he is essentially unworldly, I imagine. He has here ample opportunity for study, and he loves his books next to his children. Then, his attachment to the parsonage and to his people is strong. 'I was ambitious of distinction in my profession, once,' he said to me the other day, 'but that was before my wife's death.' It may sound like exaggerated sentiment, but I believe he means to live and die in sight of her grave. I have learned from Eunice something about his love for her, and his grief at her death.

"I have given you this sketch of the family history that you may better comprehend what passes in the household. My lodgings are at the hotel, as are yours, but most of our time will, of course, be spent at the Parsonage. I want you to know and like them all—particularly Jessie. It may be that you can be of service to her while I am abroad."

"What does she say to that scheme?"

"I have said nothing to her about it. I dread the task!" Roy looked very grave. "Her father agrees with me that it is wiser to be silent on the subject until my plans are definitely laid. I would prolong the clear shining of her day while I can."

He arose, apparently anxious to dismiss the subject. "We must go! Eunice's tea-table is ready at sunset."

"He cannot trust himself to discuss this matter of their separation," said Orrin, inly, following the rapid stride of his thoughtful cousin down the mountain. "One tear from his pert Amaryllis would reverse his decision at this, the eleventh hour. 'Lord! what fools these *lovers* be!'"

The manse meadows were gained by a rustic foot-bridge spanning the creek which skirted these. Two young men, whom Mr. Wyllys rightly supposed to be members of the "Committee upon Orator of the Day," were waiting here to speak to Mr. Fordham, probably to solicit a copy of his address for publication, the considerate kinsman further surmised, and sauntered on to the garden, leaving the other to follow when he would. Lingering among the fragrant borders, momentarily expecting Roy to rejoin him, he lost himself in a rose labyrinth, so affluent of bloom and odor, that he did not know where he was until warned of his proximity to the oriel-window by Jessie's voice. Through a crevice in the creepers, he could see her lounge set in the spacious recess, and the back of her head as she raised it to speak to some one within the room.

"Roy described him as *distingué* and fascinating!" she said, in an accent of chagrin. "I call him positively homely! Don't you?"

Orrin should have moved—assured as he was that he was the subject of unflattering remark. In his code, this was a reason why he should remain acquiescent and hearken for more. Perhaps others who make higher pretensions to the minor moralities would have done likewise.

"He is not handsome, certainly," returned Miss Kirke.

"You are disposed to be unreasonable because your expectations were unduly raised."

"By his cousin who told me he was the most popular man in Hamilton—one of the glass-of-fashion and mould-of-form kind, you know," continued Jessie, in increasing vexation. "Am I to be blamed if I lose at least the outposts of my temper when, having expected an Adonis, I behold—"

"A gentleman!" Her sister finished the sentence. "Since he is that, dear, and Mr. Fordham's cousin, he should be safe from our criticism. At least, while he is our guest."

There was a pause before Jessie spoke again.

"Darling Euna! are you displeased with me?" she said coaxingly. "I was cross and unladylike, I acknowledge. I ought not to—I did not expect that he would be Roy's equal in appearance or manner, but I am grievously disappointed."

"Not to be outdone in generous candor, I own that I am, also," was the reply.

The elder sister approached the window as she said it; and Mr. Wyllys effected a skilful retreat.

The labyrinth had its terminus in a matted arbor near the church-yard fence. Sitting down in this, the subject of the recent discussion indulged himself in a hearty but noiseless fit of laughter.

# CHAPTER III

Orrin Wyllys could afford to laugh at criticism that would have provoked a thin-skinned, or moderately-vain man to anger, if not to hatred. For he was aware that his cousin had spoken the bare truth when he represented him as the admired Crichton of the town which was their home. His features and form were as I have portrayed them. He had neither beauty nor absolute symmetry to recommend these. He was not wealthy, nor yet eminent in his profession. A lawyer in fair practice, gained principally by the exercise of other gifts than legal acumen, he was yet a person of mark in the community. The reason assigned for this would have been the same, in effect, by every acquaintance, whether the witness were the fine lady of *ton* who made sure of him before issuing her cards for the grand ball of the season, or the Milesian who "stepped intil his Honor's office to ask him could I take the law of Teddy O'Rourke for this black eye, or is it himself that will be afther taking the law of me for the two I've give *him*?"

"Not regularly handsome, I admit, my dear," Mrs. Beau Monde would say. "But there is something more potent, as more subtle in influence in his presence and speech. Do you know I think a fascinating homely man the most charming creature in the world? And Mr. Wyllys' deportment, tone, and conversation are unsurpassable. Other men may be as well-bred, but there is a nameless Something about his manner that is exquisite and irresistible."

While Murphy would expatiate by the hour upon the "satisfaction a man experienced in daleing wid a pairfect gintleman, and it was Misther Wyllys had the beautiful way wid him!"

That he danced elegantly, sang expressively, and was a pleasing pianist; that he was conversant with the current literature of the day; that the stereotyped cant known as "art criticism" fell from his tongue aptly, and as if no one else had ever used the same phrases in his auditor's hearing,—undoubtedly contributed largely to his popularity; but these accomplishments were secondary in power to the nameless Something lauded by Mrs. Beau Monde. His own sex recognized the charm more willingly than they are wont to acknowledge the claims to favoritism of one who is the woman's darling of his set. The graceful *insouciance* that artfully concealed his consciousness of the degree long ago awarded him, as "Pet of the Petticoats;" his gay good-humor, his fund of anecdote and repartee, made him as welcome at bachelors' wine and dinner-parties as in mixed companies. If his negligent saunter through the assembly-room, his deliberate articulation and grave, deferential bend before his fair vassals, provoked ill-nature to the charge of puppyism, the censor was silenced by tales of his proficiency in manly sports; how in the gymnasium and billiard-room, upon the cricket-green and skating-pond, he had few equals, so seldom found a superior, that his exploits had passed into a proverb.

After all, however, his brightest bays were gained in his character as carpet knight. Trained coquettes and professional flirts, flushed by a long course of victories, had put confident lances in rest and run vain-glorious tilts with him. He was always ready to accept the challenge; ready to become, for a few days, or, in exceptionally tough cases, a few weeks, the apparent captive of the ambitious belle. The approach of proud humility than which nothing could have been more opposed to servility of spirit or demeanor; the gradual, and finally rapt absorption of his every faculty and sentiment into his unspoken adoration of her whose chains he wore; the delicate appreciation of each shade of feeling and thought, and prescience of each desire;—above and beneath all, his singular faculty of adaptation to the various phases of character set for his reading,—could hardly fail, first, to disarm, then to flatter, finally to captivate.

Up to this period of his career, when he had entered his nine-and-twentieth year, nobody said openly of him that his business in life was to win hearts for the pleasure of breaking them. If he had broken any, his victims made no moan. In the cases of the veteran coquettes alluded to just now, sympathy would have been thrown away. There were stealthy whispers to the effect, however, that others, less wary, had been drawn into his snare; had dreamed of love, and, awakening to anguished perception of their folly, had shrouded bleeding hearts in robes of pride or Christian resignation, and lived on outwardly as little changed by the experience as was he. It is superfluous to remark that these cautious rumors lent lustre to his fame instead of tarnishing it; that dozens of intrepid damsels were wrought by the hearing into a Curtius-like spirit of self-immolation; panted to leap, bedecked in their bravest array, into the gulf which yawned to destroy the safety and peace of mind of the whole sisterhood of marriageable women in the classic town of Hamilton. The envious, nor the prudish, stigmatized him as a lady-killer. The coarse term would be an insult to his refinement, his notable honor, and equally notable kindness of heart. He was, beyond question, the most charming of men, a social diamond of the first water, although the obtuse daughters of the Dundee manse had not at once discovered it.

What wonder that he, sitting among the roses in the arbor, found infinite diversion in the recollection that he was pronounced by Jessie "positively homely"—utterly unattractive beside her handsome lover, and that her more discreet sister had mildly echoed her disappointment?

He enjoyed the novelty of the incident and the laugh it gave him—was sincere in the half-spoken regret—"What a pity I cannot publish this verdict and the manner of its delivery, in Hamilton."

With that, he pulled down a branch of musk roses nodding above his head; broke it, tore off the petals,until he had a double handful, and buried his face in the odorous mass. Roy came up with him as the sound of low, sweet singing moved the stillness of the garden and the sunset into music. The songstress was Jessie, lying within her oriel-window alone, and gazing at the amber ocean billowing above the purple hills at the outlet of the valley. Her rich contralto voice was like the colored light and the musk roses, Orrin thought, in no wise tempted to dislike or underrate her because she did not value him aright. That mistake would rectify itself, by and by. He could stay a fortnight in Dundee as well as not. Roy had pressed him to do so, and he began to think he would.

This was what Jessie sang, never dreaming of the audience, fit, but few, hidden in the blossoming thicket:

"Sleeping, I dreamed, Love—dreamed, Love, of thee;
O'er the bright wave, Love, floating were we.
Light in thy fair hair played the soft wind,
Gently thy white arms round me were twined;
And as thy song, Love, swelled o'er the sea,
Fondly thy blue eyes beamed, Love, on me."

Neither of the cousins stirred until the song was finished, when a robin in the nearest elm began his vespers.

"This is Arcadia!" said Orrin, ravishing another spray—great white roses this time, with creamy hearts.

"It is *home!*" replied the other, softly.

Orrin appeared not to hear him.

"Or the Vale of Cashmere!" he went on, drawing in long breaths of perfume. "Here are

"'Timid jasmine buds that keep
Their odors to themselves all day,
But when the sunlight dies away
Let the delicious secret out—'

roses of Kathay and bulbuls—and Nourmahal!"

Roy looked at him over his shoulder.

"If you have pulled enough of Eunice's rare, early roses to pieces to satisfy your destructive proclivities, we will go in," he said, pleasantly.

Something in his friend's eye and tone disinclined him to pursue the theme. He could not suspect him of an intention to ridicule Jessie or her home, but he felt the absence of sympathy with his own mood.

"Are they *hers*?" asked the other, brushing the wasted leaves in an unheeded shower to the floor.

Roy paid no regard to the emphasis. He was strangely averse to talking about Jessie at that moment.

"They are," he said, leading the way to the house, Orrin treading on the scattered flakes of fragrance, to gain the door of the bower. "She is an able florist. There is not another garden like hers for many miles around."

No one excepting Jessie observed that Mr. Wyllys did not accost her of his own accord while they were at tea, which was set out upon a small table near the large window in the parlor. She, used to petting, and what might have been considered by an impartial judge more than her share of general attention, and a trifle nervous withal, in her desire to produce an agreeable impression upon Roy's kinsman, did remark it, and was conscience-smitten by the fear lest her chagrin at beholding a man so unlike her preconceived ideal had been reflected in her manner. She seized an opportunity, therefore, when Roy rolled the table to its accustomed place in the middle of the apartment, to court Orrin's notice.

"So you ascended our Mont Blanc this afternoon?" she said, smiling engagingly. "I must retract my saucy innuendoes touching your fondness for ease."

He was quite near her, but he must have been inattentive, for he turned his face to her, with—"Pardon me! I did not catch your observation!"

"It was nothing so dignified as an observation," she retorted, coloring and laughing. "If I were to repeat it, you would be reminded of the poor girl whose complaint—'The soup is hot,' uttered confidentially to a deaf old lady who chanced to sit next her at a dinner-party, was the signal for the solemn production of an ear-trumpet, and the remark—audible to all present—'A very profound and interesting observation, I doubt not, my dear! Will you oblige me by repeating it?'"

Mr. Wyllys laughed in well-bred moderation that, somehow, made Jessie feel that her little story was not very amusing, and had been tamely told.

"I submit to the consequences of my deafness, rather than annoy you by the ear-trumpet," was his answer.

Bowing, in quitting her, he followed Mr. Kirke to another window.

"We were speaking of Ruskin's 'Stones of Venice,' to-day," Jessie heard him begin.

She had read the book, and would have enjoyed listening to their discussion of it, as did Eunice, to whom Mr. Wyllys appealed at her re-entrance, setting a chair for her by her father's, and establishing himself in front of them.

Roy apparently did not object to this arrangement, for he drew a stool to the sofa, and talked to Jessie, aside, of things that would have interested her beyond all other subjects, but for the sight of that group in the moonlight that now flooded the room. It kept astir the uneasy sensation produced by Mr. Wyllys' marked avoidance of her at tea-time. While her hand lay within her lover's, and her ear drank in all he said, and her heart beat, fast and warm, as he only could make it pulsate, she was ashamed to catch herself watching the slender figure, bending easily forward, his elbow upon the table at his side, his chin upon his hand, now in an attitude of respectful attention, while her father or Eunice spoke, again talking earnestly—she was sure, eloquently also,—in the low, cleverly modulated accents of which he was the consummate master. Did he then regard her as a feather-brained rattle? a forward school girl, of whose prattle he was already weary, and whom he adjudged incapable of entering into, or appreciating, intellectual conversation?

"Oh dear!" escaped her, when she reached this point.

Roy looked amazed—almost aghast—as well he might. He was in the middle of a description of their future home, prefatory of a hint he deemed it best to drop relative to a petition he had laid before the trustees of the college in which he was professor. This had asked a year's leave of absence, that he might pursue the study of the German language and literature abroad with one or two other branches of his profession. Orrin Wyllys had brought him letters of approbation from the body named, and the time had come when he must feel his way gently to the announcement of the approaching separation.

"My darling!" he said. "What is it? Are you in pain?"

"Yes! Not my foot!" seeing him look at it. "I have a desperate heartache! I shall never be good and wise enough for you, Roy! And you will discover this for yourself, one day."

"That is the only really foolish thing I have ever heard you say!" returned he, in fond raillery. "I am tormented, without intermission, by the conviction that I am unworthy of your regard, so we will let the one fear neutralize the other. Love is a powerful solvent, dear. It will melt these stubborn doubts—these flintstones of fancied incompatibility, that fret your heart when you meditate upon the chances that we shall make one another happy."

"But if I were sedate and discreet; cautious as to what I say, and to whom I say it,—more learned and beautiful—more like the blessed old Euna over there. You see"—in real mortification—"I cannot express the wish to reform without falling into my nonsensical tricks of speech!"

Roy could not preserve his gravity.

"I am not laughing at you!" he whispered, as she flung her arm over her eyes. "What has moved you to this sensitiveness—and with *me*? I could but liken my sentiments in the imaginary survey of the pattern bride you would give me to those of Jacob, who was put off with the demure Leah, when he had bargained for witching wicked Rachel."

"The comparison is an insult to Euna!" interrupted Jessie, warmly. "I said you ought to marry a woman like her—pure as a pearl, true as steel—in principle like adamant. Leah! Bah! I always detested her! She was a sly, heartless traitor—a smooth-tongued hypocrite, who cozened the pretty young sister whom she envied—becoming, as she did, a willing party to her father's fraud. She deserved all the unhappiness she got!"

"We shall not differ there. The 'tender-eyed' Jewess is no favorite of mine. But, even supposing that I were to sacrifice inclination to a sense of what you consider the fitness of things, Eunice or one like her would never elect to marry me. It is dissimilarity in certain characteristics that provides the best sauce for courtship. Your sister, for instance, would be well-mated with a man like Mr. Wyllys, the salient points of whose character are those which she has not."

"In other words, you think the interests of the drama demand that I should do the light comedy as a counter-poise to your heavy tragedy?" said Jessie, appeased. "I am sure I could never like your cousin—or one like him—well enough to think of marrying him."

"I don't ask you to do it!" rejoined Roy, playfully. "But do not, on that account, shut your eyes to his real excellence. He is to be your brother, remember—for I have no other. His father was my guardian, and while he lived, I scarcely felt the early loss of my parents. To Orrin personally, I owe much. He is four years my senior, and when we were at school, he fought many a battle in my behalf with boys bigger than either of us. Then, we were separated for seven years, seeing one another only in vacations and casual furloughs from business. He is one of the trustees of our college, and, although he will not admit it, I am persuaded that I am indebted to his influence, seconded as it was by my dear old friend, Dr. Baxter's advocacy of my cause,—for my Professorship. You will like and esteem him when you come to know him. I hope you two will be great friends in time. As a preliminary to your better understanding, and consequently your admiration for him—I am going to ask him for some music."

Orrin obeyed the call, but not with alacrity. He seemed altogether content with his location and his companions.

"Please do not order lights!" he said to Eunice who arose with him. "No illumination can be preferable to the mountain moonlight. It is radiance clarified to purity."

It revealed to him, from his seat upon the music-stool, a picture he was artist enough to enjoy. Jessie's white dress and pillows were flecked by the irregular tracery of vine-shadows, but, through an opening in the leafy lattice, the moon poured a stream of light upon her face and bust, revealing even the gleam of the betrothal ring upon the hand supporting her cheek. Roy had opened the piano, and now stood at her feet in the shade, leaning against the wall—a dark, motionless sentinel, with folded arms and bowed head, listening to the music, or watchful of her.

The player essayed no scientific surprises; no juggling complication of fingers and keys. He began with a moonlight sonata, the original theme of which might have been rung by fairy hands upon the jessamine bells, "giving their delicious secrets out" under the weight of summer dew. From this he strayed into the "Midsummer Night's Dream,"—thence to the most beautiful of the musical paradoxes, "Songs Without Words," and there rested.

"More, please!" entreated Jessie, in dreamy delight.

Both hands were folded under her cheek now, and she had not moved since he finished the fairy sonata.

"This is Elysium!" she added, softly.

"But sing, Orrin—won't you?" asked Roy.

So long as his cousin's music brought his darling more pleasure than did conversation with himself, the generous fellow would contribute in this way to her gratification.

"You wouldn't have wondered at or blamed me, if you had ever heard him sing," said a broken-hearted wife to me once, in reviewing the circumstances of her early acquaintance with the man who had married, neglected, brutally ill-used, and finally deserted her. He was bully, ruffian, liar, cheat, and drunkard, but he sang like an angel, giving to words and music a depth and delicacy of expression that sounded to the listeners like heavenly inspiration. With the visage of a Caliban and the appetites of a satyr, he yet moved others to smiles, tears, high and holy aspirations, to solemn or wild enthusiasm, religious or patriotic. His musical genius was the talisman by which he made himself popular, courted, envied, passionately beloved. Orrin Wyllys' voice, his exquisite taste in and knowledge of music would have won him social distinction had he been awkward in carriage, boorish in manner, and an ignoramus. There was not another amateur performer in his circle who could ever hope to equal him in effective and scientific execution. In the keeping of some — of many — the gift would have been a joy and a beneficence. He had none more dangerous — and he knew it, lightly as he affected to esteem it.

If his first selection on this occasion harmonized less perfectly with the hush and chastened lustre of the evening than his unsyllabled melodies had done, he was excusable since it developed the best tones of his voice. It was Mrs. Norton's sea lyric—"The Outward Bound." His auditors felt the rush of the favoring wind that had sprung up at dawn; heard the flap of the sails as they filled, and the creak of the line that strained at the anchor; saw the knot of parting friends; the close, tight hand-clasp, that helped force back the tears from eyes that would fain smile farewell.

"It is a fine old song," said Mr. Kirke. "I heard it many years ago. I thank you, Mr. Wyllys, for reviving the memory."

"This generation has nothing that can compare worthily with the music of other days," replied Orrin's voice from his shaded corner. "The true lover of the art must turn from the *potpourri* of the modern opera, the unflavored whey of fashionable ballads, with the craving of him who, having tasted the mellow wine, refuses the new — for he saith, 'the old is better.'"

Jessie moved like one awaking from a trance—spoke with feigned lightness.

"'To weep is a woman's part!' I don't like that line of your song, Mr. Wyllys. If your 'Outward Bound' had admitted mothers, sisters, and wives to the parting banquet, they would have borne themselves as bravely as did their masculine comrades, and without the aid of the 'sparkling brimmer,' which is, I suppose, the poetical name for a potion known, hereabouts, as 'mountain dew' or 'Dutch courage.' But if poets of the stronger sex are to be believed, Niobe was the prototype woman."

"Your quarrel is with one of your own sex, Miss Jessie; not with me or mine," was the cool rejoinder. "Mrs. Norton wrote the offensive line."

"There is something very like it in Kingsley's 'Three Fishers,'" said Roy, to cover Jessie's trifling discomfiture. "Let us have that next."

Mr. Wyllys sang it, giving to the refrain a weary sadness, exceeding pathos. He knew how effective this was when he saw Jessie's hand steal up to her eyes. She did not plead for "more," or cavil at "Men must work and women must weep," when he left the instrument, and went back to the window where Eunice was sitting.

"If you and your father are not afraid of the dew, I should like to see the mountains in this light," he said, persuasively. "Dare you walk for a little while upon the porch?"

The three went out together.

"Don't stay here, Roy!" begged Jessie. "The view must be fine to-night. It is not fair that you should be tied to my side all the time. I feel as if I were defrauding your cousin of his share of your society."

"You must continue to upbraid yourself with the theft, then," answered Roy, reseating himself upon the ottoman, and drawing her head to his shoulder. "Or, rather, my pet, you must cease to imagine that I could prefer any society to yours, any scene to the delightful seclusion of this, our betrothal nook. Orrin knows all. He has fine tact, and comprehends how precious to me is every hour passed with you."

This was a plausible solution of the reserve which puzzled and pained her. Jessie tried to receive it in full faith, and forgot to watch the forms strolling back and forth before the two windows which opened upon the piazza. When the party broke up for the night, she extended her hand to Orrin in cousinly freedom.

"I mean to make my trial effort at sitting up, to-morrow," she said, blithely. "And we will have some music. Euna doesn't sing, but she will play our accompaniments, since Mr. Fordham disdains the piano."

"I threw a number of instrumental duets into my trunk yesterday," said Orrin to Miss Kirke. "I did not then know why I did it. I understand now that I had some intuition of coming enjoyment. May I bring them up to-morrow?"

Jessie had never been jealous of Eunice in her life. Her disposition was as generous as it was impetuous. She did not care, she said to herself, in reviewing the evening that sent her to her pillow tired but sleepless, that Mr. Wyllys had openly preferred her sister's companionship to hers; that he had scarcely noticed her proposal about the music in his desire to play with Eunice. But she was conscious of a discordant jar in memories that would else have been all brightness, whenever she reverted to her repeated efforts to scale the barriers of the strangerhood that ought not to have existed between them for a moment after he heard Roy's story—and the adroit rebuffs that had met each of these.

Eunice had helped her undress and seen her comfortably laid in bed, kissed her affectionately, and promised to be with her early in the morning. By the time the door was shut, Jessie had propped her head upon her crossed arms, and lay with wide-open eyes gazing through the unshuttered windows at the broad, straight brow of Windbeam, black and majestic in the mountain moonlight; listening to the stealthy whispers of the vine-leaves about the casement, and living over the events of the day—an exciting one in her quiet life. Her thoughts of Roy were all of prideful joy. Her heart was very tender, very quiet in the glad humility that possessed her as she pondered upon the fact that he had chosen her—an undisciplined, unsophisticated country girl, to share the career she was sure would be noble and distinguished. Something more than usually fond in Eunice's silent caress at parting from her for the night, brought up a host of reminiscences of the motherly love with which this sister had guarded and nurtured her—the youngling of the household. Such a bright, sweet day her existence had been! In all her sky there was not a cloud, save this light vapor of discontent with herself that the introduction to Roy's relative—the first of his old friends whom she had ever met—should have been so unsatisfactory.

"His reserve actually increased as the hours went on," she reflected. "His manner was more free and cordial while I was telling him the story of old Davie Dundee than after Roy had explained to him what we are to one another. Perhaps he thinks an engaged young lady should be demure and dutiful, having no eyes or ears for any one except her betrothed. Perhaps it is as Roy says, and he fears to intrude upon our *tête-à-têtes*. I must convince him that we are not so selfish. Roy declares that his cousin approves heartily of our engagement—that he said many pleasant things of me, else I should fear that he had taken a dislike to me, from the beginning, that he thought Professor Fordham might and ought to have done better. I must make him like him for myself—not merely because I am his kinsman's choice."

From which soliloquy the reader will perceive that Mr. Wyllys had led off with a winning card.

# CHAPTER IV

A week had passed since the Dundee Centennial, and life in the parsonage had been in outward aspect like the weather—still and sunny. The oldest Dundeeian had never known before so early and genial a season. Eunice's roses were in luxuriant bloom; the clover-meadows were pink and fragrant; the forests had burst into full leafage; the strawberries upon the southern terrace of the kitchen-garden were swelling globes, white on the nether, scarlet upon the upper sides.

The ways of the household, always simple and methodical, were not otherwise now. Roy spent a couple of hours each forenoon with his betrothed. Orrin rarely made his appearance until two or three hours after dinner when the cousins came up from the hotel together, and did not return to their lodgings before ten o'clock at night. Mr. Kirke had daily interviews with Mr. Wyllys in the course of the walks and drives they took in company, and brought home accounts of his suavity, wit, and varied information, which were endorsed by Eunice, which Jessie heard with growing bewilderment at the chance or purpose that withheld her from participation in what was freely enjoyed by her father and sister. Even their music practice had not melted the ice that lay, an impassive mass, just beneath the surface of his deportment whenever he approached or addressed her. Her liveliest sallies and most friendly overtures, met with a response, ready and civil, indeed, but so unlike the gentle courtesy, the kindliness and graceful deference of his behavior to Eunice that nothing but a spirit determined and unsuspicious of evil as was our heroine's could have kept her to her resolve to win his friendship.

Roy found her very charming under the light veil of pensiveness this secret solicitude cast over her. She never intimated to him that his kinsman had not met her expectation in every respect. She was thankful, instead, that her betrothed did not see for himself that all was not right between them. Some day, when the frost was quite dispelled, they would laugh over it together—over her fears, her innocent stratagems for the accomplishment of her object, Orrin's stateliness, and Roy's blindness to her perturbation. She had patience and hope. She would await the vanishment of the mist, passing content, meanwhile, with the heart-riches that were hers beyond peradventure. She had not heard of the German University scheme. It was unlike Roy Fordham to hang back from making a revelation which must come in the end, which delays could not soften, and which could cause no more distress now than if it were withheld until the close of his vacation. His judgment said that Jessie would better endure the prospect of the separation while he was with her, to lead her thoughts to the great and manifest advantages that would accrue to him from the year of foreign study, and— overleaping the gulf of absence—to paint the delight of re-union. Mr. Kirke represented that Jessie was a girl of sense and strength; that she would be better pleased to be confided in, and consulted as his future wife, than be blinded and petted as a child; and Roy, acquiescing in this opinion, still put off the evil hour. Was it loving consideration for her—or presentiment— that struck him with dumbness?

The lovers sat on the piazza, one afternoon, just after the sunset repast. Jessie's "trial effort" had been made with ease that augured rapid recovery, but she was forbidden to walk without assistance, or to bear her whole weight upon the injured foot.

"While I feel strong enough to run a race with you down to the mill," she said, pointing to a venerable building, a quarter of a mile distant. "You can form no idea of the perversity of the restless thing that used to be a manageable member, when I had leave to walk, or sit still as I liked. I have a terrific attack of the fidgets!"

"Penalty of insubordination—a return to the lounge and oriel-window!" smiled Roy, in warning.

"That would be no punishment at all! When I am strong and active again I mean often to play helpless, upon that dear old lounge, to lie within the window and dream. I love it!"

Her voice sank in an intonation of ineffable tenderness that went to Roy's heart in a pang, not a thrill. This evening he meant to tell her that for many months she must sit alone in what he had named their "betrothal-nook;" that the year they had agreed upon as the period of their engagement must be passed apart, the one from the other. He had made up his mind to another thing. If she asked the sacrifice at his hands, he would abandon the cherished hope of years, the fruition of which seemed now so near, and she should never guess the extent of his self-denial. She was so dear to him! this incarnation of frolic, passion, and of fancies—gay, graceful, as whimsical as various—but all beautiful to him; she, whose eyes deepened and softened and glowed with the tender cadence of those three words— "I *love* it!" He had never succeeded in telling Orrin why he loved her. His spoken analysis of her character was cold and imperfect. Had Orrin uttered aloud his unflattering, "pert Amaryllis," Roy would have resented the epithet warmly, yet acknowledged, secretly, that his own portrait of her was hardly more like the reality. He could not describe her trait by trait, feature by feature. But for himself, he knew that she was the embodied glory of his life; that every ray that kept his heart warm and bright with a very summer of gladness, could be traced to her,—her love, and the influence the consciousness of this had upon his thoughts of the present, and dreams of days to come.

"The oriel is enchanted ground to me. We will build one like it, in our own home, and cover it with jessamine and wisteria," he said, noting, with loving amusement, the crimson flush that always bathed her face at direct allusions to their marriage. "Orrin shall sketch it for me. He is a universal genius, and his taste is marvellous. His bachelor apartments are a notable exception to any others I ever saw. They are furnished *almost* as well, kept almost as neatly, as if he were married."

"Isn't he a bit of a Sybarite?" queried Jessie, abruptly. "If he has a fault— or, no! you wouldn't own that he has—but, isn't his foible a love of luxury— of comfort, if you prefer to call it so—bodily and mental?"

"He is certainly not indolent. I know no other man who will work more persistently, although quietly, to gain a coveted end. And if he loves the ease of the flesh, why so do we all—don't we? His philosophy teaches that it is folly for one to be miserable, when he can as readily be happy and comfortable. His has been a prosperous life, thus far. He has known little of sorrow or trial. Should these come, they will ripen, not sour him, for the original material is good. I am the more anxious that you should know and appreciate him because—"

The gate swung open to admit a visitor—a farmer's lad, in whose attempts at self-education the young professor took a lively interest.

"I found this in the field on the other side of the mountain, to-day," he said, laying a piece of stone in Mr. Fordham's hand. "I think there's ore in it."

Roy inspected it closely.

"Miss Jessie"—he gave her no more familiar address in the hearing of common acquaintances—"is your father in his study?"

"I believe so," she replied, eyeing the intruder less amiably than her lover had done, in the anticipation of the prolonged interruption.

"Mr. Kirke has an acid that will test this in a few minutes," continued Fordham to the boy. "Will you excuse me for a little while?" turning to

Jessie with a smile loving for herself, and entreating her forbearance for his *protégé*.

Her ill-humor vanished instantly under the benignant ray.

"Certainly!" she replied, nodding cordially to the bashful lad. "He is the noblest man God ever made!" she said aloud, when she was alone.

She leaned back in her easy chair, her hands folded in blissful contentment, enjoying the breeze from the mountains, the sunset clouds, the incense from the flower-garden, and the hum of the mill-wheel, mentally recapitulating her hero's perfections, until her heart ached with happy sighs, and she saw the landscape through an iridescent haze.

"I am a baby!" was her indignant ejaculation, as she cleared her eyes with an impatient brush of her hand. "I grow more ridiculous every day!"

As a means of growing wiser, she fell to watching her sister and Orrin Wyllys, who were busy tying up wandering rose-bushes in Eunice's pet labyrinth. Mr. Wyllys had his back to Jessie, when she first observed them. He was fastening back a branch which Miss Kirke held in its place, and their hands were very close together. It may have been this circumstance, it may have been the heat of the day, or the reflection of a bunch of pink moss-roses overhead—it could hardly have been anything which her companion was saying which brought the delicate roseate flush to the face usually pale and calm. His attitude was far too dignified and respectful to hint the possibility of gallant badinage on his part. *Bonâ-fide* love-making was, of course, out of the question, since they had not known each other ten days.

"Euna is handsome!" mused her sister in complacent affection. "What a high-bred face and bearing she has! She looks the lady in her morning-gowns of print and dimity; but that lawn with the forget-me-not sprig becomes her rarely. I am glad I insisted upon her putting it on. But she wouldn't let me fasten the lilies-of-the-valley in her hair! Her only fault is a tendency to primness. She and Mr. Wyllys get on admirably together. He evidently admires her, and it is a treat to her to have the society of a cultivated gentleman. I know," smiling and blushing anew, "it is a salvo to my conscience to see them satisfied with each other's company, needing Roy and myself as little as we need them. I should else blame myself for our seeming selfishness."

Rambling on discursively, she struck upon an idea, too fraught with delightsome mischief not to urge her to immediate action. Eunice had turned her head away, and Orrin was concealed by a tall shrub. The grassy alley leading from the porch to where they were standing would not give back the sound of footsteps. How frightened and amazed the careful elder sister would be, if she were to steal down the walk and present herself before her! How solemnly Orrin would look on while she submitted to be lectured for her imprudence, and how she, in the end would triumph over her custodians, Roy included (who, by the way, was staying away an unconscionable time), when she should demonstrate that she knew better than they what she could do and bear; that she was none the worse for the escapade that had wrought their consternation. She only regretted that she must lose the sight of Roy's horrified visage when he should return to discover her flight.

Her eyes gleaming with mirth, she arose cautiously, favoring the unused joint, and stepped off the low piazza. Even when she felt the cool, delicious turf under foot, she steadied herself by grasping the nearest objects that offered a support. First it was a clump of box, then the stout prickly branches of a Japan apple-tree, then a fan-shaped trellis, which would by and by be covered with Cyprus vines. She would do nothing rashly—would come to her own by degrees. But when another step would bring her within arms' length of the florists, she trod firmly upon both feet, and feeling neither pain nor weakness, laughed aloud in wicked glee, and took that step. She saw Eunice start and grow white; saw Orrin's grave yet courtly surprise as he advanced to offer his arm. Ere he could reach her, the treacherous ankle gave way with a wrench that drove breath and sense in one quick shuddering breath from her body.

As they left her, she heard, like a strain of far-off music, a voice say in her ear, "My poor child!" had a dizzy thought that strong arms—stronger than Eunice's—received her.

Then, all was a blank until she awoke upon her lounge, hair and face dripping with wet; the scent of *sal volatile* tingling in her nostrils, and a cluster of anxious faces about her. Eunice's was the first she knew, Roy's next. He was on his knees by her, chafing her hands. She pulled them feebly from his hold, and clasped them about his neck, hiding her eyes upon his bosom.

"O, Roy! I was very wrong! very foolish! Don't scold me."

"Hush! hush!" he said, soothingly. "Nobody thinks of scolding you! If you apologize to any one, it must be to this gentleman. He brought you into the house, and I suspect his arms want looking after more than your foot does."

He laughed, not quite steadily, in saying it, and Jessie felt his fingers tighten upon hers. She flushed up rosily—was herself again, as she looked around for Orrin. He was in the rear of the family party, as was seemly, but his eyes were bent upon her with a singular fixedness—the irids closing in upon a spark that flashed and pierced like steel. Involuntarily, she shut hers, for a second, as if blinded.

He came forward at that.

"Don't believe him!" said the same voice that had sent its echo through her swoon. "I am none the worse for the slight exertion. I consider myself very fortunate in having been near enough to help you, when you fainted — am very thankful that you are better. Come with me, Roy! Here is the doctor! If *he* scolds you, Miss Jessie, please consider me your champion."

The doctor, being an old friend, did scold the "madcap," who had, he for a while averred, undone his and Nature's fortnight's work. Relenting, finally, at Jessie's pretty show of penitence, he confessed that less harm had been done than he had expected, and contented himself with sentencing the delinquent to two days' strict confinement to the sofa, and "serious meditation upon what might have been the result of her imprudence — her reckless step."

"My misstep, you mean," said the incorrigible patient. "If I had not lain here so long already as to forget how to walk straightly and squarely, and to maintain the centre of gravity, this would not have happened."

Altogether, the evening was gayer than usual to all. Jessie's spirits were exuberant to a degree her sister feared was hysterical, and Orrin seconded her sallies with a quieter humor, that amused the rest and enchanted her.

"It was worth my while to faint!" she owned to him, *sotto voce*, when he came up to say "Good-night." "I wish I had done it before!"

Her cheeks were red with excitement; her eyes laughed up into his with arch meaning that was very bewitching and very indiscreet. His pupils contracted suddenly to the blue spark, and his left palm covered the little hand he held within his right.

"You are very kind!" was all he said with his lips.

"What treason are you two whispering there?" questioned Roy.

"Nothing that concerns you in the least!" answered Jessie, saucily. "We will keep our own counsel — won't we?" to Orrin.

He was too sensible to lie awake thinking, at an hour when people with accommodating consciences and gutta-percha hearts are wont to sleep soundly. Nor had he ever contracted the unsafe and irrational habit of talking audibly to himself — one to which poor Jessie was addicted. Yet he had his thoughts as he put out the candle in his bedroom that night.

"She is either a born flirt, and over-anxious to practise her calling, or she is the most charming, because most novel compound of naïveté, cleverness, and feeling that has crossed my path for many a day. In either case, she is a study."

The best and the worst women were with him resolved into that—studies, all,—and when they had fed his vanity and ministered to his individual gratification, they were laid aside for other specimens. As the dissecter of men's bodies soon loses his reverence for whatever of divinity the common mind may discern in the human form; as the anemone and the nettle are to the botanist but different combinations of stamen, pistil, and petal,—so your professed student of character, your mortal searcher and tryer of souls, merges heart into head in the practice of his art. Sorrow has no sacredness; Love no warning purity; Pain no appeal to him. Sensibilities are interesting only as they quiver and shrink beneath his touch; Affection is his plaything; blasted hopes, withered and wounded hearts, are the unconsidered *débris* of the sacrificial honors done the ensanguined Moloch of his Self-love.

It is the fashion to call such ornaments of Society. A better, because truer, name, would be the Thugs of Civilization.

# CHAPTER V

Dr. Septimus Baxter was President of Marion College, situate in the beautiful town of Hamilton, lying two hundred miles to the northward, and in another state than the mountain-girded valley of which the Dundee Church and the surrounding village were the chief ornaments. Dr. Baxter was the nominal head of the faculty of professors, and Mrs. Septimus Baxter was virtual autocrat of his home.

He was a little man, physically, at his best, which was when he was in his own realm—the area enclosed by the walls of his lecture-room. There was, in popular phrase, "no fit" to his clothes. His trousers bagged at the knees, and his coats hung in loose folds down from his shoulder-blades, on the very day they left the tailor's shop; were shabby within twenty-four hours. He had a trick of brushing the nap of his hat the wrong way in his abstracted moods, and of twisting his forefinger in one bow of his white cravat until he dragged it into a slovenly loop, two crumpled wisps depending from it. Another and his most inveterate habit was, to tie his handkerchief into a succession of tight knots while he lectured, preached, prayed, and talked. Each marked a step in ratiocination or a rise in interest in the matter that engaged his mind until the climax of proof or animation was reached, when he would begin to untie them, one after the other, timing the process so judiciously that "Amen!" or "*Quod erat demonstrandum!*" passed his lips as the released cambric swept through his hand in a flourish prior to its restoration to his pocket. Nevertheless, he commanded respect from students and professors. His courage in grappling with crabbed or ponderous themes; the eagle eye that penetrated the vapors of mysticism, detected the insidious thread of sophistry, which, intertwined with legitimate argument, was gradually but fatally guiding the inquirer away from the truth; the bursts of real eloquence, passages of beauty and pathos, that starred the didacticism of his discourses, electrifying his hearers as the musical ring from the desiccated tortoise-shell may have startled the god who tripped over it—these made him a hero to his classes, a man to be consulted and reverenced by his co-laborers. Moreover, he had a great heart within his narrow chest, soft as a child's, generous to self-abnegation, and full of such holy and Christian graces as love the shade, while their unconscious aroma betrays their existence to all who pass.

Mrs. Baxter had been a belle, and she would hardly have cast a second glance upon the small and shabby divine, but for two weighty reasons. By some unaccountable freak of Cupid, or of Fortune, the popular Miss Lanneau had counted her thirtieth year without exchanging her celibate state for that which she languishingly avowed would be preferable to one of her dependent nature and seeking sensibilities. She laughed yet with her lips and executed arch manoeuvres with her speaking eyes, when unfeeling allusion was made in her presence to the "crooked stick" that awaits the over-nice fagot gatherer, and to the forlorn and aged virgin, also a wanderer in woodlands, who answered the owl's "To-who?" all the freezing night with the despairing—"Anybody!" But at heart she was growing restless, if not unhappy, when Dr. Baxter fell in her way. She was a *littérateur*, as well as a beauty, and her reverend suitor was a man of note—a distinguished clergyman, a *savant* and senior professor in a highly respectable institution of learning. She had longed for a "career" all her life—for a sphere of decided influence—social and literary. Would a more promising avenue to this ever be offered her? She overlooked the ill-fitting coat, the dragged cravat, the inevitable handkerchief. As she put it, she "set the subjective where it should always be placed—above the grosser objective." In direct English she married the doctor, and had for fifteen years made him an excellent wife. If his testimony were of importance in this case—and he was a sturdy truth-teller—he wanted no better.

I have said that he was a little man at his best. He was a pygmy on a certain evening in the November succeeding the Dundee Centennial summer. To begin with the most severe of the dwarfing processes to which he had been subjected. It was a reception night in the presidential mansion. Mrs. Baxter had given a party the previous week, and now sat in state, as was the Hamiltonian usage, to receive the calls demanded from those who had been the invitees on that occasion. The ceremony in its mildest form would have been purgatorial to her spouse, but she had aggravated the torture by personally superintending his toilette. This accomplished, she entreated him if he had one atom of regard for her, to leave necktie and handkerchief alone for that night; walked him into the parlor, and inducted him into an immense easy chair directly beneath a bracket-light; thrust an illuminated folio—one of her centre-table ornaments—between his fingers, and withdrew to her own chair a little way off, to examine the effect.

"You are really picturesque, my love!" she decided, in honeyed patronage. "If you can *only* remember to sit upright instead of slipping down in the lap of your chair until your coat-collar shows above the back of your neck, you will make a fine study for a sketch of 'Learned Leisure,' or something of that kind."

The poor man smiled resignedly, and began to turn the leaves of his book. It was a sacred album, the work of his wife's fair fingers, although he did not know this.

"I flatter myself you will find some choice bits there?" she said, modestly.

She was fond of talking about "bits," and "effects," and "tone," and "depth;" of "*chiaro-oscuro*," and "bas-reliefs," and "intaglios," and "antiques," —useful cant that forms the stock-in-trade of many an art-critic, whose decrees pass current with a larger circle than the clique which eulogized Mrs. Baxter's talents. She was, in feature and coloring, a pretty woman still, in defiance of her forty-five or forty-six years. Her brown eyes were lively; the red of her complexion, if a trifle fixed and hard, seldom outspreading the distinctly defined round spots upon the cheek-bones, was hers honestly, as were the glossy curls that showed no frost-lines, and the pearly teeth she had trained her lips to reveal at every possible opportunity. Her hands were plump, white, and small, and would have been smaller had she exercised them less. Like the teeth, they were too obtrusive. She could not say "Good-day" to a passing acquaintance without parting her lips in a wide smile over the milk-white treasures, tucking away their natural covering in an incredibly narrow fold above the ivory, and stretching it below into a straight line which lost itself in creases that had once been dimples. She had been renowned in her youth for her vivacity, and had cultivated it into what nobody was kind enough to tell her was frisky affectation. The extent to which the pliant fingers curved, and twined, and twinkled, and sprawled, in the course of a conversation of moderate length, was a thing of wonder forever to the uninitiated spectator of her gambols. She added to this gesticulation a way of plunging forward from her girdle upward, when she waxed very animated, that threatened to precipitate her into the lap of her fellow-colloquist, after which she would lay her hand upon her heaving bust, and swallow audibly, while awaiting a reply to her latest deliverance. To sum up description in one word—Mrs. Baxter's speciality was Manner.

Her friends were correct in one laudation. She was amiable and kind-hearted in her way, as her husband was in his. If she trafficked upon this excellence, made the most of it, very much after the style in which she showed off her teeth and hands, it was rather because display was her controlling foible, than through any design upon the answering gratitude of her beneficiaries. She was dressed in black silk, with a jaunty velvet basquine, a scarlet scarf of Canton crêpe fastened upon the right shoulder with an antique cameo, and knotted under the left, the fringed ends falling low down upon her skirt.

She was just established in her comfortable *causeuse*, when the door-bell heralded a visitor.

"My dear Mr. Wyllys!" she cried, fluttering forward to meet him. "You are doubly welcome when you come alone. One sees you so seldom except in a crowd, that it is a genuine pleasure to have a few moments' quiet conversation with you."

"It is like yourself to excuse my unfashionably early call with such gracious tact," responded the gentleman, bowing low over her hand.

He shook hands with the doctor with less *empressement*, but most respectfully, and sank upon a divan near the hostess.

"I have another engagement this evening, but I could not deny myself the pleasure of paying my *devoirs* to you in passing. I will not ask if you have recovered from the fatigue of Thursday night"—with an expressive look at her blooming face. "I believe, however, it is never a weariness to you to be agreeable, as it is to us duller and less benevolent mortals. I am horribly cross, always, on the morning succeeding a party. It is as if I had overdrawn my account, in the matter of social entertainment; borrowed too heavily from the reserve fund intended by Nature for daily expenses. But this rule applies only to people whose resources of spirits, wit, and general powers of pleasing, are limited. You are above the need of such pitiful economy as we find necessary."

"*Shall* I undeceive you?" beamed the lady. "If the doctor—dear, patient martyr!—were put into the witness-box, he might tell sad tales, make divulgations that would demolish your pretty and flattering theory. Doctor, my love! Mr. Wyllys is anxious to know what was the status of my spiritual and mental thermometer, on the morning after our little *re-union*, last week?"

"Eh, what did you say, my dear?"

He lowered his folio. His eyebrows were perked discontentedly, and his forefinger was in the doomed bow she had tied not fifteen minutes before.

Mrs. Baxter tried, unsuccessfully, to frown down the offending digit before she made reply.

"Mr. Wyllys has heard that I am like champagne, 'stale, flat, and unprofitable'—with a dash of vinegar—when the effervescence wrought by social excitement is off," vivified, by her mirthful misrepresentation of her visitor's words, into radiance that revealed every molar, and forced her eyelids into utter retirement.

"Ah!" The doctor smiled absently, and re-bent his brows over the page, protruding his lips in a vicious pout as he read.

"He disdains to notice the slander," resumed Mrs. Baxter, unabashed at her failure to elicit a conjugal compliment. "Seriously, Mr. Wyllys, I am thankful for the guidance of reason and will that counterbalance my mercurial temperament. My spirit resembles nothing else so much as a mettled steed, whose curvettings are restrained by an inexorable rein. But for my sober judgment, Impulse would have led me into an erratic course, I fear."

Relaxing the tension of the fingers and wrist that had pulled hard at an imaginary curb, and unclenching the teeth from their bite upon the word "inexorable," she sighed, reflectively.

"The combination is rare—" commenced the gentleman.

"It is preposterous!" ejaculated the doctor, closing the Russian-leather album with a concussion like the report of a pocket-pistol.

"I think not, dear," said the wife, gently corrective. "It is, as Mr. Wyllys says, a rare combination, but certainly not an impossible one."

"It is preposterous," reiterated the doctor, with a ruinous tug at his cravat, "that a rational creature, who can read and write, should waste time in disfiguring good, honest paper with such incongruous, not to say blasphemous, nonsense as I find here. It was bad enough for mediæval monks to deck the Word of Life in the motley wear of a harlequin. Greek, German, black-letter text, are, all of them, stumbling-blocks to the unlearned, diversions to the thoughtless. But when the sacred Scriptures are bedizened into further illegibility by paint and gilding, and *illustrated* by birds, beasts, and even fishes, daubed upon fields, azure, argent, and verde, the offence becomes an abomination. Such profanation is offered that divinest of pastorals, the twenty-third psalm, in this volume," elevating it in strong disgust.

Mrs. Baxter arose and took it from his hand in time to save it from being tossed to the table or floor.

"Tastes differ, my dear husband," was all she said, but her forbearance and real sweetness of temper called forth a look of unfeigned respect from the amused spectator.

"I wouldn't keep it in the parlor, if I were in your place, Jane," the doctor expostulated, seeing her deposit the folio upon a stand beyond his reach.

"I will not ask you to look at it again, love," —still amiably.

She returned to the subject when the critic had helped himself to a volume which was more to his taste.

"I saw few things when I was abroad, before my marriage, that interested me more than the illuminated missals and breviaries preserved in convents, museums, and private collections of *vertu*," she said to Mr. Wyllys. "I am the possessor of a remarkably fine specimen of the illuminator's art—the gift of a dear friend and relative, now no more. I had not looked into it for years until after I commenced my humble album, which, allow me to observe, my excellent husband does not guess is my handiwork. To return"—the hands describing an inward curve, and subsiding into an embrace upon her knee—"the best touches in my work were after my precious reliquary. I must show it to you. I am chary of displaying it to non-appreciative or irreverent eyes. Consequently it seldom sees the light."

Orrin followed her to an escritoire at the back of the room, peeping covertly at his watch as he went. Mrs. Baxter laid her hand upon her bust, and choked down some rebellious uprising of memory or regret, as she unlocked a drawer.

"This is it!" mournfully, taking out a thin volume bound in gilded leather and carved boards, and redolent of the scent of some Indian wood.

Orrin examined it in pleased surprise. He had expected to see an absurdity. He beheld a gem of its kind; a collection of Latin hymns, including the Stabat Mater, Dies Iræ, and Veni Sancte Spiritus, each page encircled by a border of appropriate design, and delicate yet rich coloring.

"I have never seen anything finer. I do not wonder that you prize it highly. I thank you for showing it to me," he said, sincerely. "By whom was it executed?"

"My friend ordered it for me of an adept in his art, then resident at Florence. I forget his name, but you will find it cleverly concealed from the common eye in some one of the convolutions of the title-page," was the reply.

The fly-leaf adhered slightly to the page designated, and Orrin read the inscription upon the former before detaching it.

"'Jane Lanneau, from Ginevra. Florence, January 1st, 18—.' I have surely seen that handwriting before! 'Ginevra!'" he repeated slowly, and the pretty name fell musically from his tongue. "There is poetry in the word!"

"You would have said so, had you known her!" Mrs. Baxter winked away two unbidden tears that glazed her eyes, without forming and dropping—swallowed anew and very hard. "She always reminded me of a plaintive poem set to music. That is, in the later years of an existence which was all song and sunniness when it was fresh and new."

Orrin fluttered a few leaves; commented upon the grace and finish of a decoration here and there, and went back to the inscription. It was strongly like Jessie Kirke's writing, but the resemblance was undoubtedly accidental. The one line had been penned, he learned from the date, before she was born.

"She was the Helena to my Hermia," pursued the hostess. "We lived the same life until her marriage, which preceded mine by five years. She was my senior by some months, but in heart and soul we were *twins!*"— pressing her hands gradually together, beginning at the wrists, and passing upward to the finger-tips, to express the idea of oneness. "And by a most extra-*or*-di-nary coincidence, we both married clergymen!"

"Another evidence of the perfect harmony of soul existing between you. Did I understand you to say that she is not living?"

"Alas! she has been in her grave for fifteen years. I never saw her after her marriage, which was a surprise to all her friends. We anticipated a brilliant union for her. But she bestowed herself, her talents, her beauty, upon a clerical widower who was twelve years older than herself. My poor Ginevra! it was a strange ending to her sanguine dreams. Mr. Kirke was a scholarly man, it is true, and a thorough gentleman, and of his devotion to her there could be no doubt. It was such worship as few women can inspire. I believe that he tried faithfully to make her happy, but my personal acquaintanceship with him was very slight."

"Kirke!" repeated Orrin, more deliberately and with less emphasis than was his wont, and he was always the reverse of abrupt. His lazy articulation now was almost a drawl. "I know a gentleman—a clergyman of that name—Rev. Donald L. Kirke, resident, now, and I fancy for many years, at Dundee—"

"It is the very same!" Mrs. Baxter started tragically, and leaned gaspingly toward him, her throat swelling like a pouter pigeon's. "And you know him, you say? Tell me something about him—about his family! My sweet cousin left a child, I know. Does it still live? Dundee! yes! that was the quaint Scotch name of my Ginevra's new home. I have always associated it with 'The Cotter's Saturday Night.' You recollect 'Dundee's wild, warbling measures'? Do sit down and tell me all!"

"You should visit Dundee," said Orrin, sauntering back to the fireplace, but declining the seat she offered. "It is a beautiful valley—sheltered from storms by a barricade of picturesque hills. I was there in May, and the climate and flowers—especially the wealth of roses, reminded me of sunny Provence. I became quite well acquainted with Mr. Kirke. He is, as you describe him, a thorough gentleman—one of the genuine 'old school'—

handsome, refined, and scholarly. His daughters, of whom there are two, are cultivated ladies. The younger—who is, I presume, the child to whom you refer—is, I have heard, very like her beautiful mother. You would be interested in her, first, for your cousin's sake, but very soon for her own. This matter of family likeness is a curious one. I see now what was the resemblance that puzzled me last Spring. Miss Jessie Kirke might easily be mistaken for your daughter."

"If she were, what a happy woman I should be!" cried the flattered lady, casting up her brown eyes, and raising her clasped hands to a level with her chin. "The relief afforded by your charming description is beyond expression. I have never dared inquire respecting my lost darling's babe. And she is really a Lanneau! Heaven bless her! I feared—*how* I feared! to hear that she had grown up an awkward rustic, whose faint likeness to her parent would pain, not gratify me. Therefore I have maintained no correspondence with Mr. Kirke since our exchange of letters immediately after his wife's decease. 'Jessie Kirke!' what a *riante, piquante,* bewitching name!"

"I wish you could prevail upon her father to entrust her to you for a time. She would be a feature in our society this winter. Her face and manners are strikingly attractive, and hers is a style of beauty that will improve with years and knowledge of the world. Her bearing and conversation have much of the fascination which is, I suspect, a family gift. She will grow handsomer until—I cannot say when. Women, like leaves, have their time to fade, and this trying season lies, with a large majority, a little on the bright side of thirty. The Lanneaus have not lost the secret they brought from fair France—the magic that purchases the gift of perennial youth."

"Fie! fie! how you digress! I am dying for information of my beloved young cousin, and you launch into irrelevant gallantries—flattery that is thrown away, let me tell you, upon one of my age and gravity!" frowned Mrs. Baxter with her forehead, her lips openly refractory, and her eyes dancing with delight. "*Do* sit down and tell me more!"

"I cannot, thank you! I have already bored you with a visit three times as long as I meant it should be. Your cousin does the family credit. I can award her no higher praise. *Au revoir!*"

"One second!" she entreated, detaining him. "The discoveries of this evening seem trifles to you. To me they are an Event! I shall write to the precious lamb to-morrow. Please give me her address in full."

Orrin dictated, and she wrote it upon her ivory tablets.

"Perhaps it would be as well not to mention me in connection with this renewal of your intercourse with Mr. Kirke's family," he said, carelessly. "Your friendship will be the more welcome if it is supposed that it has its root in your fond recollection of your lamented relative. Excuse the suggestion—but from what I have seen of father and daughters, I am inclined to think them sensitive and proud—as they have a right to be. Your tact hardly needed this hint, however. There is a ring! I have loitered here shamefully! Do you know that your beautiful drawing-room is likened, about town, to Circe's cave?"

# CHAPTER VI

Mr. Wyllys was careful not to repeat his visit within a week. He could trust to the natural growth of the seed he had sown, and he was too politic to appear solicitous, on his own account, for the resumption of cousinly intercourse between the houses of Baxter and Kirke. He did not overrate his influence with the would-be leader of Hamilton society. Four days after his party call, he had a note from Jessie.

"Dear Cousin Orrin:

"I enclose a letter received last night from Mrs. Baxter, wife of the President of Marion College. She is, I have learned from this, my nearest living relative, outside my immediate family circle, being my mother's first cousin. I never heard of her until the arrival of this communication. My father knew her, years ago, but did not remember whom she had married. I little imagined when I listened to Roy's praises of his friend, Dr. Baxter, that I had any personal interest in, or connection with his family. Mrs. Baxter writes, you see, in an affectionate strain, and is urgent in her request that I should pass the winter with her. My father and sister agree with me that you are the proper person to consult with regard to my answer to the invitation. You are, doubtless, acquainted with Mrs. Baxter, and are certainly more *au fait* to the usages of Hamilton polite society than we are.

"Tell me freely what you think I ought to do—freely as if I were in blood, as I am in heart,

"Your Kinswoman,

"Jessie Kirke."

"Here is an example of hereditary transmission that would stagger Wendell Holmes himself!" thought Orrin, scanning the epistle, letter by letter. "The chirography of the girl, who could not write at the time of her mother's death, is precisely similar to hers—as similar as it is unlike that of the sister by whom she was educated. It is a nut to crack for those who carp at the idea that the handwriting is a criterion of character, who attribute variety of penmanship to educational influences entirely. What has my fair 'kinswoman' inherited from her matronal progenitor besides her features and carriage, and these sloping, slender Italian characters, I wonder? It may be worth my while to investigate the question as a psychological phenomenon."

To secure the facilities for doing this, he resolved to run down to Dundee the next day.

The early train he had condemned in the spring, started now before daylight, and he called himself a fool, as he took his place in the cold, smoky car, for making the journey at all. Being mortal, he was liable to these spasms of prudence and faltering of purpose, during which he held serious questioning with Common-sense—leaving feeling out of the discussion—whether he were not squandering time and thought in prosecuting his favorite pastime of winning and wasting hearts. He knew that, viewed in the dead white light of sober judgment, tested by commercial rates, his ambition to stand chief victor in Cupid's lists, would be ignoble and unremunerative. He felt that he would himself thus rate it, had he no other aim in life. Aware, as he was, that he kept step with his fellows in business pursuits, that he was intellectually the peer of those the crowd called masters, he did not let the thought of adverse criticism of his *affaires du coeur* weigh too heavily with him. It was easy to persuade himself that since the world's conquerors and prophets, sages, warriors, and saints, had, each in his time, esteemed the love of woman the worthiest meed of valor, learning, and piety; had fought, gone mad, and made shipwreck of faith, to gain and wear the prize, leaving upon record the aspiration "to waste life upon her perfect lips," alongside of heroic epics and religious meditations,—his researches and successes in this field of art,—the mining and delving and polishing that attended his explorations among the curiosities of woman's affections and follies—were lawful and dignified, and should entitle him to an honorable grade in the school of philosophers.

Apart from these cold-blooded considerations (a man flirt is always more cold-blooded than a woman—coquetry and the desire to conquer hearts being oftener a passion with the latter than a deliberate plan)—apart from these I say, Orrin Wyllys was, as he would have said of himself, "not a bad fellow." He liked to give pleasure, to be useful to his kind, to be thanked and praised for his benefactions.

Finding myself, once upon a time, in the actual presence and in social converse with one of the brightest of modern (American) stars—a man I had reverenced afar off, as a mental and moral monarch among mortals, I was disenchanted and appalled at hearing him say something like this:

"I have no patience with this talk about finding one's truest happiness in promoting that of others. I believe that man is best employed who makes the most and best of Himself! My business in life is to improve Myself by every means at my command—to make Myself, spiritually and intellectually, 'round and perfect as a star,' without diverting my energies and wasting my sympathies with projects for the good of my race. This is my idea of true philanthropy."

"And the rest of mankind may go hang!" said a plain-spoken auditor.

The Star shrugged his broad shoulders.

*"Ce n'est pas mon affaire!"*

This was, substantially, Orrin's creed, but he had his own notions as to the manner in which the cultivation of Self was to be conducted, and being still some degrees below the exalted plane of observation occupied by the aforesaid Star, was not superior to the weakness of talking about philanthropy, even believing himself that he did good for good's sake, and that his satisfaction in seeing others made happy through his instrumentality, was pure benevolence. His charities were many—and open. Indeed, Lady Patronesses shook their heads, smilingly, at him while deprecating his "soft-hearted credulity" and lauding his generosity, and his name was a synonym among men for good-nature and lenient judgment.

Therefore, when he muttered—"Just like my confounded amiability, this taking so much pains to benefit those who may never appreciate my motives, nor be grateful for what I have done!" as he buttoned his overcoat up to his chin and pulled on his fur-lined gloves, he half believed that he spoke sincerely—went systematically to work to arrange his projects with the best side toward him; found substantial comfort in so doing.

Roy had left his affianced to his guardianship, and her action at this juncture might be fraught with important consequences to her and to Roy himself. He could allay Mr. Kirke's scruples, if he had any, relative to his daughter's acceptance of Mrs. Baxter's pressing offer of hospitality and chaperonage, better in five minutes' talk than by twenty written pages. He was anxious that Jessie should pay the visit. She had taken a strong hold of his fancy, and he could study her to advantage while she was her cousin's guest; be her cavalier wherever she went, by virtue of the authority vested in him by her absent betrothed. Hamilton was dull this season. There was not a woman in it whom he had not read from preface to "Finis"—and his energies were chafing for lack of exercise in his noble vocation. The prospect of Jessie's coming—the high-spirited child of nature, lively and loving, was very tempting.

But this was, he perceived, a digression, and he hastened to regain the original line of thought. His scheme—which Mrs. Baxter must be suffered to believe was her's, instead—of giving the country clergyman's daughter a season in town, was a golden opportunity of improvement of her mind and manners that should not be lightly cast aside. She had, more than once, confidentially bemoaned her inability to procure in Dundee the tuition in music and German she fancied she needed to qualify her to fill worthily the station to which Roy had elected her.

The reader of human nature smiled a little just here.

"When, if the truth were known, the practical Professor would be better pleased—aye! and better served in the long run, were his Jessamine to confine her ambition to the realms of cake, and bread, and butter making. I have seen other women as mistakenly risk complexions and eyes in poring over books, under the fond impression that they were 'qualifying' themselves to be their husband's 'help-meets'! What an age of shams is this!"

Since, however, this was Jessie's delusion, it might as well be indulged. She could have excellent music and language masters in Hamilton. He would, himself, snatch a few hours, weekly, that he might read German with her. The readings would prevent him from rusting in a language once familiar to him, as his own, and he would find further compensation for his trouble in the enjoyment he foresaw in guiding her eager mind through the rich storehouses of literature a knowledge of German would unlock for her. Waxing more complacently benevolent, he dwelt upon the comfort and pleasure Mrs. Baxter—a worthy, though ridiculous, creature—would derive from the companionship of her young friend. The Lady President was a born Patroness. The introduction of the sparkling luminary he was sure Jessie would become in the Hamiltonian firmament, would be with her a work of pride and love. She would spare no pains to make the novice's sojourn in her abode delightful to all parties interested in it.

Notwithstanding which irrefragable reasoning—such was the effect of atmospheric and other extraneous influences upon one in the undisputed possession of a sound body, sane mind, and serenely approving conscience—Mr. Wyllys relapsed into discouragement several times in the earlier stages of his journey; wrote himself down an ass for taking the trouble of a ten hours' ride into the country at this gloomy season to accomplish that, which, after all, might have been settled by letter. Breakfast by gas-light, a hard run through muddy streets to catch the train; a seat in a damp, close-smelling car, which was chilled, rather than warmed, by a stove-full of green wood, were sorry tonics for preparing spirits and temper for the duties of a new day. It annoyed the philanthropist that he could not put from his mind the vision of Roy Fordham's happy face as it shone upon his waking sight one July morning—the first of the summer vacation. Valise in hand, he had burst into his cousin's sleeping-room to say "Good-by," for he was off, by peep of dawn, to Dundee and Jessie. Orrin remembered every word that had been spoken; how he had forborne to remind the rapturous lover that this was the last visit he could pay his promised bride before his departure for Europe in August, and the calm surprise he had felt at seeing "prudent," far-seeing Roy apparently oblivious of all save present delight. Oddly, enough, it would have been more agreeable to his trusty relative to think of the absentee as a staid, studious personage, whose affections were always subservient to duty and judgment.

Few of earthly mould—such are the freaks of imagination and the complications of nervous irritation—are, at all times, superior to like vicissitudes of purpose and temper. I trust, then, that my hero will not suffer materially in the opinion of the exceptional minority when I state that it was near noon ere he finally and stably reassured his dubious mind that in this flying visit to the parsonage, he was acting wisely for Himself, and, as secondary, third and fourth rate considerations, for Jessie, Roy, and Mrs. Baxter. The lever that completed the task of elevating his self-esteem from the slough of doubt, was not the anticipation of Jessie's personal and mental improvement, or Mrs. Baxter's gratified maternal longings. It was the thought how the light imprisoned in Eunice Kirke's berylline eyes, would break up to the surface in the golden glints he had seen, at infrequent intervals, dash their placid darkness; how her slow, bright smile would greet his unexpected appearance, and applaud his vivacious sallies; the sweet monotone, many a queen of fashion would give her costliest jewels to imitate successfully, reply to his questioning. For he would have many questions to put. This was a studious autumn with the sisters. While Roy had laughed at Jessie's lamentations over her lack of learning, protesting that she "knew more already of books and men than any professor's wife he had ever met," he had, in compliance with her desire, and believing that active employment would be wholesome discipline for her in the weary months of their separation, arranged a schedule of history, ancient and modern, French, German, and general reading for her. Orrin had also visited Dundee in the August vacation, accompanying Roy back to town, and not quitting him until he waved his farewell from the pier to the slowly-moving steamship "outward bound." During those sad, precious "last days," the disengaged pair were, of necessity, often left to entertain one another for hours together, and their decorous friendship had matured naturally and gracefully into an equally decorous intimacy. Orrin had marked passages for Eunice's consideration in divers books they had glanced over in company; sent to her after his return to Hamilton, Carlyle, Emerson, and Macaulay; besides running down for a day in October, to bring a thick roll of duets, sonatas and *études,* and the whole of Mozart's Twelfth Mass for Miss Kirke's practice in the lengthening evenings.

He had taken extraordinary pains to ascertain her tastes, and displayed his customary tact in ministering to these.

"We are almost relations-in-law, you know!" had been his only apology for attentions and gifts, and Eunice had accepted all in simple good faith.

Her interest in his talk and her manifest liking for him, were a more flattering tribute to his vanity than was Jessie's frank cousinliness. I think it is always thus with the tokens of favor vouchsafed to friend and admirer by reserved, self-concentrated women. While Jessie was his especial study (or quarry) just now, he did not disdain the goods the gods offered him in the esteem and preference of the handsome elder sister. He had found her eminently convenient when his motive was to pique and mystify his cousin's betrothed by a feint of haughty indifference, and he was too wise an economist to cast aside what he had gained. He would be a clumsy diplomatist, indeed, were he to prove himself incompetent to the management of two affairs at the same time.

If my attempted analyzation of a "fascinating man's" principles and intentions has seemed prolix to the surface-reader, he will bear in mind that it is but a meagre abstract of what Mr. Wyllys thought, felt, and reasoned through the dreary November day, that did not see the sun until a break in the clouds low upon the western hills let out his light upon a sodden, wretched earth.

The late rays burnished Windbeam's coronal of cedars into golden-green, but curling fleeces of mist clung about his mighty chest and flanks, making him look grimmer and blacker by contrast; the valley was full of shadows, purple and gray; the old church was lightless save for the one dazzling arrow which was shivered against the slender tip of the spire, when Orrin undid the latch of the parsonage-gate. Provençal warmth and roses were things that belonged to the dead summer. Eunice's evergreens hardly redeemed the garden from desolation. A trim arbor-vitæ hedge kept warm the southern border, that would be gay in March with crocuses and tulips; the box-trees were the only leafy shrubs in the alley down which Jessie had crept, to faint in his arms at the other end. A thrifty holly, beaded with scarlet, mounted guard at the left of the front steps, as did a cedar, covered with bluish-white berries, at the right. A stately young pine he remembered as a favorite of Jessie's, filled the air with its solemn sighing, while he awaited the answer to his knock.

"So, Winter comes even to the Happy Valley!" he moralized. "I ought to have known it, of course, only I had not thought of it."

Patsey, the good-humored servant-girl, opened the door, and welcomed Mr. Wyllys with the broadest of smiles.

"Mr. Kirke and Miss Eunice is not at home, sir. They're a-visiting some place in the village. Miss Jessie is in, though. Be pleased to walk into the parlor, and I'll tell her you're here."

He heard swift feet skim the floor overhead as his name was repeated, and Jessie was in the room before he could take off his gloves. With a wild, scared face, lips that moved without sound, and eyes that demanded confirmation or denial of the dread that was strangling her heart, she caught his hands and looked up dumbly at him. His smile broke the spell sooner and more effectually than words could have done. She wrested her fingers from his, with a laugh so burdened with shame and happiness as to be more like a sob, testifying what had been the pressure and what was the release.

"I was sure" —

"That I was the bearer of bad news from abroad. I understand," Orrin took up the broken sentence. "You were never more mistaken. Your letter, enclosing Mrs. Baxter's, brought me. Your fears must take counsel of hope and faith another time. Roy was well when last heard from—well and happy, and, you may be sure, very busy. But what is this?" leading her to the window and scrutinizing her with fond solicitude. "What have you been doing with yourself? I am afraid he keeps his pledge of health, and resignation to the Inevitable better than you do yours to him. Are you not well? You have been sick, and I was not told of it!"

Her complexion was dead to sallowness; her eyes were leaden, the lids drooping wearily, and she was thinner in face and figure than when he had parted from her six weeks ago. Her dress, of dark, "navy" blue serge, made plainly, the long skirt heavy and still while she stood, and unrelieved save by narrow linen collar and cuffs, looked like a mourning garb.

"The *Mater Dolorosa* to the life!" said the quick-eyed lover of the fine arts to himself. "A blue hood drawn well forward would make the likeness perfect. Who would have thought that a morbidly love-sick girl could, by dreaming and fretting, stamp her features with the imprint of that divine sorrow! Marvellous are the tricks of Nature!"

All this while he held Jessie's hand; his eyes seemed as if they could not leave the countenance whose change had so pained him. The girl's faint smile was very grateful.

"I am not sick! I have no physical ailment beyond a sensation of general good-for-nothingness. I ought to be ashamed to confess it, but I imagine I have a touch of what fine ladies call the 'blues.' Papa would have in Dr. Winters a month ago, in spite of all I could do and say. He laughed at me a little, scolded me a great deal, and pronounced my malady dyspepsia, or low fever, or nervous debility—he was not certain which. In any case, his prescription was quinine, dumb-bells, and porter, ale, lager beer, or a decoction of gentian-root and chamomile flowers. Think of it!" with a grimace. "Could my cup of existence be more effectually embittered? I take quinine, and swing the bells a thousand times each day, but I do not see that the regimen increases my appetite or makes me sleep better. There is nothing the matter with me that will not yield to resolution and common-sense and—and—time! I shall be all right when I get used to things as they are," she continued, with feverish rapidity, marking his doubtful look. "I need discipline, hardening, tempering. If papa and Euna would rate me soundly for my folly and childishness, the counter-irritant would brace my system. I should need no other medicine. But they won't, unfortunately!"

She was laughing now, but not with her native glee. Orrin's scrutiny— serious and tender—was prolonged until her eyes sank and a blush of the lost color tinged her temples. A sigh escaped him as he relinquished her hand, and walked twice through the apartment to collect thoughts and words.

"My coming was timely," he said, drawing a chair to her side. "Dear child! your life is too precious to be wasted in unavailing regrets. Your peace of mind is dear to too many to be wrecked by morbid nursings. Don't think me harsh! You should have something to engage your time and thoughts beyond the routine of occupation and recreation appointed to you here; should see more of the world than that portion of it which is bounded by these mountains. You would starve upon what satisfies your sister. Duty to be performed—duty done—a straight course and strength to walk therein— these fill the measure of her earthly desires. Your temperament and your intellect demand a larger sphere—wider range for your mind and more food for your heart. You are dying of inanition, and you do not know it. You are a caged wild bird who is trying to learn to sing by note."

She shook her head wilfully.

"You are altogether wrong. I have been pampered, housed, petted, until nerve and muscle, mental and spiritual, are gone. I need a stimulant, but a moral one."

Orrin changed his ground.

"What if I supply it in the guise of a German course, seasoned with unsparing admonition whenever you are indolent or unreasonable?" he said, lightly.

# CHAPTER VII

A less vain man than Mr. Wyllys would have been flattered by the effect produced upon the spiritless, faded creature, the mocking shadow of the old blithesome Jessie, by half an hour's talk with himself. A less patient man would have been chagrined by the discovery that his enumeration of the varied and substantial benefits that would accrue to her from the proposed visit to Mrs. Baxter, and the delicate skill with which he contrived to keep before her all the while the prospect of his society and guardianship, weighed but as thistle-down with the obtuse "love-sick girl," in comparison with the circumstance that Hamilton was Roy Fordham's home.

Orrin was surprised, and not agreeably, when her own words forced this astounding fact upon him.

"It will be the next best thing!" she said, dreamily, a happy smile touching her lips and kindling up her eyes. "I have heard him talk so much of the place and the people, that it will be like revisiting half-remembered scenes—renewing former acquaintanceships. You will show me all his favorite haunts, let me see the friends he values most highly—won't you? The ocean is narrower and quieter when I think of taking the walks and drives he likes best—which he has described to me over and over; of mingling with those who were his daily associates—who knew him before I did. Though I don't like very well to think of *that*"—interrupting herself with a laugh. "I feel as if nobody had the right. It seems to me that I cannot recollect when I did *not* know him."

She mused silently for some minutes—the tender light still trembling over her face. It was as if she had forgotten his presence, until a sudden thought turned her to him with an abrupt query.

"Mrs. Baxter knows nothing of—has heard no rumors?" in shy anxiety that appeared overstrained to one who had heard the loving soliloquy Orrin was prompt to decide was in very bad taste, even when the unconsidered listener was in the confidence of both parties.

"Of your engagement?" he said, with grave directness. "Hamilton is in profound ignorance on that subject. Roy knows how to keep his own

counsel, and knowing it was his wish that your betrothal should remain secret, for the present, I have mentioned it to no one. You need be under no embarrassment on that score."

"Thank you."

Jessie was silent again, but the pause was filled with soberer thoughts. She began to fear lest she had been talking nonsense—been indiscreet and unmaidenly. Orrin kindly overlooked the lapse into selfish sentimentality, but she was ashamed that she had given him occasion for exercising forbearance on this subject. He noted, and with satisfaction, that she treated him to no more love rhapsodies that night; did not voluntarily name Roy in the ensuing dialogue.

"I am happy to learn that Mrs. Baxter is warm-hearted and sincere," she said, at the close of a searching catechism upon that lady's characteristics. "I was prepossessed in her favor, less by her letter, than because she loved my mother. My sister has been a dear and careful parent to me. You have seen what my father's fond indulgence is. But the core of my heart has ached for my mother—my own beautiful mother—ever since she died. I was not quite five years old, yet I recollect her as if I had kissed her for the last time, yesterday. My father had this oriel built to please her. I remember seeing her nowhere else until she was carried up to her death-bed. Her easy chair stood there"—pointing—"and her writing-desk beside it. When I could, by standing on tip-toe, just get my chin upon the window-sill, she would make me measure with a bit of ribbon how much the jessamine had grown in a week. She planted these vines and tended them as if they had been her children. She said to me, more than once or twice, that she hoped I would be like my name-flower when I grew up—brave, sweet, faithful—telling how one had for fifty years curtained the porch of the house in which she was born, and how dearly she loved it. She made me her companion, and, in some sort, her confidante by the time I could talk plainly, and very proud I was of the distinction. She used to take me upon her lap, or hold me closely in her arms as she lay on her lounge in the twilight, and repeat stories of her Southern home; sing ballads so sweetly sad that I could not help crying quietly while I listened—very quietly, for fear she should hear me, and stop."

It was twilight by this time. The mountain-crown was dusky as the plain; the elm-trees in the church-yard were swaying in the bleak wind that bowed the garden-shrubbery, and swept the long grass above neglected graves into brown waves. The naked, snake-like sprays of the creepers tapped monotonously against the window-panes. Orrin had healthy nerves, but as he looked through the glooming air at the shaft, standing like a sheeted

ghost at the head of Mr. Kirke's second wife, and heard in the stillness of the place and hour, the sobbing sighs of the pine boughs, he wished Jessie had chosen some other hour and spot for her weird reminiscence than the November gloaming and this haunted recess.

She was leaning back in her chair, her hands crossed, her face upraised to the sky:

"I have a perfect picture of her before me, at this moment," she went on, presently. "She had large, soft eyes, and very dark hair. She was always pale, and she never laughed. But her smile was my reward when I was good, as her kiss was the cure for every hurt. Nobody else can ever tell me such wonderful tales. Some were in prose, many in verse, more beautiful to my apprehension than any poetry I have read since. This was on her well days—my white days! when the writing-desk would, if I requested, be supplanted by the color-box and pencils, and we passed whole hours together—she and I—she sketching or painting to illustrate anecdote and fairy story, I perched in my high chair at her side, looking on in rapt delight. I believe that I was a troublesome child—noisy, wayward, passionate—to everybody else in the house. I kept away from her of my own accord in my stormy or sulky fits. The earliest lesson taught me by my father was, that 'poor, sick mamma must not be disturbed.' I suppose it was on account of her feeble health that he always heard my prayers, put me to bed at night, and nursed me in my infant sicknesses. It was he who came to my crib in the dim light of one terrible January morning, and told me that she was in Heaven. I did not understand exactly what that meant, but I gathered that it was something very dreadful from the sight of his emotion. I have never seen him weep except that once. I had sprung from my pillow to sob out my childish grief in his arms. He pressed me to his bosom until I could scarcely breathe, and said, over and over, in a strange undertone that terrified me more than did the drip of the hot tears over my face—'Ginevra's baby! Ginevra's baby!' Baby though I was, the scene is graven upon my memory for life."

The wind shook the casement, and the bare sprays tapped more impatiently upon the glass, as the spirit of the dead mother might have signalled her child to let her in.

"Mrs. Baxter will never weary of talking with you upon a theme so dear to you both," said Orrin, shaking off the superstitious fancy.

Jessie was aroused to livelier speech by the suggestion.

"You have heard her speak of my mother, then?"

"Yes, but before I suspected the identity of the 'Ginevra' who was her adopted sister, with your father's wife. By a singular mischance, she never named him to me until one day last week, when she asked if I knew him — and you."

He had equivocated so adroitly as to bar cross-examination, he hoped, but Jessie's curiosity was not easily parried.

"Was that before or after she wrote to me?"

"Probably afterward, for she told me that the sight of a keepsake given her by your mother had set her to thinking of their early and close intimacy, and that she had 'obeyed the impulse which bade her make inquiries about you, and ask you to visit her.' Those were her words, as nearly as I can recall them. She expresses herself warmly — but not, I honestly believe, more warmly than she feels."

"I would not go to Hamilton had you recalled to her mind the fact of my existence. If love for her lost friend did not prompt her to seek me out, I would not owe my recognition to the recommendation of another. No! not to yours!"

Had he not read aright her sturdy pride, her jealousy for her mother's memory and her father's dignity? With what wise pre-vision he had detected the danger, and, by his caution to Mrs. Baxter, averted it!

Eunice, the beryl-eyed, also had her confidential talk with Mr. Wyllys that night.

"Father," she said, after supper, as he tarried, for an instant, in the dining-room. "I should like to speak with Mr. Wyllys for ten minutes when Jessie is not by. Can you contrive to call her out of the parlor, by and by?"

"Certainly, my daughter," he replied, without curiosity or hesitation.

Jessie was his pride and darling — very beautiful and gifted in his eyes. He lavished upon her the wealth of a heart that had never known its own depth until he met her mother. The first Mrs. Kirke was the daughter of one of his college-professors, a little older than himself, very amiable, very discreet, and the best housekeeper in the parish. He owed much to her exemplary management since, relieved from cares domestic and pecuniary, he could devote much time, bring unjaded energies, and a free mind to the prosecution of the studies he loved so well. Without in the least entering into his enthusiasm in scholastic research, she laid down as one of the rules of her orderly household, that his study was forbidden ground to heedless or intrusive feet; guarded him when he had entered the sanctum, and shut the door between him and the living, active world — as vigilantly as she would have watched and defended hid treasure. He was "about his business," in her phrase, and to her just, practical ideas of duty and life it was but right that people should be allowed to follow their lawful and allotted callings without molestation. She did not particularly enjoy her husband's sermons, but he found her bread, butter, and cake always to his taste. He was an accomplished linguist, and would have been glad to have one under his own roof, with whom he could converse in Italian, German, or French. She had, as his correct ear continually reminded him, but an imperfect acquaintance with her vernacular, according to classical standards. But her coffee was fragrant, clear, and strong; while a whiff of her Young Hyson was as the scent of a zephyr that had wandered over acres of flowering tea-plants, and made the wishy-washy, or over-boiled decoctions of other housewives seem but weedy and rank abominations. If the refined and sensitive young pastor kept within his own breast many thoughts, dreams, and regrets he would fain have shared with a congenial mate, it should have been a compensation that the shirt-front covering the sealed repository of these was snowy and glossy as a bran-new tomb-stone; that the heels of his socks were always run before they went on his feet, and that in the years of their wedded life he never found "a button off." Mr. Kirke believed fully all his parishioners said when they assured him that he had a pattern wife, and that he ought to take good care of her, since he would never find another like her. She worked steadily and diligently—she was never "fussy"—up to the day on which Eunice's little brother was born. "Overdid herself," said doctor and gossips, while her husband blamed himself bitterly for not having taken thought to spare her who had served him to the death. The death that came so swiftly and easily, she had time for neither parting word nor kiss.

"I am tired, I believe," she murmured to the nurse. Unused to complain, she said it deprecatingly even in mortal weakness. "Do you think that I might just take a little nap? If Mr. Kirke should want for anything, don't hesitate to wake me at once." With that she turned her face to the wall and died—"fell asleep," said her head-stone. Her baby was buried with her.

This was Eunice's mother. Four years after the decease, the widower met Ginevra Lanneau at a watering-place whither he had gone for health, and she for distraction from certain troublesome memories. Whatever may have been her faults and weaknesses; whatever the motives for her marriage and the causes of her subsequent invalidism and melancholy, this good man had worshipped her with entireness of devotion; had mourned her with an intensity of anguish that bleached his locks; bent his stately form toward the earth that had swallowed up his idol; deafened him to the calls of ambition that urged him to leave a seclusion endeared to him as her home and burial-place.

But for all this, Eunice was his right hand, in Parsonage and in parish. He "really would have no excuse for a third marriage," was a common saying in the neighborhood—"with such a daughter to keep his house and 'do for him.'" If the spirit of the mother were permitted to watch her child's daily walk and conversation, it must have heightened her beatitude to be thus assured that "Mr. Kirke" was not likely, while Eunice lived, "to want for anything." Her father's trust in her discretion was implicit, and when she unblushingly asked him to "contrive" to secure for her a *tête-à-tête* with a young and attractive man, he made no demur, formed no conjectures. Nor did he doubt that the matter of her communication to Mr. Wyllys was, in some way, essential to Jessie's weal. The first and abiding thought with both was "the child," he had yet made up his mind to part with for a little while.

Eunice was sewing by the shaded parlor lamp. Wyllys, while he talked to both sisters, looked quite as often at her as at Jessie. He was in the mood for enjoying himself, and his surroundings were propitious. He had had an excellent supper. Eunice had inherited her mother's taste and skill in the domestic department. Her dainty cookery would have done credit to a salaried *chef*, said Mr. Wyllys, than whom there were few better judges of all that pertained to the gratifications of the flesh. A wood fire burned busily and gayly upon the castellated fire-dogs of shining brass that flashed back the illumination from a hundred curves and points. There was a breath of tea-roses and mignonette in the air, for the shelf running around the inside of the oriel was filled with plants; crimson curtains had taken the place of muslin, at the other windows. A November gale—"a dry storm"—was rising without. It was pleasant, while hearkening to its blustering, to bethink himself that he had not to breast it in a tramp back to the hotel, he having accepted Mr. Kirke's invitation to sleep at the parsonage. The recollection of his disagreeable journey, now that he was rested, warmed, and filled, was another element in his present content. The old-fashioned parlor with its quaint and massive furniture, were more to his liking than the polish and glow of the modern "suite of rooms," every prosperous mechanic's wife now regards as one of the necessaries of life. From his leisurely and approving survey of the apartment, his eyes came back to dwell longest upon Eunice.

She wore a brown merino, that made no noise when she moved, and fell in classic folds about her as she sat in her straight-backed chair. A knot of blue ribbon joined a crimped ruffle above the high-necked dress, and frills of the same material were at her wrists. The light, strained through the ground-glass shade, made her skin seem fair and fresh as that of a little child; while it did not blur the clear chiselling of her features. Her hands were shapely, her motions replete with quiet grace. The high-bred lady, stainless in deed as single in motive, spoke in the fearless, tranquil eyes and composed demeanor.

"She rests me!" said the connoisseur in womanly loveliness, to his appreciative self. "If I were obliged to marry either, I am not sure she would not suit me better than this restless gypsy, who keeps one perpetually upon the *qui vive* by her sharp interrogations, her repartee, and variable moods. To secure the perfection of comfort, a man should be able to flirt with one all day, and come home at evening to recover from his dazed feverishness in the cool semi-twilight of the other's presence. I must find out, some day, if she has ever been in love. I think not. There is a dewy firmness in the texture of her heart that seldom outlasts the fires of even a mild passion—such a timid flame as the pastor's daughter might conscientiously feel for some pious under-shepherd or amorous evangelist."

At this precise instant, Jessie, who had been flitting restlessly about the room, picking dead leaves from the geraniums, and seed-vessels from verbenas and mignonette, tossing them, one at a time, into the fire, and pensively watching the blaze feed upon them; parting the curtains to press her face against the glass "to see whether it rained," stopping once in a while to lean on her sister's chair and address a question to her or Orrin—obeyed her father's summons to his study. The two left at the fireside, followed her to the door with their eyes, then these met. Eunice answered the questioning of Orrin's.

"She is over-excited to-night. But there is a nervous restlessness about her of late that makes me anxious. I hope much for her from the proposed change of air and scene."

She laid aside her work, neatly folded; put scissors and thimble in their cases, and the cases into her work-box, and calmly confronted her companion.

"Mr. Wyllys, I wish to say a word to you respecting my sister's antecedents before she goes to Mrs. Baxter."

Without a symptom of surprise, he bowed, and exchanged his seat for one near the stand by which she sat. In this one action, he accepted her confidence, and put his services at her disposal should she desire them.

"From the descriptions of this lady, given by yourself and my father, I infer that she is affectionate and voluble. She will be likely to impart to Jessie all she knows of her mother's history, and question her concerning her own childish recollections. I have thought it best that you should hear the truth upon a subject that is rarely alluded to in our family. My father talked freely of it with Mr. Fordham before giving his sanction to his engagement with Jessie; but he has not spoken of it to me in many years—never to my sister. Should a garbled version of a story which is sad enough in itself, reach her ears, it would distress and bewilder her if there were no one near who could correct the mis-statement. My stepmother never recovered the natural tone of her health and spirits after my sister's birth. Her malady took the form of a gentle melancholy, indifference to domestic and neighborhood interests, varied at times by fits of wild weeping, so violent that she was confined to her couch with headache and debility for several days after each. She talked rationally when drawn into conversation, expressing herself upon every topic discussed with clearness and intelligence; but the spring of action was gone. She never complained of bodily pain; made no unreasonable demands upon the time and patience of those about her. Nor did she require to be humored and amused as is the way of most sufferers from confirmed hysteria. She read much and wrote more, burning her manuscripts, however, as fast as they were finished. She drew, too, rapidly and well, and upon these occupations expended what little energy of mind and body remained to her after the illness that had nearly cost her her life. We guarded her from intrusion and uncharitable remark as far as we could. My nurse, an elderly widow, was then alive, and was our housekeeper, her daughter being our only other servant. How the report originated, I cannot say—probably from some indiscreet remark let fall by this daughter, who has now a home of her own some miles away—but within the year, a rumor has been brought to me that Jessie's mother died a lunatic. It is possible Mrs. Baxter has likewise heard such. If she has, and should be so imprudent as to repeat it to you, so unfeeling as to hint it to the daughter of that unhappy lady, may I rely upon you to tell my sister the exact truth? My stepmother lived and died a sane woman—as sane as I am this moment. Jessie is impressible and ardent. Her love for her mother is a passion. It would nearly kill her if this slander were retailed to her."

She had made her little speech; summed up the case, and offered her appeal with such simplicity, such deft moderation, as challenged the lawyer's admiration. His reply was directly to the purpose.

"You may depend upon me, Miss Kirke. I hope, with you, that I shall never be called upon to fulfil the trust with which you have honored me. I am confident that Mrs. Baxter is ignorant of the particulars of her cousin's ill-health. She has spoken to me with apparent frankness of her early life—of her marriage, and the seclusion that followed it."

"For which she blames my father!" interrupted Eunice, red indignation staining her fair face. "Because he would not subject his wife to the indifferent or pitying observation of those who had been the associates of her brilliant girlhood; because he indulged her longing for solitude and quiet; guarded her sedulously and tenderly from all that could tax and jar upon her tortured nerves—he fell under their ban! He gave me some letters to examine and file—or burn, if I thought fit—ten years ago. Among them I found one from Mrs. Baxter—one from another cousin of Ginevra Lanneau. They were written to him, just after her death. Both reproached him—Mrs. Baxter (then Miss Jane Lanneau) gently, the other harshly, for separating his young wife from her friends and 'immersing her in a savage solitude, where, cut off from all congenial associations, a nature so refined as hers could not but pine itself to death.' I do not quote from Mrs. Baxter. If she had upbraided the best of men and most loving of husbands in these terms, Jessie should never enter her house, unless under my protest."

"You are right. But, believe me, she will be safe and happy in Mrs. Baxter's care. Her goodness of heart is undeniable; her impulses are amiable, and she is, moreover, a woman of sound principles and genuine piety. She is vain, but never unkind or censorious. She always reminds me of the pretty *bas bleu* immortalized by the 'Spectator'—or is it the 'Tattler'? 'When'—says the essayist—'she would look languishing, there is a fine thing to be said at the same time that spoils all. Thus, the unhappy Merab, although a wit and a beauty, hath not the credit of being either, and all because she would be both.' Our Hamilton Merab has sterling traits, nevertheless, and is incapable of using the language you have quoted. No one but a vulgar idiot could apply it to Mr. Kirke. The writer had, I take it, never seen him. You have every reason to be proud of your father, Miss Eunice. He is that best work of the Creator—a Christian gentleman,—I say it without reverence,—a prince of the blood royal."

The golden lights glanced up from the dark wells of her eyes; her smile was grateful and exultant.

"Thank you! I know you mean what you say, and it is but the truth."

Neither spoke for a brief space. The soughing of the pine-tree was annoyingly continuous to Orrin's ear; the fire-flashes were silent. He tried to forget the vexing sound in remarking that Eunice's bent profile showed against the dark wood of the high, carved mantel, clear and fine as a cameo cutting, but it would be heard.

"You were very young at the time of your step-mother's death to be your father's assistant and co-adviser," he said, to prevent an awkward break in their talk. "I am surprised at the accuracy of your recollections."

"I was fifteen. The elder daughter of a family early learns to assume and to bear domestic cares; is more mature at the same age than are those who come after her. I remember my own mother, who died eleven years earlier than did Jessie's. I was thirty last month."

She picked up her sewing without a flutter or a blush, and Orrin, not daring to offer her the flimsy compliment of incredulity he would have paid another woman who had volunteered a confession disparaging to her personal charms, was still casting about in his mind for words that should praise, yet not offend, when his opportunity was lost through Jessie's return to the room.

# CHAPTER VIII

"You find us, in humble imitation of Mr. Turveydrop, still using our little arts to polish — polish!" said Jessie Kirke, mimicking the famous trowel gesture of the Professor of Deportment, as Orrin Wyllys entered Mrs. Baxter's drawing-room on the evening of the fourth of January.

The Lady President's "collegiate re-unions" on the first and third Thursdays of each month had, up to this winter, been declared a nuisance by the class for whose benefit she had inaugurated the series; to wit, the homeless, graceless students whose intellectual training was committed to her husband and his *confrères*, while their polite education was left to Fate and the hap-hazard culture of promiscuous society. Now, promiscuous society — (the term is Mrs. Baxter's — not mine) in Hamilton, although less detrimental to the principles, manners, and conversational powers of unguarded youth than the same foe would have been in a region more remote from the great humanizing and refining centre expressed, to the visual organs, by the square, cream-colored mansion at the right of the college campus — was yet inimical to the best interests (another stolen phrase!) of the aforesaid matriculated youngsters. To counteract the evil, the presidential residence was converted, on the evenings I have designated, into a social reformatory, and the mistress put forth her utmost energy to render the process of amelioration pleasant to the subjects thereof. The success of her system, which had gone into operation two years before, had been less than indifferent up to the date of her young kinswoman's arrival. Simultaneously with her appearance at the pillared portal of the cream-colored Centre, the cause of elegant deportment and colloquial accomplishments began to look up in the contiguous halls of learning. The "reception" on the ensuing Thursday was well attended, the second was a "crush "—the supply of lemonade and sponge-cake inadequate to the demand.

This was the third, and the hostess, elate with past, and sanguine of prospective, victories, had, with the assistance of her guest, bedecked her rooms with New Year's garlands and floral legends. As an ingenious tribute to the learning of the major portion of the assembly, Mrs. Baxter had accomplished a Latinization of certain stock phrases of welcome, and was immensely proud of the "classic air" imparted to her saloon by these.

"I suppose they are all right," Jessie said dubiously to Orrin, when he inspected them. "My knowledge of the dead tongue is confined to the musty sayings everybody has learned by heart—'*Sic transit gloria mundi,*' '*Mirabile dictu,*' and the like."

"Salve!" blossomed into being in heather, and pink-and-white paper roses over the mantel opposite the door of the front parlor. Over that in the back—"*Jubemus vos salvere,*" while "*O faustum et felicem hunc diem!*" was tacked above the piano in the music-room.

"To polish! to polish!" reiterated Jessie, stroking her gloved left hand with her right, and looking so roguishly beautiful that Orrin had no difficulty in throwing an expression of intense admiration into his gaze.

"Stand off, and let me look at you!" said he, brusquely for him, drawing back for a better view.

She was well worth it. Native quickness, aided by the marvellous intuition as to effect, and the daring that attempts new combinations of color and untried styles of coiffure and dress, which people name "French taste," had wrought together in her attire. She had a "genius for apparel," Mrs. Baxter pronounced delightedly, adding "So much for blood! The Parisian eye and Parisian aptitude are, like the poetic afflatus, *nascitur, non fit*. You are a true Lanneau." There would be no better-dressed woman in the assembly to-night than the country girl, whose toilette had yet cost less than that of any other who laid claim to the honors of belleship.

Her maize-colored tissue had a full double skirt; the upper looped with rosettes of black lace and narrow black velvet. A bunch of fuschias—scarlet with purple hearts, drooped above her left temple. Not a jewel was visible except her engagement-ring—a fine solitaire diamond. Instead of a brooch she wore another spray of fuschias, mixed with feathery green, at her throat, and her only laces were those edging her neck and sleeves. But she was dazzling enough to turn stronger heads than those of the sheepish sophomores, pert juniors, and priggish seniors, who would compose her train, thought Wyllys, surveying her with the deliberate freedom of a brotherly friend. Her eyes sparkled into splendor, her bloom deepened, and the white-gloved fingers toyed nervously with her bouquet as his inspection was prolonged. As the finale, he offered his arm with a sweeping obeisance, and they strolled through the rooms, untenanted as yet save by themselves.

"I hardly expected to see *that*, to-night," said Orrin, touching her bouquet. "The utmost I hoped was, that it might please your eye for a moment, as it passed in review among a host of others."

"There is a degree of modesty which is laughable," she returned. "Pray, whose flowers did you suppose I would prefer to yours?"

"Perhaps I feared the rivalry of the chaste assortment of sweet alysseum and white rose-buds I saw left at Professor Fairchild's door this morning."

"Eminently suitable to my 'style'!" interrupted she, ironically. "The fear reflects credit upon your discrimination—and my taste."

"Or—" he went on—"the astounding array of camelias, azaleas, and orange-blossoms that arrived last night, duly enveloped in wet cotton, sent per express from the green-house of a city florist to the millionnaire's son—Senior Lowndes. Rumor affirms that he has neither studied nor eaten since he was first pierced by Cupid's arrows—your eyelids doing service as bows, and the sight of the magnificent offering which is to propitiate the blind god, has driven him clean daft with rapturous anticipation. Seriously and frankly, my advice is that you discard my simple gift in favor of the exotics. I am content—or I should be—with the grace already shown me by your intention to give my flowers the place of honor. But Mr. Lowndes may be offended if you do not exhibit his Brobdingnagian bouquet. It is already the talk of the place, and everybody expects to see it in your hands to-night."

"It will not be everybody's maiden disappointment," said Jessie, obstinately. "The floral behemoth has a big vase and a table all to himself in the music-room, so Mr. Lowndes can play show-man to his satisfaction. I reserve the right of wearing what I please, and my bouquet is part of my toilette. Could anything harmonize better with my dress than these scarlet verbenas, divided from the purple violets by the circlet of white blossoms, and capped by one snowy cape-jessamine—like a queen in her ermine?"

"That is the only member of your family to be had in this frozen region," rejoined Orrin. "I telegraphed to Baltimore in the vain hope of obtaining the golden bells you love."

"Did you? They do not bloom anywhere at this season, I imagine. But your effort to procure them was an evidence of thoughtful kindness beyond my expectation and desert. You do too much for me! I am humbled yet happy when I recount to myself your favors."

"Don't say 'favors!' If you knew—"

"Knew what?" queried Jessie, innocently, looking up. He held her eyes for a second by the irresistible magnetism of his, then, saying, with a short laugh that sounded like bitter self disdain—"What you will never hear from me!" commenced talking fast and gayly about other things.

Mrs. Baxter ran in, opportunely, to give Jessie time to collect her thoughts. Unobservant of the gravity of one of the parties to the broken dialogue, and the forced liveliness of the other, the hostess dashed into a profusely illustrated description of the *contretemps* that had detained her in her dressing-room. It was nothing less serious than the doctor's mistake, in taking from a closet a bottle of ink instead of the scented glycerine she asked him to get.

"For my tender skin (we Lanneaus are deplorably thin-skinned) is frightfully chapped this winter, and there is no better remedy for this affliction than bay-water and glycerine, as perhaps you know—you who are ignorant of nothing! 'Now, my dearest,' I said, '*may* I trouble you to pour it upon my hands as I hold them over the basin? Gently, doctor, darling!' When, presto! down came an inky deluge!" screaming with laughter, as she had with alarm when the mischance had occurred. "I spent nearly an hour in endeavoring to efface the murky stains, and I shall be compelled to keep my gloves on the entire evening. Isn't it a pitiable predicament?"

The scarlet scarf was on duty again to-night, but now tied about her waist, the knot at the side.

"I never feel quite dressed unless I have a speck of scarlet artfully brought into my costume," she had said to Jessie, on the evening of her arrival. "It individualizes my attire. I should not know—should not *be* myself without it."

Jessie joined in her merriment over the catastrophe that would have angered a wife whose temper was less even, but her heart was beating hard and hurriedly with vague alarms. Orrin had altered inexplicably of late. His sudden alternations of spirits and mysterious allusions were more than an enigma—they were a distress to her.

"If I knew!" she repeated mentally. "What was he about to say, and why did he look at me so intently? Why did he refuse to finish the sentence? I have wounded or offended him—but how?"

Self-condemnation was her first impulse when she noted a change in the demeanor of those she loved. Orrin ridiculed it as a morbid trick of mind that might be cured by reproof or raillery. Roy bore with it patiently and hopefully, recognizing in it an hereditary strain of melancholy which she would conquer or outlive in time. Her eyes were darker, her voice a tone lower, her smile a trifle subdued all the evening, for the incident that preceded the festivities. Nobody complained of the change. She was new, handsome, and sprightly, a triumvirate of recommendations that would have made her a star of note among her associates had her "style" been less unique, her cast of thought and conversation as commonplace as it was original. She was surrounded continually, to-night, by a group of gentlemen—most of them young, while there were some whose attentions—paid as they were by men of mature years and high standing, intellectual and social—were a compliment of which the *débutante* might justly be proud.

Orrin kept aloof from her, playing his part among the guests with his wonted spirit and grace. But his eyes followed her furtively wherever she went, until she was provoked with herself for meeting them so often. He would suspect her of impertinent curiosity, accuse her of forwardness, or feel that he was under espionage. She would not look in his direction again. A resolution she was certain to break within three minutes after it was made, tempted to the infraction by the stealthy yet piercing ray she imagined she could feel, when her face was turned away from him, and which, struggle as she might against the inclination, drew her regards again and again in his direction.

She descried a new meaning in his watchfulness before long,—a sad yearning that would not let her out of his sight; mournfulness that might signify either compassion or regret. Unused to dissemble, she must have grown *distrait*, unmindful of the gay scene and the duties it imposed upon her, but for the example of his fidelity in the performance of these. Emulating what she plainly perceived was self-denial in him, she talked, promenaded, and laughed with conscientious diligence, to the delight of her *chaperone* and the distraction of the smitten swains of three classes, the freshmen counting as nobodies.

The crowd was thinning fast when Orrin again approached her.

"We will finish our promenade now that there is room to move and breathe," he said, drawing her hand within his arm. "I want to have a moment's talk with you before I go. I leave town early in the morning."

The involuntary clasp of the gloved fingers upon his sleeve was all it should be, but the deprecating glance and exclamation were too frank and sisterly.

"Are you going away? Not to be absent long, I hope?"

"A week certainly—probably a fortnight."

"I shall be very lonely without you! absolutely lost, in fact!" replied Jessie, feeling all she said.

"I could stay, I suppose—but I ought to go," said Orrin, slowly. "Yes, it is the best thing left for me to do! Don't think, however, that it costs me nothing to leave Hamilton while you are in it. I shall carry the image of my docile pupil, my bright-faced, sunny-hearted friend, with me wherever I go. You have been a beautiful revelation to me, Jessie. Let me speak, for a moment, out of the sad sincerity of a spirit, wrung as I trust yours will never be. Should we never meet again upon earth, you will not cease to be to me—pshaw! what am I saying? I talk wildly to you, I doubt not, but there are times of battle and tempest and desolation in the which incoherence is pardonable. When you are married, you may be sorry for me in a calm, sisterly way, as people on the cliff above the beat of the surf, pity the wretches suffocating in the waves."

"Let me help and comfort you now!" begged Jessie, her tell-tale eyes glistening until Orrin was fain to halt before Mr. Lowndes' monster bouquet in the last room of the suite, and keep her back to the company, while she struggled for composure. "It breaks my heart to hear you!" came at last in a half sob from the trembling lips.

"Don't talk of breaking hearts, dear!" he returned, smiling sadly. "It is an idle phrase in the mouths of the loved and happy. May you always be both!"

He squeezed her hands until she winced with pain, took one lingering look into her eyes that seemed to compel her soul to their surface, whispered, "God bless you!" and before she could move to stay him, he was making his *congé* to Mrs. Baxter.

Regardless of the stranger and inquisitive eyes that might be upon her, Jessie watched the parting; the hostess' dramatic start, and fingers joined in hospitable supplication; the toning down of her physiognomy from tragic consternation, at the announcement of his contemplated journey, to plaintive resignation, as he declared the fixedness of his purpose; marked the animated pantomime, and felt no inclination to smile that it was over-wrought to extravagance. Assuredly, Orrin's going at all was a serious discomfort to herself. Taken in connection with his evident unhappiness, his disjointed confessions of grief and trial, that, despite the absurdity of the imagination, she could not help believing had some reference to her; finally, her inability to soothe or aid him,—these all combined to make the farewell the saddest—save one—she had ever gone through.

"You are weary, my dearest girl!" said Mrs. Baxter, sympathizingly, twining her arm around her and pulling her down upon the sofa, when she had bidden a widely smiling adieu to all her guests, with the exception of a bald, mild man in spectacles, who was penned in the angle formed by the chimney and the wall, while the doctor, planted in front of him, held to his argument and his handkerchief at such length that only half the knots were yet untied. "But you have been charming this evening! have really outdone yourself! I prognosticate a dazzling season for you—scores of conquests and troops of friends."

"I don't care for the conquests, but the friends will be welcome to one who has so few," returned Jessie. "Not that I have any enemies, but my circle of acquaintances is small."

She tried to speak brightly, lest her dispirited mood should reflect discredit upon her friend's endeavors to make her happy.

"It will enlarge rapidly within the next few weeks. The *prestige* of Mr. Wyllys' approval and friendship would ensure the success of a *débutante* whose personal claims upon popular favor were far inferior to yours, my sweet. I shall always cherish a grateful recollection of his attentions to you, as my relative and friend. It is a high compliment, as you would understand, were you better acquainted with the materials and structure of our best society. His influence in Hamilton is ex-tra-*or*-di-na-ry. I have promised to do my best to fill his place while he is away, but I am painfully conscious of my inability to prevent you from missing him continually. He was averse to going, but said the necessity laid upon him to do so was imperious. He was rather out of spirits, I fancied—but it might be *only* a fancy. Doctor, dear! do let Mr. Barnard come to the fire! The rooms are growing chilly, now that they are so nearly empty."

"Empty!" The doctor turned amazed. "Where are all the people, Jane?"

Jessie did smile now, impolite as she feared it was, at the alacrity with which the mild victim wriggled from the corner at the momentary diversion of his jailor's notice, muttered apologetically to the hostess, and got himself out of the apartment and house.

"As I was saying—" pursued the doctor, consulting his handkerchief and collecting his wits—"my objection to Darwin's theory and to the hypothesis advanced by Agassiz is one and the same. I maintain—"

"Dearest husband!" interposed his wife. "Since Mr. Barnard has followed the rest of our friends, suppose we postpone the further discussion of that point until to-morrow. Jessie and I are quite exhausted by the excitement of the evening."

Jessie was sorry for him as he began, with a rueful visage, to disentangle his cambric and his brains.

"I hope you have had a pleasant evening," she said, affectionately, going up to bid him "good-night."

His eyes cleared at sound of the frank, sweet voice, and the sight of her face. She had never been shy of him, had understood him better and sooner than young girls did generally, and made herself useful to him in many little ways. He caught himself dreaming, sometimes, in looking at and listening to her, of what his life and home might have been, if daughters of his own had graced and blessed it. Jessie had taken very kindly, on her part, to the rustic, eccentric scholar. Roy had made her acquainted with his excellences as well as his peculiarities, and bespoken for him a worthy place in her regard. He talked of "my young friend, Professor Fordham," to her more frequently than he was aware of, won to communicativeness by her deep and evident interest in the theme. She had not thought it best, up to this time, to reveal her engagement to him or to his talkative spouse, although Roy's last letter had gently advised her to do so, at the first favorable opportunity. The doctor might let slip the *morceau* of news in one of his tits of abstraction, while "Cousin Jane" would, she was sure, be in a twitter of mysterious importance, and desire to announce it formally and publicly. And Jessie, being new to the fashionable world, shrank from having her heart-history gossiped about. Her conscience was pricked slightly now for her want of confidence in Roy's dear old co-laborer, as he laid a hand on either shoulder, and gazed steadfastly at her, his hard, Scotch lineaments softening into kindliness and paternal affection.

"You are very handsome, my dear! Do you know it?"

Jessie blushed deeply, but she did not laugh or bridle, and her answer was straightforward and unaffected as was the query.

"I have been told so, sir!"

"Very handsome, but somewhat wilful!" continuing his physiognomical examination. "Undisciplined, too! A warm heart, but hasty judgment. Loving and lovable. A nature powerful for good as for evil. My daughter! when the crisis in your life shall arrive—for there is a turning-point in every human life—hesitate long and pray earnestly that you may be directed into the right path. If you take the wrong, great woe will ensue to yourself and others."

Then, with the grave simplicity that sometimes invested the quaint little man with dignity at which the most irreverent could not mock, he laid his withered hand upon her head:

"The Lord bless thee and keep thee; make the light of His countenance to shine upon thee, and give thee peace!"

After which he kissed her between the great, solemn eyes, and wished her "sound slumbers and happy dreams."

"It seems a ridiculous thing when it is put into words, but it reminded me of the way Roy used to say 'Good-night,' last summer, at the close of our happiest evenings!" thought Jessie, on her way upstairs, a mist between her and the glittering stair-rods. "Oh! I ought to be a good woman!"

Too much excited by this little episode, or the other events of the evening, to sleep, Jessie sat down by her chamber-fire, when she had donned her dressing-gown, and unbound the hair that oppressed her head by its weight of braids. She had kept up her Parsonage habit of reading a portion of Scripture before retiring each night, and her Bible lay upon her knee now—but unopened. She was heavy-hearted, notwithstanding Mrs. Baxter's congratulations and predictions.

Was it home-sickness that painted the images of her father and Eunice in the fiery bed of coals filling her grate? that showed her, in the violet-tinted flames quivering above the ignited mass, her chamber in the manse among the hills; her mother's portrait over the white tent bedstead; her mother's escritoire, between the windows, that contained Roy's letters? Was she already tired of the life that had been so pleasant four hours ago? Was this dissatisfaction with herself and those with whom she had talked and laughed within that time, satiety or chagrin? She had enjoyed every moment of her visit heretofore, with the avidity of a novice in the scenes to which her cousin's kindness had introduced her; the rides with Mrs. Baxter; the walks with Orrin, and the Hamilton girls who had extended to her a hearty and generous welcome; the parties, lectures, and concerts she had attended; the German and music lessons; the books she read aloud to Mrs. Baxter, and those Orrin had read to them both on the delightful stormy nights that kept other callers away; had caught eagerly at Fanny Provost's offer to teach her billiards, and Orrin's proposal that she should learn to skate. In fact, the day and evening had been so crowded with occupation, recreation, and incident, as to leave her scanty space for letters to Dundee, and oblige her to steal hours from sleep that she might live her enjoyments over in describing them to Roy. She had studied faithfully, too, and successfully under Orrin's direction, and spurred on by his encouragement. She was sure she could never learn so rapidly and zestfully again. Life seemed such hard and dreary labor.

She wished herself back in the quiet Parsonage, where the evening's talk, music, or reading was seldom interrupted by neighbors or strangers; where one day went by like every other, within doors; where, on snowy afternoons, the ticking of the hall-clock could be heard all through the house—by Patsey in the kitchen; by Mr. Kirke in his study; by Eunice, sewing in her room overlooking the church-yard; most distinctly by herself as she read, drew, or wrote in her favorite oriel, or, in the twilight, walked up and down the parlor, dreaming visions that put winter and gloom to flight—dreams of Roy's return and their united lives. Wished herself back, if she could be once more the girl who had left home six weeks ago. She forgot that latterly she had sickened there in mind and body, under the strain of her grief at

Roy's absence, and the pressure of her self-imposed tasks, unrelieved by the diversions needful for a girl of her age and temperament. That life seemed such a safe, wholesome one—simple, pure, pastoral. It beckoned her as might a living friend, beloved and trusted. She verily believed, after the fashion of young and ignorant dreamers, who take to misanthropic reverie at the first blast of disappointment, as a frightened deer to the water, that she had exhausted the pleasures of existence; had proved the gay world, and found it all "hollow, hollow, hollow"—the while she, a *blasé* cynic, could never return to relishful participation in the innocent joys that had once satisfied her.

The touch of Dr. Baxter's hand was yet warm upon her head; the grave accents of his admonition and blessing had scarcely left her ear, but she had no thought that the predicted crisis was upon her; that her feet stood upon the very point where turning was to be blessing or curse. No! she was fatigued in body, unsettled in spirits. The eccentric doctor's warning had joined to the reaction succeeding the excitement of the day, to put her out of conceit with her present mode of life—and Orrin Wyllys was to be out of town for a fortnight.

This was the diagnosis she made of her discontent after an hour's melancholy lucubration over the restless tongues of flame, and their scarlet substratum. All her causes of discomfort were absurd and childish vagaries, she said, severely,—excepting the last. And oh! of course, the separation from Roy! Orrin's absence would make her feel this the more—would be an actual trial. For was he not the oldest and best friend she had in America, outside of Dundee? She had thought much, tenderly, and regretfully, since she had become so dependent upon Orrin's kindly offices, of her own dead brother—the day-old baby whom she had never seen; who would, had he lived, have been to her all that her brotherly friend was—and more, if that were possible. She had mourned that little baby always. It is natural for girls to want an older brother upon whom to lean for protection and guidance. She had not guessed what a comfort and joy such would be to her until Roy's adopted brother had, in some degree, supplied this need. She had seen him every day since her arrival in Hamilton, and each interview had strengthened her regard and admiration for him. His interest in her studies, her amusements, her health—in all that went to make up the sum of her earthly happiness, was marked and unvarying. A brother in blood could not have been kinder, more thoughtful, in providing whatever could increase her comfort or contribute to her pleasure. She had learned to expect his coming on the evenings she spent at home; to watch for glimpses of his figure in a crowd of unfamiliar forms and faces; to refer doubtful questions to his arbitrament, and appeal to his sympathy in her moments of sadness and anxiety. In fine, he had gained what may be called Cupid's best vantage-ground—he had rendered himself necessary to her enjoyment and peace of mind. His going made a void in her daily life and in her heart.

Although romantic and immature, she was not weak or mawkish. Therefore, she did not repeat—"I never loved a tree or flower," as she ended her musings with a sigh to the memory of the student in foreign lands, and for him to whom she had that night said a tearful "Good-bye." But she remembered both in her prayers. If she named Orrin with more earnestness than breathed in her petitions for Roy's welfare, it was because she believed his present need of comfort to be greater. The very mystery veiling the cause of his unhappiness, led her to dwell upon the subject longer and more interestedly than if he had confided to her the nature of the trouble he was in.

With the morrow came a note.

> "Dear Jessie:—I am scribbling this before sunrise on this dark morning, to ask your forgiveness for my abruptness and moodiness last night. I puzzled—maybe, pained you—kind heart that you are! Do not let a thought of my unhappiness mar the brightness of your existence, now or ever. If you cannot think of me without sadness, forget me. I could bear that better than the thought that I had distressed you. Believe me you have no truer friend than he who signs himself in sorrowful sincerity,
>
> "Yours faithfully,
> "Orrin Wyllys."

"Doesn't he mean to write to me while he is away?" said Jessie, after reading the ten lines through twice, wonderingly and attentively. "He is evidently in great trouble. If I could only help him!"

If he meant her to forget him, he had taken extraordinary measures to secure this end. At six o'clock, every evening, a bouquet was left at Mrs. Baxter's door for Miss Jessie Kirke. Mr. Wyllys' card accompanied the first. The rest needed no other label than the snow-white cape jessamine, that, lurk in whatever ambush of greenery and bloom it might, was instantly betrayed by its subtle aroma.

Eight days went by more laggingly than Jessie had believed time could pass in Hamilton, and Eunice's weekly bulletin of home news announced that Dundee had been honored by Mr. Wyllys' presence.

"He spent the Sabbath with us," wrote she. "It was a pleasant day to us all. Mr. Wyllys kindly took my place as organist in church, and played with even more than his usual taste and feeling. His news of you would of itself have made him a welcome guest. His report of your health, sports, and progress in your studies was very favorable. He says, moreover, that Mrs. Baxter will not consent to give you up before Spring. Do not abridge your stay, for fear we shall be lonely without you. We miss you, of course, but we are consoled for the pain of separation, by the knowledge that you are improving in health and enjoying social and educational advantages such as our secluded valley cannot furnish.

"I enclose a letter from Roy, directed, as usual, under cover to Father. In the accompanying note, he alludes to his gratification at learning that you are so pleasantly situated and happily employed this winter. We are glad that he is heartily in favor of the important step we ventured to take without waiting to consult him.

"I wish you could see your oriel now. Our flowers have flourished this winter as they never did before. The Daphnes are in full bloom. The Stephanotis is almost encumbered by buds, and the fragrant petunias and double nasturtiums (the seed of which Mr. Wyllys gave me in the Fall) are thriving bravely, the latter climbing rapidly.

"Our excellent neighbors are very kind and attentive," etc., etc.

Jessie re-read this letter when she had finished Roy's; perused it with a half smile that was more mournful than amused, and an odd stricture about her heart. Eunice's round of duties and pleasures seemed to her like something she had passed—outgrown ages since; yet there was, far down in her spirit, a piteous longing for those gone days. She might be wiser—she was not better or happier for the glimpses lately granted her of a world of stormy and contending passions and mixed motives.

"He spent the Sabbath with us!" she read aloud. "And I was not at home! He said nothing to me of his intention to visit Dundee. Since he has changed his plans in one respect, he may in another, and be absent three or four weeks instead of two. Heigho!"

She folded up her sister's letter, and addressed herself very slowly to the task of getting ready for a party at Judge Provost's—the great house of the town. It was given in honor of a niece of his, who was visiting his daughter, and was to be a grand affair. Jessie had never attended one half so fine, but she was *ennuyée* in anticipation.

"There will be the stock company of beaux," she meditated. "The one unmarried professor; the ten almost marriageable seniors, and the ten utterly ineligible ones, who are without beards or moneyed capital; the whole army (I had nearly said 'herd') of juniors and sophomores; the dozen or fifteen gentlemen detailed for the occasion from the doctors' and lawyers' offices, and the higher rank of tradespeople in Hamilton. There will be dancing in one parlor, and small-talk in another; promenading in the halls and billiard-room; flirtations in all stages among the oleanders and lemon-trees of the conservatory, and a "jam"—*not* sweet—in the supper-room. As a clergyman's daughter and the guest of a clergyman's wife, I must not dance in public. I am sick to nausea of callow collegians and small-talk, and I don't care for late suppers of indigestible dainties. I would rather spend the evening with Mariana in the moated grange, for that mopish damsel would let me sit still and sulk if I wanted to. And I believe I do!"

"A little more fire, my love!" whispered Mrs. Baxter in the dressing-room, affecting to be busy in shaking out Jessie's pink silk drapery. "I have a presentiment that you are to meet your fate to-night. But you must positively exert yourself to seem less quiet and preoccupied. Repose and lofty indifference are considered well-bred, and are a very safe *rôle* for the commonplace to adopt. But they are unbecoming to *us*."

The novice did her best to throw light into her eyes and warmth into her complexion. Being a novice, the attempt was a failure; but Mrs. Baxter, perceiving that ignorance, not obstinacy, hindered the desired effect, forbore to hint that, in spite of Jessie's elegant attire and becoming *coiffure*, she had never seen her look worse. Trusting to the animating influences of the festive scene to restore that which friendly expostulation had proved inefficient to recall, she committed her to the officious homage of young Lowndes, and turned her attention to the part she was herself to play in the evening's drama.

"What a magnificent creature your niece is, Mrs. Baxter; or is she a cousin?" said an elderly gentleman—also one of the judge's visitors—to her, at length.

The pleased and amiable chaperone looked over her shoulder, directed by his gaze, just in time to see Jessie pass, treading as if on air; her eyes luminous orbs of rapture; her cheeks like the inner foldings of a damask rose; her lips apart in a smile, sweet and happy, and her hand on Orrin Wyllys' arm.

# CHAPTER IX

And you have really been to Dundee!" Jessie was saying, unconscious that she was clinging to Mr. Wyllys' arm—very slightly, but perceptibly to him, with the glad hold of one to whom something dear and rare has been restored. "Was this a part of the original plan of your journeyings?"

"No,—but my business led me within sight of Old Windbeam—('a frosty pow' his is, just now!)—and it acted upon me as did the Iron Mountain of the Arabian Nights upon the hapless ships that approached it. It drew out the nails of doubt as to the best course for me to pursue; the screws of resolution not to be turned aside by memories of the Past and the allurements of the Present. To be brief—I collapsed utterly! took the afternoon train to Dundee, and passed, in that retreat from briefs and busybodies, the happiest Sabbath I have known since last August."

"Euna wrote to me about it—the lovely, precise old darling! She never indulges in extravagances upon any subject, but her concise sentences mean much, and these said how she enjoyed the day—and your music. I was envious of her, when I read of it—just for a moment, of course. I have seen so much of you this winter it seemed mean and selfish in me to grudge her one day of like pleasure."

"Envy so groundless could not but be evanescent," said Orrin, with admirable gravity. "But tell me about yourself. What have you been doing while I was away?"

"Cultivating envy, as I said—and, I am not positive, but wrath and all uncharitableness, as well. Who is it that confesses to an instant uprising of all that is wicked in his nature at the approach of trouble, while visible blessing always moves him to thankful piety? I am afraid I am similarly constituted. I have been dull and 'dumpish' for a week and more; choosing to quarrel with the three peas under the fourteen feather-beds, rather than enjoy the good that is certainly mine. You see I also am versed in fairy-lore."

"I remember that the disguised princess, at being asked why she was haggard in the morning after the night spent in the forester's cabin, betrayed her gentle breeding by complaining of the lumps in her mountainous couch. Fourteen feather-beds! Think of it! To sleep amid the waves of one of the Dutch abominations is enough to engender dyspepsia, apoplexy, and spleen. But what were the three peas in your bed of roses?"

"It has rained four days out of eight, my Germany letter was behind time—and I missed my brother-cousin at every turn," responded Jessie bravely, vexed that anything in the enumeration should make her cheek put on the sudden flame of poppies.

"Two valid and sufficient reasons for *ennui*! As for the third, and notably the least of all, I thank you for the welcome implied by it. I have missed you, Jessie!"

"But not as I have you!" was the ingenuous response. "I have been homesick, dismal, disagreeable,—*horrid* generally. But I spare you the recapitulation. I am very, very happy that you are back again in health, and,"—faltering a little,—"in better spirits, than when you left us."

"Mr. Wyllys!" interrupted a consequential personage—a young-old bachelor. "Excuse me, Miss Kirke, but this is business of importance!"

He spoke a sentence aside to Orrin, who replied briefly in the same tone.

"Mr. Hurst is acting as master of ceremonies to-night, *comme à l'ordinaire*," observed Wyllys, moving on with his companion. "How will Hamilton parties get on after he dies—or marries—I wonder? There has been an addition to the ranks of fashion during my absence, I find. I had hardly finished my bow to Mrs. and Miss Provost, when Warren Provost presented me forcibly to Miss Sanford. I learned, before I went three steps farther, that this party is given to Miss Sanford, and now Mr. Hurst tells me that I am expected, presently, to dance with Miss Sanford. Who *is* Miss Sanford?"

Jessie comprehending, at once, that he shunned further reference to the state of his spirits at their parting, followed his lead away from the subject, with alacrity.

"Miss Sanford is the daughter of Judge Provost's sister, and *such* an heiress! An American Miss Burdett Coutts, if half the stories in circulation about her be true. She is the only child of a five-millionaire, and has, besides, a million in her own right, inherited from her mother. Poor thing! what a nuisance it must be to be so *horribly* rich!" commented the country girl who thought herself wealthy with her mother's wedding-portion of ten thousand dollars, carefully husbanded by her father against her majority or marriage.

"If another woman than Jessie Kirke had said that, I should have supposed she was in jest," said Orrin. "I believe you mean what you say. But why? Many and sweet are the uses of money."

"Why do I regard it as a misfortune for a woman to be immensely rich? Because she can never be sure of true friend or lover. Because she seldom escapes one of two evils, dupedom or misanthropy. It must be almost an impracticable task for a great heiress to satisfy herself that she is not wooed *pour les beaux yeux de ses écus*."

"But if there are no other *beaux yeux* in the case—her own being, we will say, leaden—should she not congratulate herself that she has one talisman that will win attention and regard?"

"Regard!" echoed Jessie, incredulously.

"And why not? She typifies bank stock, real estate, ready money, to the adorer of these. He worships *them*, it is true, but through her, as discriminating Romanists try to make us believe that they adore the Virgin Mary by the help of her images."

"And as Dr. Baxter told me, the other day, Aaron and his crew of apostate ingrates bowed down to the molten calf—as the representative of the Egyptian Apis," put in Jessie, sarcastically. "If a woman can content herself with that sort of worship, put herself on a par with the goose that laid the golden egg, she wants neither affection nor pity."

"Yet I'll warrant that the famous goose preened herself alongside of the most gorgeous peacock in the barnyard; accounted herself the equal of the stateliest swans. There are as many purse-proud women as men. Millionnaires of both sexes do not scorn the court paid to their money through themselves. On the contrary, they would be piqued and offended if their dollars were not duly appreciated. Novels and sentimentalists tell us that the unhappy possessors of princely fortunes desire to be loved and sought for their intrinsic virtues, whereas the great mass—especially of women—who are wedded for their riches, are quite alive to the truth that this is so, and are far from being wounded thereby. They are neither dupes nor misanthropes, but sensible practical bodies who regard their property as a part of themselves—soul of their soul—and unhesitatingly appropriate all the advantages it buys, pluming themselves, as a rule, upon their ability to command service and fidelity. You shake your head? Let me illustrate from real life. I was talking, some time ago, with a married lady whom nobody had ever, in my hearing, called weak-minded, even behind her back. I had known her for many years, and she opened up her mind to me freely, with regard to her courtship by, and marriage to, the man of her choice. 'I feared, at one time, that I had lost him forever,' she said. 'He was, quite assiduous in his attention to another young lady who was pretty, elegant, and accomplished. I was very unhappy, for he had never declared his intentions to me. But she had not money enough to suit his notions of the fitness of things,'—I quote literally. 'So he came back to me. Wasn't I thankful then that my dear father had provided for me handsomely and thus secured my happiness for life?'"

"A clever anecdote—considering it is impromptu!" said wilful Jessie, with an air of superb disbelief. "If I could credit it, and you—"

"You would cease to commiserate heiresses!" finished Wyllys. "For myself, I have an antipathy to the whole class. All whom I have had the misery of knowing were sordid, self-conceited, and rapacious of admiration to a degree that passed understanding and disgust."

He dropped his voice, for the crowd immediately about them had grown still and attentive.

Miss Sanford was going to sing. Jessie and her escort chanced to be near the piano, and had a fine view of her as she was led to the instrument by an ambitious senior, whom she loaded down with her bouquet, gloves, fan, handkerchief, and gold vinaigrette. She was probably about twenty-five years of age, but this was a difficult point to determine from her appearance; her hair, eyebrows, and complexion being so light, that, as Jessie afterwards said to Mrs. Baxter, she looked as if she might have lain for forty-eight hours in a bath of caustic soda and water—the preliminary process in the preparation of the phantom bouquets the President's lady was skilled in arranging. Miss Sanford was thin and bony. "Scraggy," one would have termed her, had she belonged to the so-called inferior animals. Her eyes were a pale, fixed blue, like those of a china doll; her lips met scantily over teeth that were unpleasantly prominent; she had a receding chin, a sharp nose, and a low forehead. A homely, shrewish-looking girl to the uninstructed eye. Yet her air showed that she was accustomed to receive court from the sophisticated multitude, the many who were awake to the fact that she was the undoubted mistress of charms not to be adequately expressed by less than seven figures. Her dress was a walking advertisement of her pretensions to this intelligent homage, being mauve satin, flounced with point lace. It was cut too low upon the flat chest and prominent shoulder-blades, but the region thus left bare was made interesting to feminine eyes by a magnificent diamond necklace. Bracelets to match loaded her meagre wrists, and were pushed up ostentatiously before she put her fingers upon the key-board, with a coquettish grimace at her cavalier.

"I don't sing ballads," Jessie and Orrin heard her say, tossing her head one-sidedly—a frequent trick with her, since it set her ear-rings to dancing until the precious stones seemed to emit sparks of real fire. "Ballad music is considered so low in refined circles. I have never cultivated any but the classical style—operas, you know, bravuras and arias, and all that, you know. Let me treat you to my favorite—just the *sweetest* thing you ever heard, from La Traviata. I perfectly dote upon it!"

She played a thumping prelude and accompaniment in villainous time; her voice was shallow and shrill; she made audacious dashes at trills and cadenzas, her feeble pipe breaking down upon the ascending, and breaking up upon the descending scale. A more lamentable and witless travestie of operatic execution could hardly have been conceived of. The Italian words were made a thing of no account whatever.

"Her resources are wonderful," said Orrin, under cover of the buzz of compliments and thanks that succeeded the song. "When she forgot what came next she substituted something of her own composition—in the Kaffir dialect, I think—with a readiness and coolness truly astounding. Honor bright, now," laughing down mischievously into his companion's eyes—"what has this little scene reminded you of—something you have hitherto viewed as a caricature?"

"I won't tell you!"

But Jessie's face was alive with fun. It might not be—it certainly was not altogether kind or well-bred in her to join in ridiculing the host's niece, but it was "only Orrin," and so long as his comments were for her ear alone, no harm was done.

"You need not! Miss Swartz has arisen above such 'low style' as 'Blue-eyed Mary' and 'That Air from the Cabinet,' but she can still 'sing Fluvy du Tajy if she had the words.' Indeed, being bent upon fascination, she sings it, words or no."

He had found Jessie and Mrs. Baxter deep in "Vanity Fair" one evening, had taken the book and read aloud several chapters, including "The quarrel about an heiress."

"Yet you will not let me say, 'Poor Miss Swartz!'" said Jessie.

"Certainly not. She is in Paradise. Reserve your pity for me, who am doomed to ask her to waltz so soon as this part of the exhibition is over. Hark! another sweet selection! This time from *Der Freischütz*—Agatha's prayer, done into boarding-school German *patois*, varied by the amazing improvisations aforesaid. For Heaven's sake! come away into the conservatory. Even 'when music, heavenly maid, was *very* young,' a baby in the cradle, she never squalled like that!"

Jessie could not help laughing at his whimsical impatience. Mirth came easily to-night. The surprise and joy of her friend's return had exhilarated her. The very freedom of his comments upon others made her feel the entireness of their mutual confidence. His talking to her in this strain was a direct compliment to her discretion. It was delightful to see him gay once more—to believe that his light rattle was the overflow of a heart as full and happy as her own.

He lingered with her in the conservatory until the indefatigable Mr. Hurst came to hunt him up.

"You will let me take you in to supper?" said Wyllys, pulling himself up with graceful unwillingness from the fantastic root seat beside the fountain. "Where shall I find you, if I survive the next half hour?"

"Here!" glancing up brightly. "It is cool and quiet, and my feet ache with standing. Don't send anybody to me, please! I shall sit here, and rest and think—ponder seriously upon the miseries of the rich, the compensations of the poor."

Orrin had chosen their resting-place in the leafy boudoir with his habitual sagacity, having an eye both to ease and the semi-privacy which confidential friends find so enjoyable in the neighborhood of a crowd. An osier frame overrun with ivy, screened Jessie on the left from any save very prying eyes; a barricade of lemon and orange trees towered at the back; in front, the fountain, showering from peak and sides of a rock-work pyramid, cast a shimmering veil between her and the archway, closing up a vista of vines and shrubs, through which issued music and the hum of many voices with the rhythmical beat of feet. Jessie listened to the merry din, the nearer dash of the glittering drops into the basin at her feet; and inhaling the perfume of the exotics behind her, smiled a happy little smile in remembrance of her scornful weariness in predicting the flirtations among the oleanders and lemon-trees. She had no pre-vision then that she should sit here with one chosen companion, talking freely and gladly of all that was in her heart; none of the gentle and lovely reverie to which he had left her.

From a great globe of ground glass overhead, effulgence like that of a midsummer moon streamed down upon the falling water; the trailing grasses and clinging mosses upon the stones were threaded with tiny brilliants; the broad wet leaves of the aquatic plants overhanging and growing within the marble reservoir were washed with silver. A single lily arose, pure and proud, from a clump of luxuriant flags. Tall ferns standing motionless on the thither margin, made a miniature brake of an alley that stretched away into cool green dimness. A bed of musk-plant yielded up languorous sighs to the warmed air. All that was sensuous in temperament and artistic in taste made response to the influence of the place and hour. Jessie gave herself up to it without resistance, laid her head against the tortuous scroll-work of the high back of the settee, and dreamed. The evening had been triumphant, intoxicating to her. The evening she would have preferred to spend with dolorous Mariana!

She whispered the familiar lines to herself:

> "'All day, within the dreamy house,
> The doors upon their hinges creaked;
> The blue fly sung i' the pane; the mouse
> Behind the mouldering wainscot shrieked,
> Or, from the crevice peered about, —'

But that was nothing! I dare say the Grange was a commodious, respectable family mansion; that it would have been as beautiful as the Alhambra to the poor girl, had the faithless lover kept his tryst. '"He cometh not," she said!' That was the key to the desolation without and within. I had not believed that I could be so glad to see any one except Roy, as I am to meet Orrin again. He has a look like his cousin sometimes. I never noticed it before as I have to-night;—a look that gives me a sense of safety and companionship when with him, which makes sadness and home-sickness impossibilities. It is *good* to have a friend upon whom I can lean my whole weight without fear of causing weariness—in whose society I can be frankly, fearlessly, joyously, *myself!*"

There were but two or three couples in the conservatory besides herself, and they, too, seemed to be lulled into silent musing by the subdued lights and odorous airs of the fairy-like haunt. Perhaps some of the dancers found fault with the draught from the archway, for Jessie saw Warren Provost and Mr. Hurst let down the damask curtains which had been looped back from it. She drew a deeper breath of content in the feeling of increased seclusion. Now that the music, the babble of human tongues, and the tramp of a hundred waltzers were muffled, a mocking-bird from his concealed cage in an acacia tree began to sing. First came a chirp of alarm as if he had just awakened from dreams of tropical skies and magnolia groves—then a trial trill, a gush of liquid melody, clear and soft as the ripple of a mountain rivulet. Next, he whistled, still softly, but with marvellous correctness and sweetness, a flute waltz Jessie had heard Orrin Wyllys play last summer. She smiled and murmured in her trance, —

"Everything associated with him is pure pleasure!"

Nobody could be moody or dull when he chose to please and interest. To her, his coming was like the spreading of the sun rays down the mountain sides and through the valley on summer mornings, steeping the commonplace in beauty; making of native loveliness a witching miracle. Dear, *dear* Roy! She owed this great happiness also to him. He had reckoned wisely and lovingly in committing her to the care of this guardian.

The band struck up a march. The blare of the instruments burst unwelcomely upon her rosy dreams. She aroused herself with a start to see the curtains pulled back. The mocking-bird ceased his song abruptly. The waltzers, panting and flushed, thronged the narrow aisles of the conservatory; chattered and flitted among the foliage like bright-plumaged, loud-voiced parrots. Miss Sanford was conspicuous among them, leaning palpably upon her escort's arm. Her affected laugh grated unpleasantly upon Jessie's ears, every few seconds. She was in exuberant spirits; in high good-humor with herself, and, presumably, with her partner.

"Oh! that darling beauty of a lily!" she cried, pushing roughly past the ivied screen, to get a closer view of the proud, pale princess of the fountain. "I wanted you should see it! Fanny Provost, my cousin, goes just crazy over it. It was brought to her all the way from the Nile, or the Ganges, or the Amazon, or some other of those stupid rivers in Europe, whose names I always forget—by her beau. You know she is engaged to Lieutenant Averill of the Navy? Everybody who is anybody announces engagements nowadays, as soon as the matter is settled by what my uncle, Judge Provost, calls the high contracting parties. It is a nice fashion. Don't you think so? I *do* think an engagement must be just the cunningest, sweetest thing in the world!"

"That depends, in a great measure, upon who the high contracting parties are, I suppose," replied Orrin, with the slightest imaginable glance in the direction of the concealed spectator, but one in which she read a drollery of appeal that wrought irresistibly upon her risibles.

Miss Sanford tittered. "I declare I am afraid of you, Mr. Wyllys! You are *so* sarcastic! Of course, that was what I meant. One takes that for granted always. But it must be just *too* sweet for two people who are devoted to one another, and who are of suitable ages and prospects, and all that, you know, to promise that they will just perfectly adore one another, till death, you know. At least, that is the way *I* look at it. I am *so* womanly, Mr. Wyllys! I often tremble at the thought of buffeting the world. Everybody is so absorbed in their own selfish interests. My cousin, Mrs. Morris—the ex-Chancellor's lady, you know—says I am a sensitive plant, not fit to meet the rough winds of life."

With the ventriloquial knack that belongs to the genuine slayer of hearts, Orrin made his reply inaudible to any one but the woman at his side, who flushed up eagerly, and fanned herself in naïve agitation.

"I wish I could think so, Mr. Wyllys! It is ever so kind in you to wish it, I am sure. But men—and I am ashamed to say it—women, too, are such awful flatterers! And appearances are *so* deceitful! Nobody would believe, for instance, that I, with everything—comparatively speaking you know—to make me happy, should pine for a kindred heart—one that would beat responsive to mine. True, one person cannot have everything, you know—There! I've torn my lace flounce upon that ugly cactus! Just see, Mrs. Saville!"—to a lady who was passing, revealing the extent of the rent. "The first time I have ever worn it, too! I don't know what my careful papa will say. It was a present from him. But, la! who cares? If he scolds, I'll punish him by paying for it myself. That will just break his heart. Nothing puts him out so much as for me to remind him that I can be independent of him if I choose. That is the way with all you gentlemen—isn't it, Mr. Wyllys?" staring boldly—she fancied engagingly—up at him. "You would have us owe everything to you. Bless me! can that be supper? And just as we are having such a sweet, romantic time! Isn't this just the most delicious bower in Christendom? I tease my cousin Fanny by insisting that Lieutenant Averill couldn't help proposing when once she had got him in here. Not that it can compare in size with our conservatory. Ours is connected, too, with the graperies, which makes it perfectly *immense*. Where can Mr. Romondt be? He saw me come in here, I am certain, for we passed him in the door. He was to take me in to supper, but I am not in the habit of waiting for my escorts. It would be just *too* funny if *I*—of all the women here—should be thrown upon your protection in the character of the deserted maiden—wouldn't it?"

"The bliss of succoring you is not to be mine, at present, it seems," said Orrin, with an adroit, backward bow, as Mr. Romondt hurried upon the scene, full of apologies, to claim his convoy.

A new caprice seized the belle.

"I protest *he* ought to be the deserted one, in punishment for his tardiness!" regaining her hold of Mr. Wyllys' elbow, and making a resentful *moue* at the derelict gallant. "I have half a mind to go off with you and leave him to solitary regrets. Suppose, if I trust myself to him, my barque should be shipwrecked on the journey?"

It was an awkward moment. The heiress' look and action plainly testified that hers was no "half mind" to commit herself to the pilotage of the man who had not invited such a display of confidence. Wyllys extricated himself promptly and creditably, and as if her proposal were entirely decorous and ladylike. He had too much sense and tact ever to patronize one of his own sex, and owed much of his popularity to the air of respectful *bonhommie* with which he now turned to the perspiring and rebuked Romondt.

"Do not try fallible humanity beyond endurance, Miss Sanford! It is hard to be just and magnanimous in the face of such a temptation, but right is right. Mr. Romondt! grant me the honor of becoming your security for the safe and pleasant transfer of *la reine du bal* to the supper-room.

Jessie was quivering with merriment in her sheltered nook.

"I have been in mortal terror lest I should not be launched at all, but be left high and hungry upon the stocks!" she cried gayly, at her attendant's approach. "And supper is one of the substantial blessings of life, when one has a good appetite."

Orrin feigned to wipe the dews of exhaustion from his brow with a despairing flourish of his handkerchief.

"At last I am at your service. You must stay me with flagons (of champagne), and comfort me with (pine) apples;" he said, profanely enough, "for I am sick of heiresses!"

# CHAPTER X

Judge Provost, whose wife and daughters were the leaders of fashion in Hamilton, was himself a social Greatheart. Having brought to bear upon various vexed domestic problems the force of his astute mind and enlightened Christianity, he had arrived at a series of conclusions equally creditable to both. The pertinence of his deductions was so obvious to the impartial reasoner as to excite his surprise, that the great body of good and sensible men and women did not adopt and practise them. For example, he maintained first, that the best way to keep men out of jails, was to provide them with abodes so comfortable that they would prefer these to stone cells and prison fare: secondly, as a modification of the same principle, that, since amusements are necessary to the happiness of the young, they should be provided with lawful diversions in their own homes, lest they should seek unlawful abroad; thirdly, in unconscious plagiarism of the wise and genial author of "Annals of a Country Neighborhood," he held and believed for certain, that the surest way to make an indifferent thing bad, was for good people to hold themselves aloof from doing it.

Acting upon these principles, the eminent jurist built a bowling-alley at the back of his garden; caused his eight children to be instructed in music and dancing, and encouraged them to pursue these recreations in his parlors,—where, also, lay backgammon and chess board in full sight. Finally, he crowned their gratification while he drew upon himself the reprobation of the zealots and puritans among his neighbors, by throwing a wing out from his already spacious residence, expressly for a billiard-room. It was a pretty place, and a cheerful, with its green carpets and lounges, tinted walls, and long French windows, and was, as may be supposed, a popular resort with those of the college students who had the *entrée*, as well as with the young Provosts and their friends of both sexes in the town. A happy, hospitable set were the young Provosts—the four sisters and four brothers—affectionate to one another, dutiful and loving to the parents to whose judicious affection they owed their sunny childhood and youth. Jessie liked them better than she did any other family in Hamilton, while Fanny, the second daughter, had taken a fancy to her at first sight, which was ripening into a cordial friendship.

The billiard-room was very bright with afternoon sunshine, and merry with the chatter of gay voices, one day late in February, when a party of six or eight girls was collected about the table—four playing, the others looking on and talking, sometimes of the game in progress, sometimes upon other subjects—all in a familiar yet ladylike way.

"Somebody mark for me, please!" said a ruddy-cheeked damsel who had never, by any chance, won a game, and whose principal points were the point she made of missing every shot. "If I should hit anything it would be a pity not to get credit for it. Now—all of you look and learn!"

She poised the cue with a superabundance of caution, pursing up her lips into an O, as she took aim; dashed at the white ball nearest her, which flew frantically from side to side of the board, rebounding twice from the cushion, and, at last, popping into a distant pocket, having dodged every other ball with a malicious ingenuity eminently illustrative of the proverbial perversity of inanimate things.

"Better luck next time!" said the player, invincibly good-humored, resigning her place. "If there is anything in perseverance and hope, I shall do it yet, some day, and astonish you all."

The others laughed—with, rather than at her—and Jessie Kirke took the stand she had vacated. All leaned forward to watch her play, her skill being already an established fact. A touch—not a thrust—to the white ball sent it against a red at such an angle that in the rebound it hit another quite at the other end of the green table, which latter rolled into a pocket. This, to the uninitiated, meaningless process, being repeated by her, with trifling variations, until she had made sixteen points, was considered a feat among the embryo billiardists surrounding her.

"So much for a true eye and a sure touch!" said Fanny Provost. "You shame us all, Jessie dear."

"So much for having a good teacher!" said another, less complimentary. "If Mr. Wyllys would bestow as much care upon our tuition as he has upon hers, we might be adepts, too."

"She has practised ten times as much with me as she has with him," answered Fanny, pleasantly. "So, I am entitled to the larger share of the praise for her proficiency. I will not be cheated of my laurels."

"Is Mr. Wyllys, then, your best player?"

The querist was Miss Sanford, who "did not care about billiards," and had even remonstrated, at the beginning of her visit with her cousin Fanny, with regard to her liking for the game—"such a queer one for ladies! She would be afraid to touch a cue for fear she might be called strong-minded."

She had discovered, furthermore, that her wrists were not stout enough to bear the weight of a cue steadily, and took pleasure in publishing their genteel fragility. Only that afternoon she had called attention to this by an exclamation addressed to Jessie, as she drew up her cuffs in order to be ready for her turn.

"Dear me! Miss Kirke! what wouldn't I give to be as robust as you are! Look at her arms! They would make six of mine. What do you do to develop your muscles so?"

Jessie smiled in quiet satisfaction with her own beautifully moulded wrists.

"I am healthy, and I lead an active life," she said, laconically, but politely.

Miss Sanford was not pleased either with smile or words, but there was apparently nothing to resent, and she returned to her sofa. She had attended a party the evening before, and was to-day "utterly worn out." While the game went on, she toyed with her rings, slipped her bracelets of dead gold and pearls up and down her thin arms, and now and then yawned behind her hand. Mr. Wyllys' name awoke her from the apathetic droning.

"Decidedly!" replied a looker-on, Selina Bradley by name—a kind-hearted, talkative, and indiscreet girl whom everybody liked, yet of whose tripping tongue many were afraid. "Decidedly the best in town. Don't you think so, Fan?"

"There are not many who can equal him among our finest billiard players," said Fanny. "I do not believe he has lost a game since Mr. Fordham went away. *He* played splendidly! His nerves were steady and his judgment nice."

"Fordham!" repeated the heiress, quickly. "What was his first name? Who is he?"

"Roy—and he is a professor in our college. He is now in Heidelberg, Germany. Do you know him?" said Fanny, in surprise. "You must have heard us speak of him before."

"Never! I used to know him," rejoined Miss Sanford, tossing her head. "He was engaged to a very dear friend of mine. No! I didn't know he was in Germany. I am glad of it!"

Selina, breathless with excitement, did not catch the meaning of the latter sentences.

"Engaged! I thought he was love-proof! Fanny! Nettie! Sue! do you hear this? Who do you guess is engaged to be married? No less a personage than our invulnerable Professor Fordham!"

The girls crowded about Miss Sanford, forgetting the game in the superior attractions of a love-story.

"To whom?"

"Who told you?"

"I don't believe it!" were the divers comments upon the intelligence.

Jessie remained alone at the table, tapping the cushion opposite her with her cue, her face flaming with indignant confusion. Taken utterly by surprise, she could not at once rally to reply to the false statement she had heard, or govern her countenance well enough to seem indifferent.

The heiress bridled at the last remark, setting back her head in a fashion she conceived was regal, whereas it was merely ungracefully scornful.

"You are not asked to believe it, Miss Barnes! I said distinctly that the gentleman was *formerly* betrothed to my friend. I am happy, on her account, to be able to state that the (to her) unfortunate engagement was broken almost a year since."

"What do you mean? How did it happen? And to think we never heard a breath of it! Go on! there's a darling! and tell us all about it!" entreated Selina, sinking to the carpet at the feet of the in nowise reluctant newsmonger.

"Perhaps you had rather not, Hester," suggested gentle Fanny to her cousin. "Such stories are painful to those interested in either of the parties to the engagement, and the telling does no good to any one. The fewer people that hear of them the better, it seems to me."

"Oh! I don't mind it in the least *now!*" Hester hastened to re-assure her. She settled the voluminous skirt of her purple cashmere peignoir about her; disposed her rings upon her fingers, and her fingers upon her lap to her liking; sighed profoundly, and looked smirkingly sentimental. "There was a time when I could not allude to it, or even think of it, without tears. My disposition is *so* sympathetic! But time deadens all griefs, and my poor friend acknowledges herself that it was best the affair should have terminated as it did. She met Mr. Fordham at the seashore summer before last—was with him there for a week or so. It was long enough for him to fall violently in love with her. He couldn't help being taken by her appearance, for she is just perfectly lovely! a blonde, with blue eyes, and a red rose-bud of a mouth, and golden hair, and the *sweetest* smile!"

"She must be a real beauty!" sighed Selina, in an ecstasy of admiration.

"She is. People pretend to see a resemblance between us. I have actually been mistaken for her more than once—but that is all nonsense," said Hester, modestly. "I should be just too happy if I were half as handsome as Maria. But I love her too dearly to be envious. We are like twin sisters in heart. I dare say that is the reason we are called so much alike. We go out so much together, you see, that the sight of one reminds people of the other, you know. But as I was saying, this Mr. Fordham pretended to be smitten with her, and, early in the winter, visited her at her own home. Her parents liked him exceedingly. He is rather an imposing man, you know, and has some reputation as a scholar. So, when he paid a second visit at Christmas, and offered himself, there was no objection raised to the match. Poor, dear, deluded Maria! how happy she was! All went swimmingly for about six weeks, when, without warning, he broke the engagement. And why, do you suppose? He had heard that one of her sisters had died of consumption several years before he knew her, and he 'could not be hampered by a sickly wife!'"

She waited until the chorus of reprobation subsided, then resumed:

"He wrote to her. Iron man as he was, he was afraid to trust himself in her presence. He 'regretted the necessity that forced him to this unpleasant step,' he said, 'but he owed a duty to himself which was not to be lightly put aside. He should always remain her friend,' and all that sort of rubbish, you know. The broken-hearted creature stooped to argue with him. She loved him devotedly, and she had had no other love. If I had been in her place, I would have died sooner than let him know how I suffered; but she was *such* a lamb-like, gentle creature! and her spirit was utterly crushed. She wrote to him, imploring him not to leave her, representing that there was not a sign of hereditary consumption in the family; that her parents were living, and that her grand-parents on both sides had all died from other diseases. But he was obstinate. He 'would never,' he replied, 'in any circumstances, marry a woman who was not, in his opinion, perfectly sound in mind and body, or who had any predisposition to scrofula, consumption, or insanity.' He pretended to believe still that she had the seeds of a fatal malady in her system, and went so far as to allude to her beautiful color—just the sweetest pink and white you ever saw!—as a hectic flush. *That's* the history of Mr. Roy Fordham's love-scrape!"

"And did she break a blood-vessel, or go into a decline?" asked Sue Barnes, her round face ludicrously elongated, while her eyelids twinkled away a sympathizing tear.

"Well—no!" Miss Sanford hesitated, then made the admission unwillingly, evidently appreciating the damage her mournful recital must sustain through the want of this orthodox sequel. "But she was in a sad way for awhile. Her family kept the miserable affair as quiet as possible for her sake. The truth was communicated to nobody except a few very intimate and dearest friends. But you can't wonder that I have hated the sound of Professor Fordham's name ever since."

"Very natural, I am sure!" murmured the plastic Sue.

Hester made a parade of wiping her eyes with a lace handkerchief.

"Not that I ever liked him. Poor Maria brought him around to our house, one evening, on purpose to have me see him. And the next morning she was in, bright and early, to ask what I thought of him. 'I don't fancy him in the least, my dear child,' I said to her, candidly. 'He has a cold, severe eye, and a stubborn mouth. He is quiet in manner because he is unfeeling. If you marry him, he will rule you with a rod of steel, and make your life a burden.' It was a trial to say it, but I knew it was my duty, and I didn't turn back, you know. She cried her eyes out over what she said was my unkindness, and left me in a tremendous huff. She would neither speak to me, nor hear my name mentioned in her presence, until the rupture came. Then she sent right away for me, and fell upon my neck, begging my pardon. 'If I had been as clear-sighted as you, Hester, what wretchedness I would have been spared!' she sobbed. I am very acute in my perception of character. My grandmother, Mrs. General Deane—my mother's mother—said to her dying day that my skill in seeing through people—especially sheep in wolves' clothing—I mean wolves in sheep's clothing—was—well! the most astonishing thing she had ever seen."

Jessie was knocking the balls to and fro, in reckless disregard of the laws controlling the game, but the sharp click of the ivory spheres did not distract general attention from Miss Sanford.

"I never was more amazed in all my born days!" said Selina, conscientiously reserved with respect to her pre-natal experience. "Mr. Fordham is so pleasant, yet so dignified, and ranks so high in the Faculty and the church, and has so much influence among the students! Who could ever have thought of his behaving in such an inhuman and ungentlemanly manner?"

"Why, people in Hamilton—everybody—out of the college as well as in, consider him a piece of perfection!" added Sue.

"He is a detestable snake in the grass, then!" Hester said, vehemently, her energy so disproportionate to the occasion, that doubts would have arisen, in an unbiassed mind, of her own belief in the affecting narration she had glibly poured forth.

"Take care, dear!" cautioned Fanny. "There may be extenuating circumstances of which we are ignorant. Mr. Fordham's character as a gentleman and a Christian is not to be lightly disputed. Every question has two sides, papa says, and those are wisest who suspend judgment until both are heard. I am morally certain there is some mistake about all this, which Mr. Fordham could clear up, if he were here."

The heiress sniffed haughtily, and her light skin was dappled with fiery red spots to the roots of her hair; her faint eyebrows met in a viragoish frown.

"I thank you for the inference, Miss Provost! Would I repeat a story unless I was sure—'morally certain,' as you say, that it was true in every particular? If you question my veracity, you can ask dozens of her acquaintances in her native place, who will confirm my statement. And you may be thankful if you don't, at the same time, hear some other ugly facts about your Christian gentleman, that I have chosen to omit. If I have a fault, it is that I am too charitable in my judgment of human nature. I am perpetually being imposed upon."

The cue that had been stationary while Fanny put in her plea for mercy to the absent perjurer, was restless again, red balls and white chasing one another aimlessly across the green cloth.

"To tell the truth," said Nettie Fry, another of the listening group, propitiatory of the mistress of a million in her own right,—"I never admired Mr. Fordham so much as many pretend to do. He was always so cool and lofty—so unapproachable and unlike other young men of his age. And as Miss Sanford says, he looked as if he might, when married, grow into a kind of Bluebeard."

"For my part, I thought him grand and good," confessed Selina. "And I liked him a hundred times better than I did the modern young gentleman, with his flattering speeches and unmeaning attentions. I didn't think he *could* trifle with a woman's affections. I am dreadfully disappointed! I wonder if Mr. Wyllys knows anything about this shocking business!"

"Of course he doesn't! How should he?" retorted Hester, tartly. "There are not three people besides myself, even in our city, who ever heard of it."

"You said 'dozens,' just now, Hester!" ventured merciful Fanny, in gentle rebuke.

Selina averted the burst of anger portended by the darkening visage of the moneyed belle.

"I thought Mr. Wyllys would be more likely to hear Mr. Fordham's side of the story than anybody else," she said, timidly. "You know they are own cousins."

"You don't say so!" ejaculated Hester, horrified; and by a simultaneous conviction of their indiscretion, the entire party was moved to glance at Jessie.

She appreciated the extreme awkwardness of the pause; felt that their eyes were directed, like so many burning-glasses, to a focus that was herself, and mechanically went on playing with her cue and balls. Only Fanny Provost was in a position from which she could see that while her features were steady, and her eyes seemed to follow the red and white spheroids in their windings and doublings, one swollen vein in her throat was beating like a clock, and the nails were bloodless where they pressed upon the cue.

"Come! we must finish our game!" said the young hostess, going back to the table. "Jessie has been perfecting her skill by a bit of private practice, while we were making havoc of our neighbors' characters."

At heart she was exceedingly displeased with the tale-bearer, but the courtesy of hospitality forbade her more emphatic expression of disapproval.

Jessie threw down the slender rod, and tried, very unsuccessfully, to laugh,

"I have done nothing except spoil your game for you. I thought you had found an occupation so far preferable that you would not care to go on with this. I give up my cue and my place. You must choose other partners and commence anew. I have forgotten how the balls were set up when we stopped to listen to Miss Sanford's thrilling romance. I must go now, Fanny. My time is up!"

Bowing a general "Good afternoon," she made her way to the library where she had left her hat and cloak. Fanny accompanied her.

"You will join us again this evening, I hope," she said, kindly. "Mr. Wyllys is to give us some music. Hester has never heard him sing. By a somewhat strange series of mischances, she has never happened to be present when he gave the rest of us this pleasure. She cannot endure contradiction, as you see; so when she insisted I should ask him for to-night, I complied, I am often thankful, Jessie, that I am not an only child, when I see how restless and irritable so much notice and petting has made her. It is a downright misfortune to be so wealthy as she is. Everything and everybody conspires to spoil her. She is more to be pitied than blamed, poor girl!"

Jessie said nothing in rejoinder to this ingenious apology for her cousin's ill-natured tattling, and Fanny was obliged to proceed directly to the point.

"I am sorry if you are leaving thus early on account of anything Hester has said," she continued, genuine concern depicted in her countenance—"sorry if the slur cast by the idle talk of a party of thoughtless girls upon the character of your—of our friend, Mr. Wyllys' cousin—has wounded or displeased you. Hester does not mean to exaggerate or misrepresent, but she has a wild, careless fashion of talking sometimes. I am convinced that there is some great mistake in the story we have heard. In details and in general bearing, it is not in keeping with Mr. Fordham's well-established character. If you knew him, you would agree with me in discrediting it, *in toto*."

"I do know him, and I quite agree with you!"

Jessie was tying on her hat, and the action might have caused the slight quaver and weakness in her voice. It was firmer when she spoke again. Fanny, in consternation at the unexpected disclosure, and the manner which said that more was behind the mere statement, could not summon words for reply.

"Mr. Wyllys' cousin"—with unconscious emphasis, Fanny imagined was disdainful—"is not a stranger to me. I have known him a long time. But say nothing to your friends about the acquaintanceship. They might fear they had offended me by their strictures. I will—I may tell you more some other time. You will comprehend then why certain things which were said just now, have excited me more than I care to show. You are always just and tender-hearted, and I thank you for speaking when I could not. Good-by!"

Her lips were set and hard to Fanny's soft kiss, and her eyes glowed dangerously as the latter attended her to the front door. The peace-maker, noting this, refrained from further endeavors to heal the breach between her relative and her new friend. Hester had been shockingly, shamefully imprudent, even if what she stated were true. Jessie was hurt and angry, and she had a right to be. Yet she, Fanny, dared not advance another step without a more distinct understanding of the case. For the present it was beyond her art. She tried to content herself by a cordial invitation to "run in to-morrow forenoon for a quiet billiard-practice—only you and myself—if you do not think better of your refusal to come to-night," and let her visitor go.

# CHAPTER XI

Greatly perturbed, Fanny returned to the circle of gossips. They had not recommenced their game, but were standing about, and leaning upon the billiard-table, busily rehearsing the late scene, accentuating their animated periods by tapping the floor with the cues, and rapping the board with the ivory balls. All except Hester, who sat still upon her lounge, twirled her rings, and looked sulky.

Selina was foremost and loudest in apologetic exclamations—being as candid in regret as she had been in censure.

"Do you know I never *thought* of his being a relation of Mr. Wyllys until just as I spoke of it? That is like my blundering tongue! There is no half-way house of meditation between the brain and it. We are ruined! you and I especially, Nettie, and Sue is almost as badly off. Jessie will tell Mr. Wyllys, and he will report us all to his cousin, and won't there be a row?"

"Why should you care?" said Hester, sharply. "If the man is away off in Germany, he can't quarrel with you."

"But he is coming back next Fall! I should sink into the earth if he were to ask me any questions about what I have said. He has always been so gentle and pleasant with me! I felt quite proud of his good opinion."

"You had very little to be proud of, I should say!" retorted Miss Sanford, losing command of her tongue and temper entirely, as the discussion proceeded. "Thank Heaven! I am not dependent upon such contemptible trifles for my peace of mind! I wouldn't recognize Roy Fordham on the street, or anywhere else; would cut him dead were he to enter this room at this very minute. As for Miss Kirke, I care less than nothing for her, or her opinion. If she chooses to play the spy upon a confidential conversation between *ladies*, and carry tales to gentlemen, she may, and welcome. I never could abide her from the first instant I ever saw her. I do hate tattlers and backbiters! But let her do her worst! I flatter myself that *I*, at least, am above her reach!"

"I should be very uneasy and unhappy, if I believed that the substance of our conversation would ever reach Mr. Fordham's ears," rejoined Fanny, very gravely. "But Mr. Wyllys is no mischief-maker. Nor, for that matter, is

Jessie Kirke. My principal regret is that we have wounded her; for I do not think a reputation so nobly earned as Mr. Fordham's has been, will suffer from our idle chatter. It is founded upon a rock. As to Jessie's playing the spy, Hester, she had no reason to believe the communication you made was confidential."

"She never opened her lips while I was talking! just stood off there, pretending to be busy with the billiard balls, and *listened*," said Hester, hotly, "If that wasn't mean and dishonorable, I don't know what is!"

"I am inclined to think it would have been well had the rest of us done likewise!" smiled Fanny, willing to give a jocose turn to the circumstance. "Since we cannot help our blunder, we will try to forget it."

But Hester had a troublesome bee in her bonnet. She looked more and more discomposed.

"What makes you all think that this Kirke girl will blab to Mr. Wyllys? What has she to do with him, more than any of you here?"

"What's he to Hecuba, or Hecuba to him!" quoted Fanny, theatrically, bent upon covering her cousin's coarseness of speech and manner. "They are old friends, and he is intimate at Dr. Baxter's, where she is staying. As I said, however, the least of my apprehensions is that she will stir up strife between us and Mr. Fordham."

She chalked her cue carefully, as if it were her chief concern at present.

"Is he addressing her?" demanded Hester, with increasing interest.

"I don't know. Selina! will you play on my side?"

"In a minute!" The volatile Bradley was off at a tangent. "I don't begin to believe that he means to offer himself to her, whatever wiseacres may say. It is well known that he is not a marrying man. He brings out girls that have the making of belles in them. It is a sort of hobby with him—a mission he has. This done, he stands back serenely, and lets other men marry them. He is a universal lover of the sex, and upon occasions like those I have named—a benefactor. Some of our most elegant matrons and handsomest young ladies were his *protégées*. His sanction of their charms made them the fashion. It is odd, but true."

Hester smiled, laid her head on her left shoulder, and peeped at an opposite mirror.

"It would be a sin were you Hamilton girls to let him marry this girl. You don't half appreciate him. I have met so many distinguished and gallant men, that I call myself a tolerable judge of true breeding and polished manners. And I can inform you that in a large, gay city such as that I live in, he would be a *star!* might have almost any girl he wanted. The idea of his throwing himself away upon a poor minister's daughter is just perfectly nonsensical. I have too good an opinion of his common-sense and his taste, to believe it for a second. He can't but know that he could look ever so much higher. What there is about this Miss Kirke that you all admire, I can't see, for the life of me. She couldn't carry it, in our place, with such a bold hand, as she does here. She would be put *down* at once and forever!"

"Jessie Kirke is my friend, Hester, and was but just now my guest," said Fanny, firmly. "Excuse me for saying that I cannot hear her spoken of unkindly in this house. She is a lady—born and bred. Papa says her family were people of rank in this country, before ours was ever heard of. I am not an aristocrat, but if I were I should rather belong to what Dr. Holmes calls the 'Brahmin caste', in America, than to any other. Jessie Kirke comes of an educated race, and the refinement of educated generations shows itself in every motion and word. I do not affirm that she will—that she would, if he offered himself, marry Mr. Wyllys. I do say that he would do well to win her for his wife. And I suspect he does not need to be told this."

The sun was an hour high as Jessie descended the granite steps of Judge Provost's mansion. The college buildings lay to her right, upon rising ground, separated by a shallow valley from the hill crowned by the Provost house and grounds. Instead of taking the street that would conduct her to Dr. Baxter's door, she turned sharply to the left, and began another and steeper ascent. There were few residences in this quarter of the town, and these were gentlemen's villas, separated by large gardens. She did not look up at the windows of the scattered dwellings in passing, although more than one acquaintance watched, from one and another of these, the straight, slender figure that held on its rapid course without sway or falter. In the plainest garb, she was conspicuous for her carriage and peculiar style of beauty. This afternoon she looked like a young forest princess in her dark green dress, and tunic trimmed with fur, the black velvet cap and sweeping green feather. She had thought of Hester Sanford's colorless countenance and Parisian costumes as she made ready for the call upon Fanny, laughed to herself at the image that smiled back upon her from the mirror, knowing how far handsomer, even more "stylish" (Hester's pet word!) she was in her simple robes. She thought more of such things now than ever before. Her enjoyment in general company was no longer the gratification of a young girl's frank vanity—often as guileless and freely uttered as a child's. The desire to be at her best looks, to attract and to hold the admiration of those whom she met abroad, had ceased to be simple and positive. There was in it the baser element of competition. She would be beautiful and brilliant because others—Hester Sanford in particular—were homely and silly. The feeling had grown upon her insidiously—so stealthily she could not tell when she forbore to laugh, good-naturedly, at the heiress' absurdities; to declare openly to Mr. Baxter and Orrin that she had conceived an antipathy to her before she had known her three hours, or three minutes,—that association with her invariably provoked her into an indescribable but intolerable state of discomfort, analogous to that a cat is supposed to feel when her fur is turned the wrong way. But she disliked the woman intensely now when she hardly ever named her to others.

There were many reasons for this. As proud in her way as Hester was vain-glorious in hers, it galled her continually that she must appear—even for Fanny's and decency's sake—to submit to the insufferable impertinence of one who was her peer in nothing save the accident of riches. She would give her no apparent advantage; would not put it into her power to boast that she had driven her out of the arena where she—Hester—believed that she reigned queen of Fashion, if not of Love and Beauty,—or she would have avoided her whenever she could. It seemed to her that the more dignified course was to overlook her—her spiteful innuendoes, her pompous condescensions, and brainless boastings—with the sublime indifference of one whose thoughts were set upon worthier and more comely objects; to mete out to the heiress scrupulously such show of regard as she would vouchsafe a peevish, painted gad-fly hissing about her ears and eyes.

The gad-fly had stung her out of her seeming of haughty carelessness, and since she could not crush or even touch it, she was fleeing before it, as for her life. The figure occurred to her as she climbed a third hill—one she had never crossed before without pausing on the summit to look back over the town—a view Roy had commended to her admiration in one of his letters. She did not stop now, or turn her head, but almost ran down the other side, her teeth clinched, and a dry aching in the throat that ought to have been relieved by tears, yet was not to be. She met no one in her walk. The day was still, and very cold; the hills beyond the ice-bound river were strongly defined against a pale orange sky into which the color seemed to be frozen, so unvarying was it, as the sun rolled horizonward. She had passed the region of paved sidewalks, but the ground rang like stone under her tread; her breath was frosty vapor as soon as it left her lips. She did not think how much colder it would be in the open country road on the other side of the bridge. She would not feel it when she got there. Two wood wagons, each with a team of four horses, were coming across the bridge, abreast, and she stepped aside to let them pass. The drivers were walking behind their loads, swinging their arms and stamping to keep up the circulation of the congealing blood in their limbs. The roadsters tramped in a cloud of steam from their nostrils, about which fine icicles clung to their shaggy hair.

They had thick woollen shields over their breasts, fur collars upon their shoulders.

"Men are tender in their mercies to the brute creation!" thought the young lady at whom the men looked with respectful but evident approbation, in going by. "When it comes to women, their pity fails them!"

She was doing more than escaping the malignant tongue that had blackened the fair fame of her betrothed. She despised Hester Sanford's intellect and inventive talents so heartily that she should have laughed to scorn the tale to which she had hearkened; dissected the ill-formed mass of contradictions, and boldly refuted her statements by a comparison of their incongruities. Three months earlier she would have covered the traducer with confusion, and rightly punished her gloating audience by standing forth as the defender of Roy's honor and truth, and proudly announcing the nature of the bond between them. She was incapable of such an attempt now. Like a cowed hound, she had crouched in a corner and suffered the outrage to him who was her other self—the gallant gentleman, whose name she was to bear some day—lifted neither tongue nor finger to save that name from obloquy. Not even to amiable Fanny (how much braver than her craven self!) had she been able to say—"This man is to be my husband! Who strikes him, wounds and makes an enemy of me!"

Why was this?

She stopped midway across the bridge; leaned over the parapet with locked hands and rigid features; stared down upon the shining black ice—still not feeling the cold—and tried to answer the question thrust upon her.

Why had she made no fight to save the character of him for whom she had once declared herself willing to die?

"How *dared* they?" she had muttered between her teeth, in leaving Judge Provost's portico. On the bridge she spoke again—a hoarse whisper it hurt her throat to sibilate.

"If this be true!" she said, letting her clasped hands fall upon the stone wall.

There was a livid bruise on both, when she removed her gloves that evening, but she had not felt it when it was dealt.

Had then her belief in her lover's integrity succumbed to the weight of the first doubt cast upon it, in her presence? Were her faith and her love made of such flimsy stuff as to be torn into wretched rags by a single gale? If these were ever well-founded, must not the inroads of distrust have been gradual in order to be effectual? Had suspicion and forebodings visited her before to-day? been harbored, but not recognized? If so, what were the grounds for doubts and fears?

"*If* it be true—" she repeated, with a desolate moan—"there is no help for me in earth or in heaven! I can never trust or love again!"

Some one was coming on behind her with quick steps, which echoed loudly on the icy planks, and she walked on hastily. Her first unwise impulse was to increase her speed in the hope of getting away from the intruder, whoever he might be. But finding, on reaching the opposite shore, that he gained on her, she slackened her pace to let him pass. She would be the sooner alone and unobserved if she allowed him to go on. It was only a chance wayfarer, of course, but she would shun all eyes, idle or searching, while her brain was in such a whirl, her heart rent and quaking. She detected nothing familiar in the footfall, but she did remark, with a sense of irritation, that it was more deliberate in nearing her. Did the unseen pursuer mean to dog her?

Annoyance was exchanged momentarily for active alarm; the angry blood welled to her face and head in one mighty throb, as a hand touched her elbow, before her persecutor had breath to accost her.

It was Orrin Wyllys' voice that said, laughingly, "Is it Atalanta, or swift Camilla scouring the plain, whom I have chased for the last ten minutes? What are you running away from?"

"The Furies!"

# CHAPTER XII

Orrin was shocked into sober sincerity by the fierce, curt utterance.

"My dear Jessie! what has happened?"

"Don't ask me!" walking on, without looking at him.

Orrin kept step with her for several moments, studying the eyes that, black and disdainful, stared straight before her, and the mouth set in a close curve of pride, before he spoke again.

"I will ask nothing just now, except that you will take my arm, and allow me to be your escort. This is a lonely road."

"It suits me the better, then!"

He waited a minute more, and, with gentle force, undid her right hand from its hold upon its fellow, and drew it within his arm.

"I see that my society is unwelcome, Jessie, but it is not right for you to be so far from home at this time of day without a protector. I shall not compel your confidence. When you are ready to give it, my sympathies or services are at your command, as they have always been since I became your guardian in the absence and with the sanction of my cousin."

The hot sparkle was a blaze as she looked up.

"Yes! and you, too, must have known it! You, who pretend to be my friend! My trust has been blind and foolish throughout. You were ready enough to counsel and warn me about other things. Why did you never tell me of Roy Fordham's former engagement? of the love-affair (save the mark!) that clashed with mine? You have said again and again that you respected me—that my happiness was of value in your estimation. Did not respect or humanity urge you to spare me this bitter humiliation?"

Unaffectedly amazed though he was at the onslaught and the information she imparted, Orrin yet refrained from explicit denial.

"Who has been talking to you?" he asked, instead.

She dashed through the story in the same impetuous strain, ending it with—"He ought to have told me this, and so ought you! I can forgive anything but deliberate deception."

Orrin mused.

"You are excited—"he began, slowly.

She interrupted him—"Who would not be? I am not a stone!"

"Nobody said that you were, or ought to be," smiling a little. "I was about to say that the displeasure you feel is perfectly natural—just what any woman with a heart would experience in the circumstances. But let us investigate before we condemn. What is your ground of complaint against my friend and your betrothed? Did he ever tell you that you were his first and only love?"

"I do not know that he asserted it in so many words," she replied, with a vivid blush. "But I certainly inferred as much from what he has said."

"Every woman's inference is the same when she listens to a declaration of affection. Who but a fool would preface such by a confession of how many times he had rehearsed it to other ears? Few men reach the age of twenty-five without having had two or three *grandes passions*. I do not maintain, as a gentleman did once in my hearing, when taxed with being engaged in his fortieth love-suit, that in this, as in most other things, practice makes perfect. But I hold that you cannot accuse Roy of deceiving you, unless he has declared expressly that he had never loved or wooed until he met you. Happy are those who are not visited by the ghosts of by-gone—and, as they deemed, buried—affections upon their bridal eves! Ghosts that are hard enough to lay, as many a miserable married, not mated one can testify."

"None such shall stand between me and him whom I marry!" cried Jessie, vehemently. "If Roy Fordham once loved—if he still regrets this girl—has one pang of compunction in the review of her fidelity and her sorrow; if he repents, never so slightly, his relinquishment of her upon insufficient cause—he shall go back to her. I will have a whole heart, or I will quit him, a pauper in love. Divided allegiance is worse than desertion."

"Be assured of one thing!" returned Orrin, emphatically. "Roy Fordham 'regrets' no past action of his own. His judgment is as calm as his measures are decided. If he suffers his heart to go out of his keeping, he does it in the persuasion that he could not act more prudently, more in accordance with his best interests, than to intrust it to her whom he has chosen. But should he, nevertheless, discover, from subsequent developments, that he was mistaken, he would recall affections and troth without weak hesitation. If Miss Sanford's story be true (which, please observe, I am far from admitting), we may still rest content in the knowledge that he pursued what he thought was the wisest course—performed what seemed to him a simple and imperative duty. He is, of all men I know, the most clear-headed and conscientious. If his ideas upon certain subjects appear to me to be over-strict, if his conduct, in cases that would be trying emergencies to me, looks like an exercise of superhuman resolution or self-denial, I do not, therefore, question his wisdom or my failings. His standard of right is so elevated, his views of duty are based upon—"

"Don't make labored excuses for him which you feel, in your soul, are paltry sophisms!" burst out Jessie, impatiently. "Is it your belief that he was ever betrothed to this girl? And, if so, did he cast her off upon the barbarous pretext Hester Sanford named? I have tried to think it all out," she continued, putting her hand to her head, like one dazed or stunned, "but nothing is fixed and clear. He *was* at the seashore two summers ago, after he visited Dundee. He *did* go to B—— the following winter—twice—both times to attend the weddings of friends, he told me. These things he made no secret of. That does not look like guilt. And yet—Tell me what to believe—how to act!"

"If I were in possession of the exact truth, you should have had it before now. I am as ignorant as yourself of all except the facts you have stated. He has friends—relatives whom he esteems—in B——. I recollect that he was with them at the sea shore late in his vacation, and that he spent Christmas before last in the city which is their home. This is the extent of my actual knowledge touching this mystery. He is reticent in the extreme with respect to his personal affairs. I never heard your name; never suspected that he was not heart-whole prior to my first visit to Dundee. I can only judge him in this, as in every case, by what I know of his principles and past conduct. He is incapable of what he would consider a dishonorable, much less a base deed! Try and trust him; forget this tale which may be a fiction, out-and-out, and hope for the best!"

"Christmas before last!" murmured Jessie, in stifled accents. "He was corresponding with me then! He had told my father that he meant—Oh!" stopping short, and stamping her foot with feverish energy upon the frozen earth—"Is there *no* way of ending this horrible suspense? no one who can put me out of this pain? I would give my right hand if I might stand face to face with Roy Fordham, for ten minutes! just long enough to bring my accusation, and hear his defence!"

"I am thankful that this cannot be!" said Orrin, composedly. I understand him better than you do in some respects. To doubt is to insult him. One sentence of 'accusation,' and your power over him is gone forever. Be guided by me, Jessie! You are not in a fit condition to decide for yourself upon your safest mode of action at this critical juncture. It is an oft-repeated maxim of human law that every man is innocent until proof brings his guilt home to him. Two things are patent from our present standpoint. When Roy asked you to marry him, he was free to do so,—the previous engagement, assuming that such had ever existed, having been dissolved some months earlier than the date of his proposal to you. Again—and on this head I can speak confidently—he is thoroughly satisfied that his choice is a judicious one. This is not the first time I have wanted to say this to you. He may not be an ardent suitor, because his is not a passionate nature, nor is he given to demonstrations of emotion. But he is more than contented. He is sincerely attached to you—"

"Which means that he will fulfil his part of the contract of marriage unless *my* sister should die of consumption before the wedding-day arrives!" Jessie checked his defence of his kinsman by saying, with a rasping laugh.

Wyllys looked deeply pained.

"We will defer further conversation about this matter until you are calmer," he said, with a manifest struggle. "You are not ready for it just yet, or you would not sneer at my well-meant, if ineffectual, attempt to set your mind at rest."

"With unfeeling arguments! with special pleadings that freeze the blood at my heart!" she pursued, unappeased and desperate. "If this is the ablest defence you can set up for your client, you do well to defer the further consideration of it. I have prayed you for bread, and you give me a stone! I have said—'Let me have the plain truth!' and you tantalize me with fine-drawn theories and exhortations to patience and faith. I am tempted to believe that you are in the league to deceive me!"

"Jessie! Jessie! take care! You do not know what you are doing!"

It was entreaty—not reproach. He seemed to crave a personal boon— deliverance from impending trial of his strength or feelings. Jessie rushed on headlong, deaf to the significance of the petition.

"Your advocacy is worthy of the cause you have espoused! And while you expatiate upon your cousin's cool head and colder heart, and recommend me to make sure of this pattern partner—yes! that is the way you put it—I am being torn by pride and wounded affection and incertitude, as by raging wild horses! It is easy for you to talk sensibly and even eloquently of what appeals only to your reason!"

"Child!" seizing her elbows, and bringing her to a stand-still in the middle of the road, facing himself, "does it cost *me* nothing, do you think, to plead this cause? There are no wild horses for me then! No 'Might-have-been' dogging my steps and haunting my pillow! No furies of betrayed confidence and remorse menacing me! I tell you, your pettish jealousy, your slight heat of resentment that will be gone before to-morrow morning, is, in comparison with what I endure, a summer breeze to a tornado,—the flicker of a match to the fires of Gehenna!"

He released her, and she walked on beside him, bewildered and giddy; almost oblivious of her individual grievances in the thought of the passion that had fired his eyes, found vent in his hurried sentences. The sun was down. They were in a rough country-road; stone fences on either hand; the naked hedge-rows seeming to shiver in the still, freezing air. The hard orange dye of the west was beginning to melt slowly into a gray as cold. It was a heartless, dreesome afternoon.

Jessie never forgot it, or the interval of awful silence that succeeded Wyllys' unprecedented outbreak. Not daring to glance at his face, she had a second surprise, when he, at length, suggested, in a tone tranquil to coldness, that they should retrace their steps. Could she be dreaming now? Or were the strange, wild words echoing confusingly in her brain, dictated by her distempered fancy?

"It will be late before we reach home, as it is," Orrin offered, in support of his proposition. "And the air grows keener every moment."

Nothing more passed between them until they were again upon the bridge, where he stayed her, for a moment, that he might rearrange her furs.

"You are not used to this biting weather! Are you tolerably comfortable?" he asked, in his usual brotherly way.

"Quite comfortable—if you are not angry with me!" she answered, enboldened by the little attention and his tone.

"You silly child! I have never had a thought of you that bordered upon unkindness. We have both been hasty and unreasonable in judgment and in language, this afternoon. Your warmth was excusable. Mine was culpable weakness. You will hate me, in time, if I forget myself in this manner. It was selfish and wicked, besides being unmanly. Don't contradict me! I know what I am saying now, at any rate. To exchange an unpleasant for a painful subject—promise me that you will not allude to Miss Sanford's narrative in your letter to Roy."

"I shall write to him by to-morrow's mail, and tell him all!" said Jessie, with a return of stubbornness.

"You will regret it all your life! If he is guilty, he will be offended at your arraignment of him by letter, which must, of necessity, be formal and incomplete as to testimony—you having but one witness, and that by no means a reliable one. Should he be innocent, you inflict severe and needless pain; put yourself in the position of a touchy, suspicious, exacting *fiancée*, whose troth he will ever thereafter hold by a slight tenure. 'Let sleeping dogs lie,' is a sage motto, unless they can bark to some purpose. If you will allow me, I shall make it my business to sift this story carefully, and apprise you of the result—if I have to cultivate an intimacy with Miss Sanford in order to get at the truth. Meanwhile, we will depend upon what we are certain of—Roy's integrity and the nicety of his honor. At the risk of being again taken to task for special pleading, let me say that he is, in my estimation, as nearly faultless as mortals ever grow to be. You cannot act more rationally than to think as much as possible of him, and as little of his *vaurien* cousin as is consistent with common benevolence."

It was silvery-gray twilight out-of-doors when they gained Mrs. Baxter's door, and they found a rosy twilight of summer within her firelighted parlors, balmy, moreover, with the spiciness flowing out in the genial temperature, from the latest bouquet presented by Mr. Wyllys.

The donor, playfully gallant, and bent, it would seem, upon effacing the memory of his late excited speech, was chafing Jessie's numb fingers before the fire, and she laughing in spite of herself at his sallies, when Mrs. Baxter tripped in.

She always entered a room bouncingly, generally with the added effect of being pushed in by some unseen hand from behind. She recoiled, momentarily, at the tableau upon the rug, and Jessie observed it with a sick, guilty qualm that made her snatch away her hand from Orrin's hold.

He was not discomfited.

"Here is a frozen wayfarer I picked up on the bridge, my dear madam, taking an *un*constitutional," he said. "Mindful of your known charity and condescension, I took the liberty of bringing her in to be treated by you as her needs require. If I may advise you in a matter in which you are so much wiser than myself, I recommend that a cup of warm drink—gruel, panada, or posset—and a reasonable amount of admonition, tempered to suit the exhausted state of the patient, be administered without delay. As an additional precaution against rheumatism, pleurisy, or bronchitis, a glass of hot lemonade, with"—affecting to whisper—"a tablespoonful of Jamaica rum or old Bourbon, at bedtime, would be eminently judicious. My impertinence culminates in the petition that you vouchsafe to bestow upon my unworthy but chilly self a cup of the nectar in common use upon your table under the name of souchong."

Jessie slipped away to her chamber while her cousin was replying in suitable terms to this nonsense, and did not reappear until the tea-bell had rung twice.

She had been crying, Mrs. Baxter saw at once, and she was still very pale. It had been a violent fit of weeping that had exhausted her to languor of expression and movement. The doctor spoke cheerily to her as she seated herself beside him.

"Well, my little girl, how are your spirits, this freezing night? Do they follow the mercury, or rise as it descends?"

An unfortunate question, but it brought a faint glow to her face.

"I shall be more lively when I have had my supper," she said, averting her eyes. "I am cold and tired now."

The doctor bent his head and raised his hand to ask a blessing, and then bade his wife "pour out Jessie's tea, forthwith. She looks as if she needed it," he subjoined, uneasily, watching her with eyes that were very keen when he was awake to what was passing in the everyday and material world.

Jessie sipped the scalding liquid, swallowing each spoonful with a tremendous effort, when it trickled down the lump that obstructed larynx and epiglottis, wishing, the while, that the doctor would subside into one of his fits of learned abstraction and knot his handkerchief, instead of staring so solemnly at her; expecting, every second, to hear him demand—"What have you been crying about, my daughter?"

She was very grateful to Orrin for his persistent and, in the end, successful attempts to draw the fire of the searching regards; and, rallying her wits and courage, she, at last, joined in the conversation. Mrs. Baxter, likewise, was less voluble than was her wont. Appreciating the fact, recognized by the majority of his acquaintances, that Mr. Wyllys was not a marrying man, she aroused herself to ponder, in serious earnest, upon what was likely to be the result of his fraternal intimacy with her ward. Orrin had made all straight with her at the outset, even before Jessie entered her house as a visitor, by representing himself as an old friend of the family, and speaking of Mr. Kirke's daughter in a grandfatherly strain, that entitled him to become the platonic cavalier of the rustic *débutante*. But platonic grandfathers did not squeeze pretty girls' hands *en tête-à-tête* in the twilight—"or they should not," reasoned the duenna; and Jessie's red eyes and pallid complexion increased her misgivings to dreads. She had been asleep all winter until to-night, she thought, shudderingly, and had awakened upon the edge of a precipice. If through her neglect or misplaced confidence, Ginevra's child should come to grief, she would rue, to the latest day of her life, the invitation that had enticed her from home and safety, to lose her heart to the designing arts of a man of the world.

Orrin had small temptation to prolong his stay into the evening. There was incipient disfavor in the hostess' eye, which was not neutralized by her stereotyped smile. The doctor betook himself to his study when he arose from the table, and Jessie shaded her face from fire and lamp-light by a hand-screen, complaining that she was stupid after her walk in the wind.

"I promised to go up to Judge Provost's to-night," he said, at the end of an unsatisfactory half hour. "Won't you join our party for billiards and music? Miss Fanny charged me not to come without you."

Jessie did not raise her regards from the screen.

"No, thank you! I have had enough billiards for one day. And I am in an intensely unmusical humor."

"I really ought to 'do' the polite to Miss Sanford," continued he, lightly to Mrs. Baxter's ears, significantly to Jessie's. "I have been shamefully remiss since her appearance among us. Miss Fanny took me to task for it, an evening or two since, and I was obliged to plead 'Guilty.' I have paid her very little attention except in public, and that has been confined to a dance or two at each party."

Mrs. Baxter, profoundly indifferent to Miss Sanford, and the degree of court he offered her, yet strove to look interested.

"That is a little remarkable, Mr. Wyllys, considering your reputation for gallantry and hospitality, and she is invested with more substantial charms than any of our Hamilton belles can boast."

"I am afraid my taste for the substantial has not been properly cultivated," was the reply.

Jessie was silent and gloomy, and Wyllys secretly lost patience with her.

"I thought her more of a woman!" he said, inly. "She acts like a fractious child, inconsolable for the loss of a toy. I gave her credit for more depth of feeling, more power of endurance."

She called up a faint symptom of a smile, in response to his adieux, and relapsed into taciturnity and the shadow of her screen, when he had departed. Mrs. Baxter flitted about the rooms like a perturbed guardian angel; poking the fire that her charge's feet might be warmer; dropping a curtain to shut out a draught from the back of her neck; pushing forward a *brioche* for her use, and giving her chair a gentle tug nearer the grate, before she essayed verbal consolation.

Finally, she leaned upon the back of Jessie's seat and made several mesmeric passes over her brow and scalp, the fringe of the scarlet scarf it was her pleasure, to-night, to sport twisted around her right wrist, brushing the chin, and tickling the nose of her young relative.

"Does your head ache *very* badly now, my sweet?" breathlessly solicitous.

"Not at all—thank you, cousin!"

"I am *de*lighted to hear you say so! You don't think you have really taken cold, my precious—do you?"

"Oh, no! I never take cold!"

"Mr. Wyllys seemed very anxious lest you had," Mrs. Baxter remarked, quite too earnestly. "I say, 'seemed,' for these ladies' men are not models of sincerity, always, however charming they may be as parlor companions. If I had a daughter, my love—and it is the great sorrow of my life, as it is of the doctor's, that we never had one—if I had a daughter, just blooming into womanhood, affectionate, susceptible, and unsuspecting, I should caution her to be on her guard against a too-ready credence in the flattering tongues and the more insidious flattery of demeanor and action of gentlemen who are honorable in all things else. I respect Mr. Wyllys"—she continued, the passes faster and more agitated, and the silken fringes bobbing up and down before Jessie's vision. "I honor his many estimable—admire his many shining qualities. But I am fearful that in his otherwise commendable desire to please and make happy, he may excite hopes—or expectations may be the better term—he never intended to engender. There is in every community, my darling Jessie, a class of men—pardon me for saying that it is fortunately a small class—who do not care or intend to marry except for convenience, or pecuniary gain—perhaps not even then. Yet they are generally the pets of their respective circles, especial favorites with ladies. Why, I cannot say, unless it be that they endeavor to make themselves agreeable to the entire sex, instead of concentrating their attentions upon one woman. Mr. Wyllys is a notable example of this order of carpet knights."

Entirely out of breath by this time, she withdrew her hand from her guest's head, to press it upon her own palpitating bosom, while her gulp of emotion was as loud as the cluck of a brooding hen.

Jessie lowered her screen with a gesture of haughty amusement.

"If your object is to warn me against attaching undue importance to Mr. Wyllys' friendly attentions, Cousin, I can disabuse your mind of fears for my peace of heart, by assuring you that it is not threatened from that quarter. I ought to have told you, long ago, of a circumstance that exculpates Mr. Wyllys from the charge of trifling, and renders the notice he bestows upon me altogether harmless and proper. I am engaged to be married to his cousin, Mr. Fordham, and he knows it. This makes all safe for us both—does it not? I am sorry I did not apprize you of this state of affairs when I first came to you. It would have been more honorable and kind to you—and an act of common justice to Mr. Fordham, if not to Mr. Wyllys."

# CHAPTER XIII

There was no prettier spot in the Dundee valley than Willow Creek, a somewhat wide, and in some places deep, stream, just where it was spanned by a rustic bridge at the bottom of the Parsonage meadows. The fringe of willows on the thither bank, and the alder and birch thicket studding that nearest the house, were reflected in the clear, brown mirror to the tiniest leaf and bud. Beneath and between these, there were stretches of turf which were evergreen; beds of wild balsam that flowered all summer; ferns in variety and profusion, from the tree-ferns upborne by their wiry black stems to a height of four or five feet, to the delicate maiden-hair, hiding in the lee of straws and stones; and on the day we are describing—the fifth of September—these alternated with borders of hoary mountain sage, blue-eyed asters, tossing plumes of golden-rod, yet taller purple brush, stiff and gorgeous, and patches of bright yellow dodder, running riotously into the water, and entangling the commoner arrow-leaf and sedge in its meshes.

Through the gorge worn by the creek in the mountains, one had a view of the upper valley, and the chain of hills that grew bluer and lower as the eye pursued their southerly course. Below the bridge was the church, benignant warder of the plain fertile as was that of Sodom, loaded with corn, ripe for cutting, and already stacked for the garner, and white, here and there, as from untimely snows, with blossoming buckwheat. The whistle of the quail in the stubble, the rattling roll of empty farm wagons over the stone bridge below the mill, on their way to the field; the duller thunder of heavily laden trains creaking and swaying from side to side behind the straining oxen, and the drowsy undertone of the mill-wheel, mingled with the nearer warble of birds in the trees and the gentle wash of the waves under the willows. It was bright, benignant weather—a day that reminded one of healthy, active, happy middle-age, for there was a whisper of Autumn in the air, the mellowness of Autumnal light over plain and water and hill.

There was nothing in landscape, air, or sunlight that should have reminded Jessie Kirke of the miserable February afternoon when she stood on the Hamilton bridge, staring down at the black ice below, and fought her first battle of life. But that other scene and the strife of that hour were very present to her, as she halted on the foot-bridge and leaned over the rail to gaze at the slow, smooth current of the creek. The narrow crossing had been designed and partly built by Mr. Kirke himself. The floor was of oak plank; the railing was composed of cedar branches with the bark left on, arranged in fantastic figures, and surmounted by a slender pole of the same wood. Many stopped to examine and admire it in passing over, and it made a picturesque feature in the view. It was familiar in every joint to Jessie, having formed a part of her favorite walk for ten years; but she chose to linger there on this morning, to hang over the parapet, pick bits of bark from the side and fling them into the creek, as an idle child might launch and watch a miniature fleet.

It was a face many removes from childhood's thoughtlessness and childish glee that looked back at her from the glassy surface. A face, wild-eyed and haggard, with bent brows betokening suffering and conflict; a mouth telling, in piteous and patient lines, of defeat.

She had returned from Hamilton in April, looking jaded and ill, said the Dundeeians, who shook sagacious heads over her winter's dissipation. Her father and Eunice attributed her loss of bloom and liveliness to too close application to her studies, and cited her improvement in music, French, and German, in proof of their theory. She did not relax her diligence when she was settled at home. Eunice, whose name was a synonym for industry, did not surpass her in strict attention to all departments of feminine work. In the kitchen and the garden, at the needle, the piano, writing-desk, and her books, she toiled from sunrise until bedtime, with energy Eunice silently likened to greediness for occupation of mind and body, while Mr. Kirke hardly recognized his darling in the decorous thrifty housewife and busy student. Intonations, phraseology, and deportment—all were altered. She was an elegant woman in appearance and conversation, but the fond parent missed the tricksy sprite who had wrought mischief and mirth in his home; missed her teasing and her follies, her exactions and her caresses. Not that she was cold or sullen. She told long and entertaining stories of her Hamilton life; gave faithful descriptions of the people and things she had seen while away from them; listened with apparent interest to neighborhood news and family plans; talked of art, literature, and philosophy to him by the hour; was attentive to his every possible want, and offered regularly the morning and evening kiss she had been accustomed to bestow from her infancy. But, having already one daughter who was an exemplar to her sex, he recollected the bewitching naughtiness of the old-time Jessie, and wished fervently that he had met Mrs. Baxter's invitation by a peremptory negative, and kept his gem as it was. To his taste, it had lost—not gained—in the cutting and polishing.

Eunice was discreet when he intimated something of the kind to her.

"She is certainly more quiet and studious," she replied, "but she says she is very well, and she has much to make her thoughtful in Roy's absence. The long separation must, of itself, oppress her spirits continually. And, Father, our Jessie has gained new views of Life and Duty within the last year. She can never be a child again. Her nature—mind and affections—must broaden and deepen with time. We would not have it otherwise, strange as the change is to us now. I fear, though, that she works too hard, while I honor her determination to prepare herself thoroughly for her future position. She will be a wife of whom Roy may justly be proud."

Again, when Mr. Kirke feared that Jessie was often depressed to despondency, although she strove bravely to conceal it, the elder sister "hoped all would be well again when Roy came back."

"He can reason or soothe her out of morbid fancies better and sooner than either you or I. His influence over her is wonderful and always beneficial."

"I wish he were home again then!" sighed the parent.

He did not guess how heartily Eunice echoed the desire. She might be partially successful in quelling his anxieties, but the beryl eyes saw that, so far from all being right with her young sister, something was lamentably wrong. Jessie's very manner of speaking of Roy and her marriage was totally dissimilar to her former frank or bashful confession. If she had lived with him as his wife a dozen years, she could not have mentioned his name more composedly, or talked of housekeeping and other practicalities in a more matter-of-fact strain. This was exceedingly sensible, but it was not, on that account, the more like Jessie. The transformation from an enthusiastic madcap, who did and felt nothing by halves—let it be loving, laughing, sorrowing, or working—into the dignified partner of Eunice's everyday cares and duties, equable in temper, reliable in judgment, and judicious in action—ought, perhaps, to have elicited commendation from one who was herself a model in all these respects; but, instead of gratification, she felt only bewilderment and alarm at the completeness of the change. It had been her habit to think and say, when her sister's crudities or extravagances were more marked than her quieter taste approved, that the discipline of life, as life went on, would rectify these; that they were but the redundant growth of a noble stock. A little pruning—a few sharp experiences, and hypercritical indeed would be the judgment that should find room for blame. She was displeased with herself in recollecting this, now that the discipline had wrought upon the free, wild spirit; the redundancies had fallen under the pruning-knife.

Something of this external change must have manifested itself in Jessie's letters, for Roy had twice written privately to Eunice, questioning her closely about her sister's health and spirits.

"Her letters are as regular as ever, and no less beautiful than punctual," he said. "But they contain so few particulars of her daily life and feelings, while they treat freely of other subjects, that I have fancied there is something pertaining to her individual experience she desires to hide from me, lest the knowledge of it should pain me. My noble, generous girl! She would bear any distress or inconvenience rather than afflict me by revealing the extent of her suffering or perplexity. I intrust my sometimes wayward—always sweet, graceful, and clinging Jessamine to you, our sister! Tend and guard it tenderly for me."

Eunice answered hopefully and with such reassurance as she could truthfully impart, and wished more ardently than ever that he would return and assume the charge of his treasure—the charge and the cure.

They had had a quiet summer, the most stirring event being a visit from Mrs. Baxter and Orrin Wyllys, who acted as her escort. They were domesticated for a week at the parsonage, and Jessie's monopoly of her cousin's society had left Orrin almost entirely to her father's and sister's care. Nobody made verbal objection to this division of hospitable duties. Mr. Wyllys held long talks with his host—scientific, theological, literary, and political—during post-prandial smokes, besides driving and walking with him in his professional rounds at such seasons as Eunice was too busy to attend to her guests. When she was at liberty to devote herself to social duties, there were hours of music and reading; long rambles among the hills—Mrs. Baxter and Jessie far in advance—for the latter always outstripped her sister in pedestrian expeditions; moonlight promenades and conferences on the piazza that left Jessie all the time she desired for conversation with her late *chaperone*. It was generally agreed at parting that the week had passed swiftly and delightfully; farewells were linked with hopes of a repetition of the pleasure, and the household relapsed into its ordinary aspect and ways. If there were any perceptible difference in those composing it, it was that Jessie worked harder and was paler than before the interruption, while Eunice grew younger and prettier every day.

"I have tried very hard!" Jessie said aloud, still hanging over the water, but clasping her hands in a sort of despair. "And I am very tired!"

Then two heavy tears rolled from her eyes and broke up the reflection of the sad face below into little dancing circles.

An hour ago, as she stood in the garden grafting a rosebush, a neighbor rode up to the fence to say, "Good-day," and inquire after the health of the clergyman's family.

"You'll have company pretty soon, I'm thinking," he said, knowingly. "I suppose that's no news to you, though?"

"We expect no one," said Jessie, carelessly.

"It will be a pleasant surprise to you, then. I saw Mr. Wyllys at the hotel as I came by."

Jessie's knife swerved slightly as she made the incision in the bark, but her voice was firm.

"Are you sure?"

"Oh, yes! I talked with him. He got up late last night, he said. Come now, Miss Jessie; I am an old friend, which of you is he after?"

"Neither that I know of. Certainly not me!" replied she, imperturbably.

She finished her task carefully, when the inquisitor had passed; carried twine and scissors into the house; gave Patsey an order as she glanced into the kitchen, and, unobserved by the servant, left the dwelling and went down through the garden into the meadow.

Her father and Eunice were away from home for the day—probably for the night also, and she had her reasons for preferring the solitude of the woods, or a retreat among the crags of Old Windbeam, to a prolonged interview with Orrin Wyllys.

Did I say, "preferred"? Does not the opium-eater, in his lucid intervals, prefer thirst and languor and pain to the drug for which his diseased appetite cries out as the dying for breath, and the fever-scorched for water? Prefer it with mind and conscience, if not with flesh and will? Jessie Kirke's will lived yet, and it had borne her beyond the reach of temptation and kept her there. But it did not hinder her from picturing Orrin pacing the portico, or, sitting in the parlor, awaiting her while she hid herself and her wretchedness among the willows. She had but to go back by the way she had come, and hours of blissful companionship would be hers; full draughts of enjoyment such as those which had intoxicated the unwary girl who, last winter, had believed that she might drink and be blameless. His eyes would kindle into the magic gleam that enervated resolution and let loose a flood of vague, delicious fancies upon her brain; his voice melt into the modulations that enchained the ear like pathetic music. Under the spell of his consummate address she would believe, for the moment, or the hour, or the day he spent with her, all that he said or looked, although dimly conscious, the while, that she would despise herself as a weak, guilty fool for the temporary faith, through weeks and months afterward.

As she did now! She was wrung by self-contempt for nursing these imaginations, yet dallied with them—sipped shudderingly, yet with avidity, of their dangerous sweetness.

"I have tried very hard!" she moaned again.

Tried to hold fast to her trust in her betrothed after the cruel shock it had sustained from Hester Sanford's story, for she still believed that it was firm and absolute up to that hour; ignored persistently the fact that other influences had previously been at work sapping her confidence in the attachment of one who, his nearest of kin reluctantly admitted, was a man of granite, virtuously severe to the frailties of others, because he was himself prudent, sage, and incorruptible by such bribes as most men found potent— love, and the hope and opportunity of making the beloved one happy. Not one word of this had Wyllys ever uttered. He always spoke of Roy with seriousness and respect, confessing voluntarily, time and again, his own moral and intellectual inferiority to his cousin, and scrupulously keeping her betrothment before Jessie's mind. Whatever might have been her lapses from loyalty, she could not deny that in this oft-repeated acknowledgment of her paramount obligation to her affianced husband, Orrin had been honorable to punctiliousness. She had not yet come to see that he had also been ingenious in pressing invisible shackles into her soul; in reminding her perpetually that she was no longer a free agent. The girl had chafed under the process, without knowing that she did so, and why. Her brotherly friend, who had seen a blooded horse, although docile by nature and well broken in, fret and grow restive under an over-tight check-rein, may have known, better than she, what he was about.

She was still uncertain how much or how little truth there was in the heiress' tale. She had contrived to see her but seldom after the scene in the billiard-room, and in this she was ably seconded by Miss Sanford when the news of "that Miss Kirke's" engagement to Professor Fordham was circulated in Hamilton circles. Jessie did not try to analyze the impulse that bade her announce the relation she bore to Roy at the very time when her doubts of him were at their height. Perhaps she felt the need of a safeguard for herself; or her conscience may have rebuked her that she had not defended him—right or wrong—when attacked; or the suspicion of his unworthiness stimulated her to a strained generosity, a resolve to leave undone no part of the duty she owed, while she was under contract to him. It had been long since her latest mention of the matter to Wyllys. He had replied to her queries by an injunction to continued confidence in Roy's integrity, which was construed by her into a charitable evasion. He promised again and solemnly to push his investigations as occasion might offer, but she believed that he was afraid to keep his word. He would preserve intact his own love and esteem for the cousin he professed to revere, and blindly declined to undertake the examination of a record he more than feared contained entries that would lower his opinion of his hero, and damage the latter's character irretrievably with herself.

Given this lever of unappeased distrust in, and latent resentment toward him, to whom her allegiance was due, and a less adroit *diplomat* than Orrin Wyllys might have so weakened the defences of her love and constancy as to make her question whether surrender were not unavoidable—even desirable. She was "tired," poor child! dismayed that her labor in "deep mid-ocean" was so tedious and severe, longing for rest in whatever port her worn heart might make.

"I shall be tamed by the time you come home," she had said, 'twixt tears and smiles, to Roy at their parting. "Quite tame and old!"

"And I am!" she thought, the jest recurring to her now. "Only life has also grown tame, and the world old and gray!"

She had swung her hat upon her arm, and pushing back her hair with the palms that supported her forehead, that the wind from the water might cool her beating temples, she rested her listless weight upon the frail railing. The woven twigs, once supple, were dry and rotten under the bark, and swayed outward with a sharp crack—a warning that came too late to save her. She caught, in falling, at the shattered panels left standing, and dragged only a handful of broken sticks with her into the creek. Coming to the surface after the plunge, she threw her grasping, struggling hands widely abroad, succeeded in seizing one of the upright supports of the bridge, and clung to it. Her head and shoulders were out of water. She was not actually drowning. In the strength imparted by this consciousness, she drew a long breath, and called for help.

A faint echo came back from the hills. The rest of the shout was lost in the spreading meadows, or overpowered by the commingled sounds that were the voice of the early autumn day.

She heard them more distinctly than when she had stood upon the bridge; the beat of the mill-wheel, the rattle and rumble of the farm-wagons, even the tread of the teams upon the oaken flooring; the now distant whistle of the quail, and, close beside her, the lapping of the creek among the sedges.

She weighed her chances of speedy release from her unpleasant and dangerous situation before she raised another outcry. The stream was the feeder of the mill-pond, and was made deeper and more sluggish by the dam, less than half a mile farther down. She remembered to have heard that the depth just under the bridge was about ten feet. It might as well be a hundred if she were to relinquish her hold. She could do nothing but cling and wait until her calls should bring rescue, or some chance passenger espy her. This was an unfrequented by-way, and it might be many hours before assistance came to her in the latter form. As to the other, the Parsonage was the nearest dwelling. The mill was no farther off, but the united shriek of twenty drowning women could not be heard above the clatter of the machinery. Patsey was alone in the kitchen, her whole soul in her semi-weekly baking, and deaf to all out-door noises excepting those from the poultry-yard. There was no one else in the house, unless Orrin had arrived. Jessie believed that she tasted the bitterness of death, as she imagined him, expectant of her coming, yet thoughtless of evil as the reason of her delay, taking a few restless turns upon the portico; then, wandering into the parlor, and standing, as he often did, for several minutes together, gazing at the picture of the girl at the wishing-well; opening the piano and running over some remembered air, or improvising dreamy, wistful strains, with absent thoughts, and eyes fixed upon vacancy.

And she was here! nearing the gates that were to shut down between them forever.

She called again—a shrill scream that scared the birds from their perches on the willow and birch boughs, and awoke a wailing echo among the mountains. Then all was quiet, save for the mill, the fainter roll of heavy wheels, and, louder than either, the lap! lap! lap! of the waves upon the grassy bank. How deadly cold the water was! And she became sensible now of an increasing weight drawing her downward—the strain of her saturated garments upon the arms wound about the rough pole which stood between her and death. There was a current, also, to be resisted, placid as the mirror had seemed from above, and her sinews were aching already. Her whole body would be numb presently—her clutch be relaxed by cold and the prostration of the nervous and muscular system.

She had decried life as tame, and the world as unlovely. She found them, in this fearfully honest hour, too dear and beautiful to leave thus suddenly. She recollected, even in this season of peril and dread, the oft-repeated story that one in the act of drowning recalls, in a flash of memory, every event of his past existence, however remote and minute; reasoned within herself that this must be an old wives' fable, since she, on the brink of eternity, had but one overmastering idea—how to avert impending dissolution. Her father, Eunice, Roy, and Orrin, were all in her mind by turns, but there was no quickening of affection now that she might be leaving them to return no more. They were, in comparison with the terrible fact of her present danger, but misty and far-off abstractions—faded portraits in her mental gallery, hardly deserving a glance. She dwelt, in agony, upon the circumstances that the stream was becoming like ice to her limbs, and the pain in her arms intense, while her soaked clothing and the current were sucking her downward. When the last remnant of her strength should fail, would she be drowned by the cruel waters where she had fallen in, or borne, conscious, and writhing in the throes of suffocation, over the dam, to be mangled by the rocks below the fall?

The horror of the last fancy drew from her another shriek. The echo taunted her by its feeble mimickry; the dull boom of the mill-wheel, the teamster's shout to his oxen, had the same meaning, and the lapping of the water was that of a fierce destroyer, hungering for his prey.

Meanwhile, the visitor at the Parsonage had been through the round Jessie had sketched for him in her tortured imagination; had paced the porch until he was weary of the solitary turns; surveyed the portrait to his heart's content, regretting, in his æsthetic mind, that the original had toned down to the level of commonplace refinement, and had played a pensive "thought" on the piano.

This performance brought in Patsey.

"Dick Van Brunt was by the gate just now, Mr. Wyllys, and he said as how he seen Miss Jessie going down toward the crick, nigh upon an hour ago. You mought see something of her if you was to walk that way."

"Thank you, Patsey. Perhaps I will if she do not come in soon. And perhaps I 'mought' make a fool of myself, clambering over those confounded mountain-paths for half a day, and not get a glimpse of her!" he muttered, when the handmaiden had withdrawn.

He stepped through the oriel-window into the garden, humming, *sotto voce*, "My heart's in the Hielands, my heart is not here;" made the tour of the enclosure, noting how Eunice's rose labyrinth had grown, and that the rarer plants he had sent her in the Spring were recompensing her for the care she had bestowed upon them; brushed both hands over a bed of bergamot until the air reeked with perfume, and plucked a sprig of rosemary from the spot where he had stood to overhear the sisters' criticisms of himself sixteen months before—smiling queerly as he did so.

"I will send the fair Una a root of 'Cæsar's Bay,' with the stipulation that she shall set it just here," he said inwardly, the smile brightening at the apt conceit. "It shall be to me a floral monument—a Cupid's Ebenezer."

He gathered, furthermore, several bunches of choice roses, rifling them of their freshest odor by ruthless handling, and strewing them to the right and left as he went from the garden into the meadow. The day was fine, and not warm enough to make walking a grievous task, and he might find Jessie at or near the bridge. He whistled "Casta Diva" as he strolled over the short, thick grass, elastic to the foot as carpets of the deepest pile, — whistled melodiously, and, one would have said, for want of thought, in remarking his roving eyes and tranquil physiognomy. He looked, as he felt, on excellent terms with himself and the rest of the world; like a man who had eaten to satisfaction, but not to repletion, of the sunny side of the peach tendered by Fortune, and who was suitably grateful to the person to whom he considered that he owed his success in life—to wit, Orrin Wyllys.

What a companion portrait to set over against this serene visage and lounging figure in the pleasant meadow-paths was that, which, with distorted limbs, and countenance eager to frenzy, hung midway over the stream he was approaching! Jessie had heard the whistle, and known it for his; caught from afar his measured tread upon the sward, and, feeling herself grow weak and voiceless in the rush of reviving hope, had painfully gathered her remaining forces to abide his coming. She could see him through rifts in the low-branching birches; counted every step with trembling impatience until he was within a stone's throw.

Then she signalled him in a husky, dissonant voice that shocked herself, fainting though she was with suspense, intent only upon watching his movements, which meant to her deliverance, sure and swift.

"Orrin! make haste! I am perishing!"

A glimpse of the broken railing told him all.

Tearing off his coat as he ran, he leaped into the creek, swam out to her, and bade her loosen her hold, and remain perfectly quiet.

"Don't seize me! I will save you! Trust me!" he said, in authority she did not dream of resisting.

In a minute more he had dragged her through the water and laid her upon the warm turf, where the sun fell in brightness that meant comfort to her now as emphatically as the wavering glitter upon the stream had signified derision of her sufferings when she was very nigh to death.

In all their intercourse, Orrin had never spoken words that came so directly from what had once been a heart, as those that stirred the languid pulses and brought back the fleeting senses of the forlorn creature who lay gasping within his arms—livid, sodden, almost lifeless.

"Darling Jessie! Precious child! Thank Heaven, I was in time!"

The blue lips were touched by a smile; her eyes unclosed upon his with a look of worshipful love and gratitude that appealed to meaner elements of his character than those that had prompted his first outburst. He was himself again as his gaze kindled into responsive softness and fire.

"*My* love!" he murmured, bending to kiss her. "May I not call you so for one blessed instant? My only love, and mine alone!"

# CHAPTER XIV

Mr. Kirke and Eunice were still absent when Orrin paid his second call at the Parsonage that day. He had conducted Jessie home in the forenoon—a drenched and shivering figure, at which Patsey screeched with terror; stayed long enough to learn from the girl that the preventives he had ordered against cold were administered, and that her young mistress was put comfortably to bed, after which he betook himself to the hotel to make the requisite changes in his own apparel.

"Miss Jessie hopes you'll stay here, sir," remarked Patsey. "She says you'll find dry things in Mr. Kirke's room. I've just laid 'em out all ready."

"I am much obliged to Miss Jessie and to you, my good girl; but I shall run no risk in going down to the village. Say to Miss Jessie that she will hear from, or see me again before night."

Three hours later, a messenger brought a note, inquiring how Jessie was, and if she would be quite able to see him in the evening.

"For I must return to Hamilton to-morrow," he added.

Jessie wrote one line in reply:

"I am up and well. Come whenever you please.

Gratefully,

J. K."

His pleasure was to delay the visit until twilight. Perhaps he had a difficult programme to arrange; perhaps he wanted to give Jessie time to recover strength and composure, or he may have thought that delay would enhance the value of his society. On the legal principle he had enunciated when Roy's prior engagement was under discussion, we ought to accept his own explanation of his tardiness.

"I could not come earlier," he said very gravely, in reply to Jessie's faltered gratitude and fears that he had suffered from the morning's adventure. "You needed rest and quiet, and I have been unhinged all day— mentally, I mean. Don't thank me again! You don't know how like mockery phrases of acknowledgment from you to me sound. Sit down. You are still weak and nervous. You are trembling all over."

If she was, it was not from cold or debility. He placed her in an armchair, brought a shawl from the hall, and folded it about her; turned away abruptly, and walked the room in a silence she had neither words nor courage to break. The piano stood open as he had left it in the morning. He stopped before it on his tenth round, seated himself, and began a prelude. Then he sang the ballad she had crooned in the amber sunset, so many, many months ago! while he listened without, and tore the hearts out of Eunice's roses.

He gave the first verse with tenderness that was exquisite; rendered the musing ecstasy of the dream with beauty and expression that thrilled the auditor with delicious pain. This deepened into agony under the passionate melancholy of the last stanza:

> "Soon, o'er the bright waves howled forth the gale,
> Fiercely the lightning flashed on our sail;
> Yet while our frail barque drove o'er the sea,
> Thine eyes like loadstars beamed, Love, on me.
> Oh, heart, awaken! wrecked on lone shore!
> Thou art forsaken! Dream, heart, no more!"

He came back to where she sat—all bowed together, and quivering in every limb—and knelt before her.

"Jessie, I have dreamed, and I am awake. I am here to-night, to ask you to forgive, not only the rash, presumptuous words I spoke this morning, but the feeling that gave them birth. I have loved you from the moment of our first meeting. You and Heaven are my witnesses how I have striven with my unwarrantable passion,—how, persuaded that the indulgence of this would be a rank offence against honor and friendship, I resisted by feigned coldness your innocent wiles to win the good-will of Roy's relative. I deluded myself, for a time, with the belief that I could control the proofs of my affection within the bounds of brotherly regard. You best know how, when your faith in the truth of your accepted lover was shaken, I became his champion; how conscientiously and laboriously I have pleaded his cause with you; tried to be faithful to the trust he had reposed in me;—how, when I had nearly betrayed myself in an unguarded moment, I endeavored to dissipate any suspicions that my imprudence might have awakened in your mind. Again and again I have avoided you for days and months together; punished myself for my involuntary transgression against my friend by denying myself the sight of that which was dearer and more to be desired in my esteem than all the world and heaven itself; have shut myself into outer darkness from the light of your eyes and the sound of your voice. The fruit of the toils, the anguish, the precautions of more than a year, was destroyed to-day by one outburst of ungovernable emotion.

"I shall dream no more, dear! I solemnly vow this on my knees, while I beg you to say that you do not despise me!"

The bowed head was upon his shoulder now, and she was weeping. He put his arm about her, and held her close, while he prayed her to be comforted.

"I have cost you many painful thoughts, and not a few tears since the day when you told me the story of old David Dundee, over there in the window," he said, sadly. "It would have been better—much better for you had you never seen or heard of me. These tears are all for me, I know. But, indeed, darling, I am not worthy of one of them. They make me feel yet more keenly what a villain I must seem to you."

"Don't say that!" she burst forth. "If you are unworthy in your own sight, what must I think of my conduct? You were under no vow; had professed to love no other, had entered into no compact in the name of God, to be constant to one—one only—while life endured; a compact you called as sacred and binding as marriage. I loathe myself when I think of my fickleness and falsehood. I do not deserve to receive the love of any true man. There is, at times, a bitter tonic in the idea that I may be better worth Roy Fordham's acceptance than I would be of another's who had never deceived the trust of the woman who loved him."

She sat upright, and laughed, in saying it. "We—he and I—could not upbraid one another on the score of inconstancy."

"I will not have you depreciate yourself. You have been true to the letter of your vow. There are some feelings that defy control. Listen to me, dearest," sitting down by her. "This is a world of mismatched plans,—of blighted hopes and fruitless regrets. But the wise do not defy Fate. They look, instead, for the sparkle of some gem amid the ashes of desolation. Let us be brave since we cannot be hopeful. I can never forget you,—never cease to think of you as the dearest and noblest of women. The memory will be more to me than any possession in the gift of Fortune. No change of external circumstances can make us less to one another than we are now, while to the world we can never be more. Nothing is further from my wishes or designs than to weaken your regard for the strength of a compact so solemn as that which binds you to your betrothed. He is a good man, and he will cherish you kindly and faithfully. It may be a hard saying, but we are dealing in no mock reserves now, love; and however weakly my heart may shrink from pronouncing the doom of my happiness, I ought not to disguise from myself or you the truth, that, as he has done nothing since your betrothal to forfeit your esteem, you should fulfil your promise whenever he shall claim it."

"Which he may never do!" Jessie interrupted the forced calmness of the argument. "I heard a terrible story a month ago—one that has driven sleep from my eyes for whole nights since. Did you ever hear that my mother was insane for many years before she died?"

It was too dark to see her features, but Orrin felt the strong shudder that ran over her; saw the gesture that seemed to tear the dreadful secret from her breast.

She went on wildly. "That the loving words and caresses, the recollection of which has fed my heart from my babyhood, the tales and songs and sketches that were my choicest pleasures then, were the vagaries of an unsettled mind; that she knew nothing aright after I, miserable little wretch! was born! Not even her own and only child! That, through all these years I have been worshipping a beautiful myth! I never had a mother! Oh! that I had died while I still believed in her!"

The cry of the last sentence was of hopeless bereavement, and the specious actor beside her sat appalled at the might of a woe beyond his conception.

She resumed before he could reply.

"I ought never to marry! Accursed from the beginning, I should finish my shadowed life alone. You talk of the gifts of Fortune. The best she can offer me now are quiet and obscurity. I have written all this to Mr. Fordham. He knows, by this time, that I am a less desirable partner for his fastidious and untainted self than was the poor girl whose only crime was that her sister had died of consumption,—that a deadlier malady is my birthright!"

"You have written this to Roy?" exclaimed Orrin, in stern earnest. "Without consultation with your sister or father?"

"Why should I consult them? Having deceived me for twenty years or more, they would not be likely to tell me the truth now. The story came indirectly to me, from the daughter of my mother's nurse, who lived here herself as a servant when I was born. Afterward I saw and talked with the woman myself. Nothing but the whole truth would satisfy me. Her account was clear and circumstantial. There is no mistake."

"The woman is a lying gossip—a malicious or weak-minded slanderer. You have acted hastily and most unwisely!" Orrin said, in seriousness that commanded her attention. "This tale is not a new one to me. Your sister informed me that there was such a figment in circulation before you went to Mrs. Baxter."

He rehearsed Eunice's description of her step-mother's invalidism, softening such portions of it as might, he feared, tend to feed the daughter's unhealthy fancies.

"Your father and your family physician will tell you that her disease was physical. Her low, nervous state and hysterical symptoms were concomitants to this, as were her indisposition to see strangers, and inability to go abroad. It is your duty to write this explanation to Roy. He had your father's version of the case, when he asked his sanction to his addresses to yourself. You must tell him that this was the correct one."

"To what purpose would all this be?" He had never heard her speak sullenly until now. "Better that he should part from me on this pretext than upon the ground which my farther confession would furnish."

She said the concluding words so indistinctly that Orrin did not catch their purport, or his rejoinder would have been different and less prompt.

"For the sake of your mother's memory!" he urged, gently. "The mother who, you are again persuaded, both knew and loved you."

She was still for a moment.

"You are right," she said then. "It would be base to screen my faithlessness at the expense of her reputation. I am cowardly—but indeed, indeed, it is not an easy task to undeceive him. He trusts me implicitly! If you had read his letters! And I do still value his esteem. I believed in him so long, you know. But I will tell him all! It is just that I should be spared no humiliation!"

To Wyllys this was sheer raving, yet it sounded dangerous.

"What do you mean?" he queried, in an altered tone.

Instead of replying, she hid her face in her hands—(how well he remembered the old action!)—and moaned.

He touched her shoulder, less in caress than admonition, as he asked, "Tell him what? Why do you speak of humiliation?"

"Because he still believes in *me*, I tell you! He will scorn me when I confess that my heart has changed—that I can never love him again, as I fancied I did once!" she whispered, as if ashamed to say it aloud. "He will cast me off—free me at once and forever."

The temptation was powerful, and the Thug yielded to it, without a struggle.

"And if he should, darling? What then?" he said, tightening his arm about her waist.

"*You* should not ask me!" in a yet lower whisper.

Had the dusk allowed, she might have seen a smile of triumph upon his face; an involuntary uprearing of the head as from the binding of the bay of victory about his brows. In affections and in spirit, she lay at his feet—her love confessed, her destiny in his power. Did he wish, for one insane instant, that his acting were reality, that, with clean heart and hands, he could fold her in his embrace, and call her by the name which is the seal and glory of loving womanhood? make her his honored and beloved Wife?

We are all human, and there may have gaped in that one wild second, an hitherto unsuspected joint in his harness of unscrupulous egotism. If this were so, he conquered the weakness before he again spoke.

"Jessie, this is sheer madness! My beautiful angel! why have you made me love you only that both our hearts should be broken at last? Do you know what you are doing? Do not injure yourself fatally in the estimation of all your friends by cancelling this engagement. Your father has talked much to me of the comfort it is to him. He loves and honors Fordham; is happy in his old age in the anticipation of giving you into his keeping. This will be a crushing blow to his pride and affection. And Fordham! you do not comprehend what a terrible thing his anger is. I, who have seen him aroused, warn you not to make him your lifelong enemy. These calm, slow natures are vindictive beyond the possibility of your conception."

"Yet you would have me trust myself and my happiness in his keeping? When I have said that I do not love him! Have you read *my* nature to so little purpose as to think that fear will drive, where affection does not lead me?"

Her spirit was rising. He knew the signs of her mood, and that the sharpest of the struggle between her will and his was to come. He made ready his last shaft.

"Leave things as they are! If I plead earnestly, it is because there is so much at stake. For me, as for you! Do not tempt me to perjury and dishonor. Help me to keep my integrity by holding fast to your own! Believe me, who have seen more of life and human inconsistency than your virgin fancy ever pictured, when I say that crossed loves are the rule, love-marriages the exception in this crooked, shadowed world. By and by, you—both of us— will learn quietness of soul, if not content, and nobody surmise the secret of the locked heart-chambers which are consecrated to one another."

"Perjury! dishonor!" repeated Jessie, bewildered. "By what oath are *you* bound? I do not understand!"

"You have heard no report, then, of the business which brought me to Dundee? Has not Mrs. Baxter or Miss Provost written to you of my engagement?"

"Engagement!" still wonderingly.

"I am engaged to be married, Jessie!" mournfully firm.

"To whom?"

He just caught the gasp, for her throat and tongue were too dry for perfect articulation.

"To Hester Sanford."

Without another word, she got up and groped her way to the mantel.

Orrin followed.

"What is it?" he asked, tenderly.

"I want the matches! Ah, here they are!"

She struck one, the blue flame showing a ghastly face above it, lighted the lamp, and motioned Orrin to a seat opposite her own, at the centre-table.

"Now!" she said, interlacing her fingers upon the table, and leaning over them in an attitude of attention. "Go on with what you were saying."

If she had expected him to show embarrassment, she was foiled. He put his hand upon hers before he began, and although she drew it back, he felt that it was clay-cold, and judged rightly that his real composure would outlast her counterfeit.

"What could I do?" he said, beseechingly. "You were lost to me as surely as though you were already married or dead. If I am to blame for obeying the reckless impulse to double-bar the door separating us—to divide myself from you by a gulf so wide that expectancy, desire, and hope would perish in attempting to cross it, you are scarcely the one to upbraid me for the deed. More marriages are contracted in desperation than from mutual love. I said: 'If I am ever cured, it will be by this means.' Miss Sanford was not unpropitious to my advances. I will not insult your common-sense by pretending that her evident partiality flattered or attracted me—much less that I ever felt one throb of tenderness for her. Since I could never love another woman, what difference did it make who bore my name and kept my house? It were better—so I reasoned—to marry one whose supreme self-love would prevent her from divining my indifference and its cause, who was shallow-hearted, insensitive, and obtuse of wit, than one who, gauging my feelings by her own, would expect a devotion I could not feign—

"But I cannot talk of Miss Sanford and my new bonds, here, and now! I thought myself armed at every point for self-justification when I came to you. One ray from your eyes showed me my error."

"Perjury! dishonor!" reiterated Jessie, without moving the eyes that were fast filling with disdain. "It is from these that I am to save you? You perjured yourself when you told that girl that you loved her—and tell it to her you did, or she would not have accepted your hand. Other men have sought her in marriage, and she would be exacting as to the form of your proposal. You dishonored yourself and the name of wedded love in every vow you made her. From this sin, at least, I am free. When I promised to marry Roy Fordham, I thought I understood my own feelings. And my heart *was* his! If I could forget the mad, wicked dream that divides me from that season of purity and gladness, I would peril my soul to do it! You speak of the sanctity of my engagement; of the integrity that bids you hold fast to yours. We will pass over the first. It *was* a sacred thing, and a precious, once, before the serpent left his loathsome trail upon it. But where was your integrity when you talked to me of love, just now? when you deliberately prefaced the announcement of your betrothal by the declaration that the memory of me must always be more to you than any earthly possession? Was this loyal? Was it honorable, or even honest? I believe that I have loved you, Orrin Wyllys! I believe, moreover, that you have tried to win my love—for what end the Maker of us both alone knows. If I have been weak, you have been wicked. I see it all now—step by step! fall after fall! And to crown the injury you have done me with insult, you adjure me to save you from temptation to perjury by heaping lie upon lie, in continuing to assert by actions, if not by direct protestation, that I love a man to whom I am indifferent. You have sold yourself for Hester Sanford's millions. You would have me sell myself, soul and body, for expediency and convenience—and to avert Roy Fordham's lasting enmity. That is the case, stripped of sentimental verbiage."

"Jessie!"

"I have no affection for him, or for any one else! No faith! no hope!" she pursued, towering above him like a lost but menacing spirit. "You saved my life this morning. You make of that benefit a wrong to-night, by robbing life of all that it held of sweetness and comfort; by showing me what a coarse bit of gilded clay I—poor fool! have worshipped. I wish you had let me drown!"

"Jessie! are you mad?"

He had arisen with her, and would have drawn nearer to her side, but she waved him off. There was a terrible beauty in her wrath that fascinated him, in spite of her cutting words.

"I was a happy, trustful child when you crossed my path. I am a hard, bitter, suspicious woman—and the change is your work. You have humbled me forever in my own eyes, by letting me into the dark secrets of my instability and idiotic credulity. I care not what others think of me. I shall write to Mr. Fordham before I sleep, and release him; if he still considers himself bound to me, shall tell him plainly that my love is dead—and my heart!"

"You will judge me more mercifully, and yourself more justly one day, Jessie. Your self-reproaches pain me more than do your vituperations against myself. Nothing you can say in your present mood can alter my feelings for you. You have had much to try you, to-day, my poor child! When you are cooler, you will retract—mentally at least—the charges you have brought against one whose heart is now—and always will be—your own. You know me better than you think. I can wait for time and your sober reason to right me. Implacable as I know Fordham to be, under his impassive demeanor, he will be more lenient to what he will esteem my breach of trust—the wrong I have done him—when once he has heard my defence, than you are at this moment."

"You suppose, then, that I am going to lodge a complaint against you?" she said, contemptuously. "I shall not mention your name. I should be ashamed to own who was the cause of my folly. You have nothing to dread from your cousin's anger."

And, although his last remark was a "feeler," designed to elicit such an assurance, this speech stung him more sharply than had the volley of invectives that preceded it.

Mr. Kirke and Eunice did not return until midnight. Jessie had the evening to herself, and the letter to Roy was sent to the post-office before she went to bed.

It was short and decisive to unkindness:

> "When I wrote to you, last week," was the unceremonious commencement,—"I said that I would await your reply before sending another letter. I believed that the information contained in the former would be the means of terminating our engagement. I have learned since that the story was a malicious or idle exaggeration. My mother died, as she had lived, a sane woman. But this matters little so far as our relation to one another is concerned. Another, and an insuperable obstacle to our union, exists in the change of my feelings toward yourself. If I ever loved you—I think, sometimes, I never did—I love you no longer. Months of doubt and suffering have brought me to the determination to confess this without reserve. I offer no extenuation of my fickleness. I ought to have remained constant, but I have not. May you choose more happily and wisely in the future!

"I write this without conference with my father or sister, — in the knowledge, also, that my change of purpose and prospects will be a sorrow and a surprise to both. But I cannot hesitate or draw back. I need hardly say that I have entered into pledges with no one else. No one desires that I should, or seeks to win my affections. It rests with you to give me the release I ask of your generosity and humanity, or to hold me to the letter of my bond. If, having learned the extent of the change that has come over me since I gave it, you insist upon the fulfilment of my promise, I shall submit to your decision.

"Foreseeing what your action will be, it only remains for me to add that your gifts and letters await your order.

"Jessamine Kirke."

# CHAPTER XV

The September nights were cool among the mountains, and as Mr. Kirke and his elder daughter drove home through the moonlight, between eleven and twelve o'clock, from the visit of mercy they had been paying on the other side of the ridge, there were white blankets of mist upon the meadows, and filling up the valleys along which their route lay.

The fire was out in the kitchen, and Patsey had been asleep for two hours and more, having made up her mind that her master would not return until the morrow. There was still a light in Jessie's chamber, and she came down, wide-awake and dressed, to admit the travellers. The servant man slept in a room over the stable, and, after calling to him two or three times without arousing him, the worthy clergyman took pity upon his weariness after his hard day's work, and groomed his horse himself. Eunice exclaimed at the dampness of his overcoat in helping him remove it, and Jessie—instructed in such appliances to health and comfort by her watery adventure, the telling of which she reserved for a more convenient season—prescribed a glass of brandy-and-water. Mr. Kirke needed nothing except a night's rest, he assured them both; pinched Jessie's cheek, in kissing her "good-night," and rallied her upon her anti-temperance proclivities, then ascended to his chamber. He came down late to breakfast, the next morning; owned that sleep had proved obdurate to his wooing; that he had had something very like an ague during the night, and that it was a violent headache which deprived him of appetite.

When he arose from table, Jessie coaxed him, almost in the old winsome way he could never resist, into the parlor; made him lie upon the sofa; tucked a shawl warmly about his shoulders, and sitting down of her own accord to the piano, played plaintive, soothing airs until he fell asleep.

This was the beginning of the spell of fever that, within twelve hours, laid him upon his bed, and which, ten days later, assumed a typhoid form.

His daughters were his nurses, by day and night. Offers of watchers poured in from the few gentle and the many simple who were his parishioners and neighbors; but the sisters courteously and gratefully declined them all. Their patient was all-deserving of the name, and needed no other care than they could give him. He slept much, and suffered little pain, and their light household tasks allowed one or the other to be constantly with him. Thus, to the kindly applicants; while to each other and their parent they said that love would not allow them to delegate a duty so dear and pious even to the true friends who sought to divide their labors. No man ever had more tender and gentle custodians. There was no perceptible difference in the assiduity and skill of the two, but visitors were unanimous in the expression of the opinion that their anxious vigils told more visibly upon Jessie than upon her sister. She wasted almost as rapidly as the sick man, while her eyes were settled in their mournfulness, and she seemed to forget how to smile days before the physician expressed any doubt as to the sequel of her parent's illness.

He had been confined to his room three weeks, when, on the morning of the 27th of September, Jessie met the doctor on the stairs, as she was carrying in a bowl of beef tea she had just made.

"Ah, doctor! I did not know you were here!" she said, more cheerfully than he had heard her speak for several days, unless when within her father's hearing. "Papa is more comfortable—is he not?"

"He is more quiet, certainly. Can I see you for a moment, my dear, when you have taken that in? I shall wait for you in the parlor."

He spoke very gravely, averting his eyes as he finished; and hope went suddenly and completely out of the daughter's heart.

She bore the basin carefully and steadily into the chamber, up to the bedside of the patient, and called his name clearly:

"Papa, dear, will you take a little of this for me?"

She watched him narrowly as he aroused himself to respond.

"He sleeps all the time, to-day," whispered Eunice.

There was a dull glow in his half-open eyes, and he put his hand to his head, confusedly, staring in his younger daughter's face, as she repeated her request.

"It is Jessie, papa! You have been dreaming, and are not yet awake. Here is your beef tea. May I give you a spoonful or two?"

"I thought you were your mother, child!" he said, smiling faintly but lovingly at her. "I was dreaming, as you say."

She fed him as she would an infant, but he would take only a few spoonfuls of the nourishment, turned his face away, and fell asleep again instantly.

The doctor's delicate and unenviable duty was half done for him before she joined him in the lower room.

"You consider my father worse?" was the address with which she opened the interview.

"I grieve to say that I do."

"Can nothing be done for him?"

He hesitated.

"I am answered!" she said, hastily. "Don't shelter yourself behind the hateful, worthless subterfuge about hope ceasing only with life. Tell me, instead, how long—"

The rest of the sentence was beyond her powers of utterance. But she did not succumb in aspect, after the wordless struggle died away in a quiver of the unmoistened lips. She was very white, but very still. The doctor congratulated himself upon the sagacity that had led him to choose this one of the twain as the recipient of his unwelcome intelligence. Jessie was his favorite, and he had always contended that hers was the stronger, as well as the more sprightly nature of the two. Since she was so collected—so well prepared for the sad probability—if not the fell certainty—he could be entirely frank.

"The symptoms are of general congestion," he said. "If this should advance rapidly, we cannot hope to have him with us more than twenty-four hours, at the utmost. I shall return, presently, with Dr. Trimble. But his verdict will, I think, coincide with mine. The indications are distinct. Your father will probably be unconscious much of the time, and suffer little, if at all. No one can doubt his fitness for the great change. I have known him for over thirty years, and I can testify that he has walked humbly and closely with his God. He has instructed you so carefully, Jessie, my dear, that you, do not require to be told where to look for consolation, for grace, and strength, in this trying hour—"

A motion of prohibition that had in it none of the grace of entreaty, checked his formula.

"You will not be long absent?" asked a voice from between the rigid lips.

The circles under her eyes were blacker and broader each second.

"I shall be in again as soon as I can find Dr. Trimble. You had better take Miss Eunice into your confidence without delay. She might think it strange—might take it hard if anything were to happen, you know—"

"Yes! I know!"

That shut his mouth, and rid her of his presence.

The day was warm for the season—so sultry that the cirrus clouds swimming in the blue ether, looked soft to April tearfulness. How still it was, as Jessie stood in the open oriel-window, and let her eyes roam through garden and church-yard,—ever returning, without volition of hers, to the gap in the long lines of gravestones next her mother's tomb! Had Nature swooned all over the broad earth? Was there nothing real left in creation save the fact of her great woe?

"My father is dying!" she said, aloud and distinctly.

And, again—"I suppose this is what people mean when they talk of not realizing a sorrow!"

As if aught but overwhelming appreciation of the might of a present calamity could crush the heart into deadness.

She was picking the faded leaves from the creepers, and crumbling them into dust, when Eunice came in. Jessie's protracted absence after the conference with the doctor had excited her apprehensions, and she stole down, while her father slept, to inquire into the cause. Immeasurably relieved at sight of her sister's attitude and occupation, she smiled as she aroused her from her reverie.

"I could not think what had become of you, dear! What does Dr. Winters think of father?"

"Sit down, Eunice, and I will tell you!" said Jessie, dreamy pity in her eyes, but no change in her hard, hollow voice.

Eunice sank into the nearest chair, laying her hand quickly upon her heart.

"You cannot mean—"

"That he is dying? Yes!" interrupted the other; and in the same awful composure, she repeated the doctor's verdict, *verbatim*.

"Now"—she concluded—"I will go back to him. You may come presently, when you have had time to think over the matter."

The beryl eyes were washed with many tears before they again met Jessie's across the sick-bed, but, after that, Eunice bore herself bravely. Hour after hour, they sat in the hushed upper chamber, facing their nearing desolation, without a plaint or an audible sigh. Below stairs, all was silent as the grave. Patsey, with an indefinable idea that the house should be set in order for the coming of the grim guest, had dusted the furniture, set back the chairs in straight rows against the walls in parlor and dining-room, and closed all the blinds on the lower floor; made her kitchen neat as Miss Eunice could have wished; then seated herself upon the upper step of the side porch, her arms wrapped in her clean apron. Jessie's orders were positive that no one besides the doctors should be admitted, and as the servant's lookout commanded the front gate, she intercepted the many callers who flocked to the Parsonage, at the swift rumor of the pastor's extreme illness.

"We will keep him to ourselves while he stays with us!" the younger sister had answered the other's fear lest this proceeding should give offence to "the people." "He has belonged to them for thirty years. At the last, we may surely claim him!"

"But they love him dearly!" expostulated Eunice. "He is their spiritual father and guide."

"He is our *all!*" was the curt reply, and Eunice forbore to argue further.

In the midst of her grief, she was slightly afraid of Jessie. The wide eyes that were caverns of gloom; the tuneless accents that never shook or varied, cowed her into quiet and obedience.

There was little to be done. The sick man slept—if it were sleep—except when aroused to take medicine or food. At these periods, he recognized his children, and spoke coherently, although briefly. His kind heart and gentle breeding were with him to the end. His utterances were of thankfulness for the services they rendered, and love for those who bent over him, that not a word should be lost of that they felt, at each awakening, might be the last sentence they should ever hear from him.

He spoke once intelligibly and calmly of the nearing separation.

"I am going fast!" he said to Eunice, who was lifting his head upon her arm that she might adjust the pillow. "The Father is very good. The 'precious blood' avails—even for me—for me! I go empty-handed, but rich—for there is the 'unspeakable gift!'" Closing his eyes he murmured softly to himself.

Eunice bowed her ear, and held her breath to catch the words.

"'The token was an arrow, with the point sharpened by love, let easily into the heart!' God is good—very good!"

It had been the testimony of his whole life.

"Jessie, dear! my little girl! you are wearing yourself out for me!" he said, at another time. "I wish Roy were here! But His will be done! He knows my darling's needs—her temptations—her trials. Like as a Father pitieth his children, dear! And it is true! Recollect that I told you so, this—and when—and how!"

She was to recollect it in the Father's good time. Now the words meant little, after she had heard the dying parent's wish for Roy's return. She said something in her own heart that was like a thanksgiving that her father was spared the one pang which the coming of the man he would have her marry, would bring,—that the sea rolled between them.

"We shall be cared for, Papa!" she replied, quietly.

"I know! The promise is sure," and he slept again, like a child at eventime upon the mother's breast.

"The 'great peace' is his!" said Eunice, in pious gratitude.

Jessie was mute.

So the afternoon went by, and the shortening twilight of Autumn drew on apace. The shutters of the southern windows were unclosed to admit the air which evening had not made raw. The fleecy clouds were packed in a cumulose mass upon the horizon, and this began to rise in portentous majesty, as the sun set behind it. Dun, while day lasted, with ragged, brassy edges, it darkened and thickened as Jessie watched it from her seat at the bed-head, into a banner of blackness absorbing the light from the rest of the heavens, and blotting out the earth from her sight. The silence was breathless. Not an insect chirped or leaf rustled. Even the pine boughs were motionless. The mill wheel was still; the roar of the waterfall was the only sound abroad under the inky sky. The sisters could no longer see each other, but all the waning light in the room seemed concentred upon the pallid face between them. The effect of the pale radiance and the brooding quiet about them was weird—unearthly. Eunice could bear it no longer.

"I will bring the night-lamp!" she said, rising.

She had hardly reached the foot of the staircase, when Jessie heard the garden-gate shut, and steps upon the gravel-walk leading to the kitchen; next, a stifled scream from Patsey, and a low, manly voice in rebuke or reassurance. Listening, as for her life, the deadly cold of hands and feet creeping up to her heart, she caught a faint exclamation from Eunice; then, the cautious tread of feet in the hall to the parlor-door, which was shut behind those who went in; after which all was quiet again.

For one moment, the darkness was Egyptian, and the night more freezing than winter. The watcher struggled to arise, to raise her hands to her madly throbbing head, but a dull paralysis was upon her limbs. It was not more than three minutes, but it seemed an hour, before will asserted its sway so far as to call back the blood in a tingling rush to the heart and extremities. Her trial was at hand. This—the *coup de grace* of the appointed torture—was not to be spared her, and she awaited it dumbly. But for the moveless face upon the pillow beside her, she must have rushed away to hide herself in thicket or cave—perhaps in the river-bed from which she had been rescued so lately. *That* she could not leave. Her father slept on, the pale, unearthly glimmering abiding still upon the broad brow and noble features. He was beyond the reach of earthly solicitude—the swimming and buffeting, the toil and anxiety, were forever overpast; his feet already touched the solid ground. He was very far off from her—bruised, struggling, condemned to endure the consequences of her own and another's wrong-doing.

A weary season of sickness and dread elapsed ere Eunice entered with the lamp. She put it down upon a stand in a distant corner, came around to Jessie's side, and stooped to listen to her father's breathing before she spoke.

Her voice was husky and uneven, and there was the shine of fresh tears upon her cheeks.

"There is some one down stairs who wishes to see you, dear," she said, laying her hand upon her sister's, to support her in case she should be overcome by the great joy in store for her. "Some one you will be glad and thankful to meet again!"

"Is it Roy Fordham?" asked the hard voice, while Jessie did not start or stir.

Eunice saw that her prefatory measures were thrown away.

"It is! He sailed a fortnight earlier than he expected; arrived in America but yesterday. Dear sister! our Heavenly Father has sent him to us in our sorest need. He is waiting, love!"

"Then let him come up. I shall not leave this room."

# CHAPTER XVI

Every object in the dimly lighted chamber seemed, to Jessie's strained eyes, to stand out with painful distinctness, as her long-absent lover entered. Most clearly of all, she saw his familiar figure; noticed even the full beard and gray travelling-suit, while he crossed the floor toward her. She arose, mechanically, and went forward a step to meet his fleet, noiseless advance.

"My own one! my precious darling!"

He had her in his arms before she could resist, if she had meant to do so. There were tears in his eyes and voice as he kissed her, and he held her closely, warmly, as a mother would a suffering child.

She undid his embrace with fingers strong and chill as steel.

"My father is very ill!" she faltered, and retreated to his pillow.

Disturbed by the movement and sound of his name, Mr. Kirke awoke. The recess in which his bed stood was in partial shadow, but his gaze rested at once upon Roy, and he tried to lift his head.

"Is that the doctor?"

Jessie replied:

"No, Papa! It is Mr. Fordham."

Instead of welcoming him, the sick man looked heavenward, and his lips moved in prayer. Only the daughter who had crept nearest to him, interpreted the burden of his thanksgiving.

"Lord! now lettest Thou Thy servant depart in peace!"

When he moved, it was in an effort to hold out his arms to the returned voyager.

"Roy! dear, dear son!"

Roy took the emaciated hands in his, with one answering word.

"Father!"

"Leave us for a little while, my children!" said the dying voice. "We have much to say to one another, and the time is short!"

He was obeyed; Eunice going to her room, to weep and pray in mingled gratitude and sorrow; Jessie flying down the stairs into the hall, thence out into the garden.

The sky was one expanse of cloud by this time. The wind moaned fitfully in the tree-tops; brought down showers of dry leaves into her face and upon her uncovered head. They whispered drearily to her as they hurtled by and crackled under her feet, and each thicket had its sigh of desolation. She heard and felt all—her soul in unison with the night and its voices of woe. She had fled from her father's presence, feeling like one accursed, forsaken by God and man. The return for which the dying saint's praise had gone up to heaven, was the event she had anticipated with shame and terror that made her long to bury herself in the wilderness or the grave, to escape the sight of him whom she had deceived. To him, her father was now bequeathing her—his dearest earthly treasure. Would Roy let him, indeed, depart in peace, or would his stern sense of truthfulness and honor impel him to a revelation of her perfidy? True, he had taken her in his arms and kissed her, but she had received this as his farewell, not his salutation;— seen in it the resistless overflow of the old-time fondness at sight of her and her affliction. Better—a thousand times better—that he had not come until the eyes that had lighted into gladness at sight of him were sealed in death, than to plant thorns in the painless pillow of the death-bed by relating how she had betrayed the trust of her betrothed, and disappointed her father's hopes.

If she could have warned him! If she had had the presence of mind to make some sign of caution before she left them together!

Would Roy—"the man of granite"—have mercy? or must her father's last words to her be reproof and not blessing? regret and not thankfulness?

Up and down! up and down! she trod the long alley, looking at the faintly illuminated windows of that upper chamber; wringing her hands in her dry-eyed agony, longing yet fearing to hear the summons that should end her suspense.

It came at length! Roy's step upon the piazza, and his call, guarded that it should not reach the sick-room, but audible to her as would be the trump of doom.

"Jessie! where are you?"

She went toward him without hesitation. Women have gone to the hall of sentence and to the block in the same way. He met her, guided by her rustling tread among the leaves.

"This should not be!" he said. "*You* will be ill next!"

He led her into the house, and to the parlor where there were lights.

She was not surprised that he did not let her pause until they reached the deep window—where she had not sat, for months, until that morning after the doctor left her. She had not expected a violent outbreak of anger or recrimination; had felt that, even in becoming her accuser, he could not cease to be a gentleman.

Orrin had told her, more than once or thrice, that his kinsman was just to calm severity. He would grant her a chance of self-exculpation; would judge her out of her own mouth; make her rehearse to him the story of her falsehood upon the spot where she had plighted her vow of eternal constancy. And she would meet it all—say it all, save the name of her tempter—that she was pledged not to reveal—if he would but let her go back the sooner to her father—the father who was dying upstairs!

"Don't think me cruel, dear, or ungenerous," began Roy, when he had seated her, and himself at her side.

Had her wretchedness moved him to leniency?

He continued: "But this is no season for useless delays and mistaken reserve. Our dear father is passing away from us. I met the doctor on my way to you this evening. He thinks that he may leave us very, very soon. One moment, dearest, and you shall go to him"—for she had started up. "He has made a dying request of us—of you and me—the fulfilment of which depends upon you. I say nothing of the eager happiness with which I have given my consent to the proposal—only of the comfort you can shed upon his last moments by marrying me in his sight within the next hour."

"No! no! *no!*" She slid from her seat to her knees, and hid her face, crouching to the floor in horror and humiliation. "I cannot! It would be a sin! a fearful sin!"

Roy would have raised her, but she shrank away from him.

"Anything but that! Ask me anything but *that!*" she repeated.

"It is not I who ask it, dear. Our father has decided what shall be the time and place of our marriage. It is not selfish—much less is it sinful in us to yield to his wish—his last earthly desire. It has been his prayer from the commencement of his illness that he might live to join our hands; give you into my keeping before you should close his eyes. Surely, knowing this, we may not fear to repeat in his hearing the vows we made long ago in this, our betrothal nook."

The simple, sad sincerity of his appeal sounded like pitiless will in the ears of the distracted girl, but she could not gainsay his reasoning. The decision was then thrown upon her! Hers was the power to cast a ray of light upon the even-time of the life which had been to her a constant benefaction, or to cloud it with disappointment.

"It is not selfish in us to yield to his wish!"

The words stung like venomed sarcasm. Not selfish to accept the fate against which her nature—physical and spiritual—had lashed itself into revolt for weary months past! Not selfish to bind upon her neck the yoke of the scorned and unloving wife!

The last thought moved her to action. She dragged herself to her feet, still rejecting his aid, and, for the first time since their meeting, looked into his face.

"Did you get my last letter? that in which I asked you to release me from this engagement?"

"Yes."

He would have drawn nearer as he said it, but she kept him off—less by her gesture than with her eyes—so unlike the sweet wells at which he used to drink his fill of love!

"And knowing all, it is still your wish to marry me! Think well before you answer. This bond is for life, remember! and life is long! Oh, how long to the miserable!"

"This is my answer." Before she could avoid him, he had gathered her in his arms, had pressed the reluctant head to his bosom. "We have been wedded almost a year and a half already, my Jessie. I am claiming my wife, not my betrothed. Did you imagine that I could be frightened from my hope and my purpose by that morbid little note, written by a half-sick, over-sensitive woman? Recollect! you left the decision to me! If, instead of this, you had ordered me to stay away forever, I should have come to you all the same; have taken you to the old resting-place and kissed away the gloomy fancies that had tempted you to banish me. I know your heart better than you do yourself—and it is *mine*! The Lord do so to me, and more also, if aught but death part you and me!

"Now, beloved, what shall I say to our father? The minutes are precious."

"It shall be as you and he desire. I will tell him this myself," replied Jessie, calming all at once into mournful composure Roy deemed altogether natural in the circumstances.

"One word more!" detaining her. "I met Dr. Baxter this evening at the station, on his way to pay you a visit, promised, he said, ever since last winter. Stopping at the hotel while the stage set down other passengers, we heard of your father's illness, and our dear old friend, with characteristic delicacy, would not present himself—a stranger—to your sister, in the circumstances. He remained at the hotel until I should bring further intelligence. Am I right in supposing that it is your wish, as well as mine, that he should perform the ceremony which is to make us one in name, as we have long been one in heart? If so, I will go for him without delay."

"Do what you like—whatever is best," she answered, hurriedly. "By all means, bring Dr. Baxter here! My father will like to see him."

"His arrival just now is providential," said Roy, walking upstairs at her side, his arm still supporting her. "There is light, even from the earthward side, upon this dark river, love!"

He beckoned Eunice from the sick-room as Jessie went in, exchanged half-a-dozen sentences with her relative to his plans, and ran down the steps lightly and swiftly. He had ordered Mr. Kirke's horse to be harnessed to his buggy before he sought Jessie, and Eunice heard him drive off in the direction of the village by the time she returned to her post.

The sisters awaited him and the clergyman where they had sat all day, the one at the right hand, the other at the left hand, of their father. Eunice ventured to suggest to her companion the expediency of making some change in her dress before the ceremony.

"I thought perhaps you would like to be married in white," she said, timidly. "I am almost sure Roy would prefer this."

"I have not time to dress. I have left *him* too long already," returned Jessie, pointing to her father.

She tried to keep her promise of apprising him of her acquiescence in his will, but was partly baffled by his increasing drowsiness! He spoke, it is true, when she told him that she had heard from Mr. Fordham of his request, and determined to grant it, but it was not clear that he quite understood her.

"Good child!" he said, with closed eyes. "God bless you both!"

Did "both" mean his daughters or the two who were to be wedded presently? She could not bring herself to ask.

Mr. Kirke lapsed into slumber or stupor, and the room was silent again save for his irregular breathing, showing that his semi-insensibility varied in character from that of the day. Once, Jessie got up with the remark that it was time to renew the mustard-poultices that stimulated the curdling veins into action, and the pair did the office deftly and mutely. Eunice saw her sister, as she reseated herself, lay her cheek to the almost pulseless hand that rested on the coverlet, and close her eyes, while her lips were stirred by an inaudible sentence. The observer was thankful for this token of a more subdued and natural frame of mind than the suffering girl had yet exhibited. It was meet that she should seek the blessing of Heaven upon the union she was about to form, and that thoughts of prayer should be linked with loving ones of her earthly parent. And Eunice, too, prayed in her gentle, pious heart for the happiness of the child she had reared as her own, and for that of the true, fond brother, whose arrival in this their darkest hour, was like a direct answer from on high to the petitions she had offered, during their long days of watching and anxiety. With Roy to console and care for Jessie, the smitten household would be rich even in temporal comfort.

Was Jessie praying? She had proudly flung the charge of perjury at another, saying—"Of this sin, at least, I am innocent." What was the act to which she had given her consent—which the next hour would render irrevocable? It was when this question was forced upon her by some taunting demon, that she kissed the lifeless hand, and whispered the formula she had said aloud that morning at the open window, and repeated inly hundreds of times since.

"My father is dying!"

Since she could not lie down and die in his stead, she would sacrifice the poor hopes of peace that were spared to her from the wreck of her early dreams, to purchase for him what gratification she could still give him. Eunice might well eye her apprehensively, all that day and evening. Many with steadier brains and cooler blood than were hers have been consigned to insane asylums.

The wind was so loud, the roar of the pine outside the window so continuous, as to drown the sound of returning hoofs and wheels. They were ignorant of Roy's second arrival until he knocked at the chamber-door. Eunice said, "Come in!" and he whispered a few words to her before he approached Jessie.

"Are you quite ready?" he asked, softly.

She bowed her head in assent.

He disappeared for a moment, then came back with Dr. Baxter, Drs. Winters and Trimble. The physicians, with difficulty, aroused their patient so far as to swallow the stimulant they administered. Patsey brought in more lights, and retired, with the doctors, to the background—an interested spectator of the singular scene.

"Father!" it was Roy's voice, sonorous yet pleasant, that reached the senses and reason which were fast slipping away with life. "This is Dr. Baxter, of whom you have often heard—Jessie's very dear friend—and whose wife is the cousin of Jessie's mother."

The double reference was talismanic. Mr. Kirke opened his eyes to their full width—all recognizing, in them the glassy stare of dissolution—and tried to move his hand toward the person thus introduced.

"He is very welcome!"

Dr. Baxter pressed the cold hand between his.

"Brother in Christ! we should have met before. We shall meet again. In that safe world there are no crossed purposes or partings. There we shall know even as we are known—of one another and of the Master. You are very near the entrance upon that perfect life. I have been sent hither by our Lord to bid you, 'God speed!' on the short and easy journey, and to ask your blessing upon these, our children, who would walk after you, hand in hand. Is it still your wish that they should be married here beside you, before you go from their sight?"

"Yes; by all means!"

The emphasis was faint, yet perceptible, and he shut his clammy fingers feebly upon those Jessie slipped within them, as she obeyed Dr. Baxter's injunction to join her right hand with that of her betrothed. She felt their loose hold more plainly than she did the warm, strong grasp that signified loving protection, tenderest sympathy.

It was a strange, sad rite,—stranger and more melancholy than burials usually are. The bride's gaze never left the sunken face and closed eyes that rested among the pillows, and her assent to the interrogations put to her was so slight as to create a passing doubt in the mind of the catechist as to whether she had given any. The mountain storm burst overhead in thunder, wind, and rain, as the bridegroom spoke his reverent and stead-fast response, and when the benediction was pronounced, Jessie stooped to kiss her father, apparently forgetful that Roy's was the paramount right to the token of affection.

"Dear Papa! It is your little Jessie! I have done as you wished. Will you not bless me?"

The cry sounded in the ear deadened by the death-stupor as a faint and far-off call. Mr. Kirke's eyelids quivered without rising, and the muscles of the mouth were moved. Then, the gray calm settled down again upon his countenance.

"He must speak to me! I must be sure that he hears me—that he understands how I have obeyed him!" said Jessie, frantically. "He *must*!" to the physicians who advanced to the bedside with restoratives.

They were useless. The dying man was beyond the reach of human skill. The lips were parted, the throat did not contract. Dr. Winters shook his head despairingly and turned from his old friend and pastor, the untasted glass of brandy in his hand.

"He does not see or hear me!" cried the daughter, throwing up her arms in a passion of despair. "I did it for him, and he will never know it."

She sank to her knees beside the bed and buried her face in the coverings. Roy leaned over her, and whispered something the rest did not hear. He might as well have addressed her father with words of consolation. When he touched her to recall her attention, she shivered violently, but gave no other sign of consciousness of his presence.

"I am glad you are here, Mr. Fordham—-heartily rejoiced and greatly relieved," said Dr. Winters, as Roy attended him down the stairs. "Your wife needs very delicate and judicious treatment just now. Her whole nervous system is unstrung. I saw it in her manner and eye this forenoon. When the unnatural strain is relaxed, she will break down completely, I am afraid."

Mr. Kirke died at midnight. He had noticed no one, and said nothing since his feeble rejoinder to Dr. Baxter's query whether the marriage should proceed, until half an hour before he breathed his last, those about him saw a change in the face that, in stillness and beauty, resembled a fine Greek mask. Jessie perceived it first; was quick to take advantage of the tinge of color, the tremor of features.

"Papa!" she prayed, raising his head to a resting-place on her arm. "Can you hear me? If you can, kiss me."

The stiff lips moved under the pressure of hers, and a smile, ineffable in radiance and tenderness, remained when the kiss had been given.

"You do know me—do you not?" said his daughter, breathlessly. "Who is it that is speaking to you?"

All present heard the reply:

"*Ginevra!*"

# CHAPTER XVII

The "breaking down" predicted by Dr. Winters, took the form, not of hysterical emotion, as he had anticipated, but of physical languor and spiritual apathy, which were more alarming. Jessie moved, spoke, and thought like one in a trance; acquiescing in every proposal made by her sister and Roy; obeying every request without demur or inquiry. If left to herself she asked nothing except to be allowed to sit or lie passive for hours together; her great eyes closed or blank; her countenance set in the gloomy weariness that had marked it from the moment her hand left her dead father's forehead—a look that said she had henceforward nothing to hope for or to fear.

Few husbands would have had tolerance with this excessive grief for the loss of a parent, however beloved, and worthy of filial attachment. One might search far and long without finding a man whose sympathy with the demonstration of this would incite him to warmer love and fonder care for her, who, for the time, overlooked his claim to supreme regard in her devotion to a memory.

"You could not mourn more bitterly for *me!*" I once heard a man say in impatient reproach, upon surprising his wife in tears within a week after she had committed an indulgent parent to the grave.

He was a good man, and an affectionate husband, but he could not endure the semblance of a divided allegiance.

Had Roy Fordham's love been of this sensitive and exclusive type, it would have been chafed threadbare before the honeymoon was one-tenth wasted. The new bond between them she ignored entirely—not, it was evident, in wilfulness or shyness, but because it had no place in her thoughts; was a matter of no moment in comparison with the event that steeped her whole being in despondency. It was well that neither he nor Eunice had any knowledge of the continuous warfare of the summer, the fiercer struggle of that early September day, the morrow of which had brought a fresh sorrow in her father's illness. Had they comprehended all this, superadded to their fears that her three weeks' watching and its *finale* had seriously affected her nervous system, they would have had small hope of the curative power of Nature and of Love. She was, in reality, insane for the three days immediately succeeding her marriage, if lack of feeling, thought, and connected memory signify mental aberration. In after years, this period was almost a blank in the retrospect, a confusing dissolving view that defied her scrutiny. While it lasted it was a nightmare from which she had not strength to awaken.

When she was led by Roy to take a last look at her father's face as he lay in his coffin ready to be transported to the church, her eyes were vacant and dry, her features emotionless.

"He looks very natural!" she said slowly, like one trying to recall the conventional phrase in such circumstances.

When Eunice bent weepingly to kiss the frozen lips where still lingered the smile of ineffable peace with which he had named his wife, Jessie eyed her with a mixture of wonder and perplexity; and remarking again, "Very natural! almost life-like!" turned away, with the air of one who had said and done all that could be required of her.

In an agony of alarm, Roy sought Dr. Winters, who had called to inquire after the health of the family, and to see if he could be of service in their affliction. Eunice had taken charge of her sister at night, and reported that what little sleep had visited the latter had been won by the use of anodynes. Had the physician—asked the bridegroom—a sedative, potent enough to induce slumber for several hours, the after effect of which would not be increased cerebral excitement? Come what might, Jessie must not witness the obsequies appointed for that forenoon. Her mind seemed, to him, to need but a touch to complete its overthrow. While the two gentlemen held counsel, Eunice entered with the welcome news that Jessie had, on leaving the parlor where the remains lay, gone voluntarily to her own room—-she having shared her sister's since their common bereavement—thrown herself upon the bed and fallen into a deep sleep.

The church-bell was not tolled for the pastor's funeral, and a band of trusty yeomen, stationed fifty yards up and down the road, prevented vehicles from approaching the gate of Parsonage or church-yard. The reason was quickly disseminated, and the value of the precaution universally admitted. Mingled with the tears that fell upon the bier of the faithful servant of God, were earnest prayers for the restoration of health and reason to the daughter—"the people's" pride and pet as she had been his—the merry, popular "little Jessie," who was known to every household in the parish. Many wistful eyes sought the closed blinds, behind which she lay wrapped in death-like slumber.

"The only hope for life and brain!" Dr. Winters had pronounced, and the dictum was repeated far and near with awed looks and subdued breath.

Within the manse, all was hushed and dark. Eunice sat with the sleeper while the services at the church went forward.

"Do not separate us this morning!" was her petition to Roy, who would have taken the post himself. "I have nobody left but her!"

She interpreted correctly the meaning of the imperfect sounds that penetrated her seclusion—the funeral psalm, the dull tramp of many feet from the front to the back of the church; the awful pause—like no other upon earth—-that told the coffin was sinking to its place—the voice of prayer—the brief, reverent utterances with which the dear dust was committed to the keeping of the Lord of Life, through all the coming ages of Time—then, the muffled tumult of departure. She sat quiet until the end; restraining sob and sigh that the beloved living should not be disturbed; staying her heart upon the Father of the fatherless, the God whose goodness the expiring saint had charged his children never to forget.

Roy relieved her as soon as the Services were over.

"Thank you," he said, kissing her with a brother's fond sympathy. "Go now, and leave her to me. I will call you, should you be needed."

Alternately, and in company, they watched her until Dr. Winters' third visit that day brought hope that was confidence to their tried souls.

"If she sleep, she shall do well!" said Dr. Baxter, when Roy carried the glad tidings to him, that the stupor had changed to natural slumber. He was sitting in the window of Mr. Kirke's study; for a wonder, without book or paper before him, but absorbed in contemplation of the mountain scenery.

"You are wearing yourself out," he added, observing that Roy's complexion, tanned by the sea-voyage, was fast regaining its natural hue, and that his eyes bore evidence of grief and anxiety. "Jessie is safe in her sister's care, and while she sleeps cannot miss you. Bide here a bit with me"—he often relapsed into the Scotch dialect— "and refresh yourself by a survey of this picture. I must quit you all to-morrow, and I would have a few words with you before I go."

Jessie was alone when she awoke. Eunice had been called to the parlor to see a parishioner from the other side of the mountain who had not heard of Mr. Kirke's decease until that morning, had ridden twenty miles to attend the funeral, and arrived too late. Eunice had been too long the obedient servant of the congregation to hesitate as to the course she should pursue in the dilemma. Jessie slept soundly and peacefully, and Roy would be back soon. She closed the door noiselessly, and obeyed the summons of her father's friend.

Summer zephyrs were coquetting with the sombre pine-branches; summer-scents were stealing up to Jessie's windows from the garden. To such wooing whispers and goodly odors had she awakened many mornings during many years. She mistook the colored light visible through the shutters for dawn; marvelled sleepily that her limbs ached and her head was weary.

"It must be time to get up!" she meditated, 'twixt sleeping and waking. "Yet I am not rested. I have · not heard Eunice or Patsey go downstairs."

In tossing her arm up to pillow her head for a second nap, she saw her sleeve. How had she happened to fall asleep without undressing? She sat upright, and tried to remember when and how she had gone to bed overnight. How queerly her head felt!

"As if it had been dead and was coming to life again!" was her simile.

She was at home, and in her own room; everything about her was in its usual order. Yet something had happened. What was it? A Bible lay on the stand by the bed. Between the leaves was a handkerchief. She drew it out, and saw Eunice's name in the corner. How came it there? Had Eunice sat with her, last evening? If so, why? Her feet were oddly numb when she stood up; she was weak and dizzy as from illness or fasting; but she walked to the door, opened it, and hearkened for movements upon the lower floor. It was so quiet, she heard the droning of a humming-bird moth which had come to look for untimely blossoms in the honey-suckle draping the hall-window. Another sound, almost as monotonous, blended with this—the steady flow of a man's voice talking or reading in the study. Who was her father's guest? And what hour of day was it? It must be morning, since she had just awakened, yet looked, and felt like evening.

A draught from the open door she had left blew that opposite slightly ajar. Surely, that was Dr. Baxter's voice! Had she dreamed of his arrival! A fearful dream, the dim recollection of which made her sick and faint? Sinking to a settee that stood outside the study-door, seeking to stimulate her half-dead brain by rubbing her temples hard, she endeavored to gather the meaning of what Dr. Baxter was saying. He was in the middle of one of the monologues which were sometimes a bore; sometimes a delight. A gleam of amusement flitted over the wan, vacant visage of the eavesdropper as she pictured to herself—still as if she were somebody else and not Jessie Kirke—the knotted handkerchief she doubted not was on active duty.

"Is it consistent with the Divine economy for an immortal being to spend twenty-five, fifty, threescore and ten years, in the acquisition of knowledge and experience for which he is to have no use in the world to come? Believe me, they are in grievous error, denying themselves the abundant consolations which the hope of a continued and eternal existence should bring, who overlook the plain teachings of the word and the almost divine intuitions of the human soul on this question. The Future Life! What is it but the stretching into regions yet unknown to us, into the Eternity of which we have but imperfect conceptions, of the life which now is? the Present, which is the journey toward the continuing City. Into that state we shall, it is true, be born as spiritual babes. But not idiots! As the instincts and actions of the babe prefigure the disposition and appetites of the man, so the habits of thought and feeling, the inclinations and aspirations of the newly disembodied spirit will bear a certain relation to that which it will at length become—the perfect man in Christ Jesus. As hereditary taints and hereditary virtues are reproduced in the mortal babe, we shall find definite traces of our earthly individuality in the heavenly nurseling. And that the proportion which the loftiest attainments of the profoundest philosopher will bear to the infancy of this celestial creature will be less—far less than that which the mere instincts of the earthly infant bear to the wisdom and strength of the adult, I also believe. We shall have to begin with the rudiments of infinite knowledge. But we shall have Eternity in which to learn."

Jessie still chafed her forehead, where wrinkles of pained perplexity gathered and deepened, as she tried to put word to word and sentence to sentence. She lost what came next in vainly attempting to get the sense of these last sentences. Perhaps she should understand better when she was quite awake.

"Such proportion as the seed sustains to the mature plant, the ovum to the living, moving creature, you will tell me—" Dr. Baxter was saying, when she again lent attention to his dissertation. "I grant it. But like produces like in vegetable and animal generation, and why deny the spiritual analogy? What we call Death is but the threshold—and a narrow one—separating the vestibule from the temple. It is all one building—the Life which God has given. When I cast off the cumbrous shell I have borne so long that I foolishly fancy it is *myself*—a part of my being without which I should be naked, shivering, and helpless; when it slips from my soul by reason of its own weight and rottenness, I shall enter upon no new existence. It will be *I* still—not a different creation. For a moment, perhaps, I may not know what has happened. Thus, I have seen a butterfly trembling with the strangeness of his position, clinging with damp, untried wings to the bough that supports the little pendant coffin, now broken—from which he has just crept. A delicious sense of liberty and space there may be as one breathes more freely in leaving a close room for the outer air. I shall miss the incubus of the body, and the fleshly desires I have sloughed off with it. Then will dawn upon me gradually—as I have strength to bear the revelation, that I have *passed*! Not been made over, mark you! We are nowhere taught that regeneration is a posthumous experience. 'He is gone!' some one will say. And perhaps another—'He is dead!'

"Dead! I tell you, my friend, I shall be the *livest* man in that room! Not until that hour of glorious emancipation shall I know what life is!"

There was an interval of stillness. Jessie had staggered to her feet. Her eyes, no longer blank, were dilated with intensest and eager inquiry. What did it signify—this talk of death and the life to come? Who was the speaker's companion? Her father? Oh, why did he not speak?

Another voice, deeper and sweeter, made reverent response:

"Thanks be to God, for His unspeakable gift!"

She flung the door widely open; faced the astonished man with the demand, shrieked, rather than spoken:

"Where is he? He said *that*! my father! *Where is he now?*"

"Jessie, love!"

Roy caught her in his arms, but she pushed him from her.

"I will know! I am going mad! Where is my father?"

Dr. Baxter secured her fluttering hands; looked steadfastly, yet not sternly, into her eyes.

"He may be *here*, my child! We cannot tell. Be sure he remembers and loves you still, he, who, while in the flesh, held you so dear. Believe this and be still under the mighty but loving hand of God!"

Her head sank upon his shoulder.

"*You* would not deceive me! You are a good man, and speak the truth always!" she sobbed, excitedly. "Is my father *really* dead? Oh, I remember it all now!"

With the resuscitation of the torpid intellect, came a flood of tears, mingled with anguished exclamations—an hysterical attack that only abated with her strength. By nine o'clock she was asleep, exhausted, but free from fever and the nervous spasms that had made the seizure alarming at first. The danger was tided over, for the present, and ere the rest separated for the night, Dr. Baxter returned thanks for "the signal deliverance," kneeling between the husband and sister; besought comfort and peace for the smitten household in fervent, affectionate words, which showed that however his thought might stray from the subjects to which his acquaintances would hold him, his heart was always in the right place.

"I cannot thank you as I should for all you have been to us—all you have done for us!" said Eunice, as they talked of the morrow's parting.

"Do not, my dear! The privilege and the gratitude have been and are mine. God sent me to you. I bless Him for it!"

It was after sunrise when Jessie unclosed her eyes. Eunice's chair was still by her pillow, but it was empty. Her mind was clear. She had no difficulty in recalling how the gentle hands had laid her to sleep; the mellow voice read to her from The Book—"A prayer of the afflicted, when he poureth out his heart before God." Dear Eunice! her love—tried as it had been by her perversity and reserve, her late violent and selfish distress— was more precious than ever before. She would arise and share, if she could not lighten, her labors and her burdens. As she sat up in bed, she espied upon a lounge near by, a gentleman's dressing-gown. The blood sprang to her cheeks in a burning torrent, for the truth flashed instantly upon her. Roy had asserted his right to the exclusive guardianship of his wife; had sent the weary sister to take the rest she needed, and himself kept watch over her through the night. There came to her no softening thought of the anxious affection that had held his eyes waking while others slept. She was only angry—desperately indignant that he had dared sit there and watch her without her knowledge or consent. The blind, mad moment passed, she stood, for many more—white as death—thinking! Then she locked the door. Roy might enter at any instant, or Eunice glide in to ask how she was, and she must be alone while she thought it all out! No mortal eye witnessed the fight of the next hour. The woman—torn and dashed by a legion of passions verily believed, while they had the mastery, that she would not survive it. She never told the tale of her hurts to her dearest earthly friend. It was something she would not renew by relating, even when time had almost worn away the scars.

She was made of sterner stuff than she knew. Ere she quitted her chamber, her resolution was taken—every trace of the strife put out of sight. She had "light enough to see the next step." If she were bound for life against her will and conscience, Roy was basely wronged—and through no fault he had committed against her. If her course were to be joyless—a strait and rough path, his was no smoother or more delightsome. Recompense him for what she had lost for him, she could not, but she could and she would appear dutiful and resigned.

Fordham coming in from the brisk walk in the early morning air by which he had tried to make up for his vigil, found her in the parlor, arranging the books upon bracket-shelves and dusting the rare old china bowl and vases which the sisters let no one but themselves handle. Her breakfast-toilette had been carefully made, contrasting strikingly with yesterday's *négligé*. Her rich hair was braided as she used to wear it, and banded with black ribbon; her white cambric dress was belted with the same, and loops of narrower hung from her mourning brooch. She comprehended all that had happened within the week; accepted the expediencies and proprieties of her position with its sorrows and duties, and he honored her for it. Her attire showed that she consulted his taste, wished to be fair in his eyes, and for this he loved her better than ever, if that could be. He did not know it, but the woman he had wedded never, in her previous or subsequent life, gave another equal proof of strength of mind and purpose, as when, physically faint and mentally distraught by the frightful ordeals she had already sustained, she lifted this, the heaviest cross of all, and adjusted it to her shoulders for a lifelong journey.

The greeting between them was affectionate on his side—grave upon hers—very quiet on both, as befitted the circumstances of the household.

"Ah, Jessie, darling! I am glad you are well enough to be down stairs! But are you not exerting yourself too much?" he exclaimed at his entrance.

And—"I am much better, thank you! entirely able to be about as usual," was the reply, uttered without the flicker of a blush.

Then he kissed the cheek that was neither averted nor offered.

Dr. Baxter and Eunice appearing, a minute afterward, saw nothing amiss. There may have been nothing, yet the young husband had looked for a different reception—now that his Jessie was declared to be "quite herself again."

He was a patient man and a considerate, and the secret disappointment was condemned as soon as recognized. This was not the time for love-making—or—this was clearly Jessie's feeling. To oppose her scruple while her grief was so fresh and her nerves unsettled, would be persecution. She deserved all grace and indulgence at his hands, and she should have it. Their life—as *theirs* was all before them. He would be a help not an embarrassment, to the orphans. Jessie loved him! Jessie was his wife! That was enough!

# CHAPTER XVIII

Roy Fordham remained ten days longer in Dundee in consequence of an arrangement made by his brother professors by which they divided his duties among them. Dr. Baxter, whose partiality for him was proverbial, taking a double share upon himself. The furlough was not accepted by him without misgivings. He felt that he ought to be in his place at the beginning of the college session, and that to avail himself further of the generous kindness of trustees and faculty, after a year's absence, was an abuse of the same. Dr. Baxter wrote him two strong, short letters to refute this idea, and he found additional solace for his conscience in the discovery that he was needed by the sisters. Eunice and he were joint executors of Mr. Kirke's small property. To Jessie were left her mother's dowry with the accumulated interest; her mother's picture, and certain articles of jewelry, dress, and furniture, which had been hers. Everything else was Eunice's—a portion that did not nearly equal her sister's, but with which she was more than content. The settlement of the estate was easily accomplished. The just man had no debts, and the few legal papers needful to secure the title of his possessions to his children were in perfect order.

At the end of a week the only open question was that of Eunice's residence. Roy had engaged a house in Hamilton, and was urgent in his desire that she should live with Jessie and himself. The conscientious elder sister hesitated in the knowledge that her income would not support her in like comfort anywhere else.

"My inclination leads-me to follow Jessie," she confessed to her brother-in-law. "My sense of duty to myself and to you makes me doubt the propriety and justice of living in comparative idleness, when, if I had not the shelter of your roof, I must work to eke out a maintenance."

Which quibble Roy pronounced absurd and far-fetched.

"Quite unworthy of sensible Eunice! To say nothing of the manifest unkindness to our poor girl here," he said, as his wife entered the room where he was sitting. "Come here, Love, and convince this unreasonable and sceptical woman that she is indispensable to our happiness."

Jessie yielded passively to the arm that drew her to his knee.

"What is it?" she asked, listlessly.

Roy gave an abstract of the situation.

She looked confused—uncertain whether she had heard him aright. It was an effort to understand anything, sometimes. Roy and Eunice glanced from her to one another. They saw that dazed look, heard her stammer oftener than either liked; dreaded nothing else so much as they did the repetition of the scenes attending their father's demise and burial.

"Of course she will live with me—with us, wherever we go!" she rejoined. "Unless you object"—to Roy. "But I was under the impression that you wished it,—that the matter was definitely arranged."

"It is, now!" said Roy confidently, and Eunice did not dispute it.

There was a clear, more constant light in her eye, now that the responsibility of the decision was removed from her, and the step determined, upon without her vote. The prospect of separation from her sister was very painful, and there were other reasons why Hamilton should be a pleasant home to them all. This was her representation of the case to herself and to the friends who lamented losing her.

"Mourning is very becoming to Miss Kirke!" was the usual remark of these visitors upon leaving the Parsonage.

And—"She is really a most lovely woman. What will the congregation do without her?"

Roy was to leave them for a fortnight, to attend to his classes, and forward the preparations for the reception of his bride. When all was ready for their removal, he would return to superintend the sale of furniture, stock, etc., then take the sisters back to town with him.

"My family!" he said, in forced gayety, on the morning of his departure. "I assure you, my consequence in my own eyes is mightily augmented by the acquisition of my new honors."

Eunice called up one of her slow, bright smiles in acknowledgement. Jessie appeared to heed the compliment as little as she did the parting, that drew tears from her sister's eyes and choked Roy's farewell directions as to the care she must take of herself while he was away.

"I shall write to you every day, my sweet wife," he promised. "And it will not harm you—it may help you to while away the time, if you can scribble a few lines to me in return, now and then."

"If I can I will. If you wish it I will write certainly. But don't expect to hear every day from me. There's very little here to write about, you know," answered Jessie.

Eunice wondered, to reverent admiration, at the love and forbearance with which he thanked her for the concession.

They attended him to the porch. The morning was foggy, and Roy put Jessie back in the shelter of the hall-door.

"It is too damp for you out here! Don't stand there to see me off!"

Eunice—maybe he—would have been better satisfied had she disregarded the loving command. As it was, when he waved his hand from the carriage-door, Eunice stood alone in the doorway. Yet she was sure Jessie did not mean to be ungracious; that she was not really insensible to the devotion of the husband of her choice; that but for the stay of his presence she must have gone mad or died in her overwhelming grief. What she mistook for unwifelike reserve was an incessant effort to control herself to play the woman and not the child. It was best not to interfere even so far as to hint that Roy's kindest schemes for her comfort and pleasure as often as not were unnoticed by verbal thanks or grateful look from her whom he aimed to benefit. As Jessie's interest in the outer world and passing events revived, this blemish would vanish. Older people, who had known more of the discipline of life, had fallen into the mistake of idolizing their sorrows while they were new.

The sisters were at tea on the third day of Mr. Fordham's absence, when a letter was brought to Jessie.

"From Roy!" she said, quietly, and laid it down by her plate until the meal was finished, — Eunice hurrying through hers in the belief that the wife wished to be alone when she read it.

Instead of this, Jessie broke the seal, and read the four closely written pages by the lamp upon the supper-table, while her sister washed the silver and china in the same little cedar-wood pail, with shining brass hoops, her mother had used for this purpose a quarter of a century before. Eunice was inclined to be scrupulous in the matters of extreme cleanliness and system in housekeeping, and neatness and fitness of apparel; and had other and quaint, but never unpleasant, peculiarities that leaned toward what the vulgar and unappreciative style "old-maidism." But she was a bonny picture to behold to-night, her black dress setting off her fairness to exquisite advantage; her features chastened into purer outline and a softer serenity by sorrow; her eyes more beautiful for the shadows that had darkened them.

She was younger in appearance and feeling than her companion, who scanned, without change of expression and complexion, the love-words that had streamed, a strong, living tide, from the writer's heart. She read it all, from address to signature; then handed it to her sister, who had just summoned Patsey to remove the hot water and towels.

"There are several messages to you in it," she said, languidly. "You can read them for yourself."

Eunice drew back.

"I don't think he meant it for any eyes but yours, dear. Tell me what he says to me."

"I should have to go all over it again in order to do that," returned Jessie. "They are scattered sentences—business items and the like. You may look for them at your leisure. I shall leave the letter upon the table here."

She put it down under her lamp, and turned her chair to the fire.

This was their sitting-room, now that the two, with Patsey, composed the household. By tacit consent, they avoided the parlor, as recalling too vividly the gatherings and the happiness of other days. Jessie had leaned back in her cushioned seat, staring, in a blank, purposeless way, at the fire for five minutes or more, when Eunice took her place with her work-box on the other side of the hearth.

"You insist, then, that I shall read your love-letter?" she asked, pleasantly.

Faithful to her promise to Roy to do all in her power for the restoration of Jessie's native cheerfulness, she compelled herself to wear a tranquil countenance in her sight, to speak hopefully, and, when she could, brightly, in addressing her.

Jessie neither smiled nor frowned. She looked simply and wearily indifferent.

"If you please," she said, without withdrawing her eyes from the blazing logs.

Eunice skimmed the first three pages cursorily, on the watch for any mention of her own name, beset, all the while, by the idea that her act in opening the letter at all bordered upon profanation, and affected almost to tears by stray sentences she could not avoid seeing, eloquent of the young husband's tender compassion for his loved one, his longings to be with her, and fond prognostications of the peace and joy of their future life.

At the top of the fourth page, a passage seemed to dart up at her from the sheet, and, leaping into view, to be changed into characters of red-hot flame:

"What a discreet little woman you are, never to hint to me your knowledge of Orrin's engagement! The communication took me completely by surprise. He would scarcely believe that you had not told me; said that he went down to Dundee on purpose to impart to you the agreeable and important secret. The marriage is fixed for December. I always prophesied that he would marry in haste when he had once selected the lady, whom I am extremely curious to meet. He has floated from flower to flower so long that his selection ought to be worth seeing. You know her, he tells me. I shall expect a full-length description of her—done in your finest style, when I return. I own I should be better satisfied that he is to be made as happy as I would have him, if Miss Sanford were not an heiress. While we—you and I—and others who know him well, will never suspect him of selling himself for money, the above fact may give occasion for scandal-mongers to rave and exult. The father of the bride-elect is in town. I met him on the street to-day with Orrin. Rumor has it that his business here is to purchase the new house opposite Judge Provost's, as a residence for the happy pair. It will be a handsome home, but I hope and believe that we shall be as content with our love-nest of a cottage."

Jessie did not look around as her sister refolded the letter, tucked it into the envelope, and laid it upon the table. But while each believed herself to be separated from the other by a fathomless gulf of memories, every one of which was an anguish, both were pondering the same section of the epistle that lay between them. The announcement of Wyllys' approaching marriage was, in itself, nothing to the wife. The thought of it had lost the power to wound when she parted with her faith in him. The wrong he had done her could never be forgiven; he had misled her purposely; deceived her cruelly; had robbed her life of love and hope, and given her self-contempt and remorse in their stead. But she did not regret him—as she now knew him to be—or linger fondly upon recollections of their by-gone intimacy. Hester Sanford was welcome to the suitor her gold had bought.

The phrases that had found a sentient spot in her breast were these: "Whom I am extremely curious to meet." "I shall expect a full-length description of her." The apathetic misery which had locked brain and heart with fetters of ice since her father's death had not rendered her totally unmindful of her husband's long-suffering and gentleness, his unselfish love and care of herself. She was persuaded that the girlish passion that had made of him a demi-god was gone forever. Her flesh fainted, and her spirit died within her, at the caresses to which she had turned herself in the days of her idolatry, as roses open to the sun—as innocently and as naturally. She could never love again. The fires had scathed too deeply for that; but she had begun to believe that she might find comfort in esteeming and liking her only protector; might seek, and not in vain, in a calm, true friendship for this good man, forgetfulness of the storms that had wrecked her early dreams. In his frank and noble presence suspicion stood rebuked. It was easier to discredit the evidence of one's own senses and judgment, than to doubt his integrity.

But here was a deliberate deception. He—Roy Fordham—had known Hester Sanford before she—Jessie—ever saw her. She was the intimate associate and *confidante* of his former love;—of the woman he had renounced heartlessly and without compunction,—and whose name had never passed his lips in his wife's hearing. She recalled faithfully Hester's account of the call "Maria" had paid with her then betrothed at Mr. Sanford's house—a statement she would not have dared to make, had it been groundless. Whence this affectation of ignorance, on Fordham's part, of the person and character of his cousin's intended bride, if not as a further means of keeping the knowledge of the affair from *her*?

"To whom it should have been told, more than a year ago!" she reflected, a dreary loneliness creeping over her, with the conclusion—"He is like the rest of them! I would have believed in him if I could!"

The door shut quietly. She did not hear it, or miss her sister from her place. It was not an uncommon occurrence for them to sit together without speaking, for an hour at a time, Eunice's fingers busied with some article of useful needlework, Jessie's holding a book which she pretended to read as a cover for her griefful musings. Much less was it in the imagination of the younger sister to follow the elder in her progress up the staircase, her face more stony and eyes more desolate with each step, to the fair, large chamber she had occupied from her childhood.

It was cold and dark, but for the light of the taper she set down upon the mantel. There were none of the fanciful ornaments,—none of the luxurious devices, the patches of bright coloring that reflected the owner's tastes and whims in Jessie's apartment. All the draperies—those of the windows, the dressing-table, and the antique chairs, were pure white, as were also the walls. The carpet was a sober drab, checkered with narrow lines of blue. The aspect of the whole was so chill and grave on this bleak night, that Eunice shivered as at the breath of winter, as she drew up a seat to a stand in the middle of the floor, and leaned her head upon the hard wood. Not a tear or word escaped her, but a deft and an invisible engraver was at work upon her features, sharpening outlines, deepening here a stroke and there a furrow, until the father would not have known his child.

I said, many pages back, that Orrin Wyllys' victims made no moan. Least of them all, was this one likely to publish her case to the world,—to shriek out her great and sudden woe in the ear of heaven and of her kind. She had never loved before she met him, and the discovery of this curious fact had stimulated his professional zeal—animated his pride in the honor and success of his vocation. He had found the key to her heart, and had used it. Love is no holiday romance when it comes thus late in life to a woman of large capacity for affection, and a will, the strength of which has hitherto made the repression of such seeking instincts and needs as win for weaker girls the reputation of lovingness and dependence, appear even to those who know her best like tranquil contentment with her allotted share of love and companionship. She had heard herself called, "a predestined old maid," ever since her mother left her, a demure infant, apt and serious beyond her years—to become her father's co-worker and comforter. Her calm smile at the nickname looked like conscious superiority to dread of the obloquy—a fear that infects all classes of her sex. Her love was as reticent as her longing for affection had been. Orrin's most insidious arts had not sufficed to surprise her into confession. Of marriage he had never spoken, nor she permitted herself to think. Her attachment was artless and uncalculating as a child's. He had convinced her that the subtle sympathy of their souls had made them one from their earliest meeting; that he had then recognized in her his spirit-mate. The seductive cant came trippingly from his tongue with the fluent convincingness of much practice, and she was listening to it for the first time. His dual game was adroitly conducted, and the result was a triumphant cap-sheaf to his harvest of hearts. His bride-expectant would have torn her flaxen hair—natural and artificial— with rage had she guessed how tame he found his pursuit of herself; how deficient in the flavor of excitement that had marked his courtship of the beautiful but fortuneless country girls.

The hall-clock rang out nine strokes when Eunice shook off her reverie, and unlocked a drawer of her bureau. It was lined with silver paper, and the odor of dried violets stole into the still, cold air when she opened it. A bunch of withered flowers; a small herbarium filled by Wyllys and herself in their woodland and mountain rambles,—the vignette on the title-page, from his pencil; all the inscriptions, names of specimens, and poetical legends, penned by his hand; a thin bundle of letters and notes; five or six books—favorite works with both of them—composed the contents. She took them out carefully, one by one, and laid them in a heap upon the table. Then, she sought in the closet for a walnut box, one of her childhood's treasures, an oblong casket with a sliding top and a strong lock. Without audible evidence of suffering, she arranged the relics within it, with the nice regard to neatness and order which was, with her, intuitive as it had become habitual. The last article was a volume of Spenser's "Faerie Queene"—an English edition elegantly illustrated. Wyllys had sent it to her, the Christmas Jessie passed with Mrs. Baxter. His pencillings were upon several pages, and one of the fly-leaves bore an extract from Tennyson. He had apologized for transcribing it, there, in the letter accompanying the gift, by saying that it was ever in his mind, when he watched or talked with her. No eyes save his and hers had ever seen the lines as written upon that page, and they were the more precious to her that this was so.

> Eyes not down-dropt, nor over-bright, but fed
> With the clear-pointed flame of chastity;
> Clear without heat, undying, tended by
> Pure vestal thoughts in the translucent fane
> Of her still spirit; locks (not wide-dispread)>
> Madonna-wise on either side her head;
> Sweet lips, whereon perpetually did reign
> The summer calm of golden charity, —
> Were fixed shadows of thy fixed mood.

She unclosed the book and re-read them before consigning it to its place. How vividly arose before her the scene of that Christmas Eve, when the parcel was brought to her! Her father always spent the evening of the twenty-fourth of December in his study—and fasting. It was an anniversary with him; scrupulously observed for many years, of what event or crisis in his life his daughters never knew. Eunice had made her preparations for a lonely evening by her chamber-fire; collected her books and work about her that she might not feel too sadly the want of human converse. But she had touched none of these; was sitting, her head on her hand, gazing into the fire, hearkening to the wind as it flung fierce dashes of sleet against the windows, and longing, how hungrily! for some visible evidence that she was remembered and missed by another, as she thought of and missed him. Into her solitude had come his gift and letter, and the night was all light about her; the world was no more dark and cold and tempestuous. She walked in Paradise, hand in hand with the good genius who had wrought the spell.

The idealistic character of woman's love is at once her blessing and her curse. Orrin Wyllys, at that hour dancing at a Christmas rout, the gayest of the season, looking meaning but unuttered flatteries into other eyes; feigning—as he best could feign—to wait as for the sentence of life and death, upon other "sweet lips," would have laughed in unmixed amusement had he seen, in a magic mirror, the representment of himself before which a pure, fervent soul was laying votive offerings of her best affections and richest fancies;—to which she was looking up as to the highest of human intelligences, the embodiment of manhood's virtues and graces. While to her the delusion was happiness without stain or shade, while it lasted.

It was over now! Returning from the pursuit of these shadows—dearer and fairer than any real joy and positive delight that would ever visit her solitary life,—she let the leaves of the book she still held unfurl slowly under her fingers, reading a line here, a paragraph there, always those marked by the hand that must never meet hers again with the lingering touch which said more than the most impassioned words from other tongues. A blue ribbon was inserted at one place, where a passage was encircled by pencilled brackets, while in the margin was written, "E. K."

> Her angel's face
> As the great eye of heaven shinéd bright,
> And made a sunshine in a shady place.

Eunice shut her eyes in a throe of memory that ploughed deep pain-lines in her visage. Hell may keep, but earth has not a keener torment than the contemplation of what was once sweetest joy,—now changed into shameful agony.

The book had fallen to the floor and lay still open at the page marked by the ribbon. In picking it up, her eye rested upon another line—unmarked.

At last, in close heart shutting up her pain.

The rest of Eunice Kirke's life was a commentary upon that passage.

The travail of concealment began when she turned the lock upon the mementos—few and innocent—of her only love-dream. Hitherto, it had been a pearl, too priceless and pure to be exposed to other eyes.

Defaced and crushed by one rude blow, it was something to be thrust out of sight, kept beyond the chance of suspicion or detection—buried in a nameless grave.

The key of the casket was a tiny thing, at which she looked for an instant in irresolution that ended in her raising the window, and flinging it far into the garden. The rain would soon beat it into the loose mould. It would be rusted into uselessness before the spring plough-share brought it again to the surface. Upon the lid of the box she fastened a card.

"*To be buried with me,*" she wrote upon it with fingers that did not tremble.

The grave seems near and welcome in the ague-fit that shakes the soul from the divine illusion of reciprocal affection. There was not a symptom of sickly sentimentalism in Eunice's nature; but she did feel that she could have said farewell to existence and the few she loved, with less effort than was required to dress her countenance in its wonted serenity, and go back to her sister; to speak and act as if a thunderbolt had not riven the ground at her feet; to consult her rustic and unobservant handmaid about homely details of the morrow's housekeeping. Confirmations all of them—of the stubborn fact that the business of life—its tug and sweat and strain, halts not for broken heart-strings.

If the iron be blunt, a man must lay to it more strength. If the spirit refuse to bear its part in the appointed work of the hour, or day, or life, the muscles and brain must be educated to perform double duty. This toiling and reeking at the galley-oar may bring power to the sinews, and hardness to the flesh, but woe to him by whose offence the burden is bound upon the guiltless!

# CHAPTER XIX

The third Sabbath in October was bland and bright as June. Roy, who had arrived in Dundee on Saturday evening, invited his wife to a stroll in the garden with him after the dispersion of the afternoon congregation. There were more sere than green leaves in the rose labyrinth, but one side of the arbor was covered by a thrifty *micra phylia* that had been known to keep its foliage from Autumn to Spring when the winter was not severe, and which had put forth, within a week, a few large milk-white roses, warmed into delicious fragrance by the sunny day.

"Sweets to the sweet!" said Roy, cutting a half-open blossom and a bud, and fastening them in Jessie's brooch. "I wish they did not match your cheeks so nearly, Love!"

She smiled faintly.

"I am gaining strength rapidly. There is nothing the matter with me, except that I have not enough to do to keep me from moping. There is one thing you must let me speak of while Eunice is not by,"—she continued, hurriedly. "I may not have appeared grateful for your permission to remain here until her arrangements about the school are completed, but I am thankful! I feel your goodness—your generosity, deeply! I wish I were more worthy of it!"

Unconsciously, she had laid hold of the lappel of his coat, and was fingering it nervously. Then—a girlish trick she used to practise when coaxing or bantering her father, and, occasionally, when talking saucily with himself—she began with deliberate fingers to button the coat from the throat down. "Making a mummy of me, Madcap!" was the alliterative comment Mr. Kirke usually made when the process was finished. Roy recollected it now, and smiled to himself. The action—her first voluntary caress since his return from abroad, thrilled him with ecstasy. Her downcast eyes and trembling lips recalled, in one rapturous rush, thoughts of the shy dalliance of the girl he had wooed amid these bowers. He was winning her back to her true self,—or, rather, nature and affection were recovering from the lethargy induced by the shock she had sustained.

"My wife must never speak to me of gratitude!" he said, restraining the pæan the heart would have sung through the lips. "Your happiness should be—if I know myself—is my chief consideration. Much as I regret Eunice's refusal to share our dwelling, I should be savage in my unkindness if I were to add to your disappointment by denying your request that you might be left together a week or two longer. Nor do I wish to punish her, or, in any manner, express my chagrin at her determination. She is actuated by motives which are weighty in her estimation. The sight of her glistening eyes when I told her, this morning, that you were not to be separated while she remained in the Parsonage, went far toward compensating me for my self-denial. By and by, my bird will nestle in my bosom, settle herself in our home. The knowledge that you are, indeed and in truth, mine, dear one, renders me patient, almost satisfied, in your absence. If I say hourly, in the thought of your coming to and dwelling with me—'God speed the day!' the aspiration does not incline me to force your inclination, to withhold from you a reasonable indulgence, that I may see you the sooner in your right place. I would be your husband—not your jailor, my pet!"

It was impossible to look into his moved face; to hear the cadence of passion and yearning that trembled along the last sentences, and not believe that, whatever might be the record of his past loves and defections, his whole heart was now given to her who bore his name. The listener's paroxysm of humility bowed her in spirit to his feet. He was heaping burning coals upon her shamed head.

"And God make me fit for that home!" she said, solemnly, lifted in the exaltation of high resolve above the mental apathy and physical repulsion which had, up to this hour, made this enforced union an ever-present nightmare. "Indeed, Roy, I will strive to be a good wife! I have nothing to live for except the hope of making you happy. You know what I am, weak and faulty—a spoiled child from the beginning, to whom, everything like discipline was unknown until lately. And then—one stroke followed another so rapidly that I have hardly been sane, I think. But I do want to satisfy you in every respect, or so far as one like me can!"

"'So far as you can!'" his whole soul in the eyes that beamed into hers, and in the sweet, proud smile irradiating his grave features. "The work is done, dearest! My cup runneth over. It will scarcely bear a rose-leaf this evening,—only this seal of our renewed covenant, my angel of blessing, my good, true *wife!*" bending to kiss her.

He remembered afterward, how she clung to his shoulder and hid her face there, when he placed her beside him on the bench in the arbor, where they sat out the half-hour of sunset as they had so many others in days gone by.

Eunice, seated behind the tea-urn when they obeyed Patsey's summons to supper, noted the lessened gloom of her sister's mien and Roy's expression of radiant content; saw, when they gathered about the hearth for the evening's talk, that Roy took in his clasp the hand which generally lay listlessly across its fellow in Jessie's lap, and that she allowed him to retain it. Saw and was thankful for these slight harbingers of the return of the love and brightness which were once her child's life. Tried to comfort herself in her isolation with the belief that the night was passing from her darling's spirit.

"Wounds soon heal in hearts young and healthy as is hers!" she thought. "For this, at least, I may return hearty thanks."

Within two days after the receipt of Roy's first letter, Eunice had announced to Jessie the reverse of her plans for the winter. Instead of removing with them to Hamilton, she had decided to hire a cottage in the village, and open a school for girls. She had partially engaged both house and pupils before she broached the subject to her sister. Thoroughly aroused from her selfish languor by the startling intelligence, Jessie had opposed the scheme with might and main. Accustomed as she was to Eunice's calm but resolute measures, and her taciturnity respecting her own views, wants, and plans, this retreat from a position which had not been taken without much and serious thought, filled her with consternation. Having plied her unsuccessfully with arguments and entreaties of her own devising, Jessie wrote to Roy, begging him to use his powerful influence to avert the threatened evil.

"I cannot do without her!" she said, without staying to reflect upon what might be the husband's feeling on reading the avowal, "unlike as we are and reserved as we have been to one another on some subjects, our hearts are knit together by bands which are all the stronger for our late loss. In the anticipation of this parting, my only sister seems to me like my second soul—the other part of myself. I shall be less than half a woman without her. You can do more with her than any one else. If you desire my happiness, and I know you do, entreat her not to leave me!"

If aught in this letter wounded Fordham, nobody knew it. He wrote to Eunice forthwith and urgently; did his best to dissuade her from the novel project, partly because he loved and respected her, chiefly because the matter was one that concerned Jessie's comfort and happiness. He accomplished nothing, except to elicit from Eunice the admission that she had no counter-reasoning to offer, and a mild but firm repetition of her unalterable resolve. He made a second attempt on Saturday evening, during Jessie's absence from the room. Eunice sewed on steadily without a word, while he set forth the disadvantages of her present plan—the advantages of the former. Finally, brought to bay by his argument and searching questions, she confronted him abruptly.

"I must have work, and plenty of it, just now, Roy! I *dare* not be idle! When it shall be safe and best for me to rest and think, I will accept your offer. I beg you to believe that I act from principle—not caprice. I am sure that I am doing right. And now, please say no more."

He desisted at that, and with characteristic magnanimity, undertook to reconcile his wife to the separation, by holding out the hope that it was but temporary, besides inquiring into the minutiæ of her design, and lending her what assistance she required in the furtherance of it. All was in train when he returned to his post of duty on Thursday morning. Repairs were in progress upon the leased cottage, which was pretty and convenient; twenty pupils engaged to begin lessons early in November; the sale of the surplus furniture was over, and the sisters, with Patsey, were busy getting the rest of their effects in order for transportation. Jessie was to follow in two weeks, when she had seen Eunice and the faithful servant domiciled in their new abode.

It was the longest fortnight Roy had ever known, although he kept his loneliness and longing to himself, concealing their existence most carefully from his wife. She would come to "him and home," on Wednesday of the second week, and he passed every hour he could spare from college duties and sleep, in getting the house ready for her reception. On Monday, arrived boxes from Dundee which he unpacked with his own hands. They contained Jessie's personal property—books, books and *bijouterie*, and the most delightful occupation of his solitude was the arrangement of these in parlor and sitting-room. He slept at "home," as he proudly called it, after these were brought in. They were too valuable to be left unguarded.

On Tuesday night, Orrin Wyllys, who had just returned from a visit of three or four days to his *fiancée*, chanced to pass the house, and seeing lights on the first floor, rang the bell.

Roy answered it. He was in dressing-gown and slippers—a cigar in one hand, a book in the other.

"A domesticated Benedict to the life!" laughed his cousin, as he followed him into the library. "Aha! there is an old and valued acquaintance."

The portrait of the girl at the wishing-well hung opposite the door, and, he observed, in exact range of Roy's vision as he sat in his chair.

"You will find many more if you will use your eyes. Come with me."

The dining-room adjoined the library, and the parlors were just across the hall. A bronze statuette of Pallas—four feet high, mounted upon a column of Egyptian marble—presented to the popular professor by the students, was the most conspicuous ornament; but scattered here and there were many interesting works of art selected by him in foreign lands—always with reference to Jessie's tastes and wishes. The piano was Orrin's bridal gift—a surprise held in reserve by the fond husband to brighten the coming home of his household deity. But the sitting-room back of the state apartments, was the one on which he had expended most care and time. A bay-window did duty for the more roomy oriel, and the shelf, which was an extension of the sill, was filled with plants.

"Next Spring we will set a root of jessamine outside," remarked Roy, when Orrin praised the infant creepers—ivy and passion-flower—on the inside of the casement.

The carpet was mosses, green, gray, and russet, specked with red-topped lichens; the walls were flushed with pink. Jessie's escritoire was in one corner, her work-stand in another. A reading-lamp, with its alabaster shade, was upon the centre-table, and a low lounging chair beside it. The picture of Jessie's mother hung over the mantel; Jessie's books strewed the stands, and were ranged in rows within a handsome bookcase at the back of the room. Choice engravings were hung in good lights, and within the fireplace lay long, well-seasoned logs ready for lighting.

"Beauty's bower!" said Orrin, gazing about him with unqualified approbation. "Who would have given you credit for such a genius for furnishing? For the individuality of your appointments shows that you are not indebted to the upholsterer for the charming effect. But perhaps you have worked under orders. Did Mrs. Fordham and her sister give you general directions?"

"None. I am happy to have the approval of a connoisseur," rejoined Roy, lightly. "I knew, of course, what Jessie would like, and have tried to please her. Upholsterers and *cartes blanches* from papa, and the toils of magnificence are the luxuries (and nuisances) of men who marry heiresses. As perhaps you have discovered."

"Sagely guessed! I heard little besides millinery, dressmaking, and upholstery talk while in B— —. Ponderous preparations, so it struck me, for such everyday events as marrying, giving in marriage, and going to housekeeping. I had come to the conclusion that I was anti-domestic in my proclivities, but a sight of this idyl of a home has staggered the belief. I am glad you are married, old fellow!" clapping him on the shoulder. "I could not tell you in a month *how* glad!"

"Don't begin, then!" Roy led the way to the library. "Else, not to be outdone, I must take at least a year in which to express my gratification at the event."

Orrin eyed him furtively while he affected to be engrossed in the delicate operation of lighting the cigar tendered by the host. Roy's clear, open brow, sunny smile, and the hearty ring of his voice were indubitable signs of the sincerity of his happiness. It was with a lighter spirit—I leave conscience out of the question—that his kinsman threw himself back in his comfortable chair, and prepared to enjoy the evening.

"The last of my *quasi* widowerhood!" said Roy. "I wish it were the last of your bachelor days, Orrin!"

"*Ca viendra!*" returned the other, his cigar between his teeth. "Next month is December."

"I hope your wife will take as kindly to me as mine does to you!" pursued Roy. "And that I may, one day, have the opportunity to prove by services rendered her, my appreciation of the care you have taken of my interests in my absence."

"Don't speak of it, my dear boy!" said Orrin, hastily.

Even he colored slightly at the unintentional sarcasm. He coughed to emit the smoke that had gone down the wrong way, and this gave him time to rally his ideas. No harm had come of his innocent pastime. Roy was none the wiser, and his bride had had the advantage of a new sensation in the development of her latent capacities for loving and suffering. She would be better and stronger all her life; her character would gain breadth and fibre for the emotion that had stirred the depths of her being. It was wholesome, if sharp, discipline—a sort of spiritual subsoil ploughing, without which she might never have developed aright. Women were a marvellous and an entertaining study. Their powers of craft and concealment were beyond man's ken or imitation. The most imprudently passionate of them acted sometimes with circumspection that would put a Talleyrand to the blush. Jessie, mad and desperate as she was at her last interview with himself, had nevertheless reconsidered her resolution to reveal her inconstancy to her lawful lover, and judiciously judging that the Past was gone beyond recall, had taken up with the old love so soon as the new one was off. She could not have done better for all parties. "Scenes," except when sentimental and *en tête-à-tête*, were a vulgarism to be eschewed by refined people.

"Jack shall have Gill,
Nought shall go ill."

he repeated, mentally, thus salving the smart caused by Roy's thanks. "Jessie and I will be capital friends and neighbors. She will like me none the less because she knows that, had she been possessed of the fair and fond Hester's wealth, her destiny would have been changed. She is too acute of perception not to comprehend that, in that case, my sense of what was due to her and myself would not have let me resign her, even to my honored cousin, here. But what is, is best, I suppose.

"You have never met my Dulcinea, I believe?" he said aloud, both cigar and windpipe being in good working order by the time he reached this consolatory sequel.

"I have not had that pleasure. Jessie gave me a slight sketch of her—a mere outline, which I hope to fill up for myself, shortly, from life."

"Then," meditated the cool and candid bridegroom-elect, "my tow-headed divinity lied egregiously about that old affair! I must cross-examine her in earnest, and if my suspicion is correct, make her retract certain counts in her indictment against Jessie's husband. I owe him that much reparation. Since they are a wedded unit, things should go upon velvet so far as is consistent with the fact of human imperfection. I'll send the lovely Hester to make amends to Mrs. Fordham, some time. If I do not forget it."

He was in one of his gracefully indolent moods to-night, and did not hurry himself in speech.

"She is not handsome. You would not, I fear, consider her even pretty," he resumed, after a few lulling puffs, such as might be necessary to temper loverly exaggeration. "But she is a dear, affectionate, pliant little thing, and will make just the wife a *blasé* world citizen like myself needs. I hope—I think you will like her. But I don't expect you to see in her the peer of your glorious Jessie, however well she may suit me."

Roy, when left alone again, pondered this speech dissatisfiedly.

"I am not quite content with this match, nor with Orrin's tone. I had not looked for a lover's rhapsodies, knowing his critical taste in these matters, but he ought not to acknowledge or feel the need of apologies for his choice. I am afraid his love does not leave him as little to wish for and to fear, as mine does me."

He looked up at the portrait with a smile.

"But there is only one Jessie in the world, and she will be here to-morrow night."

Still standing before the picture, he made an involuntary gesture, as of folding something in his arms.

"My darling! soon to be my angel in the house! I think it would kill me to lose you now."

His sudden motion had struck a book from the corner of the table, exposing a letter that lay beneath. It was a foreign envelope, and had probably been given to the servant by the postman that afternoon, and placed there by her with the book on the top, for safe-keeping. An enclosure fell out as he opened the cover—a letter that had arrived in Heidelberg after he set out for home, said a line from a fellow-student in the University. The smile lingered lovingly about mouth and eyes, while he tore off the inner wrapper.

The superscription was Jessie's; the note the short and cold farewell she had indited after her parting with Orrin Wyllys, on the 6th of September.


"No harm done!" reiterated the affectionate kinsman, walking slowly along to his lodgings, under the pure moon. "I should have been sorry had she carried her threat into execution; spoiled her own prospects, and made Roy wretched. But I could find it in my heart to regret the witch even now that I am on the eve of beatification. The affair was interesting—most engaging while it lasted—had more cayenne and wine in it than this very lawful and eminently remunerative love-making. My 'lassie wi' the lint-white locks,' says it is 'just the sweetest thing in the world.' *Peut être!*

'An excellent piece of work, Madame Lady!
Would it were done!'"

# CHAPTER XX

Roy was at the dépôt Wednesday afternoon to meet his wife.

"You are not well, I am afraid!" she said, when they were in the carriage that was to convey them home.

"I am not sick, but I have had much to think of and to do, lately, and I may look somewhat jaded," he answered. "You left Eunice well, you say?"

"Quite well, thank you! You have overworked yourself in getting the house ready for me. You should have left that for me to do."

"It was not necessary. As it is, you will find much room for alteration and improvement, I doubt not. You were fortunate in meeting with a pleasant escort on your journey. Are you much fatigued?"

"No, but my head aches a little," turning her face to the window.

She was disappointed in her reception. The parting from Eunice had been a grievous trial; the journey filled with mournful thoughts of the past that now lay so very far behind her. In turning her back upon her parents' graves and her birthplace, she seemed to have parted company forever with the blithe girl who had been born and had grown up to woman's estate, careless and joyous as the swallows that had for a century built their nests in the belfry of the church-tower. She had almost forgotten how Jessie Kirke felt and acted. Yet she was thankful that in the midst of melancholy and dazement, her appointed way lay clear and open before her; that she had still a sure staff on which to lean,—the hope and resolve that she would do her duty bravely and well in the sphere for which her marriage-vow had set her apart. It was indicative of the generous temper and sound sense that never failed to assert themselves when the momentary tumult of passion had passed, which neither her faults nor the influence of the tempter had warped, that she had never, for one moment, blamed Roy for hurrying forward their marriage. They were "troth-plight," as her Scottish ancestors would have put it. She had said, "If you insist upon the fulfilment of my promise, I will submit to your decision." And she had not said it idly. He had taken her at her word, as he had the right to do, and by that pledge she would abide.

Lonely and tired, the sight of Roy's face in the crowd of strangers upon the platform of the Hamilton station had cheered her heart like a cordial. She forgot that he was her husband; remembered him only as a noble and faithful friend in whose presence she would be no longer solitary and sad. She was even conscious of a proud sense of proprietorship in the fine-looking, dignified man who was the first to enter the car when it stopped,—a consciousness that flushed her cheeks faintly, and quickened her pulses, as she introduced him to the gentleman who had acted as her escort and heard his well-chosen words of acknowledgment for the favor done him. He had not kissed her then—she supposed because there were so many looking on; but after taking his place beside her in the carriage, he might surely tell her that her coming gave him joy; repeat something of the rapturous anticipations that had overflowed his heart in writing his last letter, received by her the night before. His face was very pale, his eyes abstracted, his voice constrained. Anything more unlike the Roy she had known in Dundee could hardly be imagined, without changing the identity of the man. It was not surprising that a qualm of home-sickness weakened her heroic resolutions; put to flight her dreams of forgetting her unhappiness in the sustained effort to be and do all he wished.

Roy saw the struggle and surmised, in part, the cause of it; but what could he say to assuage or encourage? The caresses and fond words with which he had sought to console her in the earlier days of her desolation must, he now saw in the lurid light shed upon his honeymoon by that terrible letter, have aggravated her sufferings.

Professing to be her protector, he had played the part of a brutal ravisher; had torn her,—shrinking and crying out against the loathed union she felt would "be a sin—a fearful sin," from her free, happy girl-life, and bound her, soul and body, in fetters more hateful and enduring than manacles of steel. After the first shock of horror and of grief, he forgot the wrong he had sustained in his overmastering compassion for her. And he could not free her! Loving her better than he did his own happiness and life, he was powerless to ensure her peace of mind by restoring her to liberty. Had he been other than the true Christian and true man he was, the distracting anguish of that conviction would have driven him to madness and to suicide, as a sequel to the fearful vigil that followed the discovery of his real position.

Light came with the morning, and strength for the day. His course was plain—to mitigate the rigors of her fate by such kindly deeds as a brother might perform for the promotion of a sister's welfare; by abstaining from even such manifestations of affection as are a brother's right. There should be no formal explanation until she had recovered from the fatigue of her journey, and begun to feel at home in her new abode. Thus much he could and would do, and await the result.

"What a pretty, pretty house!" exclaimed Jessie, as the carriage drew up at the gate of a cottage on the southern slope of one of the hills on which the handsome town was built.

She had meant to praise his selection of a residence however ordinary its appearance, but her enthusiastic admiration was genuine.

Roy smiled, but not with the glad gleam she looked to see.

"It is good and kind in you to say so! If you can be satisfied here, I ask nothing better or grander."

A tidy girl opened the door, whom Jessie recognized with pleased surprise as a former servant in Dr. Baxter's family.

"Why, Phoebe! This *is* homelike! How very generous in Cousin Jane to give you up to me!"

"She said you might find me useful, Miss Jessie! I beg your pardon— Mrs. Fordham!" replied the girl, dropping a courtesy.

Jessie colored, Roy thought, painfully, at the as yet unfamiliar name. He interfered to save her further embarrassment, in the shape of congratulations.

"You will show her to her room, if you please, Phoebe. And then let her have a cup of tea. She has a headache. Your trunks will be sent up in the course of half an hour, Jessie, but I would not advise you to wait for them, or take the trouble of changing your travelling-dress. You must begin your life here by doing just as you choose in such matters."

He met her in the hall when she ran down, ten minutes later, fearful lest she had kept him waiting, and led her into the supper room; letting her take her place behind the tea-tray without one of the tenderly gallant speeches with which a bridegroom would naturally install his bride in the chair always appropriated by the mistress of heart and home. He was attentive to her wants, and talked as much as usual—perhaps more—in the endeavor to put her at her ease; telling how the flowers upon the tea-table and in her chamber were sent over at noon from Judge Provost's conservatory; that the silver service was a present from the Baxters, the bronze mantel-clock from Fanny Provost, who was very anxious to see her and resume their old intimacy. Selina Bradley had sent the chased silver butter-bowl, and other Hamilton families had testified their good-will by elegant and suitable gifts.

"I am every day more glad that you spent last winter here," he said. "You do not come as a stranger; have already pleasant associations with our town and its inhabitants, and gained a foothold, I find, in many hearts."

He had unwittingly dealt as direct a blow at the secret panel that hid the skeleton in her heart, as he had at Orrin Wyllys' indurated conscience the previous evening.

Jessie had no words in which to reply; sought to conceal her confusion by steadfastly regarding the pattern on her plate—one of a set of china Roy had purchased in Dresden, she discovered, presently, when she remarked upon its beauty.

"I had no idea you had such exquisite taste!" She made a bold attempt to break through the nameless but powerful constraint that kept down everything like easy or merry converse on her part. "I expect to be in a state of perpetual astonishment on that score for a long time to come. I did not know that learned scholars ever condescended to consider such petty details of domestic life as porcelain and carpets."

He put back his chair without replying directly to the compliment, at which, to her mortification, he looked rather pained than pleased.

"If you have finished your supper, perhaps you would like to go over the house?" he said, politely. "Or, if you are tired, we will postpone it until to-morrow."

"I should greatly prefer going now!" catching at the prospect of some mitigation of the growing stiffness.

The survey was a quiet progress for the most part, certainly not accomplishing the end she had hoped for. Roy said little, and Jessie felt very awkward, as door after door was opened, and she appreciated the thoughtfulness that had ministered to her comfort, from first to last, yet was forbidden by the mysterious spell chaining her tongue, to thank him who had wrought it all. But when they reached the sitting-room, where the flames were crackling and curling among the wood on the hearth, and her chair and fire-screen awaited her, the home-restfulness of the scene broke down the ice wall. The feelings that had gathered to oppression upon her heart, overflowed her eyes and choked her articulation.

"This is too much!" she exclaimed, catching Roy's hand in hers, and gazing tearfully into his face. "Oh! what am I—"

She could say no more.

"The mistress of this room and this house!" responded Roy, in kindly seriousness. "One who has a right to expect every attention I can bestow. This is your sanctum. Nobody shall enter it without your permission."

Jessie tried to smile playfully.

"Excepting yourself!"

"When you want me, I shall come!" was the evasive reply.

"Surely you will not wait—"

The remonstrance was cut short by a tap at the door, signalling Mrs. Baxter's impetuous entrance.

"My dearest lamb!" she cried, with a strangled sob, clasping her cousin in her embrace.

"The doctor *would* come the instant he had swallowed his tea!" she tried to cover Jessie's emotion and her own by saying, when she could speak clearly. "I told him it was barbarously unfeeling and unromantic; that, according to all rules of etiquette and sentiment, you should pass this evening without the intrusion of company. But he was obstinate. I don't believe you two have the *remotest* conception of his favoritism of you!"

Meantime, the doctor had, in his odd fashion, slipped his hand under the young wife's chin, and raised to the light a strangely agitated face— eyes swimming in tears, forehead slightly puckered with the effort after self-control, and little eddies of smiles breaking up around the mouth. Roy saw in it the whole history of the shipwreck of her heart and life, and her womanly determination to keep the knowledge of the disaster to herself. Would the physiognomist's keenly solemn gaze detect as much?

Neither of the lately wedded pair was prepared for the remark with which he released the blushing Jessie.

"I wanted to see if the heart of her husband could safely trust in her. My daughter! do you know what a good man you have married?"

"Do not raise her expectations to an unreasonable height, my dear sir!" interposed Roy, in time to forestall her reply. "And let me thank you, in her name and in mine, for the honor you have done us in this early visit."

The doctor accepted the compliment and the chair that the host wheeled forward, in profound silence. The conversation had been carried on by the others for several minutes before he again joined in. He was aroused then by his wife's laudations of Orrin's generosity as displayed in his bridal present.

"I don't see how you can take it so quietly!" she berated the recipient. "One would suppose pianos were given away every day! And you should value the instrument the more highly because it is the gift of your great admirer and true friend, Mr. Wyllys. I assure you, Mr. Fordham, nothing could exceed his care of and devotion to her, for your sake and in your name, of course! while you were over the seas and far away."

"True friend!" echoed the doctor's dryest, most rasping tones. "Humph!"

"*Now*, my love, I do *implore* that you will not drag forward that most unjust and unreasonable prejudice in the present company!" cried his wife, in a nervous flutter from her bonnet-crown to her gaiter-tips. "If I *have* failed to convince you that it is groundless and absurd, oblige me by withholding the expression of it, here and now!"

"My good Jane!" returned the imperturbable spouse—"Where else could the truth be so fitly spoken as in the hearing of judicious friends? I am sorry to say, Mr. Fordham, that my excellent wife and myself do not agree respecting Mr. Wyllys' character and actions."

"Doctor! doctor!" ejaculated the frantic woman, plunging forward, at an angle of forty-five degrees, to pluck his sleeve. "You forget that you are addressing Mr. Wyllys' cousin!"

"A candid man, and a fair judge of human nature and motives, nevertheless," her lord went on to say, with a stiff little bow in the direction of the person named. "The only safe rule among friends is candor. It is seldom I attribute sinister purposes to one whom I do not know certainly to be malevolent or hypocritical, but when I declare it to be my firm conviction that Orrin Wyllys—(of whom the best thing I know is that he has descended physically from the same stock that produced your husband, my child!)"—this to Jessie—"when I affirm that I believe him to be a wolf who ravens safely and reputably under the cowardly cover of sheep's clothing, I am not, as my dear Jane here would persuade herself and you, the victim of causeless prejudice."

"Dearest, I entreat!" broke in the wife, at her last gasp of distress.

His discourse moved on majestically. There were four knots in his handkerchief already.

"From the moment I heard Mr. Wyllys caution Mrs. Baxter not to allude in her letter of invitation to our Jessie, to information he had supplied relative to her person, residence, and education, I distrusted the singleness of his desire for the resumption of Mrs. Baxter's intercourse with the family of her early friend. When the invited guests arrived, and I learned that the terms of their previous intercourse entitled him to become her cavalier on all occasions; her preceptor and referee in doubtful cases of conscience and conduct;—when I compared this circumstance with his careless and apparently accidental mention of her to Mrs. Baxter, and his pretended indifference to her coming, I made up my mind that he was particularly interested in her for some reason he did not care to divulge. I believe still that this was the case. I believe that, knowing her to be betrothed to his cousin, he strove, consciously and systematically, to win her from her allegiance. I thank God that he did not succeed; that she has given herself and her happiness into the keeping of a true and honorable gentleman!"

"I am grateful to you, doctor, for your staunch friendship for myself, and your paternal guardianship of my wife!"

Roy Fordham's full, pleasant tones reached Jessie's ears like an angelic benediction through the seething chaos that was swallowing her up.

"I am glad, moreover, that you have, in the present company, introduced the subject of your misgivings regarding my cousin's behavior while I was away. I appointed him my proxy before I left my betrothed and my native land. The attentions that misled you into doubt of his right dealing were paid in that character. I cannot have you undervalue the 'true and honorable gentleman' I know Orrin Wyllys to be. He is my *friend*!"

The doctor tugged at his cravat-bow and stared into the chandelier. Mrs. Baxter gulped down all the solicitude she could swallow, and threw all the rest into the deprecating look she cast upon Roy. He stood before his zealous old superior—courteous, kind, but earnest in defence of his absent friend—the model of gallant manliness, thought the abject creature, cowering in the shadow of Mrs. Baxter's chair, half dead with remorse and the dread of additional questioning.

The love of this man she had trodden under foot! forgotten affection and duty to him in the mad, wicked delirium wrought by the wiles of one whom Roy, in the simplicity of his integrity, still accounted honest and faithful. A cheat and a coward Jessie had written Orrin down since that early September day when he confided to her the fact of his engagement, and shrank visibly at the suggestion of Roy's anger at his shameless breach of faith. She stigmatized him now, in the council of her thoughts, as a liar from the beginning. He had manoeuvred, then, to procure Mrs. Baxter's invitation for herself, while he denied to her that she had ever been named between them until after this was sent; had inveigled her away from the shelter of her father's roof and the guard of her sister's care, that he might establish his fell influence over her. Would not Roy, with all his generous trust in his cousin's honor and friendship, compare the doctor's mal-apropos statement with her confession of the change in herself, and arrive at a tolerably correct perception of the truth that would blast her forever in his sight, as not merely weak and fickle, but forward and unmaidenly?

When the throbbing of her heart would let her listen intelligently to what was going on, the doctor had been beguiled into a dissertation upon Druidistic history, by Roy's exhibition of a paper-weight in the form of an altar, encircled by a wreath of mistletoe, graven out of a bit of stone he had picked up at Stonehenge. His considerate spouse carried him off before one-third of the knots in his handkerchief were untied. Her valedictory, like her salutatory, was a diffuse apology for their intrusion upon the sacredness of the installation-eve.

"But the doctor—dear, blundering man! is amenable to no laws of conventionality," she subjoined, with an indulgent shrug and sigh.

It is questionable whether either of the persons addressed regretted the breach of etiquette. The time had gone by more swiftly and comfortably than if they had been left to themselves. As it was, an embarrassing silence followed the visitors' departure. Roy stood on the rug, facing the fire, motionless and thoughtful. Jessie, trembling in a nervous chill that changed her fingers into shaking icicles, durst not attempt to speak.

Fordham finally came out of his reverie with a start, and turned toward her apologetically.

"You are sadly tired! Our good friends were very welcome, but they have kept you up beyond your strength. May I take you to your room?"

She murmured a disclaimer of the imputation of excessive fatigue, but took his proffered arm, and they mounted the stairs together.

A bright fire burned in the large front chamber, flashed gayly back from the gilt fleur-de-lis of the delicately tinted wallpaper and the frames of the few pictures. A cosey armchair stood ready for Jessie, with a foot-cushion below it, and the marble slabs of bureau and mantel bore fragile wealth of Bohemian and frosted glass and Parian ornaments.

"Is there anything I can do to make you more comfortable?" inquired Roy, not offering to sit down. "Wouldn't a glass of wine do your head good?"

"I think not. I need nothing, thank you!" without raising her eyes from the carpet.

"I hope you will be quite rested by morning," he continued, with the same ceremonious gentleness. "I may as well explain to you that, foreseeing how frequently I shall be obliged to sit up late at my studies, I have had the chamber opposite prepared for myself. So I will bid you good-night now."

He held out his hand. She placed hers within it, silently, eyes still averted.

"Good-night, and pleasant dreams!" he repeated, with a kindly pressure of the chill fingers.

An impulse she could not control or define drew her to her feet. "Won't you kiss me, Roy?" she asked, in sorrowful humility.

She did not see how bloodless were the lips that obeyed. The salute was, to her apprehension, cold and reluctant, and, without another syllable, he passed on to the outer door. There he stopped—hesitated, with a backward glance at the drooping figure, standing where he had left her—and returned.

"I had not intended to say it yet," he said, agitatedly. "There have been times when I questioned the propriety of any attempt at self-justification. But I would not have you think worse of me than I deserve for my selfish recklessness in hurrying on our marriage. I received this letter"—giving it to her—"last night. It furnishes the clue to much that I now see ought to have checked my unseemly impatience to claim the right I believed was still mine. This was the communication to which you referred when you pleaded that the contents of your last letter should have hindered my proposal. I supposed, in the haste and excitement of the moment, that you meant the false rumor of your mother's insanity which had been treated of in a former communication, the receipt of which, let me say here, hastened my return. Not that I dreaded insanity for you, but because I gathered from your letter that you were unhappy and a prey to morbid fancies, and I hoped to be able to do you good by diverting these. If this 'last letter' which you hold had reached me in season, your request should have been granted."

He paused to master his own emotion, or to give her opportunity for reply. He may have hoped yet, in the face of the evidence to the contrary he had had, that she would retract her declaration. "I love you no longer" might represent that she was possessed by "morbid fancies" when it was penned; that under the sharp tutelage of sorrow, her affections had regained their balance.

She only sat still, her face hidden in her hands. There was a crouch in her attitude that suggested an unpleasant idea to the observer. It was that she *feared* him—his wrath and the results of this explanation. He forgot his sufferings in the desire to remove this apprehension if it existed.

"My only hope now is, that since I know what I should have perceived from the beginning, I may spare you annoyance, if not misery, by consulting your wishes and respecting your repugnances. If I could set you free, I would. My heaviest burden is the consciousness that this is impracticable. But it is my desire that, from this time, you should cease to regard me as your husband, and try to think of me as your friend. For we may still be *that* to each other—may we not, dear Jessie?"

She was moaning as in mortal pain.

"This kindness kills me! I had rather you should say that you hated me!"

"But that would not be true," said the gentle voice. "And henceforward we will be very frank and just in our dealings with one another. We will try, moreover, to put vain regrets out of sight, and to do the duty of the day; to serve our fellows and honor Him who has some merciful intent in leading us through these dark waters. Now, my child, this subject need never be renewed. Our Father knows our sorrows. To Him we will look for strength. He knows, too, the sincerity of my sad heart when I say how deeply it afflicts me to feel how much more grievous is your trial than mine."

Folding in his the hands she extended in a speechless passion of tears— her lips trying vainly to form a petition for pardon—he prayed the God of all consolation to have her in His holy keeping; to give her joy for weeping, the garment of praise for the spirit of heaviness. Then, bidding her again "Be comforted and sleep," he went out.

# CHAPTER XXI

"I knocked at Mr. Fordham's door, ma'am, as you bid, and he said that he wasn't well enough to leave his room, and would you be pleased to eat breakfast without him. And he said, ma'am, that you needn't be uneasy the leastest bit in the world, for it's only a cold and sore throat he's got, and, indeed, if I may make so bold as to say it, he's that hoarse I could scarcely hear him at all."

Phoebe eyed her mistress slyly and keenly when she had delivered her message. Although not particularly given to prying and gossip, her curiosity was excited by certain peculiarities in the home life of Mr. and Mrs. Fordham, for which the supposition that the master of the house had "picked up German ways," while abroad, did not fully account. They had distinctly separate apartments, carrying the rule of division so far that Mr. Fordham never entered his wife's sitting-room without knocking at the door, and if she invaded the library when he was in, she not only asked admittance in the same way, but apologized for interrupting his studies.

"They are too polite by half!" Phoebe estimated, judging them by her not very extensive observation and experience. "There's Mrs. Baxter will make more fuss over her dried-up atomy of a man in one day, than Mrs. Fordham does about her fine figure of a husband in a year."

She had never seen Mr. Fordham kiss or otherwise caress his bride, or indulge in any of the romping fondling which the lately wedded are prone to forget may be less interesting to spectators than to themselves. Yet, she was ready to affirm stoutly that, in her parlance, "they thought the world and all of one another;" that Mr. Fordham studied his wife's inclinations, anticipated her wishes, and ministered to her comfort more than any other gentleman she knew; while "Mr. Fordham likes this," or, "he is not fond of that," were decisive phrases in Jessie's mouth in the conduct of her domestic affairs, and her many devices to make his home-coming at noon and evening, an ever-new pleasure, called forth the continual admiration of the handmaiden.

It was a puzzle past her finding out. But here was a test that could hardly fail. The wife should, according to Phoebe's creed, fly on the wings of love and anxiety to the bedside of her sick lord; become his nurse and servitor until he recovered.

To the girl's grieved disappointment,—for she was sincerely attached to the whilom "Miss Jessie," and wanted to think well of her in all things— Mrs. Fordham said, composedly, if not coolly—"Very well, Phoebe! Bring in breakfast!" and turned again to the window at which she was standing, when the news was brought to her of her husband's sad case.

"I'm right down sorry—that I am!" grumbled the servant over the kitchen range. "I did hope she'd show some feeling for him when he's maybe took for dipthery or quincy or something else awful. And he such a good provider and well-spoken gentleman, and never so much as raising his voice in a temper with her, but treating her like a queen! I've a mind to slip up myself, and ask what he'll have to eat. These are the beautifullest muffins ever I see! She is a master hand at the like. And I know she made these, as she does all sorts of nice things, because he likes 'em. Queer she never lets on but what I get up the dishes he praises. Mistresses mostly is glad enough to pocket the compliments as belongs to their girls. She's a genuwine lady, and no mistake, but it cuts me to see her so cold-hearted to *him*. I suppose they're what folks call a 'fashionable couple.'"

While this soliloquy was going on, the subject of it stood still at the window, gazing into the street. It was a bleak December day. There had been rain in the night; then the thermometer sank abruptly, and by morning the sidewalks were glazed with ice. The earth was black and grim, the clouds, grayly sullen, seemed to rest upon the chimney-tops, and while Jessie looked, it began to snow, gently for a while, then so fast that a wavering sheet soon shut out her view of distant objects. The cottage was on a corner, and this being a side-window, gave upon the college-grounds on one hand, Judge Provost's house, garden, and lawn on the other. By changing her position never so slightly, the lady could have beheld the balconied front and imposing cupola of the Wyllys' residence, of which the happy pair had taken formal possession ten days before, postponing their bridal tour until Spring. "For," as the bride eagerly explained to everybody—"both of us have been everywhere on this side of the water, and winter-travelling is an awful bore. To be sure, we've been abroad, too, and seen everything that is worth seeing. So we are beating our brains to devise something *recherché*" (pronounced *rechurchy*) "in the way of a wedding-trip. And it is *so* sweet and romantic to come to our own home, right away! Indeed, as I told Orrin, it isn't safe to leave such carpets and furniture as ours unprotected."

Jessie had heard all this fanfaronade, and much more from Mrs. Baxter, but she was not thinking of it now. Nor did she move so as to bring the "new and superb mansion of our popular fellow-citizen, Orrin Wyllys, Esq.," within the range of her vision; only seemed to watch the falling snow, and the few passers-by who dotted the whitening streets at this early hour. In reality, she was speculating upon the meaning of the stillness in the chamber overhead. Was Roy, then, too ill to get up? Was his room comfortable? What attention from nurse or physician did he need? How was she to learn and supply his wants? It would be barbarous unkindness, if he were very sick, to stand aloof and leave the charge of him to hirelings. Yet her personal attendance would be awkward for both. She was not sure that he would approve of it, so fastidious had been his care to excuse her from such offices. He had spoken, in an off-hand way, overnight, of feeling chilly, and apologized for not offering to read the new number of a magazine to her by saying that his throat was sore. Without consulting him, she had brewed a pitcher of hot lemonade, and insisted upon his drinking it after he went to his room. He had thanked her with the invariable courtesy that met her every effort to serve him, and "was sure it was all he needed. A most agreeable prescription too!" he added, as he bore off the pitcher. It was a shock, after this pleasant parting, to hear that he was sick in bed. What if he were to be seriously ill? Her heart gave a great bound, then ceased moving for a moment. He was so robust, so full of life and energy, that this could not be.

What if he were to *die*! She too thought of diphtheria. There had been several fatal cases of it in Hamilton recently. She was pale and faint; her limbs giving way under her as she admitted the frightful supposition. What would she be—what would she do if the strong staff of his protection, the solace of his companionship, were reft from her?

For she knew that, little cause as she had given him in the circumstances attending their marriage, to cherish her as all men should—as some men do the women who love them fervently and constantly, there was hardly a wife in the land who was surrounded by the atmosphere of chivalrous devotion which encompassed her in the secluded life she led as the nominal mistress of Roy Fordham's home. Her deep mourning was a sufficient excuse for declining to enter the gay circle in which Mrs. Wyllys fluttered and her diamonds and husband shone. But Roy saw to it that she was not lonely. The Baxters, Provosts, and others of his friends were often with them during the day, and he spent his evenings, as a rule, at home.

"Will you favor me with your company in the library, or shall I come to your sitting-room?" he would ask, when supper was over.

They wrote and studied together as two friends of the same sex might; talked freely upon all subjects suggested by either—each watchful that no chance touch should wound the other; make him or her swerve quickly aside lest the next step should be upon the fresh grave that lay ever between them. In all their intercourse, Roy's apparent ease far surpassed his wife's. Cheerful, cordial, always kind and more than kind in manner and language, he yet comported himself as if there were nothing abnormal in this sort of association; as if passion and regret were alike things of the Past, to which he had said they need never again recur. No warmer love-name than "Jessie, dear," ever passed his lips, and after the night of the home bringing, he had never offered to kiss or embrace her. A hand-clasp, night and morning; a smiling bow and lively phrase, when he came in to dinner and tea, were the most affectionate courtesies exchanged. But no distraught lover, at the height of his lunacy, ever studied his mistress's fantasies, sought to penetrate and fulfil her will, as did this quiet and courtly husband that of the woman who had confessed that her heart was none of his when he married her. Flowers, fruits, birds, and books were lavished upon her; passed into her hands through other than his, but were always procured by him in response to some expressed liking on her part, or in accordance with what he imagined were her wishes or needs. Nor was his unobtrusive attention to her health less constant. In the same friendly style, he regulated exercise, diet, and work; saw that her habits were not too sedentary, and that she did not expose herself imprudently to cold, damp, or fatigue.

Her review of all this was rapid and circumstantial.

"He deserves all that I can do for him. False delicacy nor pride shall keep me back from ministering to the wants of one who is to me father, brother, friend. I may, at least, wait upon him as a hostess might tend an honored guest—a housekeeper the master of the house!" she had decided by the time Phoebe set coffee, muffins, and steak upon the table.

Then to the serving-girl's increased chagrin, she sat down, with Roy's vacant chair opposite her, and break-fasted alone.

"Not much of a breakfast, to be sure!" said Phoebe, returning at the end of ten minutes, to find the room deserted. "Half a muffin, and a cup of coffee, and she clean forgot to carve the steak! Looks like she was in love— but that can't be!"

"Come in!" said the changed voice that had wrought upon Phoebe's womanly compassion, as Jessie awaited the warrant to enter the sick-room—a faint-hearted lingerer upon the threshold. She buoyed up her courage by remembering that she was the housekeeper who had come for the orders for the day; the diffidence she railed at inwardly, as ridiculous and uncalled for, had no visible effect, except to heighten her color, and make her carry her head a trifle less loftily.

Already Mrs. Wyllys had been heard to say that, "if Mrs. Fordham were worth a million in her own right, she could not look more haughty and indifferent to people who were richer and better bred. When, as everybody knew, she was a poor preacher's daughter with just money enough to buy her wedding-clothes. Though, pity knows, they couldn't have cost much! Was there ever such awful taste, as not to lighten her mourning to suit the circumstances? Who ever heard of a bride's wearing crêpe?"

There were red spots upon Roy's cheeks, when he saw who his visitor was—probably hectic, for his demeanor was natural. With instant thought of her probable embarrassment, he put out his hand, smilingly.

"Ah! Jessie, dear! Good-morning! You are very good to visit a poor fellow in his affliction. For such a throat and head as I have to-day *are* an affliction. I seldom strike my colors to a common cold."

"This seems to me to be an uncommon one!" Jessie said, feeling his pulse with the practised touch she had learned in her parish-visiting. "You have fever. You ought to have medical advice. Who is your physician?"

"I have never had occasion to call in one since I came to Hamilton. Suppose we 'bide a bit,' as our worthy President says, and if I am not better in the course of an hour or two, we can send for Dr. Bradley. I had a trying day yesterday. Professor Fairchild is sick, and I had some of his classes in addition to my own. It is well this is Saturday. I can lie still, and rest my throat with a clear conscience. Provided"—smiling in her grave face—"provided you do not let me trouble you!"

"Trouble me! you should know better than that! But"—hesitating—"if you will let me say it"—

"Go on! there is nothing you may not say to me," he said encouragingly.

"I do think it would be better to see Dr. Bradley, at once—if only as a precautionary measure."

He started—looked at her intently.

"You are thinking of diphtheria! You ought not to have come in until that point was settled. There may be danger to you. If, through my carelessness—"

He turned his face away, unable or unwilling to finish the sentence.

"I never thought of *that!*" said Jessie, simply. "If I had, I should have come all the same. Whatever may be the doctor's opinion, I shall stay here, and take care ofs you. It is my place."

She rang the bell for Phoebe, and in Roy's hearing, ordered her to go for the doctor. She would not have her charge suspect that she was unduly alarmed, or believe there was occasion for a hasty summons. Then, she brought a sunshiny face to the bedside, and put a fresh pillow under the hot, heavy head.

"You don't know what a famous nurse I am," she said, blithely. "My father" — her voice sinking with the sacred word — "used to say that nursing was a talent, and that I was born with it."

She set to work, forthwith, without waiting for permission. Roy, regarding her silently from his bed, heartily endorsed Mr. Kirke's verdict. Not Eunice herself could have moved more soundlessly, wrought more efficiently to alleviate, so far as she could, the pain and discomfort of his situation. The doctor was at home, and obeyed the call promptly. Roy glanced inquiringly at Jessie when he was announced.

"Show him up!" was all she said, and when he followed Phoebe into the chamber, she met him with high-bred ease as the lady of the house; as the patient's wife discussed his symptoms; heard, with marked gratification, that her fears of diphtheria were unfounded, and received his directions gratefully and attentively.

"A fine woman, and a most devoted wife!" pronounced Dr. Bradley, at his luncheon-table, that day. "Let me hear no more gossip about her, girls. Remember!"

"But, Papa, they do say they live queerly!" ventured the irrepressible Selina. "Mrs. Wyllys—"

"Is a fool! see that you don't become another in listening to her twaddle!" was the peremptory reply.

Orrin Wyllys, hearing accidentally of his cousin's indisposition, called at noon, and was conducted by Phoebe, by warrant of the relationship, into Roy's presence. The chamber was heated usually by the furnace register, but Roy lay in bed gazing at the glowing pile of coals in the grate. There was a happy ray in his eyes, spontaneity in the gayety with which he welcomed his guest, that did not accord with the latter's preconceived ideas of the dolor of a sick-room.

"You look like an invalid—don't you?" was Wyllys' second remark. "This is the cheeriest place I have been in to-day. It is what the English call beastly weather, out-of-doors. I don't blame anybody for keeping his bed. I thought you showed me the room across the hall as yours when you took me through the house, that night, 'the last of your *quasi* widowerhood.'"

"We changed the arrangement afterward," rejoined Roy, carelessly. "But it is a luxury—is'n't it? to lie still on a stormy day, and stare a fire like that out of countenance; especially on a holiday, when there are no phantoms of unsaid lectures to torment one's reveries. I am enjoying it amazingly. I hadn't the remotest conception that being sick was so delightful."

"By Jove! I should think you would luxuriate in it, unless you have less brains than I give you credit for! With an *houri* for head-nurse, too! I say! get out of that! I can play the sentimental sufferer as well as you, and I have a native bias for lazy luxury, which you haven't. I dare say, you cunning dog! if all were told, there is some dainty mess preparing for you below stairs,—a triumph of conjugal affection and culinary skill, that should be tasted by none but an educated appetite. A Teuton like yourself would be as well suited with bretzels and sauerkraut, washed down by a gallon of lager. I am a devout predestinarian, and here lies the case. I have a canine hunger upon me. I am on my way home to luncheon. Without, 'the day is dark and cold and dreary.' I am *led* to this corner of cosiness and comfort and fairy fare to dispossess you. Impostor! how dare you lie there, and grin at my emptiness and agony! Confess! what did you have for breakfast? What do you mean to devour for lunch? What do you hope to consume for dinner?"

Roy could never resist the infection of this merry banter, seldom indulged in by Orrin except when with him. It brought back their early days—"when you thrashed the big boys for bullying me"—he liked to remind the other when they slept, played, and studied together. Orrin had his foibles, and a graver fault or so, but he was his *friend*, as he had told Dr. Baxter, and the boyish love for his gallant senior was still strong upon him. His laugh now was hearty and mischievous.

"Such a breakfast!" he said. "Gotten up in strict conformity with the injunction—'Feed a cold'"—

"And you will have a fever to starve!" interjected Wyllys. "*That* would be poetical justice! But go on!"

"Imprimis;" resumed Fordham,—"a cup of Turkish coffee,—fragrant and clear. Item, cream toast. Knowest thou the taste thereof? Of real cream toast? light, rich, smooth, that sootheth the inflamed membrane of the throat, and maketh the diaphragm to rejoice exceedingly? Item, broiled chicken—a marvel of juicy tenderness; an omelette *aux fines herbes* which was an inspiration"—

"For Heaven's sake!" Orrin feigned to tear his hair. "If you don't want to be murdered in your bed, hold your tongue!"

Roy was in a paroxysm of laughter; Wyllys, scowling horribly, had snatched the poker and was making adroit passes at him, like the cunning master of fence he was, when Jessie, ignorant of the liberty Phoebe had taken, and supposing her patient to be alone, entered. She had a waiter in one hand containing a silver pitcher and goblet, and a plate in the other, heaped with hothouse grapes. Transfixed with astonishment at the spectacle within she stopped on the threshold. Her amazement was not lessened when Orrin, replacing his weapon on the hearth, threw himself into a chair and covered his face with his handkerchief.

"A victim of covetousness!" exclaimed Roy, trying to check his merriment.

"Of misplaced confidence!" uttered Orrin, gloomily, removing his cambric, and arising with a show of melancholy composure. "I hope I have the pleasure of seeing you quite well, Mrs. Fordham! I should judge so from your blooming appearance, but having just had a notable lesson in the deceitfulness of outward seeming, I am sceptical as to the evidence of the senses and human reason."

"A dash of scepticism is like vaccine virus,—a useful thing, where there is fear of infection," said Jessie, not comprehending what had gone before, and not choosing to ask questions of him.

She bowed in passing him, making of her full hands a tacit excuse for the cavalier salutation,—a pretext that was transparent to the person she intended to slight. Depositing her burden upon a table, she bent over it, pretending to rearrange the grapes and stir the contents of the pitcher, that her face might cool before he had a chance to scrutinize it. His presence in this place was odious to her. What had she, in her self-abasement and earnest reachings after a nobler life than he had ever thought of, or aspired to, to do with his masquerading tricks and *persiflage*? His mummery, then and there, was more than heartless—it was an insult to her, with the recollection of her broken vows and blighted life, dogging every thought of possible happiness. Her residence in Hamilton had no severer trial than these chance encounters with him—her husband's nearest of kin.

"Nectar and grapes of Eshcol!" he exclaimed in a tone of calm despair, referring to the contents of waiter and plate. "You may not believe it, Mrs. Fordham—in fact I don't expect you to, for it is the nature of your sex to trust and trust again,—but you are nourishing a serpent! a base trickster! yet one of whose want of originality I am ashamed. The interesting invalid dodge is the stalest and flimsiest known to the guild of artful dodgers. Now, if I were in his place—"

"I am heartily glad you are not!" escaped Jessie, against her will to treat him with civility for Roy's sake.

Her emphasis of sincerity was unmistakable and wrought with various effect upon her two auditors.

"So am I!" laughed Roy, his eyes alight with more than mirth. "The grapes you cannot touch, my grasping friend! They were a present to me, not an hour since, from Miss Fanny Provost—a basketful, wreathed with exquisite flowers. *She* believes in the reality of my interesting invalidism. As for the nectar—give him a sip—Jessie, please! It is *not* fair that one man should monopolize all the good things of life."

Jessie poured out the draught, without jest or smile; then stood back with a gesture that bade him help himself if he would. She would not be a party to the sport, Orrin perceived.

"A missish, spiteful show of disdain!" he thought, contemptuously. "She is hardly worth a scene!"

To show that he was not repelled or overawed, he advanced a step; took up the goblet with a profound obeisance; stared her in the eyes, and swallowed a mouthful. Roy's shout of exultation and the uncontrollable grimace of the dupe, moved Jessie to a smile, but she did not speak.

"Witches' broth?" queried Orrin, with the tragical gravity of one who has made up his mind to die like a man.

"So Socrates might have glared and growled!" said Roy. "'The hemlock, jailor?'" mimicking the other's tone. "Not this time, my dear fellow! Only sage tea, sweetened with honey and stiffened with alum—an incomparable gargle, according to such eminent authorities as Miss Eunice Kirke, her sister, and, last and least, Dr. Bradley."

Orrin took up his hat, undismayed to the last.

"*Sage* tea! I go home a wiser, if not a better man! I am glad to see there is nothing the matter with you, Roy, while I lament, as one of your blood and lineage, over your unblushing hypocrisy. Mrs. Fordham—"

"You used to call her 'Jessie,'" interrupted Roy. "I said, 'Cousin Hester,' yesterday, to your bride. Shall I imitate your formal address?"

"No! But my little wife is august in nobody's eyes. Whereas, Mrs. Fordham—Cousin Jessie—I beg your pardon! Which shall it be?"

His back was to Roy; his meaning gaze upon herself was, to her perception, audacious insolence. Not daring to resent it in Roy's hearing, she yet obeyed the wifely impulse to seek his protection.

"That is for your cousin to decide. My name belongs to him!" She said it proudly, flashing her wide eyes from one to the other, and moving involuntarily nearer to Roy.

Wyllys caught up the last words.

"His relations should be yours, if the partnership be in good faith, and on equal terms."

"That is for him to decide!" answered she, precisely as before.

"Thank you! I do not shirk the responsibility," said Roy putting himself in the breach as usual, when he saw her non-plussed or disturbed. "Another sip of nectar, Orrin, before you breast the storm?"

A wry face was the response, and the most fascinating man in Hamilton bowed himself out. As he drew the door to after him, he glanced across the hall. The room Roy had showed him as his was opposite, and the door open. There was fire in that grate also; a lady's sewing-chair in front of it, and a work-box he recognized as Jessie's on the small table beside it. On the back of the chair hung a linen apron, with pockets, such as he had seen her wear when engaged in household tasks in Dundee, or gardening. He guessed directly that she had stopped in there to lay it off when she brought up the gargle. That this was her apartment, he was sure, when another step revealed a bureau with a ladies' dressing-case open upon it.

"Separate apartments!" he mused, picking his steps lightly down the cottage stairs. "Very unsentimental! Very un-American! decidedly independent and jolly. But, in this case, what is the meaning of it?"

He believed he had the clue to the mystery before he inserted his latch-key in the door of his—or his wife's—house. Jessie Fordham could not forget that Jessie Kirke had loved him. The decent show of conjugal felicity he had witnessed that day was a hollow crust below which the lava still surged and seethed. Jessie was more faithful to the one great passion of her life, and less philosophical than he had been ready to believe. Her scrupulous avoidance of him whenever this could be done without awakening suspicion; the half bitter retorts that fell now and then from the lips she would train to the utterance of conventional lies; the indignant sparkle of the eyes that answered the searching appeal of his—what were all these but the ill-concealed tokens of an attachment that had so inwrought itself with the fibres of heart and being as to defy her strenuous attempts to pluck it forth, or keep it out of sight. It was a revelation to him, and a flattering one—one that merited serious consideration.

The devil gat hold of him in that hour; sifted him as wheat, bringing all that was base in his nature uppermost. Heretofore, he had shunned everything that could secure for him the reputation of a *cicisbeo*. When a woman was once married, she became an object of indifference to him. He accounted the pursuit of such, a hazardous and flavorless exhibition of Lothario-ism which the refined age should frown down. He was not a *gourmand* or libertine, he had often proudly asserted to himself. Pleasures of that stamp he left to men of grosser tastes and coarser grain. He had meant to allow his cousin all the domestic peace which should honestly fall to his share, and to cultivate amicable relations with his cousin-in-law — Roy's wife, who had given conclusive evidence of intelligent appreciation of himself.

But if Jessie were unhappy; not on terms with her respectable husband, cleverly as both dissembled — if Jessie still loved him —

"*C'est une autre chose!*" he muttered between his teeth, and complacently knocking the snow off his boots upon the marble steps of his "mansion."

His most heartless propositions always sought cover in the facile foreign tongue.

A writer in the last generation defined an egotist to be "One who would burn down his neighbor's house to boil an egg for himself."

Orrin Wyllys was an Egotist.

# CHAPTER XXII

The snow-storm waxed furious as the day wore on.

Jessie unclosed the blinds of the windows opposite the bed, that Roy might see it in all its might and beauty.

"It is a foot deep in the street," she said. "The evergreens in the Campus are loaded; the firs and junipers are like enormous sugar-loaves, and some of the slighter trees—cedar and arbor-vitæ—are bowed nearly double. There is one"—laughing with almost her olden glee—"the ambitious arbor-vitæ near the east gate, which you said last Sunday, 'carried too much sail aloft for a gale,' whose crown not only touches the ground, but is frozen there, while the roots hold firm. I wish you could see it! It reminds me of the poor lady who, in her rage to be ultra-fashionable, had her hair dressed very *à la Chinoise*,—dragged up so high and twisted so tightly on the back of her head, that she could not get her heels to the floor. I do enjoy a grand old-fashioned snow-storm! None of the petulant flurries with swirling flakes, that spend their strength in an hour, but such a tempest as this, that does not abate under a day and a night. One has such a delicious feeling of home comfort and seclusion—the almost certainty that strangers will not intermeddle with fireside joys and interests while the household is shut in—I was about to say—tucked in snugly by the great white veil."

Roy liked to hear her talk. Her girlish prattle was more charming to him than the profoundest disquisitions of scholars, or the brilliant repartee of literary coteries. Aware of this, and that part of her nursely duty was to amuse the patient; ignorant that his heart was leaping with a new-born hope, so sweet and sudden that his head whirled dizzily under its influence, and the world took on rarest robes of beauty, she rambled on, her eyes bent upon the driving fleeces without. She had never been handsomer than now. Every trace of the shock that had prostrated nervous forces and reason, three months before, was gone from figure and countenance, while she thought only of gratifying her companion and her own fancy for a wild, winter day. Not dreaming of the impassioned gaze that dwelt upon her, she stood in an attitude of careless grace, a half smile playing about her mouth.

"As she used to stand in the oriel, at sunset!" thought Roy, with an unheard sigh. "Is all that, then,

"'The tender grace of a day that is dead'?

Can it 'never come back to me?'"

"I can think how Old Windbeam would wrap this mantle about his head and shoulders," resumed Jessie more softly. "How blackly the pines show against his sides! The meadows are an immense *méringue*; Willow Creek is frozen and invisible under the snow—so tightly locked within its banks that its groans can be heard, in the pauses of the storm, all the way to the Parsonage. I used to lie awake on sharp, frosty nights, and hear the rumble of the imprisoned air running all the way from the upper bridge down to the falls. The holly-berries on the tree by the front porch peep out saucily from the little woolly piles that collect upon the spikes and leaves; the church-yard is level from fence to fence—oh, Roy!"

With the cry, she sank down upon a low seat, weeping as from the depths of a riven heart.

"Under the snow! under the snow!" she reiterated, in a transport of distress. "I cannot bear to think of it!"

"Come to me, dear Jessie!" said Fordham, in gentle command. He hardly expected that she would obey, but she did, groping her way by reason of the blinding tears, and sobbing unrestrainedly. He had not seen her weep before since the night of her arrival at the cottage.

"Sit here!" he said, designating a chair at his side. "I have something to say when you can hear it. These tears will ease your burdened heart, and they are due to the memory of the dear ones who are for a little while out of our sight."

She had stifled her sobs, but her head was still bowed; her frame heaved in the ground-swell of the passing storm.

"For a little while! Out of our sight!" he repeated, thoughtfully—longingly. "We shall be together—all of us—very soon. Did you ever ask yourself if you would be able to await the call of the Master—all your appointed time;—ever imagine what a crushing load mortality and its ills would be to you, if, 'while in the body pent,' you could be a witness of the blessedness of those who are 'forever with the Lord'? Dear child! The Father leads us as wisely as lovingly!"

The expression of his religious faith and experience never sounded like cant, even in the ears of the scoffer. It was a part of his life. His utterances were fearless, simple, fervent, enforcing respect for their author, although the listener might not be in sympathy with their spirit. Jessie ceased to weep or sigh while he talked; presently showed her tear-stained face, tremulous with sad smiles, and laid her hand timidly upon his.

"Thank you! Every word is a drop of comfort. But so much talking is bad for your throat, and the fever will return if you are agitated. It was childish and selfish in me to give way as I did. But," her lip quivering anew—"it came in upon me like a flood! the happy by-gone hours and the dear old manse! Just how it all looked, as I had seen it, a hundred times in the winter weather I always loved. And the changes—and where *they* are now!"

"I ought to thank you for allowing me to sorrow with and try to console you. Don't be afraid of me, dear! afraid to bring your trials, with your pleasures, to your friend. If left to yourself, just now,—if I had not called you to me, you would have rushed away to hide your tears in your own room. You never wound me except when you act and look as if you stood in dread of my displeasure or criticism. Won't you be candid and tell me why this is so? Am I a very cruel taskmaster? Do you not believe me when I say that I desire no other earthly good as I do to make you contented—happy, if that can be."

"I do believe it! I should be slow to see and to be convinced if I did not!" began Jessie, the truth trembling upon her tongue. The temptation to unbosom herself without fear and reserve was very strong. "But I feel myself to be unworthy of your regard, and the goodness you show me. And you are so wise and discreet—so self-contained—"

A pang changed his features. He stirred restlessly, biting his lip to keep back a repetition of the word "self-contained!" that would have been a groan.

"You are suffering!" said Jessie, anxiously. "I have made you worse!"

"No; a passing pain—that is all! You always make me better. What should I have done without you, to-day, my kind nurse?"

A perverse fit, one of her spoiled-child freaks, seized Jessie.

"Phoebe would have taken excellent care of you!" she said, demurely, casting down her eyes to hide the gleam of mischief darting up to the surface. "She wanted to make brown gravy soup, and roast a fat duck for your dinner, with mince-pie—'to leave a nice taste in his mouth, ma'am.' And she persists in the belief that a gargle of red-pepper tea, with mustard-draughts upon your feet, and a cayenne poultice about your throat 'would pull you through,' when doctor's stuffs fail. As to society, your cousin, or, maybe, Dr. Baxter would have come in to cheer you up. What a godsend a big linen sheet would be to the good President, on a day like this, with a listener who is *hors du combat* with a hoarse cold!"

"I have not needed to be cheered up, since I saw the first glimpse of your face, this morning!" answered Roy, unguardedly. Conscious that he was trenching upon forbidden ground, he diverted the conversation. "What a flow of spirits Orrin has! I *did* hurt my throat laughing at his tragico-comico envy of my surroundings. I wish he had a *home*, one like this, if it were shared by a congenial companion, a woman who was more nearly his equal, mentally and morally, than the one he has chosen. He would be much happier than he can hope to be in the splendid pile he calls by that name."

"He seems perfectly satisfied with wife and house," returned Jessie, dryly. "And the marriage was certainly one of preference on Miss Sanford's part. Not that I admire or like her, and I know her better than you do. But I am persuaded that we waste our pity when we expend it on either of them."

They chatted, then, of various matters in the familiar style in which their conversations were generally carried on, until the day closing in about them, the fire spread a mellow radiance over the area immediately around it; the white bed and the noble head laid high on the pillows; upon Jessie's earnest face and crown of raven hair. It was the hour and the scene for the confidential talk of husband and wife; the outpouring of true soul to true; the only unrestrained heart-communion this side the Land where subterfuge and disguise are unknown; speech as far more excellent and satisfying than the language of unwedded lovers as the perfume from the unfolded lily surpasses that which steals from the bud.

Between these two, love was neither named nor hinted at. The wife's hands lay crossed upon her knees, and the husband did not offer to hold or touch them, or stroke the beautiful hair with which the betrothed had toyed unrebuked. It was an anomalous intimacy, the restraints and courtesies of which would have been laughed at as affectations, if the story of them were not totally discredited by the world outside "the great white veil" that shut them into their home,—theirs in name and in fact.

Jessie got up, at length, stepping over the carpet without rustle or jar, "the poetry of motion," thought the looker-on, and laid more coals upon the fiery mass in the grate. Many-colored flames shot up through and darted, like living serpents, along the pile; the low crackling and hissing of the igniting lumps awoke a cricket in the chimney-corner. Jessie, kneeling on the rug, glanced over her shoulder, on hearing the cheery chirp, and smiled at Roy.

"You don't treat the crickets on your hearth as Gruffand Tackleton boasted that he did—'crunch 'em, sir!' I like to hear the little busybodies—don't you?"

Without rising, when she had seemed to hearken for a while, she began to sing. Roy had not heard a note from her, even in church, since their marriage, and he held his breath, lay motionless, lest she should awaken from her reverie. It was an old ballad she was crooning—half Scotch, and with a thought of pathos in the melody, although the words were not plaintive.

"Tis rare to see the morning bleeze,
Like a bonfire, frae the sea;
'Tis fair to see the burnie kiss
The lip o' the flowery lea.

And fine it is on green hillside
Where hums the bonnie bee,
But rarer, fairer, finer far,
Is the Ingleside to me."

A light roseate film hid her from Roy's eyes. The Ingleside, where she now knelt! his and hers! did she really love it so well as not to pine for the haunts of her girlhood? And what had pressed that cry from her that was still echoing through his heart-chambers? the appeal that would have meant in a loving wife uncontrollable yearning for the sympathy of him who best knew her needs and her sorrows?

"O, Roy!" she had said, hands outstretched as if to fasten upon his for support in the deep waters. It imported more—a million times more, that childlike wail—to him than all she had afterward expressed of gratitude and esteem. In that hour, consecrate forever by what his musings brought forth, he resolved to woo and win a second time the only woman he had ever loved; who he had believed was lost to him for all time, chained as she was to his side, forced into a relation she abhorred by vows her dying father and he—impatient, ruthless lover!—had put into her mouth. He would be very wary, very patient, but love like his must conquer in the end. Doubts might oppose him in the broad light of day and common-sense, but he would not be turned aside. He did not underrate the difficulties that lay in the way of this novel wooing. Jessie was no longer the fresh-hearted, impetuous girl who had laid her hand confidingly in his (his palm thrilled now in the recollection!) as he sat by her in the oriel-window, the shadows of the tossing jessamine-bells— "joy-bells," he called them—cast upon her white dress and the carpet by the April sunshine; the dewiness and scents of the Spring morning in the air; the "light that was never on land and sea" glorifying the eyes uplifted to his.

Faulty, but frank, with a mind stored with crude riches, a heart whose capacity for love and Love's sacrifices even he had divined rather than discovered—she had been easily won, though not lightly sought. Now, the luxuriant womanliness, the growth of which he marked from day to day in her *physique*, had not kept pace with the chastened development of her inner nature. If he had said in that early stage of "Love's Young Dream"—"She is like no other girl I ever met!" she was now a veritable unique—a gem a monarch might be proud to set in his diadem.

For all that, he would win her! Should she arise from her lowly place by the ingle, and without a word of explanation or excuse for what was past, again give him her hand, saying merely, "I love you!" he would let all that had been enigmatical in their intercourse go from his remembrance at once and entirely; would trust her with his honor and affections, above all and through all that might stagger his faith in another. Was his a pitiful, cringing spirit? Was it a high or a mean type of human love that made him, possessing his tried soul in more abundant patience, say in the prospect of the tedious and cautious, it might be the arduous, approach to the goal of his desires, that must be his, if he would make success a certainty;—

*"And they seemed unto him but a few days for the love he had to her!"*

# CHAPTER XXIII

Mrs. Orrin Wyllys had "run in very sociably" to chat for an hour with her dear cousin, Mrs. Fordham.

"Orrin brought me to the door," she said, divesting herself of her fur cloak, and untying the coquettish hood that half covered her head. "I knew Mr. Fordham would be at the meeting in the Town Hall. Orrin promised to meet him there. He can't bear for me to be alone, so he offered to leave me to a comfortable dish of gossip with you while he attended to the interests of the 'dear people.' Of course, it is very gratifying to have one's husband so popular, but I often tell Orrin that I don't see one-tenth nor one-hundredth part as much of him as I ought to. I don't believe there is another man in the United States who is so run after. Not that this surprises me," tittering and trying to blush. "I, of all people alive, ought to have most charity with such devotion. It is a consolation to be assured that he regrets these numerous draughts upon his time as much as I do, and I am not disposed to be jealous. I do think mutual confidence is just the sweetest thing in the world. Between married lovers, I mean. What are you so busy about?"

Jessie's work-basket was heaped with calico and flannel.

"Making clothes for some poor children," she answered. "If you will excuse me, I will go on with my work, as the garments are sadly needed."

"Certainly! I shall be more at my ease if you do not seem to mind my being here. You are the most industrious woman I know. It positively fatigues one to watch you. I suppose, though, there is everything in being trained to such habits from childhood. Now, I haven't a thing to do from morning to night, which is lucky, for I have always been *so* carefully waited upon from my cradle up to the present hour, when my darling husband will hardly let me put my foot to the ground without his assistance. You can't imagine how *aux petits soins* he is in the retirement of our sweet, sweet home! True, the house is large, preposterously large—as I told my dear, indulgent father when he bought it. And as Orrin is fond of style, and I have always been used to it, we keep up a ridiculous establishment when one considers the size of the family. Now, I dare say, you keep but two or three women-servants, and maybe no man at all, as you have no carriage of your own?"

"Phoebe is our only servant," said Jessie, unperturbed at having to state the mortifying fact with which Mrs. Wyllys was already acquainted.

"Is it possible!" looking curiously about her through her gold eye-glass. "Yet everything about your little place is as neat as a pin. What a valuable creature she must be! I declare I must tell Orrin that! 'Five servants to wait upon two people, my love!' I said to him this very evening. 'It is frightful extravagance!' But he insists that I shall be relieved from all drudgery, knowing how delicately I have been reared. If I were fond of work, I should be puzzled how to employ myself at the hours when there are no visitors. When I am *ennuyée* in Orrin's absence, I have only to run across the street to my uncle's, Judge Provost's, to find plenty of society. What a houseful of children they have! I told Orrin yesterday, that it was lucky he never fancied Jeannie Provost (who, to whisper a secret, was just perfectly crazy after *him*!) My uncle has a large fortune, but it will be cut up by the rule of long division at his death. How fast you sew! Your *protégés* are some of your Dundee parishioners, I suppose?" condescendingly to the woman of low estate.

"No. The few poor there are so well cared for by their neighbors as not to require my help. This is work allotted me by the Managers of the Hamilton Charitable Society. There is much suffering here this winter."

"Ah!" indifferently. "Orrin doesn't approve of my attending these Women's Societies. He says it would unsex me—that he so admires my thorough womanliness! And, after all, when people can give money to the collectors and visitors and agents, and all that kind of nuisance, there is no use in doing anything else. The demands upon us in the name of charity, are just perfectly *awful*! I said to Orrin—dear, generous soul! this very morning—'My sweet love, you must positively bear in mind that we are not *quite* made of money!'"

A photograph upon a handsome easel attracted her attention, and the eye-glass was on duty.

"Is that a fancy picture, or a portrait?"

"It is a likeness of my sister."

"Indeed! Is she single or married? What is her name?"

"Her name is Eunice Kirke."

"Ah! a spinster! She is a very nice-looking person! As you were saying, the winter is severe! But the skating and sleighing are superb! I was on the ice several times last week with Orrin. He's such a *splendid* skater: I am so proud to be seen with him! I suppose you must have heard how much attention we attract whenever we appear?"

"I see very little of general society, this winter," Jessie politely evaded the inquiry. "I am not in the way of hearing about gay assemblies of any kind."

"Oh, yes! I forgot you were wearing black. But you shouldn't bury yourself too much, even to keep your house in this lovely order. I have seen you out driving several times with Mrs. Baxter, and said to Orrin what a convenience you must find her carriage. And while I think of it, do let me call by for you some day in the sleigh! Orrin and I have spoken of doing it, scores of times, but to confess the truth, we are just a *little* selfish! We *so* enjoy riding together, that we neglect our friends. Before I married Orrin, some officious friends advised me not to expect much attention from him after the wedding, 'because he was a ladies' man.' Such were notoriously indifferent to their wives' comfort, I was informed. Even my cousin—the Attorney-general's lady—said to me, 'My dear Hester! Mr. Wyllys is charming—but I am afraid he is too charming to take kindly to domesticity!' I nearly cried myself sick! But I turned a deaf ear to the croakers, and obeyed the dictates of my own heart. Now, I am reaping the reward of my wise action. It may sound boastful in me, but I don't believe my Orrin has his equal as a husband in the universe. His devotion to me is miraculous. I understand that we have the reputation of being the most love-sick couple in town, but I don't care! Let those that laugh win—and I have won! The women try to ridicule us because they are envious. It is not for *me* to say why the men do it!" A giggle and a violent sidewise toss of the head. "The worst they can say is, that we are more in love with one another now, than we were before our marriage. It is true, and we glory in it. My only fear is, that my darling husband may become too domestic in his perfect content with his wife and his home. It is very sweet and beautiful in him, but I often force him to go abroad, both with, and without me, to counteract this tendency."

Jessie stitched on diligently, with a half smile the visitor mistook for pleased interest in her theme, when it was in reality, made up of amusement and contempt. She could have had no surer evidence of how completely she had outgrown girlish foibles and unworthy rivalries; how firmly established she was upon her new plane of principle, reasoning, and views, than the equanimity with which she suffered Hester's patronage and open exultation over herself. Her contemptuous amusement in retrospection, embraced the would-be belle, who, although "nothing but a poor minister's daughter," had vied with the heiress in style and popularity. She even had a passing thought of ridicule for the memory of the dark-green walking dress, trimmed with fur, and the sweeping green plume. Such paltry contests as they looked to her now! such an insignificant opponent was this brainless, conceited creature before her!

Her boasting Mrs. Fordham valued at its true worth. Through Mrs. Baxter she had learned that the exactions, caressings, and braggadocio of Wyllys's bride made him the laughing stock of his associates. Her fortune was settled upon herself in terms that put it beyond his management, and his graceful *insouciance* had occasionally proved insufficient to cover his chagrin at her unsparing use of the power this arrangement gave her. Elated to rapture at her success in securing him, she paraded their mutual affection *ad nauseam* in whatever company they entered; people said, dragged him abroad against his will in order to do this. In the large circle of her husband's acquaintances, she was received with a degree of distinction, she chose to believe was homage to her charms and worth, and superadded to the egregious vanity and pretension of the heiress, her complacency in the dignity of the married woman was ludicrous beyond description.

She was arrayed to-night in a blue Irish poplin, bordered on overskirt, sleeves and basque with ermine; there were diamonds in her ears, upon her fingers, and clustered in her brooch, and artificial flowers in her hair.

"How I envy you for the easy time you have with your dress;" she remarked, incidentally to Jessie. "That is the only advantage one has in wearing mourning. You cannot imagine what a deal of time and labor I must expend upon my toilette. Orrin is even harder to please in these matters than I am. If he had his way I should always be in full dress."

Her voice had always upon Jessie a peculiar and unpleasant effect, akin to that produced by the touch of some viscid substance. But she was Mrs. Orrin Wyllys. This was the end of his "dream of fair women!" to become the petted henchman of a homely, selfish, arbitrary, silly, and wealthy wife.

"How can you endure to touch that coarse work?" was her next essay, with a gesture of her be-ringed fingers like filliping off an obnoxious insect. "Why, that is a flannel petticoat—isn't it?"

"Yes."

"Does Mr. Fordham ever catch you at that sort of sewing?"

"Sometimes."

Jessie had her quiet little smile of satisfaction at the thought of the delightful evenings she had had since this task was commenced, for Roy read aloud to her while she sewed.

"I am astonished he tolerates it! Orrin is *so* fastidious; has such an exalted appreciation of my refinement, that I wouldn't dare let him see me handle such a garment. I think the more careful we are to maintain a certain degree of modest reserve in the presence of our husbands, the more we shrink from all things common and unclean, the better they will love us. I dread lowering myself to the level of a commonplace woman in my beloved Orrin's eyes; would keep myself his divinity while I can. But I know I am an exception in this respect, that with most married couples, disenchantment comes with the wane of the honeymoon."

Jessie understood the thrust conveyed in the borrowed phrases, enunciated with monkey-like gravity. She had had others like it from the same source. The narrow soul and heart of the speaker had never let her forgive Mrs. Fordham for having once played in her sight the part of chief favorite upon Orrin's list of belles. He had glossed over the circumstance of his pointed attentions to the country girl, by representing her relations to his cousin; had sworn sounding oaths, more loud than deep, that he had never whispered to her of love—and his wife listened and disbelieved. At any rate, the Hamilton wiseacres gave the poorer woman the credit of the conquest, and the knowledge of this was the Banquo at Hester's coronation-feast.

"But you and our good cousin Roy are such awfully practical people!" ran on the chatterer. "I have told Orrin twenty times that I didn't believe your husband kissed you once a week. I should be disconsolate if mine did not kiss me whenever he went out and came in—not to mention dozens of times besides. However, as my blessed, charitable old love says, people differ wonderfully in temperament. Now, we are *so* ardent!"

"As you say, diversity of temperament accounts for much that seems singular in action," remarked Jessie, composedly.

There was a strange aching at her heart as she said it. Looking at the flat, flaccid visage of her interlocutor, she would have declared it to be impossible for her to wound her by this inane twaddle, peppered with weak spite. Yet she had set a nerve ajar.

"If I had a husband—"the "practical" woman was saying to herself— "his kisses would be too dear and sacred to be counted over and boasted of to others. If I had a husband! Heaven help me! I have none!"

The china-blue eyes of the shallow pate over there would have glittered with malicious delight in her own shrewdness, had she guessed how near to the truth was her description of the external intercourse of those whom the church and the world named as one.

"It is awfully nice to be married!" she rattled on, growing more and more confidential. "There is such solid comfort in the reflection that your destiny is accomplished. No more need for anxiety and setting one's cap, and all that. I shall never forget the delicious peace that filled my whole soul when I first heard myself called 'Mrs. Wyllys!' when I appreciated that the irrevocable step was taken. Still, it seems very sudden. It is just a year since I heard Orrin spoken of as your beau—a funny mistake, as you know, but I didn't then. Oh! how angry I was! for I had determined, even then, that he should fall in love with me. Maybe you recollect the time? It was one day when we were playing billiards at Judge Provost's, and somebody—Fanny, I believe—said he was your teacher. Afterward, the girls began talking about Mr. Fordham's attentions to another young lady—never supposing that he was engaged to you all the time. By the way—did I ever tell you that my dear, upright, kind-hearted husband charged me to mention to you that *that* was all a foolish mistake?"

"What was a mistake?"

Jessie looked up, arresting the swift, even motion of her fingers.

"Why, the story of Mr. Fordham's engagement to Maria Dunn, a young lady of our city."

"I recollect that you stated it as a fact," returned Jessie, pointedly. "She was an intimate friend of yours, you said, and that you had the tale directly from her. You said, moreover, that Mr. Fordham had called upon you, in company with her."

Hester's thin skin was mottled with mulberry.

"Well, yes! we were a good deal together, at one time, and she certainly did lead me to believe that Mr. Fordham was in love with her—now I come to think of it. I have forgotten the exact circumstances, but there was some talk about it and she did all she could to excite sympathy, until she took a fancy to marry another man. A miserably poor match she made—a clerk upon a salary of two thousand dollars! and her father with seven children! *Then*, she vowed there had never been any attachment between herself and Mr. Fordham. She was related to the friends he was visiting, and he happened to act as her escort once or twice. For my part, I am sure he never gave her reason to think that he cared a rush for her. She was one of those girls who are always running after the men, and fancy that every gentleman who looks at them is going to propose on the spot. If there is one creature whom I despise above all others, it is a woman who thinks marriage the chief end of her existence. I really thought I had spoken to you about this, long ago. Dear Orrin told me to do it, just after we were married. He said you might allude to the affair in talking with Mr. Fordham, and I might be drawn into a libel-suit or fuss of some kind. I can't see how I came to forget it—I am usually so particular in following his advice!"

Jessie gathered nothing intelligible from the monologue after this. The gleam of her needle was a dull spark before her eyes, and the viscid drawl had some vague association in her mind with the slimy trail of a snake. Once, the slender steel broke between her fingers. Twice she understood, from the other's interrogative intonation that she waited a reply, and she supplied one at random.

A sharp thought aroused her at last, to put a question in her turn.

"You say Mr. Wyllys told you to correct the unfavorable impression he fancied this story might have produced upon my mind. When did he first refer to the subject?"

"O, for that matter, he asked me about it before we were engaged. And, wasn't I properly frightened when I found you had told tales out of school? Of course, I made as light of it as possible, and when he paid his first visit to B— —, I set it all straight by telling him I was certain it was a fabrication. I had had reasons for doubting Maria's veracity and honor in other respects. Would you believe it? The girl actually tried to attract Orrin's notice, after she knew he was engaged to ME!"

Jessie had no means of determining how much, or how little truth there was in this statement. It mattered nothing to her who had been the more culpable in the deception practised upon her—the intriguing husband, or the foolish wife. It was probable both had prevaricated grossly and maliciously. It was certain that they had together wrought her great and irreparable harm. The long-delayed explanation was worse than useless. The one maligned by the mischievous gossip had been cast off, and alienated. She should never have the courage to confess the whole wrong to him now.

Unless—

# CHAPTER XXIV

When Roy returned his cousin was with him.

Mrs. Wyllys launched herself into the hall at sound of their voices, her bright azure train 'wide dispread;' her arms extended like the yards of a ship.

"My darling!" casting her entire weight against his chest, a hand upon each shoulder, and putting up a tight knot of a mouth for the kiss marital. "What an eternity you have been absent! I have been ever so uneasy about you!"

She re-entered the sitting-room, hanging by her clasped hands upon his arm, and warbling in her thin falsetto, —

"Now you have come, all my fears are removed,
Let me forget that so long you have roved!"

It was not in human nature, even such a gentlemanly nature as Roy's, to remain unmoved by the spectacle. His risible muscles were still rebellious when he invited Orrin to seat himself near the fire, and observed in tones that would waver, despite politeness and pity, that "the night was very cold."

An awkward little pause ensued. Orrin's chair was at Jessie's right hand, and he turned slightly in that direction while stooping to warm his hands at the blazing hearth, as if expecting some hospitable demonstration from her. She folded her work as neatly as if handling satin instead of flannel, laid it within her basket and set it back, and, with a word of apology, left the room to order refreshments for the guests. On her return, she entered from the parlors that she might more easily reach a divan on the opposite side of the hearth from Orrin. Hester was whispering to her husband, and Roy, whose seat was next that Jessie had taken, glanced down at her with a smile of cheerful greeting, as she made the exchange. She met it with eyes that well-nigh destroyed his composure. Mournful to wretchedness; appealing to supplication, they seemed to lay her soul open to his regards; to ask of him—was it succor or forgiveness? it could not be affection!

She, at least, ought to have known Wyllys too well to imagine—if she thought of him at all—that the silent by-play would pass unnoticed and uncomprehended by him. In his bachelorhood, the expression of aversion to his proximity, and the mute resort to her husband's protection, would have amused and incited him to the exercise of more potent fascinations. But Jessie's demeanor, of late, had irked him unreasonably. He could have supported an overt show of vindictiveness better than the dignified indifference that baffled his attempts to re-establish their confidential relations. Manoeuvre as he might, and as he did, he could never see her for one instant alone, and this, he was sure, was not accidental. Upon one pretext or another, he called at the cottage at all hours—most frequently when he knew Roy was engaged in his professional duties. "Mrs. Fordham begged to be excused," occasionally; oftener kept him waiting below until the, to him, inopportune burst of Mrs. Baxter into the parlor, or Fanny Provost's entrance through the side-porch next her home, prevented a *tête-à-tête*.

He could not believe that she had taken her, whom he swore at inwardly as a "chattering cockatoo," into her confidence in a matter so delicate as her unextinguished passion for himself, but it was plain that the coincidences which damaged his plans were somebody's work. For a while he derived some compensation for his disappointment from the additional evidence thus furnished him by the short-sighted novice in scheming, that her shyness was the fruit of cowardice; that lively coals of love for him still lurked beneath the ashes with which she would fain keep them smothered. But his best powers of *finesse* had not elicited a flash from these. Adroit references to scenes and words which she could not recall without emotion, if the wonted fires were still there, had produced as little visible effect as did his ardent protestations of cousinly attachment. She treated him as she did a dozen other gentlemen—neither worse nor better. Mortification and amazement at his non-success were but human. Displeasure and the inclination to retaliate upon the instrument of his discomfiture were unprofessional, and the display of them impolitic to the last degree. That he admitted these feelings, was to be accounted for plausibly only upon the hypothesis that contact with the sour whey of his wife's temper had not improved his own. In times past, he had been too rational, as well as too firmly entrenched in his self-appreciation, to descend to serious meditation upon the practice of a quality so vulgar, and usually so unremunerative as revenge. Two whole months had gone by since he laid his plans of advance upon the fortification of matronly propriety and womanly pride, and he had not gained an inch that he could discover.

It was fortunate for Jessie's self-respect that in her harshest judgment of his motives and character, she never surmised what was his present purpose. With her natural propensity to blame herself for the sins others committed against her, she would have leaped to the inference that he had seen warrant in her former indiscretion and inconstancy, for the belief that neither moral nor religious principle would serve her successfully in resisting his declaration of undiminished attachment; that she who had played false to the lover, would be unfaithful to the husband, if a similar magnet were presented to her vacillating heart. She saw, indeed, that he courted her notice and friendship; believed that she read in his conduct lingering fears that she might yet betray his perfidy to Roy, if she were not propitiated by such sugarplums of attention as other women liked. The conviction of his cowardice had dealt the heaviest blow at the idol that crumbled into common dust on that September day. All vestige of godhood had departed beneath the shock. A brave man might sin; a good man might, under extreme provocation, be cruel. The caitiff who slunk away, whining, at sight of the lifted scourge which should punish him for the crime he could not deny, must forfeit love with esteem.

Wyllys' mood, at sight of the rapid signal or query that passed from husband to wife, was the exact reverse of amiable, and he was not pacified by Hester's conduct. Hitching her chair close to her lord's, she stroked his hair and beard, smiling affectedly, in amorous languishment, at her lately purchased vassal, and purring like a cat. So soon as he could decently seek deliverance from the absurd situation, Orrin slipped from under the crawling fingers, and began to examine the books upon the centre-table.

"Isn't he looking well?" said his tormentor to Roy, showing all her prominent teeth in the affectionate leer she sent after him.

"Very well. His health has always been excellent, I believe," rejoined Roy. "Although his active habits have hindered the gain of so much as a pound of superfluous flesh."

It hurt him to see his gay and gallant clansman in the humiliating position of a led bear, at the mercy of a marmoset, but he could not be anything but civil in his own house.

"Oh! Oh! don't hint at the possibility of his ever getting *fat*! I think lean people are just *too* sweet! I wouldn't have him altered by the change of a single hair in his mustache. Women ought to think their husbands perfect, oughtn't they, Cousin Jessie?"

"If they *are* perfect!" was the reply.

Mrs. Wyllys accomplished a compound toss of her head; her ear-rings fairly jingling, and the flowers in her sandy braids and frizettes quivering like aspens in an east wind.

"That is rank heresy! Love that isn't blind is no love at all. I wouldn't give a fig for the constancy of a wife who could detect the slightest flaw in the man she has promised to love, honor, and obey. Would you now, Mr. Fordham?"

"If you would have my candid opinion, I should prefer intelligent and discriminating esteem to blind adoration," was the courteous rejoinder, at which the lady bridled.

"I might have expected some such answer in this staid, matter-of-fact household! Now, Orrin and I—"

"You are true to your *penchant* for Mrs. Norton, I perceive!" Orrin interrupted her unceremoniously, looking across at Jessie. "This is a handsome English edition of her poems."

"Yes! I have had it for several years."

"Is that an implication that you would not procure it now, if you did not possess it?"

"I imply nothing, except that she is popular with most young girls."

"Woman, then, in her maturity of mind and affection, grows out of the taste for the 'female Byron'—for that is Mrs. Norton's *sobriquet* in the literary world?" he said, interrogatively, and in suave deference to her judgment. "What some contend poetry should be,—the lyrical, expression of passion,—sounds extravagant to one who has studied life for herself. Must this be so? Are there no recesses far down in the heart where the dew will lie all day? Because we have learned to think in sober and weighty prose, must we blush to remember that our souls once melted through our eyes as we sang, 'Thy Name was Once the Magic Spell,' or read, 'The Tryst,' and 'I Cannot Love Thee?'"

"I have a song, called—'I do not Love Thee,'" interposed Mrs. Wyllys. "It is just the sweetest thing you ever heard. Let me see! How does the air go?" humming. "I do not love thee! No! I do not love thee!"

"I am tempted to doubt the decline of your admiration for our poetess," pursued Wyllys to Jessie, with royal disregard of his beloved's vocalization. "The book opens of itself at the last-named poem."

"**Do read** it aloud, lovey!" begged Hester, eagerly. "I should *so* like to hear it! And he *does* read poetry so exquisitely!" to the Fordhams. "It is just perfectly delightful to listen to him! I tell him that was the way he captivated me, with his reading and his singing. They are *too* sweet!"

"Let us have it, Orrin!" said Roy, good-humoredly, desirous to relieve him from the saccharine shower. "I never read it, I think. But I was always 'matter-of-fact,' as Mrs. Wyllys has already discovered. Perhaps the 'lyrical expression of passion' had less hold upon my adolescent imagination than it generally has upon impressible youth."

He resigned himself patiently to the hearing of an ultra-pathetic love-song.

Jessie knew every line of the poem already. She had said it over to herself, scores of times, last Summer, tossing wakefully upon her pillow at midnight, until the pine boughs seemed to have caught the rhythm; or pacing the garden walks with hurrying feet; or hanging over the railing of the rustic foot-bridge. But she could not help listening, as the cunning modulations of the reader drew out the simple fervor of each line.

A steely-blue ray shot from beneath his eyelashes in her direction, as he turned a leaf. She did not see it. Perfectly still, yet attentive, she had leaned her head against the high back of her husband's chair, and was looking straight before her.

> The cold disgust,
> Wonderful and most unjust,

found no expression in attitude and feature.

The reader's voice mellowed; the emphasis of suppressed emotion was more artistic and effective.

> Seems to me that I should guess
> By what a world of bitterness,
> By what a gulf of hopeless care,
> Our two hearts divided are.
>
> And I praise thee as I go,
> Wandering, weary, full of woe
> To my own unwilling heart, —
> Cheating it to take thy part,
> By rehearsing each rare merit
> Which thy nature doth inherit;
> How thy heart is good and true,
> And thy face most fair to view;
> How the powers of thy mind
> Flatterers in the wisest find,
> And the talents to thee given,
> Seem as held in trust for Heaven,
> Laboring on for noble ends,
> Steady to thy boyhood's friends,
> Slow to give or take offence,
> Full of earnest eloquence.
>
> How, in brief, there dwells in thee
> All that's generous and free,

All that may most aptly move
My spirit to an answering love.

"Was'nt it *too* funny that she didn't give in to such a splendid fellow?" queried Hester, sniffing away the emotion she had tried to sop up with her laced handkerchief. "I never can hear dear Orrin read without crying, no matter what the subject is. I couldn't have helped falling in love with him, I know. It *was* queer, now!" fretfully, as she saw Jessie's countenance. "I don't see what there is amusing about it!"

Jessie held her head erect—a movement full of spirit and gladness—and laughed. It was no mirthless sound, but a ripple of real joyousness.

"Very queer!" she answered, merrily. "Mr. Wyllys! we must call upon you to explain the phenomenon. You evidently understand it. You read the poem *con amore*."

She sprang up to serve her guests from the waiter Phoebe had placed upon the table. Roy followed her.

"They tell me you make a delicious article of domestic wine, Mrs. Fordham—of elderberries, or grapes, or currants—or something," said Mrs. Wyllys, bent upon patronage at every turn. "I hope you are going to treat us to some of it now."

"'They' are mistaken!" returned Jessie, the merry ring yet in her voice. "I never attempted anything of the kind. The best substitute I can offer you for the beverage you had promised yourself, is Rhenish or Marsala which Mr. Fordham procured abroad."

"I can answer for her, I believe, Mrs. Wyllys, that her efforts in that line have been confined to the brewing of flax-seed lemonade, and sage tea!" chimed in Roy.

Whereat Jessie laughed again, as she had not done at Orrin's adventure with the gargle.

Wyllys arose to receive a glass of wine from her hand, and, in taking it, looked steadily, reproachfully, passionately, into her eyes. They sustained the scrutiny without quailing, a glint of roguish defiance playing within them, and her lips curling at the corners, as she turned away. He had a misgiving then that his power over her was at an end. This was not acting, but the flashing of a stream where the sunshine reached to its bed; was filtrated through pure, sweet waters. If she were disenchanted, he knew whom he had to thank for it. He could have hated his Hester for the over-fondness that had made him ridiculous to optics which erst surveyed him with timid and worshipful reverence, as Semelé may have regarded high Jove.

He was not sorry he had wedded as he did. He had too just an appreciation of the inconveniences of living beyond one's means; the difficulties that environ a man of expensive tastes and a moderate income, and the thousand goods of wealth, to regret the investment, which had assuredly yielded more than cent. per cent., whether he estimated either the affection or the money he had put into the speculation. He was wise in his generation. Hester was the richest spoil that had ever been laid in his way, and he had not hesitated as to the line of duty. But he did wish she had not wheedled him into this visit, that she might have another opportunity to play the fool herself, and force a like part upon him. Jessie's laughter had stung him unreasonably, and in his avarice of the praise of his kind, he grudged the loss of a moiety of Roy's affectionate admiration.

Fordham did not return to the sitting-room when he had escorted his guests to the outer door. He bade his wife "Good-night," in the hall.

"Must you work to-night?" she asked, imploringly. "I meant—I hoped—that is, I thought we would have a pleasant chat over my fire."

Her manner was agitated, her eye restless; but he scarcely noted this, or that she stammered strangely in preferring the petition.

"Don't tempt me!"

He would have made his answer playful. It was a sickly show, and repulsed Jessie more effectually than sternness would have done.

With a burning blush, she dropped the hand she had laid lightly on his sleeve; murmured an apology, and hurried upstairs, forgetting that she had intended to sit for a while longer in the lower room. In her own chamber, she walked the floor in an agony of shame and despair.

"He would never have my love now, if it were offered him!" she said, wringing her hands. "He knows me too well! The glamour of that happy love-summer has gone! gone! To-night, I feel further off from him than ever. He despises me as I deserve! But righteous punishment is as hard to bear as unjust condemnation. And I have suffered so much, and so long! I could have been wholly frank with him, if he had but gone and sat with me ten minutes—if he had been *himself,* instead of shrinking from my touch—rejecting my companionship."

"The book opened of itself at that place!" Roy was thinking at that moment. He had been to the sitting-room for the volume, carried it into the library, and re-read the poem again and yet again, detecting what he imagined was a tear blister on the second page. "What can I do? What course is left to me save that which I am pursuing? Am I still odious to her?"

The girl at the spring smiled down upon him from the wall; seemed to hold out the green leaf-cup for his acceptance. He could see the glisten of the water upon it; fancy that he heard in the stillness the tinkle of the bright beads as they fell into the basin. The eyes that gave back her look were very patient, but just now it was a patience that had in it much of the weariness of hope deferred.

"I have put a cup of bitterness to your lips, my bird of beauty!" was his unselfish lament.

Mr. Wyllys "had builded better than he knew," that evening.


"I wouldn't be as cold-blooded as that woman, for all the gold of Golconda!" exclaimed Hester, before the steps of the Fordham cottage were cold from the touch of her Parisian gaiters.

"Maybe you mean diamonds," said her husband curtly. "It is a safe plan not to use terms unless you are certain they are correct."

"Gold or diamonds, it makes no difference! I don't pick my words when I am out of patience. It's precious little she has of either commodity, I guess!" laughing spitefully.

"Take care of that rough place in the crossing," cautioned Wyllys, in a less acrimonious tone, thus reminded what store his spouse possessed of the valuables specified, and, by inevitable association of ideas, of his profitable investment.

"She frets me always!" continued the sweet creature, hanging, according to custom, basket-wise upon his arm. "This evening she was positively rude. How provokingly she laughed at that sweet piece you read so divinely that I was in tears all the way through. You meant it for her, I could see well enough, you smart, sly creature! And it served her just right! I as good as told her she did not care a snap for her husband, before you came in. And she took it as coolly as if I had paid her a compliment. It is *awful* what scared consciences some people have. I take to myself the credit of having seen through her from the beginning, when that horrid old matchmaker, Mrs. Baxter, who always puts me in mind of a grinning hyena, was trying to put her off on you. As if you would have married a girl who was next door to a beggar! What is it, petty?"

"I trod on a pebble!"

He had almost flung her arms from their hold. For he remembered the story he had told Jessie in the conservatory, of the woman who was married for her money, and gloried in it.

"What a pity!" gabbled his owner. "I am morally certain that she married Mr. Fordham, poor fellow! to get a home. If that isn't disgustingly immoral—a perfect sale of one's self in the shambles, as you may say, I don't know what is. To be sure, your cousin is one of the very quiet, non-exacting kind, and I *hope* doesn't suffer as you would, darling love, if she were your wife!" pinching his arm with her claw-like fingers. "For you and I are *such* turtles, dearie!"

# CHAPTER XXV

Spring was forward in Hamilton that year. Mrs. Baxter, walking on the presidential portico at noon of a bright day in the third week of April complimented the extraordinary benignity of that usually coy month, by sporting the first white dress of the season.

A knot of irreverent students collected about the window of one of the college dormitories, catching glimpses of her snowy draperies fluttering from pillar to pillar of the porch, made merry over profane pleasantries, touching, "flourishing almond trees," and "antique angels."

"Wonder if she wears that red flannel night-cap to ward off the rheumatism!" said one, directing his puny arrow of wit at the "individualizing" scarlet scarf, now wound into a turban about her classic head, the silken fringes sweeping her shoulder.

"It is a piratical flag!" rejoined another. "And there! she is signalling some poor wretch on to his doom!"

The Lady President had waved her handkerchief to some one in or near the college, and halted at the top of the front steps to receive him.

"Who is the latest victim?" asked those in the rear of the party, as the foremost craned his neck to peer upon the campus.

"One who is able to take care of himself," was the response. "No less a personage than his Royal Highness."

This *sobriquet*, let me explain, was applied to Professor Fordham in no unkind or depreciatory spirit by his classes. Originally intended as a play upon his Christian name, it grew into popular esteem as descriptive of their pride in his manly carriage and knightly demeanor. The quintette at the window watched him with interest and admiration now, as he strode along the gravelled avenue leading to the Presidents' house.

"He would march up to the cannon's mouth in the same style," commented the chief speaker. "Did you ever see better shoulders?"

"Did you ever see a better *man*?" interrogated the fifth of the group—a grave senior, who had not spoken before.

And to the honor of the watchers, as of the watched, be it recorded that a hearty acquiescence in his verdict followed the question.

The goodly man found abundant favor, likewise in Mrs. Baxter's eyes, as she invited him to enter her abode.

"'Will you walk into my parlor?'
Said the spider to the fly."

Sang one of the graceless rascals in the dormitory, as a commentary upon the, to them, dumb show.

It was to Fordham anything but dumb. Mrs. Baxter was excruciatingly voluble in excusing herself for "what you must, I am certain, regard as an unparalleled liberty, my dear Professor!" she continued, when he was seated.

"I am gratefully at your service whenever you can make use of me, madam," was the reply, which was more sincere than professions of the kind usually are.

Mrs. Baxter's genuine love for her young cousin, and her numberless acts of neighborly kindness, had greatly endeared her to Jessie's husband. Her peculiarities of manner and phraseology weighed nothing with him when compared with her sound principles and generous heart.

"*Thank* you! I knew I might make the venture with *you!* My own mind being ill at ease, I could not resist the impulse to waylay you and unburden"—making as though she would clutch her heart, then sprawling both hands, her arms widely divergent lines from her heaving bust—"unburden myself to you, as the person most likely to sympathize with and ameliorate my anxieties. I had nearly said, my maternal anxieties. And indeed, Mr. Fordham, I could scarcely love your dear wife more, if she were, in truth, my child. Dear to me as the representative of the beloved friend of my youth, she has enhanced that partiality a thousandfold by her own worth and loveliness. This is my apology—this and the solicitude to which I have referred, for what may appear to you indelicate interference with your domestic affairs."

The polite interest with which her auditor had received her prefatory remarks was supplanted by uneasiness, instant and intense, as he perceived the drift of her speech. He had made a motion to rise when the words, "your dear wife," passed her writhing lips.

She hindered him with outstretched hands.

"Not that there is any cause for new and immediate alarm," she hastened to assure him. "But I was in to see her this morning. She keeps bravely up when you are at home, I dare say."

"She never complains. I have had my apprehensions that the untimely heat of the weather has been prejudicial to her strength. Her appetite is variable, and she is paler than she was in the winter, but I attributed—"

"Yes! of course!" interrupted Mrs. Baxter. Once bent upon an harangue, she was about as easily checked as a Yellowstone geyser in full play. "I am not surprised that your fears have not been awakened. I taxed her, to-day, with having deceived you as to the extent of her lassitude and depression. I surprised her lying on the sofa in her room, with the traces of fresh and copious tears upon her cheeks. She tried to laugh me out of my fears by talk of nervousness and hysteria, and would doubtless have succeeded, such are her spirit and address—but, Mr. Fordham! her precise likeness in look and manner at that moment to her sainted mother sent a poignant fear through my soul! Far be it from me to censure the dead, but I have always maintained—I shall ever believe that my precious Ginevra's life might have been spared—prolonged for *years*—had her husband conferred with those who were conversant with her idiosyncrasies—spiritual and physical. Although—I will reveal to you, my dear sir, under the seal of a secrecy you will see the expediency of respecting, what I have never lisped to her daughter, or even to the best of husbands and men—Dr. Baxter. My cousin Ginevra carried a blighted heart to Dundee when she went thither as Mr. Kirke's bride. An unfortunate misunderstanding had alienated her from one to whom her girlish affections were given. It is needless to enter into particulars. It is enough to say that they had loved and they were parted. She had not seen or heard from him for two years, most of which time she had passed abroad; indeed, she believed him to be the husband of another when she accepted Mr. Kirke. I own to you that my instinct and my reason opposed this fatal step. I expostulated with her.

"'Jane!' said she (you can imagine how Jessie would utter it!) 'say no more. My resolution is taken. This is a *good* man, and he loves me! In this union I shall—I *may* find rest, quiet, and in some measure, peace. I have been storm-tossed until I have no strength left for struggling!'

"Upon the eve of her marriage, the man whom she loved returned and sought an interview. I was with her in her chamber when his card, requesting this favor, was handed her. At sight of the familiar characters the buried love sprang up alive, strong, importunate! It was a fearful scene—that resurrection! What should she have done?"

"Confessed all to her promised husband!" came low and sternly from the man's heart. "He would have resigned her to her lover without a word of blame. I knew Mr. Kirke well. I do not speak unadvisedly."

"Such was my counsel. But she would not heed it. She refused to look again upon the face of him whose heart was breaking with love and vain regrets, and went right on to her bridal. And her daughter, if subjected to a like test, would act as she did."

"You say that Jessie is not well?" said Roy, shortly.

There were limits to his fortitude. He could not hear other lips tell what would be Jessie's action were an abhorrent marriage forced upon her by conscience or honor.

"In my estimation, she is very *far*" — arms again divergent — "*very* far from well, even taking into consideration the provocatives to languor you alluded to, just now. Furthermore — and again let me *beg* you to receive this intimation in the spirit in which I offer it! — furthermore, she is homesick for Dundee and her sister. I adverted to them casually to assure myself that my views on this point were correct, and her eyes filled again directly.

"'I had hoped to see Euna this month,' she said, 'but the change in the college vacation, abolishing the intermediate, and making one long term instead of two short ones, has prevented it.'

"But when I remarked—'I wish Eunice could pay you a visit, were it only from Saturday to Monday!' the loyal wife (such a stanch advocate as you have in her, Mr. Fordham!), took alarm.

"'Indeed, Cousin Jane, no one could take kinder care of me than Roy does!' she said, warmly. 'He spoils and pets me beyond reason, and when he is in the house, I desire no other society.'

"'But my precious girl!' I remonstrated; 'he cannot be with you all the time?'

"I wish you had seen the smile with which she replied—'Ah! but I have the memory of his goodness to live on in his absence!'

"She is true and fond, Mr. Fordham! Nevertheless, she does need change of air and scene. Her mother pined herself into an untimely grave in her longing for a sight of her old home and the faces of beloved ones."

Roy was silent; his eyes downcast, his lips whitening with the pressure this story had brought to bear upon him. It was not so much the consciousness that, in sending his wife away, he would rob his life of repression and self-denial of the little sunshine left to it, as the thought that she was sickening of his companionship; could not live and grow in his shadow. This was the naked truth, disguise it as she might from her cousin; deny it to herself as she probably did. In every point of Mrs. Baxter's description, he recognized this terrible sense of bondage, crushing spirit and life; heard, even in her tribute to his loving watchfulness over her health and bodily comfort, the plaint embodied in the poem he had learned by heart:

"Like a chainèd thing, caressed
By the hand it knows the best,
By the hand which, day by day,
Visits its imprisoned stay,
Bringing gifts of fruit and blossom
From the green earth's plenteous bosom;
All but that for which it pines,
In these narrow, close confines,
With a sad and ceaseless sigh,—
Wild and wingèd Liberty!"

With a deep inspiration which was the farewell to more hopeful dreams than he knew, until then, he had nursed, he collected his senses to reply.

"It was my intention to take Jessie to Dundee in June, at the beginning of my vacation. She set the time herself—I can see now, in compliance with what she believed were my wishes. But she shall go at once. I thank you for your more than friendly concern for her, your frank dealing with me."

He arose to go. The lady scanned his face somewhat uneasily. There was something there that foiled her penetration.

"You understand, my dear sir, that *nothing* would have tempted me to intermeddle in this affair, were the case precisely what you have supposed. But there is an undercurrent, Mr. Fordham, the effect of which I can trace, that seriously complicates anything like hysterical depression. And loving the child as we do—as every one does, it behooves us to watch her warily, minister to her intelligently as tenderly. The affection between the sisters is unusually strong, and we should remember that the dear lamb has known no other mother."

"I have offered, several times during the winter, to take her to visit Eunice. We were to have gone at Christmas, but Jessie had a severe cold that confined her to the house a fortnight."

"I remember! To be *quite* sincere with you—not that I consider it a dangerous symptom—but I *wish* she were rid of that little hacking cough. She makes light of it. Says it is nervous, or from the stomach. But I do not like it!"

She attended him to the portico, disclaiming, cautioning, and thanking him,—gesticulating through it all—as the wickedest of the wicked quintette of observers had it—"like a lunatic windmill." They espied no change in the Professor's gait or air. He walked firmly, head erect and countenance composed. And their distance from him was too great to allow them to note the want of color in his complexion.

He entered his own house, more slowly than he had trodden the pavement. Jessie had fallen into the habit common to wives who hail their husbands' return as cheering events, of meeting him in the hall, sometimes at the front door. She appeared from the sitting-room, while he was hanging up his hat and dusting his boots. He was particular in all that pertained to personal neatness.

"Your step sounds weary," she said. "It is very warm, really debilitating, to-day—is it not?"

During his brief answer he surveyed her narrowly, the dread that had been gnawing his heart all the way home sharpening his vision in the search for signs of debility and disease.

She, too, wore a white dress, but a black grenadine shawl was folded over her chest, and Roy's eye rested aghast upon the thin hand that held it together. What had he been thinking of, not to discern the inroads of the destroyer in this, and in the finer oval of her face; in the slight cough that succeeded her question, and the hurried breathing he could hear in approaching her? If his awakening should have come too late!

"I believe I have the Spring fever," he said, affecting to suppress a yawn. "This weather puts one in mind of country delights; makes him crave the smell of the freshly upturned earth, and the sight of green land growing things."

"Then take a look at my conservatory," she returned, playfully, leading the way to the open bay-window.

The sill, without and within, was crowded with plants. She had been at work among them for an hour, and they were in their freshest trim. The pruning-scissors lay upon the shelf, and, taking them up, she clipped a sprig of heliotrope, another of mignonette, a rose-bud, and a bit of citron-aloes, bound them together with silk from her work-basket, and offered them smilingly.

"Thank you. They are very sweet, very beautiful! How does the jessamine thrive?"

"Not so well as it should—ungrateful little thing!" touching the leaves of a stunted vine which was honored with a china flower-pot and the sunniest stand in the window. "I am afraid it cannot flourish in this high latitude.

It needs warmer earth, less fitful sunshine. Or it may be that I am killing it with kindness," she added, shaking her head pensively.

Roy detected another meaning in her thoughtfulness. Ungenial influences, unwelcome assiduity of attention, were sapping her vitality, and the analogy between her lot and that of her fading favorite was wearing upon her imagination.

"We will try again."

He had to clear his throat before he could speak. Jessie smiled slightly, with no misgiving of the communication that awaited her. She even stooped to pick off a few withered leaves that had previously escaped her notice. The two were side by side within the recess; so near together that the warm breeze blew the light folds of the wife's dress over the husband's arm; but she recked no more of the wretchedness kept down by his strong will than if a thousand leagues of ocean divided them.

"I have been thinking seriously all the way home of taking you to Dundee, and leaving you in Eunice's charge for a time," continued Roy, presently. "You are not so rosy and light-footed here as you were among the mountains. And the sudden variations of our climate affect the human Jessamine also! You should have a change, and without delay."

"I am very well—entirely contented!" she interposed, reddening vividly.

"You are kind to say so!" gratefully. "But there are other reasons why you should anticipate the date originally set for your visit to your old home. Eunice has been very self-denying and patient, and she should have her reward. While you are regaining health and strength, winning back your lost roses, you can accumulate a plentiful supply of seeds and roots of all descriptions, besides studying floriculture with your sister—if it be true, as you would make me believe, that she excels you in skill. For in your absence I shall have a real conservatory built back of this room, and our long talked of oriel run out here."

Jessie made a desperate effort to jest away the discussion.

"Oh! as to the oriel, I have quite abandoned the project since Mrs. Wyllys told me—having learned from the Provosts that we meditated something of the sort—that oriels had 'gone out entirely; that no stylish house nowadays is disfigured by them.' The only thing resembling the obsolete excrescences that would be admitted into a modern 'establishment' is a mullioned window, my good sir! I should never hold up my head in Hamilton again if I were to offend so boldly against the rules of art governing the best society!"

The toss of her head and her tones were Mrs. Orrin's to the life. But Roy had hard work to smile. In his state of mind, badinage was like jesting over a death-bed.

"Mrs. Wyllys must look the other way, then—at the majestic proportions of her cupola, if she likes, for the oriel is to be a fact next month. The work will be better done if I am on the ground to oversee operations, and it would not be pleasant for you to remain in the house while it is in confusion, not to mention the risk of taking cold from the damp walls and the open room, while the wall is down. It will be a convenience all around, you see."

"If you really think that I will be in the way—"

"I did not say that!" The correction was so prompt as to sound sharp. "But my judgment tells me that the plan I suggest is the best for both of us. My mind will be easier with regard to you if you are safe and happy in Eunice's care."

Jessie had turned her face quite away, and seemed to be gazing at some object in the street.

"I see!" she said, finally. "When do you wish me to go?"

"Whenever it suits your convenience. If you desire my escort, we had best leave Hamilton on Saturday of this or the next week."

"I can travel alone easily if it is not convenient for you to leave your classes. If you go on Saturday you lose Monday also. This is Tuesday. I can be ready by Thursday morning. If the change be as needful as you suppose, the sooner it is made the better. As to an escort, a lady needs none when there is no change of cars."

Roy pinched the succulent stems of his flowers until the perfume was hot and sickly. How impatient she was to be gone! She had gasped when he opened the door of escape from her cage, as if she already saw "wild and wingèd liberty" beyond.

"You do not think it necessary to notify Eunice of your coming, then?" he inquired.

"You can telegraph on Thursday morning, when you are fairly rid of me. Euna is always at home, and always ready and glad to see me. My visit will make her very happy."

The rising tears broke through her assumed lightness. She struggled to drive them back, and failing, walked abruptly from the room.

And thus the question was settled.

Jessie began to pack that afternoon; working so diligently as to be wan and appetiteless by supper time. Fanny Provost and her betrothed, Lieutenant Averill, who was in Hamilton on furlough, called in the evening. Warren Provost and Selina Bradley came in afterward, and the hostess revived visibly in their society. Her eyes and color were brilliant; her laugh ready; her repartee pointed and felicitous. The young people, regretting the near prospect of her departure, fell to rallying her upon her partiality for country life, and she defended the preference with spirit. Then, at Fanny's earnest request, she told the authentic legend of Dundee and "auld Davie," appearing to forget herself and her slavery (thought Roy), in her enthusiasm.

"The women fought too!" ejaculated Selina, when it was finished. "They were made of different stuff from me, or any other young lady of this generation that I know. I go into convulsions at the sight of an empty gun."

"They were warring for home and freedom!" rejoined Jessie. "To avoid captivity I would fight in the open field in the ranks. And so would you. But the love of liberty is oftener a passion with us mountaineers, than with lowlanders."

She caught her breath strangely—something between a sob and a laugh—which she tried to cover with a cough.

"A sad and ceaseless sigh!"

repeated the haunting demon in Roy's heart.

The hilarious talk went on, unchecked by his occasional fits of abstraction. Jessie was like another being in the anticipation of liberation.

"Heartlessly cheerful!" said Selina, with her usual aptitude for making unlucky observations.

"One would think you two were tired of each other already!" she subjoined. "And you haven't been married more than half a year! I shall tell this to papa. He raved over your mutual attachment and your devoted attentions to Mr. Fordham when he was sick, Jessie!"

"Say, at the same time, that she does not go, of her own accord!" said Roy—"but because I try to be as careful of her health as she was of mine. Although, if you had ever visited Dundee, you would not be scandalized by her desire to revisit it."

Fanny, observing Jessie's quick, hot blush and averted eyes, and divining that something was ajar, came to the relief of the hardly pressed couple.

"Did Jessie ever tell you, Mr. Fordham," she said, in her liveliest tone— "of the astounding poetical effort put forth by her admirer, Mr. Lowndes, the rich student, they used to call him—entitled, 'Jessie the flower o' Dundee'! The graceless youths of his class set it to the good old Scotch tune of that name. It was in a different metre—very uncommon, I believe, and the fun of the joke was in fitting the words in, after the manner of 'Ancient Uncle Edward.' I will get you a copy, and Warren here shall teach you how to sing it."

# CHAPTER XXVI

The weather changed on the morrow.

Coming home at nightfall, Roy found Jessie standing at the western window, surveying sorrowfully the unfavorable aspect of the heavens.

"It will be very unpleasant travelling in the rain!" she remarked as he entered. "The sun went down behind a portentous bank of clouds. And the wind is veering to the storm-quarter."

It was evident that the possibility of a single day's delay made her restless and anxious.

"The signs portend nothing worse than April showers, I hope," he encouraged her to believe. "Or, should there be a steady rain, you will soon run out of it into the region of blue skies and milder airs. I see no reason for altering your arrangements. You will be sheltered and dry in the cars."

"True!" she answered, musingly, returning to her contemplation of the unpromising horizon.

She was perturbed, however, and unusually taciturn while they were at supper; dull and spiritless during the hour they spent together in the sitting-room; arousing herself with apparent effort to reply to his remarks, and rarely offering one of her own accord. Roy's attempts at cheerful conversation were less evenly sustained than was customary with him in her presence. It was not his intention that this last evening should be one of gloomy constraint, but it approximated this more nearly every moment. Both were abstracted, and each was unwilling that the other should discover the direction in which his and her thoughts were straying. So the pauses in the sluggish flow of talk became more and more frequent, until, at nine o'clock, Jessie arose, with a sigh of relief.

"I must get a good night's rest, if I am to travel, to-morrow. Will you excuse me if I go upstairs, thus early?"

"Do not let me detain you a moment. Is there nothing I can do to assist you?"

"Nothing—thank you! There will be time to strap my trunks in the morning. You still think I had better go—whatever may be the weather?" stopping with the door in her hand.

"I do, certainly; that is, if you are not afraid of adding to your cold—if you are well enough."

"My cold is nothing. I have ordered breakfast at half-past six. I am glad the train does not leave so early as it did last year. Good-night!"

The cold, indifferent accents sank to the bottom of his heart like lead. What a millstone about this woman's neck was her marriage vow! His endeavors to make it lighter, and her existence endurable—the work to which he had given his best energies and wisest deliberations; the self-abnegation and prayerful struggle he had accepted as the penalty of his grievous indiscretion, had proved futile. He had guarded eye, tongue, and action for five months; drilled them in friendly looks, words, and deeds, lest a glimmer of the affection that glowed—a pent but consuming fire in his soul—should offend or dismay her; had ministered to her with a lover's constancy and tenderness without a hint of love's reward. And this was the end! Some significant glance, an intonation, an excess of solicitude for her welfare, had betrayed his design to win her anew, and she had taken the alarm; was terrified and reluctant, without the power of escape. Or her constitution—physical and spiritual—had succumbed to the attrition of duty against womanly instinct. With vain care he had kept her shackles out of sight. Everything in her surroundings; the very pronunciation of her name by acquaintances, had reminded her continually of her anomalous position. Neither wife, nor maid, she stood, according to her morbid perceptions, alone and banned, without so much as a title to the shelter of his roof, except as a bondwoman. She could not forget that she was a slave. The untamable heart—in which the "love of liberty" was a "passion," was beating itself to death against the bars he had foolishly hoped to cushion and wreathe until she should cease to feel them as a restraint.

She had not loved him when she married him. That this change in her sentiments was not a passing girlish caprice, he had evidence in the words she had written to him while the right of free speech remained to her.

"Months of doubt and suffering have brought me to the determination to confess this without reserve."

"Doubt and suffering!" What were these to the horrors of her actual bondage?

"From which I cannot release her!" he repeated, for the thousandth time.

His habit was to go to the library when she left him for the night, but he lingered, this evening, in the apartment he had fitted up for her with such fond pride; which she had made a sacred place by her abiding. There was a cruel pleasure in noting the tokens of her recent presence; in inhaling the odors of the flowers she had tended; in touching the books she had handled. She could never be more to him than she was now. He believed that she must, from this hour, be less; that the solace of her friendship would be withheld. Else, why her anxiety to be away from him? her chafing at the threatened delay of a day in her flight back to the only real home she had ever known? Was the memory of the evanescent phantasy of her girlhood— the brief space during which she had deluded herself into the belief that she loved him, so sore and hateful that she would shun the sight of one who kept it in constant remembrance? Could it be true that he had, in the face of these frightful odds, cherished a hope that he might yet persuade her into a preference for his companionship?

A loud ring at the door-bell startled him into consciousness of the hour and place. Phoebe had gone up to bed, and Mr. Fordham went himself to admit the unseasonable visitor.

"Good-evening!" said a familiar voice when the door was unclosed, and Dr. Baxter walked in as naturally and coolly as if it were not ten o'clock at night, and he plentifully besprinkled with rain. "I was out thinking— and walking, after the warm day—and chancing to observe that I was at your door, I stopped to say 'Good-bye' to the lassie—to your wife. Mrs. Baxter mentioned to-night, at tea, that she was-going to Dundee to-morrow."

He had obeyed Roy's impulse in the direction of the sitting-room, but declined to take a chair. His cravat was a damp string; the handkerchief twisted about his left hand bore marks of terrific usage, and when he removed his hat, every one of his stiff gray hairs appeared to have gone into business on its own account, so distinct was its independent existence. His eyes were like those of a partially awakened somnambulist, and his voice had dreamy inflections. Had his own mood been less sad, Roy must have smiled at the grotesque apparition, uncouth even to one so familiar with the peculiarities of the good man, as was his coadjutor in the business of his life. As it was, he appreciated gratefully the love the old scholar bore his former ward, and the new proof of this, evinced by his stepping without the charmed circle of metaphysical or scientific lucubrations to pay this, for him, rare visit of neighborly courtesy and affectionate interest.

"I am sorry Jessie has retired," he said, sincerely. "She would have been happy to see you. But, in view of to-morrow's journey, she went up to her chamber an hour ago. I am afraid she is asleep by this time."

The doctor shook himself out of a menacing relapse.

"Eh! asleep—is she? Ah, well! that is as it should be. Don't disturb her! I merely called to kiss her, and bid her 'God speed.' She is a dear and a good girl. Her price is above rubies. She carries our love and best wishes with her into her retirement. Since she is not up, I will leave my message with you. I believe—it seems to me that I *had* a message"—with an ominous twitch of the handkerchief, and a dreamier accent.

"She will appreciate your kind remembrance of her, sir. She prizes your friendship very fondly."

"Ah!" another mental shoulder-jog. "We shall hardly see her again until autumn, I presume? I infer as much from what Mrs. Baxter has told me of her plans."

"There has been no definite time set for her return," said Roy, evasively, his heart heavier than before at the thought that Jessie had expressed to her cousin a desire for a long sojourn in the country.

Yet if he had failed to keep her with him now, what warrant had he for confidence in his ability to lure her back?

"You will be lonely without her!" the worthy President observed, something in the atmosphere of this, her especial apartment, conveying to his straying wits an indistinct perception of the void her absence would make in the daily life of the man before him. In his own way, he missed his restless and faithful Jane when she was not at home.

"I shall!"

Not another word before the lips were closely sealed.

The doctor looked at him quickly and keenly, then put out his hand to pat his shoulder.

"Keep up a brave heart, my lad! although the desire of your eyes be removed from your side, for a few weeks. Nothing cheats time of heaviness, like work and hope. One you will find here in your accustomed avocations. The second will culminate in fruition when you are reunited to her you love, and, please God—in the blessedness of a father's love and delight, when your firstborn is given into your arms. It is a joy He has seen fit to deny me. I shall take my name down into the grave with me. His will be done! But I have not, on that account, the less sympathy with you at this juncture. Say to our Jessie that our prayers will follow her. You will go to her at the beginning of vacation, of course. And should you wish to run down to Dundee, for a day or two, each week during the remainder of term-time, I will gladly take your classes. You can recompense me by letting me christen the heir" —a fatherly smile overspreading the dry face. "The advent is expected towards the last of July, Mrs. Baxter says."

Conscious that, in the drunkenness of his astonishment, he returned a lame and seemingly ungracious reply to offer and congratulations, Roy made no movement to detain the eccentric guest, when he, after another dazed look around the apartment, as if wondering how he had got there, espied the door, and approached it with the briefest of "Good-nights." While the master of the house stood rooted to the floor, the visitant accomplished his exit, unchallenged and unattended. Another man would have taken mortal offence at the lack of respectful ceremony. The doctor, in his semi-trance, had not an idea of the commotion he had excited.

"I am not surprised that I am an offence in her eyes—that she must accuse me in her heart, of being less than man," muttered the husband, at length, passing a shaking hand over his pale forehead. "She ought to hate me for my seeming indifference—my unfeeling silence. She would if she were not an angel. My poor girl! And she has borne it all, without a murmur; like the brave, true woman she is. God forgive me! I can never pardon myself!"

He was sitting, his arms crossed upon the table, and his head laid upon them, when Jessie glided in stealthily. Over her white wrapper she had thrown a crimson shawl, and her long hair was loose upon her shoulders. Whatever resolve had drained her cheeks and lips of bloom, and lighted the steady flame in her eyes, had been acted upon with precipitancy, lest her nerve should fail.

She halted upon the threshold, on seeing the bowed figure; then advanced more rapidly, but without noise.

"Roy! are you awake?"

"Yes."

But he did not lift his face.

"Are you sick?"

"No!"

"Can you listen to me for a few minutes!"

"As long as you wish."

His voice was hollow and tremulous to plaintiveness; but she took heart from its exceeding, if mournful, gentleness.

"I cannot sleep to-night," she commenced, hurriedly, "still less can I leave you to-morrow, without expressing to you, however feebly, my sense of the goodness and mercy you have showed me from the hour I entered this house, until now. I may have appeared unobservant and unthankful; may have seemed to accept your benefits as if they were my due, when, in reality, I was unworthy of the least of them all; but it was because I did not know in what form to express my gratitude. If, in my acquiescence in your proposal that I should go to my sister for a season, I have used few words; have not thanked you for this fresh proof of your delicate watchfulness over my comfort and happiness, I beg you to attribute my shortcomings to other reasons than insensibility or misconstruction of your motives. I was entirely unprepared for the suggestion. It was a shock to me, because I had dared to believe that you would see fit to let me remain here with you until vacation, when we could go to Dundee together."

Standing on the other side of the table, she saw a slight but eager change in the expression of the mute form. It was as if his hearing were strained for her next utterance, but the features were still concealed.

On the roof of the bay-window, the soft, large drops of the April shower were beginning to fall in musical whispers.

Jessie put out a hand upon the marble top of the table to steady herself, as she resumed. There was that in this continued silence that awed and made her incoherent. It was unlike Roy's usual reception of her advances— his ready and indulgent courtesy. Her heart beat painfully and fast, but she did not swerve from her resolution.

"I know you so well—your purity of purpose; the standard of excellence you set for your motive and deed; your earnest desire to make me happy— that I fear you will, when I am gone, accuse yourself of want of skill or judgment in your treatment of me. I want you to remember then, that I broke through the reserve we have aided one another to maintain, to assure you that, in no one particular would I have had your action different from what it has been—that, in language and demeanor you have been alike noble. Deserving your reprobation, I have received tender respect; having forfeited by my fickleness and falsehood all claim to kindness, I have been cherished as the truest wife in the land might hope to be. Something tells me that, when we part to-morrow, it will be to meet no more in time. It may be that the presentiment is born of my distempered imagination; but it has drawn my whole soul out in a longing I cannot frame into speech, to be at peace with you; to feel your hand again upon my head; to hear you call me once—just once more, by the holy name of Wife!

"For I am your wife, Roy! Unworthy as I am of the title, it is the only glory I have. Until yesterday, I had dreamed of saying this to you in very different language and circumstances. It is just that this expectation should be disappointed. I do not appeal from my sentence of exile. But, by the memory of the love you once had for me—and I was full of faults then as now—do not send me away, unforgiven, and *starving* for your affection—my husband!"

When he looked up, she was kneeling at his side, her eyes streaming with the tears that had impeded her utterance.

Still dumbly, he drew her to him; put back the hair from her face, every line of his own astir with a passion of pity and adoration she hardly dared to look upon. It was a minute before he could articulate. Then the tense lips were moved into womanly softness.

"You can forgive *me*, then, my Wife! Thank God!"

He laid his cheek to hers, and she felt the great sobs of the breast against which she leaned.

But for a long time, there was nothing more said.

Except by the rain-drops whispering over their heads, broken, now and then, by the wind into little gushes that sounded like laughter, happy to tearfulness.

# CHAPTER XXVII

In the plenitude of her cousinly compassion for the lonely husband, Mrs. Baxter coaxed her spouse into escorting her to Mr. Fordham's, on Thursday evening. The wind had settled into an easterly gale, after yesterday's genial warmth; the day had been unpleasant, and the clouds were still dripping at irregular intervals, as if wrung by impatient hands.

"But it is an act of common humanity to visit the poor fellow in his solitude, my dear, while his desolation is fresh upon him!" she sighed, sympathetically.

"Mr. Fordham was in the library," said Phoebe, with an air of bewilderment at the lady's query, and to the library the consoler accordingly tripped, with footfall of down, and countenance robed in decorous and becoming pensiveness.

Her light tap was unanswered, but uncertain of this, she took the benefit of the doubt, and entering bouncingly, as was her habit, she surprised Jessie, sitting upon her husband's knee, one hand buried in his hair, the other clutching his beard, in a fashion at once undignified and saucy. Both were laughing so heartily that their neglect of the warning knock was explained.

When the confusion of mutual explanations was over, Mrs. Baxter learned, to her amazement, that the journey to Dundee was postponed until after the College Commencement.

"I *wouldn't* go when I found that Roy wanted to get rid of me!" said the transformed wife. "When I put him into the confessional, he owned who was his fellow-conspirator in the scheme for my banishment. For shame, Cousin Jane! I have long suspected you of a weakness for the handsome Professor, but you sit convicted of a deliberate attempt to remove him from the guardianship of his legal protector, that your designs upon his affections might be more vigorously prosecuted. And no sooner do you suppose that the coast is clear, than you present yourself, arrayed in your best dress and choicest smiles, and with actually a rose-bud in your brooch! to make sure of your game. I shall never trust in human friendship again!"

"You are ungenerous to triumph over me so openly—and in the poor, dear doctor's hearing!" returned her cousin, holding her fan before her face, with a theatrical show of detected guilt.

"I ought to have some compensation for the excruciating anguish the discovery cost me," retorted Jessie. "Tongue cannot describe the tremendous struggle I went through before I could bring myself to undertake the investigation of your perfidy and his susceptibility. I know just how Esther felt when she screwed her courage to the sticking-point, and made up her mind and her toilette to face Ahasuerus and a possible gallows."

Roy was pretending to listen to the doctor's elaborate disquisition upon an important political question, but he stole a sidelong glance at the sparkling face, across the hearth, and smiled, in gladness of content.

She was his blithe, lovesome witch again. The baleful enchantment that had ensnared her fancy and distracted her thoughts from dwelling upon him and his love—(he refused to believe that he had ever lost her heart)— was destroyed, and, by him, remembered no more as a thing of dread. More to spare him pain than to shield Orrin, Jessie had not entered into the particulars of her estrangement, or revealed who was the prime agent in bringing it about. Wyllys' name was not mentioned by either.

"I had a bad, wild dream—" she thus explained her defection. "A dream that made me doubt you—Heaven—myself—everything! that robbed me of love and hope, with faith. I was susceptible, giddy, undisciplined; and I was grievously tempted by an evil spirit. Maybe"—humbly—"I am no better or wiser now; but I am ready and thankful to give myself up to your guidance. I ought to be a good woman in future; for I have been dealt with very tenderly by my Heavenly Father—and by you, my best earthly friend!"

Roy had no fear. His second wooing was, he felt, crowned with richer, more enduring success than the first had been. He cared not to ask, or to conjecture by what art his image had been clouded over, since he saw it now clearly mirrored in a heart tried by refining fires.

The christening feast was not held until December, at which date Master Kirke Lanneau Fordham was four months old.

Eunice had taken her school and cottage for a year, and the interesting *fête* could not be appointed until she could make her arrangements to be with her sister. Work for the good of others, and wholesome meditation, had brought to her, as they must to all healthy, God-fearing souls, healing and peace during the months she had spent in her new domicile. With the June vacation had come Jessie and her husband; and when the little claimant upon their love and care arrived, the lonely woman, who had put thoughts of her own wifehood and maternity from her forever, when she turned the key upon the souvenirs of her one love-dream, opened her heart and took in, with the babe, comfort and hope that were, to her, fresh and beautiful life. What Roy's arguments and Jessie's entreaties could not accomplish,

the innocent young eyes and clinging baby-fingers effected within a month after her nephew's birth. If Kirke went to Hamilton, she would follow, she promised, and early December saw her domesticated in the Fordham household.

"I wish Orrin Wyllys and his wife were not coming, this evening!" said Jessie, confidentially, to her sister, as they were arraying the boy for the grand occasion.

Eunice looked in no wise surprised at the impetuous exclamation, albeit it was the first avowal of dislike of Roy's relative she had ever heard from Jessie's lips.

"It would not have been expedient to omit them from your list of invitations, my dear!" she returned, with her slow, bright smile. "For Roy's sake, you must disguise your antipathy."

"Antipathy isn't too strong a word, Euna! You cannot understand what reason I have to distrust that man! to despise both himself and his wife! And the *début* of Papa's boy ought to be all brightness to Mamma!" suspending the process of the toilette to strangle him with caresses.

"He cannot hurt you now, love. Even poisonous breath soon passes from finely-tempered steel."

The look and tone silenced the other. Eunice's insight of the tempter's true character was deeper than she had imagined. Even she never dreamed how, and at what cost, the knowledge was gained.

Miss Kirke was an attractive feature of the assembly that night. Many thought her handsomer than her more lively sister. There was not one present who would not have ridiculed the idea of a comparison between her classic beauty and Mrs. Wyllys' shrewish physiognomy. Once, the two ladies talked together for five minutes, near the centre of the front parlor, the light from the chandelier streaming on both. Eunice was dressed with her usual just taste, in a lustreless mourning silk, a tiny illusion ruff enhancing the fairness of neck and face, her abundant hair arranged simply without ornament. She possessed the rare accomplishment of standing still without stiffness, and no nervous play of fingers or features marred the exquisite repose of her bearing, as she listened to or replied to her companion.

Hester was in the full glory of brocade, diamonds, and point lace, with French flowers twisted in her pale tresses, and trailing bramble-wise down her back. She fidgeted incessantly; her skin was muddy with biliousness and discontent; she perked her faint eyebrows into a frown, every other minute; her laugh was forced, and the viscid tones had a twang of pain or ill-humor. She was getting very tired of keeping up the appearance of conjugal felicity

with so little assistance from her lord; growing bitterly conscious of the motives that had impelled him to the uncongenial marriage, and disposed to eye jealously every woman to whom he paid the most trifling attention.

"I suppose you are baby-mad, like the rest?" she said, pulling viciously at the golden chain of her bouquet-holder. "I am in a deplorable minority here, to-night. Christening-parties are always a bore to me. I am *so* sincere, you know, so apt to say what I think, that I can never go into raptures over the little monkeys, as everybody else does. I presume, now, that it is considered rather a nice child—if there is such a thing—isn't it?"

"We think him a noble little fellow; but we do not require the rest of the world to agree with us," replied Eunice, with unruffled politeness.

"I *detest* children! just perfectly abominate babies! I wouldn't have one for a kingdom. And Orrin loves his own ease too much to want them. He is an *awful* hypocrite, Miss Kirke. You were very wise not to get married. He can't abide children"—raising her voice—"although he *is* making a fool of himself over that bundle of lace, lawn, and flannel yonder."

Eunice, inwardly provoked at the irreverent and inelegant description of the royal cherub, could yet respond, with apparent composure.

"He does it from a sense of duty, or a desire to please, probably."

She followed the direction of the wife's scornful eyes.

The folding doors were open, and through the archway, they had a view of the mother, tempting her boy with a flower she had taken from a bouquet, near by, laughing at his open mouth, starting eyes, and fluttering arms, as he tried to seize it. Orrin had approached her while his wife was speaking to Eunice; accosted her before she was aware of his vicinity. His remark, delivered with his most insinuating smile, and in his inimitable manner, was evidently a compliment to the beauty of the child; but she met it with lightness bordering upon contempt. Dropping the flower, she lifted the babe from his temporary throne on the stuffed back of an easy chair, and walked away.

Mrs. Wyllys tittered shrilly, and clapped her hands.

"A decided rebuff!" she sneered, more loudly than good breeding would have counselled. "It is strange, Miss Kirke, that your lady-killer is so slow to learn the mortifying fact that he ceases to be irresistible when he has been guilty of the mistake of matrimony."

Orrin, nervously sensitive to her tones, heard and saw her, while he affected to do neither; saw, likewise, by whom she was standing, and that she showed beside her neighbor as a tawdry, artificial rose, faded and tumbled, does when near a stately, living lily.

Seeing and admitting all this, he heaved an inaudible sigh that did not touch his eyes or chasten his careless smile. His inward moan was not—"Me miserable!" or "Fool that I was!" or anything else poetical or tragic; but—"If I could have afforded it!"

"The fair Euna will wear better than *mia cara sposa!*" he owned, candidly. "But money outlasts beauty, and is more necessary to a man's happiness. Love is only a luxury; an indulgence too costly for the enjoyment of most wedded pairs. Beryl eyes and a Greek profile would not have paid my debts, nor the future claims of carriage makers, and horse-jockeys, and yacht-builders, No! I have done all that man could, in the like circumstances. Better bread buttered on both sides by Hester, than a dry slice with Eunice."

He owed Miss Kirke no grudge; found placid satisfaction in reviewing their intercourse, akin to that he experienced in the contemplation of a fine, mezzo-tinto engraving or a moonlit landscape. But Jessie irritated and piqued him. If her gay insensibility were bravado, he would yet make her drop the mask. His wife was right in affirming that the passion for conquest was not extinct after a year of married bliss.

"She did worship me in those days!" he ruminated. "Worshipped me madly and entirely, as men are seldom loved, as few women are capable of loving. Does she take me for an idiot in supposing that I credit the thoroughness of her cure!"

Lounging in a desultory way through the rooms, bowing to this, and exchanging a pleasant word with that one of the friends collected to do honor to the infant scion of the house, he contrived to waylay Jessie in the hall. She had transferred the baby to the nurse's care, and was returning to her guests. A fierce impulse possessed him as he marked her happy face, flushed by excitement into loveliness that had never been hers in her girlhood. She was passing him with a slight and nonchalant bow, when he arrested her.

"Can I speak with you for a moment?"

"Now?" she said, dubiously, looking toward the parlors crowded with company.

"*Now!* I can wait no longer! Is any one in the library?"

Before she could reply, he had pushed the door back, and led her in. The room was not needed for the use of the guests, and was unlighted except by the low fire in the grate.

"I will light the gas!" said Jessie, trying to withdraw her hand from his clutch.

He tightened the grasp. It is said that every man is a savage at some time of his life. The brutish devil was rampant now in the polished citizen of the world, the indolent epicure. If he were ever to regain his lost influence, it must be by a *coup d'état*—by threats, rather than flattery. He would show her what she risked in attempting to dupe and foil him. A desperate expedient, but the case was not a hopeful one.

"What affectation of prudery is this?" he asked, roughly. "Time was when you were less scrupulous about granting me interviews in the firelight. Do you imagine, silly child, that your overacted farce of wifely devotion blinds me as it does the fools you have called together to-night to witness this pretty display of domestic felicity? Or"—his tone changing suddenly—"that any amount of coldness and cruelty can extinguish my love for you? the love you once confessed—in my arms—was reciprocated by yourself, then the betrothed of him, who now believes you to be his loyal consort? You have found it an easy task to deceive him, because it is not in him to worship you as I do. You may struggle to escape from me, but you know I am speaking the truth, and leaving half of it untold. Don't drive me to distraction, Jessie! or I shall divulge that which your husband, with all his phlegmatic philosophy, may resent. Resent, possibly, upon me—certainly upon you—in treatment you will find it hard to bear. I have warned you before, that generous forgiveness of an offence to his dignity and self-love is a height of virtue unknown to Roy Fordham. I warn you that you are dealing with a desperate, because a miserable man!"

"This is a specimen of the superior manliness, the lofty magnanimity you vaunt as your characteristics—is it?"

She had wrested her hand from him. The faint, red glare revealed the outlines of a figure drawn up to its full height, and instinct with anger and defiance. The clear accents were stinging hailstones.

"I am not afraid of you, if I do shrink from your touch. I am glad you have given me this opportunity to say what you ought to know. You played upon my inexperience and loneliness, when I was committed—a too trustful child—to your care by my betrothed and my father. You tampered with my active imagination and my credulity, until you wrought in my mind false and florid views of life; and when your train was ready to be fired, insinuated suspicions—which you knew were groundless!—of Roy Fordham's honor, and his fidelity to me."

"I suggested no suspicions!" he interrupted.

"You nourished the germs planted by Hester Sanford's slander. And when I did not know where, or upon what I stood; when my brain was teeming with unhealthy fancies, and my heart sick with fever and thirst, you offered me what you called love—dragged from me the admission that it was returned."

"Since perfect frankness is the order of the day, allow me to observe that the 'dragging' was not a difficult process!" interjected Wyllys, offensively.

"I am willing to allow your amendment—if you will consent to have me repeat this story in detail to all who are assembled in the other room," she returned, undaunted. "I should enjoy the task, because it would pave the way for an avowal I should exult in proclaiming to the universe. It is that I value the least hair of my husband's head more than I ever did you—body, soul, and what you denominate as your heart; that I had rather serve him as a bond-slave, and never receive a word or glance of affection, if I might live near and for him—than to reign an Empress at your side; that I never comprehend the height, depth and fulness of his condescension and love at any other time as when I reflect that these are bestowed upon a woman who was once misled into the conviction that you were a true man, and that she cared for you. I stand ready to say all this—and more. I am no weak girl, now, to be terrified by bugbears. There is a perfectness, even of human love, that casteth out fear. You forget this when you threaten me with my husband's displeasure."

She laughed, and all the corners of the quiet room caught up the mirthful echoes.

"Why, if Roy stood where you do, I could tell him all you have said, without a blush or tremor. That I have never done this, you owe to my reluctance to betray to the baseness of one in whose veins runs the same blood as in his. I would spare him the pain and shame of seeing you for what you are. But I wish he knew everything!"

"I think he does!"

While she was speaking, a shape had loomed into motion from a recess formed by two bookcases at the further end of the library, and was now at her side. As her husband's voice greeted her astonished ears, she felt his supporting arm about her.

"Hush, my darling!" he said, at her stifled scream. "I came in for a book just before you entered. After hearing Mr. Wyllys' preliminary remark I thought it best to let you vindicate yourself without my help. Not that I needed to hear your justification, but I meant that he should. We will go back to our friends, now. Shall I tell Mrs. Wyllys that you are waiting to take her home?" to Orrin.

"If you please," was the equally formal reply.

A week later, Selina Bradley brought Mrs. Baxter a piece of startling news.

"It is certainly true!" she insisted, as the other looked her incredulity. "The house and furniture are offered for sale. It is very doubtful when they will return. They may reside abroad for years—take up their permanent abode in Paris. Mr. Wyllys affects to treat the plan as one they have been considering this great while, but there are queer stories afloat. Hester is indiscreet, you know. They had a violent scene in the hearing of the servants on their return from the Fordhams' christening party. The most unlikely, but a popular, rumor is that Hester was furiously jealous of her husband's attentions to Jessie, or her sister, that night. She threatened to leave him, and go home to her father, unless he would take his oath never to speak to either of them again."

"You may well say 'unlikely!'" Mrs. Baxter said, eyeing the doctor apprehensively, as he sat up to his eyebrows in a book at a distant window. "They are going to Paris, you say?"

The doctor had lowered his volume, let go his cravat, and pushed up his spectacles.

"So Hester says, and is in ecstasies (apparently) at the prospect. As for Mr. Wyllys, he professes to think American society a very wishy-washy affair compared with Parisian circles."

"Humph!" snorted the doctor. "They could not choose more wisely and consistently. Paris is the world's repertory of gilded shams!"

He tied a double knot in his handkerchief.